Sense of Deception

Sense of Deception

· · · · · · · · · · · · · · · · · · · ·

A Psychic Eye Mystery

· · · · · · · · · · · · · · · · · · · ·

Victoria Laurie

AN OBSIDIAN MYSTERY

OBSIDIAN
Published by the Penguin Group
Penguin Group (USA) LLC, 375 Hudson Street,
New York, New York 10014

USA | Canada | UK | Ireland | Australia | New Zealand | India | South Africa | China
penguin.com
A Penguin Random House Company

First published by Obsidian, an imprint of New American Library,
a division of Penguin Group (USA) LLC

First Printing, July 2015

LIBRARY OF CONGRESS CATALOGING-IN-PUBLICATION DATA:

Laurie, Victoria.
Sense of deception: a psychic eye mystery / Victoria Laurie.
pages cm.
ISBN 978-0-451-47386-8
I. Title.
PS3612.A94423S46 2015
813'.6—dc23   2015003214

Printed in the United States of America
1   3   5   7   9   10   8   6   4   2

Set in ITC Galliard Std.
Designed by Alissa Theodor

PUBLISHER'S NOTE

This is a work of fiction. Names, characters, places, and incidents either are the product of the
author's imagination or are used fictitiously, and any resemblance to actual persons, living or dead,
business establishments, events, or locales is entirely coincidental.

For Lilly, who was the whole of my heart

Acknowledgments

You'll notice a little more of Abby's dachshund, Tuttle, in this story. Tuttle is based on my own dachsy, Lilly, who was diagnosed with terminal cancer in May 2014 and, after an amazingly valiant effort to stay with me as long as she could, finally lost her battle and crossed that rainbow bridge in November. Honestly, I'm still a bit gutted and destroyed by her passing. In her final months all I did was love on her. I nurtured and took care of and exercised patience I never knew I had with her, and they were perhaps the best six months of my life. But also the worst.

I wrote much of this story with Lilly nestled on my lap, cuddled there quietly, while I escaped the heartbreak of slowly losing her by writing about my favorite character, the Abster, inserting Tuttle a little more into the fabric of the story as I went. There is a scene late in the book that I wrote on Lilly's last day, and, although it's a very special scene to me, with Abby cuddling with Tuttle while gazing up at the stars, it's been very difficult for me to reread and edit that passage because I remember so clearly finishing the scene, then shutting down the computer for one last car ride with my baby girl, who was so brave right up to the very end.

This book is absolutely a tribute to her, but it's also about love and its many forms. Personally, I don't think there's anything that makes us more human than loving and nurturing another species. I was definitely made more human by Lilly, and I'm left a little less so in her passing. She'll live on as Tuttle, and Abby will have the benefit of loving her sweet pup for many years to come. Honoring her that way is the only thing I have left to give my baby girl, which is a blessing I'm so grateful for. Still, I would consider it a tremendous gift if, while you read this book, you'd do it cuddled around your favorite furbaby. I can think of no greater tribute to the sweetest, most adorable, amazing, loyal, enthusiastic, comedic, happy, nurturing, intuitive pup I've ever known. Also, I'm quite sure that Lillers would love it too. ☺

Very special thanks go to: Sandy Harding, Jim McCarthy, Michele Alpern, Diana Kirkland, Danielle Dill, Claire Zion, and Sharon Gamboa.

Additional thanks go to: Sandy Upham; Brian Gorzynski; Katie Coppedge; Leanne Tierney; Karen Ditmars; Steve McGrory; Mike and Matt Morrill; Nicole Gray; Jennifer Melkonian; Catherine Ong Kane; Drue Rowean; Nora, Bob, and Mike Brosseau; Sally Woods; John Kwaitkowski; Matt McDougal; Dean James; Anne Kimbol; McKenna Jordan; Hilary Laurie; Shannon Anderson; Thomas Robinson; Juliet Blackwell; Sophie Littlefield; Nicole Peeler; Gigi Pandian; Rachel Herron; Maryelizabeth Hart; Terry Gilman; Martha Bushko; and Suzanne Parsons.

Sense of Deception

Chapter One

• • •

There was chaos in the courtroom as I was dragged kicking and screaming from it by two beefy bailiffs. After I landed a pretty good kick to someone's kneecap, the number of bailiffs "escorting" me out of the courthouse increased by two. It would've been humiliating if I'd paused long enough in my struggles to consider it. Mostly I yelled my head off and wrenched my limbs back and forth until one of the big and beefies put a can of Mace right next to my nose and threatened to let loose. I piped down quickly after that and settled for glaring hard at my captors before being handed off to a couple of deputies. The deputies made quick work of handcuffing me and placing me into a van for a short road trip to a large loading dock, where I was unloaded and moved inside a big ugly building. After that I was put through the process of getting my butt thrown in jail.

On the plus side, there wasn't a strip search (thank the baby Jesus!), but I did have a panicky moment during which I seriously regretted my decision to go commando that morning. Some days it just pays to wear underwear.

Still, I had to give up my dress slacks and blouse for an orange jumpsuit, and I don't care what anyone says: Orange is *so not* the new black.

After demanding my right to make one phone call for the eleventh time, I was handcuffed and led down a dark, narrow, claustrophobia-inducing hallway to a bank of phones attached to a wall. The husky woman in uniform who'd led me there growled, "You have ten minutes," before moving a little way down the hall to eye her watch and then glower at me.

Charming.

After squinting meanly at her retreating form, I turned to the phones and called my hubby. "Rivers," he said when he picked up the line.

"Hi, honey, it's me."

"Edgar," he said with honeyed tones, using his favorite nickname for me. I love the sound of my husband's voice. So rich and seductive. It soothes me like a morning cup of coffee, heavy on the cream and sugar. "How was court?"

"Oh, you know. Not quite what I was expecting."

"Was it tough on the stand?"

"A bit."

"Yeah, this defense counsel of Corzo's . . . he's a slick bastard. Did you get beat up a little?"

I swallowed hard. "Um, yes, actually. You could say that it went exactly like that."

"Aw, dollface," Dutch said. "Don't let 'em get you down. You did great on this case. Gaston even pulled me aside yesterday to say how happy he is with the work we did to nail Corzo. And, between us, I think he's especially proud of you."

I winced. Dutch's boss's boss was Bill Gaston. Regional director for the Central Texas FBI office. Former CIA. Totally great guy, until you got on his bad side. Once on said bad side, you might as well pack a bag and leave town. Quickly. "Speaking of Gaston," I said, trying to keep the waver out of my voice, "could you maybe get him to come down to the county jail for me?"

There was a lengthy pause; then (after adopting a slight Cuban accent) my hubby said, "Edgar? What did you do?"

I took a deep breath. "I sorta outed the judge to a packed courtroom and then he attacked me and then I was thrown in jail for contempt of court."

Another (longer) pause. "Please tell me you're kidding."

"I'm kidding."

"Really?"

"No."

There was a muffled sound, which I suspected was my husband trying to quiet a laugh. "Tell me *exactly* what happened."

I opened my mouth to give him the 411, but at that moment the guard tapped her watch and gave me a stern(er) look. "Actually, honey, maybe you should just call Matt Hayes. He can give you the play-by-play. But please also call Gaston. I have a feeling we're going to need his clout to get me out of here."

I thought I heard my hubby stifle another laugh with a cough. After clearing his throat, he said, "I'll call Gaston and Matt. We'll have you home for dinner, sweethot."

Dutch had slipped into his best Bogie impression for that last bit, and it actually made me feel a little better, even though he thought my getting tossed in the clink was high-larious.

After hanging up with Dutch, I shuffled down the hallway to the waiting guard, and she led me by the arm back down the corridor, to a window with a redheaded, freckle-faced inmate standing ready behind a counter in a little enclosed room with lots of neatly packed supplies behind her. I was pushed up to the window and a pillow, sheets, a thin blanket, and some toiletries were shoved into my chest. "We're out of toothpaste," she said, as if I'd already noticed and had copped an attitude.

"Okay," I replied.

"Are you on your period?" she asked.

I felt heat in my cheeks. I'm a bit modest when it comes to discussing bodily functions. "Not presently."

"Good. We're out of tampons, too."

"Got any aspirin?"

"Yeah. You got a headache?" she said, reaching behind her for a small packet of one-dose Tylenol.

"Yep."

"Here, but that's all you get," she said firmly before jotting down the added item on a clipboard in front of her.

"Thank you very much."

She rolled her eyes and turned away. I wondered if we'd end up braiding each other's hair later.

Stern Eyes then led me to a set of doors, which required us to get buzzed through. Once we were through the doors, the conversations and shouts and jeers on either side of the hallway from the inmates currently jailed there echoed and bounced off the concrete walls like a mad game of Pong.

I tried not to tremble as Stern Eyes pulled me along, but I might have let out a whimper or two.

I'd been in jail before. Trust me on this: It's not a place you *ever* want to be. It's loud, it's jarring, and it smells like a mix of Pine-Sol, BO, and perhaps a soupçon of desperation.

Plus, it's dangerous. I mean, it's *literally* wall-to-wall criminals. Think about that the next time you want to jaywalk. (Or out a federal judge to a packed courtroom . . . ahem.)

Stern Eyes walked me down the length of the open section of the jail, and I ignored the catcalls and whistles from cells to my right and left. I suspected that new prisoners got paraded in front of the other inmates like this on a regular basis. It was meant to scare the newbies—and make them easy for the guards to handle initially—and I can tell you for a fact that it's effective.

About midway down the length of the open section, Stern Eyes tugged my arm and directed me to the right. "You're here," she said, coming to a stop in front of a closed cell door with only one inmate inside. Using the radio mic at her shoulder, she ordered the cell door to be opened, and after a rather obnoxious buzzing sound, it slid to the right. She didn't even wait for it to get all the way open—she merely gave my back a hard shove and I stumbled forward, barely able to stop myself before my head hit the top bunk on the right side. "You have a new roommate," Stern Eyes said. It took me a minute to realize she wasn't talking to me.

I turned cautiously to look across the cell at the other inmate and did a double take. She wasn't at all what I was expecting.

Tall and willowy, she had very long, very curly blond hair, big blue eyes, and the kind of heart-shaped face that would break a man's heart. (Or a woman's, depending on which team you're playing for.)

She considered me without a hint of expression, and I wondered how I measured up in her mind. I tried to square my shoulders to show her that I was cool, yo. All she did was blink.

The guard then turned to me, and with a thumb over her shoulder to the inmate across the cell, she said, "That's Miller. Play nice with her or we'll send you to solitary. You missed lunch, so dinner's at six. When the doors open, move out into the corridor and stand to the left of the opening to wait to be counted by one of the COs. Then move single file to the cafeteria. It'll be your only chance to eat for the rest of the day, so make it count. Lights out at nine p.m. Sharp."

With that, she motioned for me to raise my arms, and after dumping my assigned goodies on the metal frame of the top bunk, I held my hands out so she could undo my cuffs.

After pocketing the keys, Stern Eyes got up in my face and glared hard at me, as if she alone could scare me straight (good luck with that), and then she simply turned on her heel and walked out.

A moment later the door buzzed and slid mechanically closed.

I looked meaningfully at my new bunkmate and said, "Well, she's not getting a holiday card from *me* this year."

The corner of Roomie's mouth quirked, but there was no real humor in her eyes. Instead, I noticed for the first time a rather profound sadness there. Like all the mirth had been sucked right out of her, and what remained was something hollow. Broken. "So you're one of those, huh?" she asked me.

I stiffened. "One of whats?"

"One of those people who makes a joke out of everything as a coping mechanism."

I laughed and waved my hand. "No. I definitely have a serious side."

"What'd you do to get in here?" she asked.

"Used my charm and quick wit when I should've used diplomacy."

That quirk came back to her mouth. "Well, whoever you pissed off, they must've been high up the food chain. I'm on death row and I'm not supposed to have roommates."

I stiffened again. "Death row? I'm on death row?"

"Relax," she told me. "I'm down here from Mountain View, for my appeal. Normally they'd put me in solitary, but that's full up from the last fight in the cafeteria, so they moved some people around and I got the luxe digs here."

I gulped. The urge to ask her what she'd done was heavy on my tongue, but I wasn't sure that was (a) polite or (b) a question that could get me shivved in my sleep, so I simply nodded and said, "Well, I shouldn't be here long. My husband's gonna get me out, hopefully before dinner."

Her brow rose skeptically, but then she went back to a rather blank expression. "So, what do you do when you're not expelling lots of charm and quick wit?"

I struggled with her question for a moment; no way was I gonna reveal that I worked with the Feds, especially not in here. But I also wondered if it was a bad idea to let her know that I was a psychic. I mean, maybe I was bunking with the only serial psychic killer in all of Texas. "I'm an accountant."

She squinted at me. I had a feeling she could smell the smoke from my liar, liar, pants on fire. "Ah," she said. And then she sat back on her bunk and picked up a paperback. In jail only ten minutes and I'd already failed my first test.

"Actually," I said, taking a seat on the lower bunk, "I'm not an accountant."

"*Quelle surprise,*" she said flatly. She didn't even look up from the book.

"Okay, I deserved that. The truth is, I'm a professional psychic."

Her gaze slid over to me, as if she were waiting for my orange jumpsuit to actually explode in a ball of flames. I made sure to hold her gaze. "For real?"

"For real."

"You make a living at that?"

"Yep."

"So . . . what? You just look into a crystal ball or something?"

I grinned. "No. Crystal balls, head scarves, and lots of bangles are for amateurs. My technique is to focus on a person's energy—

their electromagnetic output, if you will. We carry bits of our future in the energy we expel, and someone like me can focus on that energy and tell a person about what's likely to happen in the future."

I waited for her to ask me what I was picking up about her, but she surprised me with her next question. "Can you look back at something?"

I cocked my head. "Back? You mean, can I look back in time?"

She sat up and put her feet on the ground, resting her elbows on her knees after setting the paperback aside. "Yeah. If I told you about something like a break-in, could you see who did it?"

"That's actually a more complicated question than you'd think," I told her. "If you're asking me if I could see how a crime unfolded, and give a description of the offender, yeah. I could do that."

Tears welled in her eyes and I couldn't imagine what I'd just said to upset her. "Have you ever worked on a crime before?"

I thought about lying again, but her sudden display of emotion and those sad eyes got the best of me. "Yes."

"How many?"

"Several dozen."

"You work with the police?" she asked, a hint of suspicion in her eyes.

I was quick to shake my head. "My business partner is a private investigator. We work quite a few cases together." And that was not a lie, albeit not exactly the whole truth either.

My roommate took a deep breath and looked away from me to stare out the bars of the cell. It was a long moment before she was able to compose herself. Putting a hand on her chest, she said, "My name is Miller. Skylar Miller."

I got up and extended my hand. "I'm Abby. Abby Cooper. Rivers. Cooper. Cooper-Rivers."

She took my hand and that small quirk at the corner of her mouth returned. "You sure?"

"I still can't decide if I want to take my husband's last name or not."

"How long you two been married?"

I returned to my side of the cell. "It'll be a year in November."

She nodded. "Keep your own name," she said. "Don't give up your identity."

"Word," I said, and put my fist out for a bump, but she didn't raise her hand or acknowledge the banter. My hand dropped limply back to my lap. "You okay?" I asked her after an awkward moment. She still looked so sad, and she hadn't asked me about this break-in she'd mentioned earlier. I'll admit that she'd more than piqued my interest.

"Yeah," she lied. Then she reached under her pillow and pulled out a Twix. Opening the wrapper, she shook out one bar and offered it to me.

As someone who never turns down free chocolate, I was quick to get up and retrieve it. "Thank you."

"Can I ask you something?" she said, looking thoughtfully down at the remaining candy bar.

"Sure."

"How much would you charge me if I wanted to ask you about something that happened a while ago?"

"That break-in you mentioned?"

Her gaze lifted to mine again. Her expression was still so sad, but for the first time since meeting her, I swore I saw the smallest glimmer of hope. "Yeah."

I took a good bite of the Twix and held what remained up. "You're in luck today. I'm running a special. All glimpses into the past are priced at one Twix bar."

"I'm serious," she said.

"So am I."

She nodded, but she didn't rush to ask me her next question, and I thought maybe a demo of what I could do was in order. "You've been in jail for . . . ten years, right?"

She squinted at me and nodded slightly.

I assessed her for a bit before continuing. "This is your last appeal."

Again she nodded.

"You don't think it'll go well."

"No."

"You're right. Your lawyer is shit."

"He came cheap."

"When's the appeal?"

Skylar sighed. "It was supposed to be today, but it got postponed to the nineteenth."

I nodded. That wasn't even two weeks away, and in Texas, when your last appeal doesn't go well, you'll have an IV filled with lethal toxins in your arm by midnight.

As I sat there, I took in all of Skylar's energy, which was extremely complex. She carried a whole lotta baggage and it was tough to riffle through it all. "You've had a pretty tough life," I told her. "But a lot of it you brought on yourself."

She squinted skeptically before waving a hand to indicate the cell we were in.

I ignored that and kept going. "You struggled with addiction. It got the best of you for a lot of years, but then I feel like you worked really hard and overcame it."

Her expression softened. I'd just struck a chord.

"You're divorced," I said next. "And your ex is still *really* angry at you."

She gave me one short nod.

I closed my eyes to better concentrate, feeling my way along her energy, looking for bits of information that I could talk about. "You lost someone," I said. I didn't know why I hadn't touched on it sooner. It was the loudest thing in her energy. "Someone very close to you was murdered." And then I gave a small gasp and opened my eyes. "Your son?"

Her eyes had misted again, but she didn't look away from me. Instead she asked, "Can you see who murdered him? Can you tell who it was?"

My brow furrowed and I stood up. The energy from my roommate had shifted dramatically; it was as if the floodgates had been opened and there were now waves of guilt rolling off Skylar—an ocean of regret filled the space between us and it was so intense that I had to withdraw my intuitive feelers. "Skylar," I said, because I needed to get her to close those floodgates. "What are you in here for? Why are you on death row?"

"Cooper!" someone yelled at the door to our cell, and I jumped a whole foot. Stern Eyes was back, handcuffs dangling off her index finger. "Step forward with your arms in front of you and put them through here." Stern Eyes was indicating a small square open section of the bars next to the lock, where she wanted me to stick my hands.

"What? Why?"

"Someone's here to see you," she said. "Someone with big brass balls and a whole lotta pull, so hurry it up."

Gaston. It had to be him. I gulped. God, I hoped Dutch was with him. Especially after what I'd pulled in court. I shuffled over to the door and put my wrists through the small window so she could slap the cuffs on me.

Glancing over my shoulder, I saw that Skylar was staring at us, and I tried to offer her an apologetic look. "Let me go meet with this guy and when I get back, we'll talk," I said.

"What if you don't come back?" she asked, and that small glimmer of hope that I'd seen in her eyes vanished.

"I will," I promised.

"All right, Cooper, step back and I'll have them open the door," Stern Eyes said.

"I will," I repeated to Skylar as I moved two steps back and waited for the buzz.

It came, and as the door began to slide open, Skylar said, "That question you asked me about why I'm here?"

I nodded.

"You know why, don't you?"

I nodded again—reluctantly, though. She was here for her son's murder, and those waves of guilt still sloshed around the cell. I didn't quite know what to think about that.

Skylar studied my face for a moment before she turned her gaze to the wall. As the door clanged to a stop, I turned, still feeling the sticky residue from the Twix bar heavy on my fingers.

Chapter Two

. . .

I was partially right about who'd come to visit me at the county jailhouse. In a small room with a table and two chairs, Gaston was waiting for me, along with two other men: my husband and U.S. assistant prosecutor Matt Hayes.

Matt looked bad, like maybe he himself had gone a few rounds with Judge Schilling, the man I'd outed to a packed courtroom a few hours earlier, who'd then leaped across his bench and grabbed me by the shoulders, shaking what little sense I had left right out of me. To make matters worse, I'd been found in contempt and thrown in jail.

Seeing Matt, however, I started to feel really bad about what I'd done, but we'd been about to lose the case anyway, and my (infamous) temper had gotten the best of me. When I'd been up on the stand, Judge Schilling had flat out called me a charlatan, a faker, a fraud. Where I come from, them's fightin' words, and I'd unleashed the kraken, pinging Judge Schilling with all his secrets, including his biggest—the affair he was having with his cute male clerk. Judge Schilling was a happily married pillar of Christian values in the community. At least, he had been that before I'd gotten through with him.

I hadn't really wondered what'd happened in the aftermath, but here in the little room I could clearly see more stuff had gone down, because Matt was as furious and worked up as I'd ever seen him, his tie askew, his shirt wrinkled, and I bet he'd been pacing a small section of the room right before I came in. Meanwhile my husband was leaning against the right wall, one arm crossed over his beautifully broad chest while he rested the other elbow on it so he could hover his index finger over his mouth.

I narrowed my eyes at him because I knew that stance. He was doing his best to appear serious while trying to tamp down a chuckle.

Hayes expended no such effort. Visibly seething, the second I came fully into the room, he let go. "What the hell were you *thinking*, Abby?!"

"Can I at least get my cuffs off before you start in on me, Matt?" I asked more calmly than I felt. I then turned slightly so the guard could undo the cuffs, but she simply offered me a mocking grin and started to leave. At that moment Gaston cleared his throat and with a one-finger wave toward me, he said, "Hey, CO. Her cuffs. Now."

Stern Eyes turned slowly toward Gaston, as if she couldn't believe he'd just given her a direct order. He casually opened his blazer to expose his badge and said, "Warden Hoffman is an old friend. I was godfather to his son, Quinn. If you'd like to have me call him and order you directly, I can do that."

Stern Eyes paled and her face slacked into a decidedly less stern expression. I had to work to hide a smirk. She stepped forward and undid my cuffs, then left us alone, closing the door behind her.

For a minute nobody spoke. I think we were all waiting for Gaston to say something else, but he merely eyed me coolly, so Matt took it upon himself to get back to yelling at me. "Do you realize what you've *done*?"

I pulled the seat out from the table and sat down across from Gaston. "It looks like I blew your case to kingdom come." I don't think Matt was prepared for that answer, because all he did was bob his head up and down with his mouth hanging open like, "Yeah you did!"

Swiveling in my seat, I turned to Dutch and said, "How bad is it?"

He lowered his hand, all hidden mirth vanishing. "Schilling called a mistrial."

"He did?" I said. "That's awesome!"

"*How* is that awesome?!" Matt shouted.

"He was going to rule against us," I said calmly.

Matt glared at me. "You don't know that!"

I tapped my temple. "Yep. Yep I do."

Gaston said, "Abigail, I haven't heard the full story yet. Tell me what happened in court. And please, start at the beginning."

For the next thirty minutes I told Gaston all about what'd gone on in court. The whole thing had been so ridiculous, so slanted against me, as if I were the one on trial and not Don Corzo, a serial killer who'd murdered at least three women in two states that we knew of.

I'd been brought on to the case late in the game. The trail had long since gone cold after the March night two years earlier when Misty Hartnet's body had been found in a small park. She'd been raped and strangled, but forensics had been unable to pull DNA off her from the rape, for reasons that were a bit too graphic to get into.

Anyway, we knew that her murder was linked to two other murdered girls by the way she'd been posed holding a white carnation over her heart.

I'd looked through the other girls' files first and hadn't gotten a lot from their cases, but when I opened Misty's case, I felt strongly that something at the crime scene had been overlooked. And yet, in the file was a stack of photographs that documented the scene in infinite detail.

Still, I couldn't shake the feeling that something about or at the crime scene had gone unnoticed, so I, along with Dutch and two other investigators, headed out to the park to check it out.

That's when I'd had the strong sensation that we were looking in the wrong spot, and I'd then spied a gazebo next to a running path about four hundred yards away. I'd been drawn to it and I'd called the boys with me as I went to check it out.

As we poked around the area near the gazebo, Oscar Rodriguez—one of the other FBI investigators—discovered, after digging through some leaves, three items perfectly preserved, as if they'd just been waiting for us to find them. A license, a bank card, and a charm with Misty Hartnet's DNA on it, which also perfectly matched the one her sister had given her for Christmas. The license and the bank card belonged to one Don Corzo, an air-conditioning repair guy who'd worked in Oklahoma—where one of the other girls, Wendy McLain, had been murdered—and in Texarkana, where Donna Andrews had been murdered. We knew we'd hit pay dirt with the circumstantial evidence, especially when the DNA results came back confirming the charm's owner.

The problem was, somewhere along the line when we'd all been preparing for trial, the defense got wind that I'd been the one to alert the FBI to the second crime scene, and he'd come up with the rather convenient argument that I was a big fat faker. He submitted a motion to suppress all evidence collected at the second crime scene under the premise that I'd actually stolen Corzo's wallet, planted it at the scene, and pointed the FBI boys right to it.

To prove that I was a fraud, he called in a former client of mine,

Stephanie Snitch. (Swear to God, that's her real name.) Stephie wasn't a fan of mine. Of course, she wasn't a fan of anyone, except perhaps herself.

On the stand, Stephie had lied her ass off. (I'll gladly pay that quarter to the swear jar.) At the end of her testimony she'd even gotten in a little jab: "You don't have to be *psychic* to know Abby Cooper *isn't* psychic."

The defense attorney, Jack Reiner, had laughed.

Corzo had laughed.

The courtroom had chuckled.

Even Judge Schilling had grinned.

Me and Matt? Not so much. It was a cheap shot, and I wondered how long it'd taken Stephanie Stoopid to come up with it. (Okay, so that's just me being petty, but seriously? How many eye-roll-worthy bad psychic jokes can a person bear in her life?)

Anyway, we had a whole ton of clients willing to testify that I was, in fact, the real deal. And I even had a recording of the actual reading I'd done for Little Miss Snitch to show how accurately I'd predicted what would happen to her in the following months. The problem was, I'd never gotten written or verbal consent on the tape to record the session. That the session was going to be recorded wasn't in my disclaimer form. And I'd only said to Stephanie at the start of our time together that I'd record it and e-mail her a copy. She'd said, "Okay," and *then* I'd hit play.

All of that forced us into the rather awkward position of having to ask Stephanie if we could play the recording of her session in court. She'd said no faster than you can type the word.

So the judge ruled that the tape was inadmissible; he'd rely on testimony alone. Stephanie had given hers (liar, liar, pants on fire), and in rebuttal, I'd been called to the stand. The judge had actually interrupted Matt's initial questioning to insert several questions of his own. After he flat out told me that the Bible itself condemned the false prophet, it was abundantly clear to me exactly where the judge stood on psychics in general.

It'd gone downhill from there as he goaded me with a few more truly insulting inquiries into my sanity, and . . . well, I'd lost my cool. And then he'd lost his. It'd been a mess.

After I'd finished telling Gaston all that had happened, for which he'd remained patiently quiet, he said, "Did you really get dragged from the courtroom shouting, 'You can't *handle* the truth!' at Judge Schilling?"

I gulped. "Uh . . . yes, sir. I might've said something to that effect."

Dutch made a barely stifled snorting sound. I turned steely eyes to him and he swiveled to the wall, his shoulders shaking with mirth.

"It's not funny, Rivers," Matt said.

He and I were fighting a losing battle, because Director Gaston also chuckled. "Oh, counselor, I think it is a little," he said.

Of course, that made me crack a smile, but Matt wasn't in a mood to think lightly about any of what'd happened today. Honestly, I couldn't really blame him.

Dutch cleared his throat, got hold of himself, and turned back to face us with only a slight quirk to his lips. "Matt, how soon can you refile the charges?"

The federal prosecutor shook his head. "You guys don't seem to get it," he said. "The defense knows how to beat us. We can't go marching back into court with any of the evidence that Abby led us to. If Corzo's attorney found one former client of Abby's willing to testify she's a fraud, the next time we go to court, he'll have a parade of witnesses claiming she's the biggest scam to hit Texas since Enron."

"Hey!" I snapped. "My clients are awesome. There's no way he'd find a parade of them to come out against me."

"Yeah?" Matt said, putting his hands on the table and hanging his head a little to look angrily at me. "Well, Corzo's team doesn't really need a parade, Abby. Today, in fact, they only needed *one*."

"We'll get you more evidence, Matt," Dutch said, back to being serious again, and sounding so sure, but Corzo was a pretty slick guy, and we'd gotten very, very lucky with the second crime-scene evidence found in Misty Hartnet's case.

Matt considered Dutch skeptically. "The first team worked these files for years with no hard evidence against Corzo, Rivers. Your team worked it for another three months before the ID and bank card were found. What makes you think there's any evidence left to discover or that we have time to let you look for it?"

"In point of fact, Hayes," Dutch countered, his tone frosty, "it was three months before I assigned the case to Abby and asked for her impressions. We had the ID and the bank card within a *day* after I asked her to look into it."

Matt shook his head. "But that's the problem. She can't touch this case from here on out. All evidence brought in by her psychic abilities is out. If I'm gonna file new charges against Corzo, then I need brand-new evidence without the fruit from her poisoned tree."

Dutch opened his mouth to protest, but Gaston held up his hand and said, "Mr. Hayes is correct, Agent Rivers. Corzo's attorney will have the jury convinced that Abigail is a fraud and that we planted any additional evidence discovered simply to avoid embarrassment for having hired her in the first place. They might not all believe we did that, of course, but all he needs to create here is reasonable doubt. And as long as she's officially on the case, she's a reason to doubt its credibility."

I squirmed in my chair. Coming from Gaston, that stung. "Sir—," Dutch said, but Gaston cut him off by holding up his hand.

"That's my final word on the issue," he said. "Abigail may not formally comment on this case moving forward. All future evidence must be the direct result of your team's strong investigative skills. Look through the files. See if you missed something. I have confidence in your keen eyes in particular, Agent Rivers, to find something we can use."

Both Matt and Dutch appeared a little stunned, Dutch to have lost the argument and Matt to have won it so easily. I settled for pouting in my chair, feeling deeply ashamed that I'd disappointed the director. I really liked Gaston, and it felt bad to let him down.

"Now," Gaston said, as if the matter were settled and there was nothing left to do but shake on it, "if you'll excuse us, Mr. Hayes, I'd like a moment alone with Abigail and Agent Rivers."

Matt nodded and offered me a rather resigned look before heading out. Gaston waited a moment after the door was closed and then he focused on me. "I'm working to get you out of here, but it might be tomorrow morning before I can arrange it."

"What?!" I gasped. "Tomorrow? Are you serious? Director, I was *attacked* in a packed courtroom!"

"Yes, and you also severely embarrassed a federally appointed judge to that same packed courtroom. That's a blow he won't soon recover from."

My shoulders sagged and I dropped my chin. As much as I wanted to say that Schilling had it coming, and that lying to his lover and to his wife and to himself about who he really was had been a crummy way to conduct himself, I could now see how my actions and outing him were nothing but petty, unwarranted, underhanded moves. "Yes, sir."

"It upsets me too that you'll have to stay in here overnight," Gaston said, squeezing my arm good-naturedly.

I lifted my chin. "Yeah. It's not so bad. My cellmate is nice at least."

"Good. That's good. Still, I'll be dropping off copies of the case files of Wendy McLain and Donna Andrews to your house as soon as you're free."

I stared openmouthed at him. "Wendy McLain and Donna Andrews, sir?"

"Yes."

"As in the two other girls murdered by Don Corzo?"

"Yes."

I looked at Dutch to see if he understood what Gaston's angle was. Dutch seemed as puzzled as I felt. I turned my attention back to the director. "But . . . I thought I wasn't supposed to comment on the case against Corzo, sir?"

"You're not. However, if you notice anything in the case file that might be of interest to us, or something you feel we should pursue, please pull it out and attach it with a paper clip to the front of the file. If a map is needed, please get one and attach it the same way. Agent Rivers here will be tasked with studying the files in the evening to see if anything sticks out that will need to be followed up on. Agent Rivers, perhaps what should jump out at you are those items paper-clipped to the front of the file."

Dutch offered the director a sly grin. "Yes, sir. I understand perfectly, sir."

"Excellent," Gaston said, pushing his chair back and getting to his feet. "And now, if you'll excuse me, I will wait outside for you, Agent Rivers, and give you some time with your wife."

"Thank you, sir," I said, so relieved that he'd forgiven me.

Gaston stepped to the door. "You're welcome." After opening

it, however, he paused and eyed me over his shoulder. "By the way, Abigail, try not to incite a prison riot before we can get you out of here, all right?"

I nodded. Vigorously. Because I knew that the director wasn't even close to kidding.

After he'd gone, Dutch stepped forward to scoop me up into a hug. I sighed contentedly and he kissed the top of my head. "Sorry we can't spring you from this joint until tomorrow."

I smirked against his shirt. "But a small part of you is sorta hoping that a night in jail is gonna teach me a lesson, huh?"

"It's like you *know* me."

I rolled my eyes and looked up at him. "What're you gonna do with your night off?" The image of an impromptu poker game and a cloud of cigar smoke blossomed in my mind's eye.

Dutch held me tighter, folding my head back into his chest. "I'm gonna miss my wife," he said. "Lots."

"Good answer, cowboy. You been saving that one up?"

He chuckled. "No. It just came to me. But not bad for one off the cuff, huh?"

"I'd give it more brownie points if I didn't know that invites for an impromptu poker game have already been sent out."

Dutch stiffened and I knew I had him. At that moment his phone buzzed from his back pocket and he stiffened again. "That'll be Oscar," I said, my radar homing in on the message as well as if it'd come to me directly. "He can make it."

Dutch's chest shook again with quiet laughter. "I can't get away with anything around you, can I?"

"Nope," I said, tilting my head back to stare up into his gorgeous midnight blues. "And don't you forget it."

He stroked my cheek and then his good humor seemed to leave him and he got all serious on me. "You gonna be okay in here, Edgar?"

"I'll be fine," I assured him. "I even have a nice cellmate. She gave me a Twix."

He cocked his head. "Only one cellmate? I figured county would put at least four to a cell."

"She was supposed to have a cell all to herself, but solitary's all booked up and I guess they're really overcrowded in here."

My hubby's brow shot up. "Why is she supposed to have a cell all to herself?"

I shrugged again. "She's on death row and they don't like those guys to mix with the general population, I guess."

Dutch gripped me by the shoulders. "What the hell do you mean they put you in the same cell with a death row inmate?" And then he looked to the door, ready to hurtle through it and cause a big scene.

"Hey," I said, grabbing his arms in return. "It's okay, Dutch. She's cool. I swear."

"Abby," he said, his voice very stern, "you don't understand. The reason they don't mix death row inmates with the general population is because they have nothing left to lose. They can kill without fear of retribution because there's no stick left to hold over their heads."

"Yeah, but I swear, she's cool. We had a good chat and she's really nice."

And then Dutch blinked and if it was possible, he appeared even more alarmed. "You haven't told her that you work for us, have you?"

"No," I said quickly. And yeah, you probably noticed that was one of those not-quite-a-lie but not-quite-the-truth statements again.

He narrowed his eyes. "You're sure?"

I held up three fingers. "Scout's honor."

"Okay, well, don't. The last thing I need is for you to get your ass kicked while I'm having the guys over for a poker game."

I grinned. "True dat, pal. I'd *definitely* hold that over your head for the rest of your life."

He let go of my arms but hugged me to him again. "Please be careful, okay?"

"I will, honey. I promise."

After Dutch and I said our good-byes, I was handcuffed and led back to the cell I shared with Skylar. When I got there, it was empty and Stern Eyes informed me that I'd missed the call to dinner. She dumped me at the door without offering to take me down to the cafeteria, and I understood pretty quick that I was being punished for the way that Gaston had ordered her around.

"Bitch," I muttered after the cell door closed and Stern Eyes had walked away. My stomach grumbled to let me know that it would also be contributing to the swear jar quarter collection. After listening to an hour of Stoopid Stephanie Snitch's testimony, and then my go-around with the judge, my total for the day had definitely risen into the double digits, so what was a few extra quarters?

I looked over the cell for something to do or read, but it was fairly sparse as jail cells go. My gaze eventually landed on Skylar's side of the space and I saw that she had just a few items on the small shelf behind her bunk. I glanced toward the door, but then realized that I'd have plenty of advance warning if I wanted to do a little snooping. I'd hear the inmates coming back from the cafeteria and the door would of course give that loud buzzing sound before it opened.

Moving over to the small shelf, I bent double, hoping to find a book or something to read while she was away. Luck was with me when I spied a well-worn paperback with the image of a man and a woman embracing in a passionate kiss. I smiled. I'm a sucker for a good romance novel.

Picking up the book, I snuck back across the cell and settled into my bunk for a little reading time. As I opened it, however, something slipped out onto my lap.

At first I thought it was Skylar's bookmark, but then I saw that it was actually a photograph of Skylar in younger, happier days with her arms wrapped tightly around a boy, who resembled her, grinning from ear to ear. He'd lost several of his teeth, but in front of him was a birthday cake with the words *Happy Birthday, Noah!* There were nine candles on the cake.

My chest constricted a bit as I took in his image, which was flat and plastic looking—a clear sign to my intuitive mind that Noah was deceased.

My gaze drifted to Skylar and her radiant smile. She was beaming at the camera; holding her son close, she looked like someone who had everything in the world she needed to be happy.

I then scanned the background looking for the other party guests, but the shutter had been trained only on Skylar and her son. I flipped the photo over and read, "May 29, 2004."

I didn't know when Noah had died, but I did note that he would be nearly twenty years old now if he'd lived. Flipping the photo back over, I gazed for a time at Noah's sweet face, with his bright blue eyes, lean features, and broad smile, which mirrored his mother's. I wondered how long after this photo had been taken that the vibrant young boy's life had been snuffed out. It pained me to think that someone so young, with such promise, could have met such an abrupt and untimely end.

"You poor little guy," I murmured, caressing his image with my fingers. I wondered if his mother had done the same thing in the years she'd held on to the photo.

At that moment there was a loud buzz and my cell door began to roll open. Accompanying this was the sort of sound that large crowds make—a sort of milling of voices that blend together to make nothing that's said discernible except for the occasional higher pitch of laughter.

I scooted out of my bunk and rushed the paperback and the photo back to Skylar's side, setting it back exactly as I'd found it before darting for my bunk again. When Skylar walked into the cell, I was lying back, idly staring up at the ceiling.

"How was dinner?" I asked, my stomach giving a little gurgle.

She wore a small smirk and she came over to my side, unzipping her orange jumpsuit to pull something out of the T-shirt underneath. "Here," she said, handing me two packages of peanut butter crackers. "I figured they wouldn't escort you down for dinner. They're mean here at county. They never cut the newbies a break."

I took the crackers greedily before remembering my manners. "Thanks," I said. "I really appreciate it. I'm starving."

Skylar shuffled over to her bunk and lay back on her cot. It was quite obvious that her mood had shifted. She'd been somewhat open to me before I'd been taken away to meet the boys, but now I could see that she had withdrawn again. I couldn't tell why, but maybe it's just what happens when you spend a decade in prison on death row. Pretty soon, I would imagine, mentally you just fold in on yourself, and it becomes hard to interact with people or even to show a spark of personality.

Skylar closed her eyes as if she were tired, but I had the impression that it was more of a meditative posture than anything else. I crossed my legs on the bunk and nibbled at the crackers, watching my cellmate studiously. "Hey, Skylar?" I said.

"Yeah?"

"Will you tell me about your son?"

She didn't answer me for a long time, and I was beginning to think she wasn't going to when she said, "He was my whole world. He was my sun and my moon and everything I lived for. Now that he's gone, I have nothing left and I just wish the state would hurry up and get it over with."

I scanned her energy for the second time and I didn't like the signals I was picking up. Skylar's energy indicated that her life would come to an abrupt end—soon. And what really, really bothered me was the specific energy surrounding her death, because there was no justice to it. In fact, it felt like a murder. I should know—I've been around enough murder investigations to sense exactly when a death goes from something that feels energetically "justified" to something much darker.

Now, I have my own views on capital punishment. I'm definitely not a member of the "Let 'em all burn in hell!" camp, but there are instances when I'm not wholly against the idea of sticking a needle in the arm of a serial killer either. Some crimes are just so heinous, so cruel, so unspeakable, and the people who commit them so inherently evil that when it comes to snuffing out their lives, I think, "Yep." And I can tell you that there's a feeling in the ether—the spiritual energy—surrounding these particularly evil doers when they are put to death that reads, to my intuitive mind at least, that justice has been served. And yet, I've also come across instances when someone has been convicted of a capital crime and put to death and the ether surrounding that capital sentence felt somewhat unfair, if not quite unjust.

Capital punishment is not a black-and-white issue, even spiritually, it seems.

With Skylar, however, when I focused on her impending death, it felt like she was about to actually be murdered unjustly by the state, and that really bothered me.

"How old was Noah when he . . . passed?" I asked her.

Skylar's chest lifted with a deep breath and she sighed out her reply. "Nine."

My mind flashed back to the photo and I felt that pang in my heart again. "That's a great age," I said. I knew I was probably being a pest, but I wanted to keep her talking. I felt the strongest urge to figure out her story and see if I could help her. Why, I couldn't quite put into words, but it was there, that feeling that I was somehow mingled with her future—that I might even be her last hope. "So tell me what happened," I said softly.

She opened her eyes and turned her head a little to look at me. "What do you see?"

"About what happened to your son?"

She nodded.

I concentrated, focusing my gaze on the opposite wall away from her face. "It's a little murky, but I keep seeing a knife."

I heard a tiny gasp escape her lips. "That's true."

"As for who was wielding it, I swear it's someone you know."

My gaze traveled back to Skylar. She sat up and looked me level in the eyes, but all I saw there was confusion.

"Miller!" my favorite guard yelled. Skylar and I both jumped as the CO appeared at the bars again. "Stand up, grab your personal items, come to the bars, and put your hands through the window."

Skylar and I exchanged a look before she got obediently to her feet, pulled up her bedding—folding it quickly and putting her book into the space between her pillow and blanket—then shuffled over and obeyed the command to put her hands through the opening, while balancing her belongings on her arms.

"Where're you taking her?" I asked.

"None of your business," said Stern.

"Ah," I said. "Tomorrow, I'll be sure to sing your praises to the FBI director so that he can pass them on to the warden."

Stern Eyes glared hard at me. Good thing I'm immune to that whole "if looks could kill" thing. "A spot opened up in solitary," the CO said grudgingly as she snapped the cuffs on Skylar. "And since you seem to have friends in high places, you get this ten by ten all to yourself."

"Lucky me."

"Let's see if you still feel that way in the morning," the charming CO replied with a smirk. She then moved a bit down the corridor and the cell door buzzed and began to slide open. Skylar kept her head down, submissively waiting for the cell to open all the way before stepping through. It upset me to think that prison had taken that sunny, bright-eyed woman from the photo and turned her into a beaten, battered shell of a person. She seemed so resigned to her fate—unjust though it might be.

"Skylar," I called, right before the door clicked to a stop.

She didn't look at me, but I felt like she was listening.

I stayed on the bunk, but I leaned out a little while Stern Eyes waved Skylar forward. "I'm gonna help you," I called to her. She made no acknowledgment of it. She simply took two steps forward out of the cell, and I knew that she put about as much faith in my words as she had left in the justice system.

The cell door buzzed again and it began to close. I got up and waited for the bars to slide across the threshold. Skylar and the guard quickly disappeared from my view. Grabbing the bars, I put my mouth between them and called out again. "I will, Skylar. I will!"

I wanted so much to reach her. To give her something to hold on to. A tiny light in the darkness. But as I extended my energy out toward her, all I felt was an empty sort of resignation.

That bothered me more than I could say.

Chapter Three

. . .

I'm pretty sure that Stern Eyes wanted me to spend a night in jail totally freaked-out and unable to sleep, but the truth is I slept like a rock. I woke up hungry as hell, but instead of getting ready to grab some grub with the other prisoners, I got up, made my bunk, and paced the floor until a new CO appeared at the door to my cell.

I held my wrists out in front of me, and when she nodded, I scooted forward and slid my wrists through the small window by the lock. "Time to go home!" I sang, even before she could tell me. Some days it really pays to be psychic.

As happy as I was to be let out of the cell, my psychic sense didn't predict what would come next, which was basically a lengthy sit-down with Matt Hayes while he pleaded for my release with Judge Schilling's clerk on the phone in the same small visiting room from the night before. In the end I was forced to write a lengthy apology to the judge and agree not to press charges against him for assaulting me in the courtroom. It irked me that Judge Schilling was coming out ahead in the deal, but Matt offered me little sympathy when I protested both the required written apology and the agreement not to press charges. "What can I say, Abby? You pissed off a federal judge to the point where he lost his temper and wanted to *end* you. Even if he ultimately gets tossed off the bench for it, no judge who hears about what you did will welcome you back in the courtroom until you show some remorse for your part in provoking Schilling and respect for the post in general."

With Matt's words weighing heavily on me, I typed out the sincerest apology letter I could, which Matt then e-mailed directly to the judge. It was rejected three times, so I suppose my sincerity needed to be *slightly* more earnest. The fourth time was the charm. Or the judge just got tired of reading about how very, very, very, very, very, very, *very* sorry I was.

Twenty minutes after the judge lifted the contempt-of-court charge against me, I was free and racing out the door to throw my arms around my BFF, Candice Fusco. "FREEDOM!" I shouted after hugging her and stepping back to raise my arms high.

Candice laughed. "Goofball," she said, nudging me with her shoulder.

I looked around. "Where's my hubby? And for that matter, where's yours?"

Candice snaked an arm around my shoulders. "The boys send their regrets. They were here earlier, but it took you so long to write an apology to Schilling that they got called back to work by Gaston. He wants them to get cracking on finding some other evidence to nail that son of a bitch Corzo."

"Is he back on the streets?" I asked.

"Last night," she said grimly.

I hung my head. "I feel like it's my fault he's out."

"Shocking."

I glanced up at her. "You think it's my fault too?"

She gave my shoulders a squeeze. "No, honey, but in any case we lose, you always assign the blame to yourself. You gotta stop doing that. It's not healthy."

"I'll work on that," I said, shushing my inner lie detector.

"You probably want something to eat, huh?" she asked.

"Nope," I told her. She raised her brow. "I want *many something* to eat."

Candice chuckled again and tugged me toward the parking lot. After leaving county, we shot over to one of my favorite Mexican joints, Mi Madre's, which serves THE best giant burrito ever put together, and you can order it at any time of day, which meant I'd be able to have at it even though it was only ten a.m. I've never been able to eat a whole burrito in one sitting, but that has never stopped me from trying.

While we waited on our food, Candice and I nibbled on chips and salsa. I did my best to restrain myself from gobbling down the entire basket. "So tell me," Candice said with a slight twitch of her lips. "Anyone in county make you their bitch?"

I suppressed a grin. "No," I said with an exaggerated sigh. "Do you think my looks are fading?"

"Yes," Candice said without hesitation. I narrowed my eyes at her and she broke out into a hearty laugh. "You're too easy, Sundance."

Sundance is my nickname. Well, one of my nicknames. Candice calls me Sundance, Dutch calls me Edgar, and I'm Abs to my sister. The guys at the bureau call me Cooper, but the director almost always calls me Abigail. To our handyman I'm the Abster, but when I look in the mirror, all I see is me. Abby—a girl with long brown locks, a nice enough nose, high cheekbones (thank you Gram!), and mildly moody sea blue eyes.

Our lunch arrived and I tucked in with relish (but not before requesting more chips). "So how was it, really?" Candice asked.

"What?" I said after savoring the mouthful of my giant burrito (spicy beef, French fries, avocado, lettuce, tomato, and creamy chipotle sauce all wrapped in a light flour tortilla). "You mean, jail?"

Candice nodded, having just taken a bite of her modest egg, cheese, and potato taco.

I shrugged. "It was fine. I mean, I knew I wasn't staying long, so it didn't freak me out much. But I did meet someone who left quite an impression on me."

"Was she pretty?" Candice asked, with a bat of her eyelashes.

"Will you quit it?"

Candice chuckled. "Sorry. I'll stop. Who was it you met?"

"This woman named Skylar. Skylar Miller. She's on death row, in county waiting for her appeal. We shared the same cell."

Candice's brow furrowed. "How did you get to share a cell with a death row inmate? That's not supposed to happen."

"County's crowded."

The frown on Candice's face remained. "Still, I can't believe they allowed that."

"It wasn't a big deal," I insisted.

"Sundance," Candice said, reaching out to put a hand on my arm, like she just realized I'd escaped some sort of terrible danger. "Death row inmates have nothing to live for. They're dangerous to the rest of the population for a reason, because there's usually nothing you can threaten them with to keep them in line."

"Skylar's not like that," I told her. "She gave me half her Twix bar and a couple of peanut butter crackers when the CO refused to let me go to dinner."

"Most people on death row are also masters at manipulation."

I sighed. "Candice, will you please listen to the rest of the story before deciding that I just lost one of my nine lives?"

Candice lifted her hand from my arm. "Okay, tell me the rest."

I took another bite of the burrito, moaned—it was so good—but chewed quickly before saying, "From what I could ascertain mostly through my radar, Skylar was convicted of murdering her son. He was nine. Stabbed to death back in two thousand four or the first half of two thousand five."

Candice winced. "Ouch."

"I don't think she did it." The minute that came out of my mouth, I felt a lightness in the center of my solar plexus. That was my intuition telling me I was speaking a truth.

Candice set down her taco and looked hard at me across the table. "You think she's innocent?"

"Yes."

"Is that your gut talking or the Twix bar?"

I frowned at her and tapped my temple. "My radar says she's innocent."

"How innocent?"

"What do you mean, 'how innocent'? Isn't innocent *innocent*?"

"Well," she said, "if I'm hearing you right, I think what you're saying is that she didn't wield the knife in her son's murder."

"Yes. That's what I think."

"But what if she was indirectly responsible?"

"I'm still not following."

Candice shifted in her chair. "What if she had a motive to kill him and contributed in the form of conspiracy to commit murder?"

My jaw dropped. "Candice," I said. "What *reason* could a mother ever have to directly or indirectly kill her own child?"

Candice shrugged. "Off the top of my head I can think of a couple of reasons—"

"Such as?" I demanded.

Candice ticked them off on her fingers. "Munchausen by proxy, to collect an insurance settlement, or because she was an impatient woman who decided she was sick of caring for a young child and wanted her life back. Or even that with him to feed and clothe, it left her less money to buy alcohol and/or drugs. I mean, what do you know about this woman's background?"

I frowned. I'd picked up on the addiction issues in Skylar's past right off the bat. "Okay, so you might have a point," I conceded. "But here's the thing: I don't think she was indirectly involved either. I think she's been falsely accused, and she's on her last appeal and the state is prepared to give her the needle at the first opportunity."

Candice folded her napkin and dropped it on her empty plate before leaning back in her chair to let out a sigh. "You're gonna ask me to help you look into the case, aren't you?"

"Yes."

"A case that won't pay our rent or even the electric bill."

"Yes."

"A case where the clock is ticking and the odds are very long that we'll be able to make any sort of progress before time runs out."

"Uh-huh."

"A case that's a decade old and cold as the polar ice caps."

"Yep, although global warming and my intuition might make things a tad more optimistic."

Candice looked hard at me before she dropped her chin and shook her head. "Sundance, I'm gonna say this as someone who loves you—you're great company, but you're also a giant pain in the ass."

"Would it help if I said please?"

"Couldn't hurt," she said.

"Please?"

My best friend lifted her chin, a slight grin on her lips. "Fine. But you'll only get my help if you agree to a few conditions."

"Shoot."

"First, if we lose, I mean, if the clock runs out and we don't find anything that can clear this woman, you're not gonna go around blaming yourself for not figuring it out in time."

I sat with that. I'm good with guilt. We're buddies. We've spent an awful lot of time together, but I could see what Candice was saying. When I get involved with a case, I'm all in. And this woman had struck such a weird chord with me; I felt so compelled to do what I could for her and I wasn't sure why. Keeping my emotions in check—especially if we couldn't clear her in time—wasn't going to be an easy task. "I'll try," I told her, because that's all I felt I could promise.

"Okay, I guess that's honest. Condition number two is that we follow the evidence, and wherever it leads, we go there to find out the truth. I know you feel strongly about this woman's innocence, Abs—"

"It's not just my feelings, Candice. It's a solid knowing. My intuition is *insisting* that she's innocent."

"And that's good enough for me to agree to get involved," she was quick to say. "But, honey, if she were somehow indirectly involved, we can't turn a blind eye to that."

I sighed. "Agreed."

"Condition three—," Candice started to say before I interrupted her again.

"You come with a lot of conditions for a girl who prides herself on keeping it simple."

She flashed me a toothy smile. "I like to adapt to whatever the situation calls for. Condition *three*, we take paying cases and clients during the day and work on this in our off time. And speaking of paying clients, as you know, at the moment I have that huge cheating-husband case that I'm wrapping up, which is gonna hog most of my time for the next couple of days, so I'll only be able to help you with this part-time. At least at first."

"I guess that's fair," I said. "We both have to bills to pay."

"Condition four . . ." I sagged dramatically in my chair. Candice continued as if I hadn't moved an inch. "Cases like this always kick up a lot of dust. We're bound to piss someone off, from the prosecutor to the detectives who worked the case, to any of the extended family. We're gonna encounter a lot of hot tempers, Sundance. It's inevitable. And that means that you need to rein in that hair trigger of yours." My BFF pointed to my mouth for emphasis.

"I'm not *that* bad," I growled.

Candice reached for her purse. "Honey, you got your ass thrown in *jail* yesterday because you did what you always do when someone pushes your buttons. You come out swinging with that radar of yours, dropping little bombs of best-kept secrets all over the place until the room is full of casualties."

I crossed my arms and glared at my best friend. I hated that she'd so easily pegged me. I'd learned to fight back against the onslaught of bullies that had populated my youth by publicly revealing their darkest secrets, pulling away their carefully held facades to expose them for the little weaklings they were. It'd been incredibly effective, and I'd done that even before I'd consciously known that I was psychic. Candice didn't look at me while I pouted; she simply dug out her wallet, took out a twenty, and then waved to our waiter for the check.

He dropped that off and Candice took a quick peek before enclosing the twenty in the small leather binder and handing it to him with her thanks.

"Fine," I said quietly. "I'll rein it in."

Candice focused once again on me. "That a girl," she said, beaming. "Now, come on, we've got some work to do."

Candice dropped me at home to shower and change, promising to meet me back at my place after she ran an errand. My car was still at the office, because Matt had come to collect me for court the previous day, so I'd need Candice to give me a lift to retrieve it.

Lucky me, I didn't have any clients scheduled for the day, as I read for clients only three days a week on a floating schedule, depending on what's going on with my FBI consulting duties, or what cases Candice and I are working on. I read for only about eighteen clients a week in total—any more than that and I'm too drained to work on the cases that Candice and the FBI bring in. Even that many, however, can leave me craving a nap in the middle of the day.

When I got in the door of our beautiful home on the far west side of Austin, I wanted nothing more than a quick power nap, followed by a quick(er) shower and some quick(est) quality time with our two miniature dachshunds, Eggy and Tuttle. But as I stepped into the foyer, I was struck by the overpowering scents prevalent in a typical man cave: smelly cigar mixed with eau de gym bag. "Gah!" I said, waving a hand in front of my nose. "That is *ripe*." At the sound of my voice, Eggy and Tuttle rushed out from the kitchen and I got down on all fours to hug and kiss and cuddle with their wriggly selves. Then I got up and opened all the windows in the living room, even though the mercury was already climbing into the mid-nineties.

I found the source of much of the smell in the kitchen, where an ashtray sat in the middle of the table with the remnants of three cigars, and glasses containing a few drops of scotch were parked at each of the six chairs. Poker chips were displayed like polka dots across the surface of the table, along with some dirty paper plates and wadded-up napkins. In the corner by the door, pizza boxes were stacked atop the stainless steel garbage can. Crumbs littered all four sections of our granite counter. "Ground zero," I said, putting my hands on my hips and offering the disastrous scene a frown.

Dutch is normally a very neat guy, but on occasion he likes to take a holiday from the domestic orderly bliss that is our home-sweet-home, and from what I could tell, the night before, he'd taken that license to extremes.

I nearly left the mess for him to take care of, but then I thought about some advice my sister had given me shortly after Dutch and I had come back from our honeymoon.

"Abs," Cat had said with that stern look that all older sisters adopt when dispensing advice to a younger sibling. "The key to a happy marriage is this: Every day when you wake up, commit yourself to making him feel like Superman. Light up when he enters the room. Let him know as often as you can how much you appreciate him and everything he does for you. If he wants to get it on, honey, get it on. And when he's tired, or ill, or grouchy, take care of him in any way you can." When I'd offered her a (very) skeptical frown, she'd added, "That doesn't mean turning yourself into June Cleaver, Abby."

I'd arched an eyebrow. "Sounds a little Stepford Wife–ish to me."

Cat had shaken her head and laid a gentle hand on my shoulder. "It's not. It simply means being his partner. His champion. His other half. Find ways every day to appreciate him, to love him, to let him know he's your one and only, and you two will be the married couple that all other couples dream about."

I'd thought about what she'd said off and on for several days afterward, when I'd actually taken her advice as an almost defiant challenge, as if I wanted to prove her wrong. But the darnedest thing started happening. From the very beginning, Dutch had been the one to take care of me. He'd always been the one to clean up my messes, cook for me, come find me when I didn't make it home at the usual hour. Soothe me when I was sad. Tell me how beautiful I was when I felt schlumpy. He'd always been there for me and my needs, but I began to see how little I'd been there for him and his.

It was a sobering thing to realize that in all the time we'd been together, I'd been avoiding getting too close to him. Oh, sure, I loved Dutch more than anyone in the world, but I'd held him at arm's length for our entire courtship, never really, truly letting him in.

It didn't take a degree in psychiatry to know why. I'd been terribly abused by my parents growing up. My mother and father, Claire and Sam, were somewhat despicable in character and they'd adamantly and consistently withheld their love and affection for my entire childhood. My mother especially had done little else but tear me down both physically and mentally from the time I was a toddler through to when I finally escaped home to go to college. So of course, as an adult, I remained a little guarded. A little distant. A little unobtainable.

But Cat had known that's what I was doing, and she'd likely known how hard that would be on a marriage. After all, Cat had been raised by the same two people, and her marriage had been through a rough patch or two. At times, Cat also knew me better than I knew myself.

Her words affected me like no advice I've ever been given, because in realizing why I kept Dutch at arm's length, I clearly saw for the first time that I was doing exactly what my parents had done to me. I was withholding.

So I began to follow her sage words. I immersed myself in my relationship with my husband, in little ways at first. Dutch would come home from his morning workout and I'd bring him coffee as he stepped out of the shower. He'd slip into a crisp white shirt and dark slacks and run a little goop through his hair, and I'd eye him in the mirror with desire and a sultry smile that he couldn't miss. He'd head to work and I'd put a love note in his bag—just a line about how proud I was of him. How beautiful he was. How happy I was as his wife.

He'd come home and cook dinner and instead of camping out in front of the TV while he fussed in the kitchen, I'd keep him company at the kitchen table and we'd talk about our days, about our future, about whatever came to mind. After dinner, he'd clear the table and I'd do the dishes, making sure to compliment him on the meal. On those weekends when he'd head outside to mow the lawn, I'd bring him an ice-cold beer. And, in those times when Dutch was in the mood and maybe I wasn't, well, I got in the mood and we had fun.

As the weeks passed and I kept discovering little ways to open myself up to him, the most amazing thing happened. I found myself falling madly, deeply, passionately, head-over-heels in love with my husband. I'd loved him as much as I thought I could love anybody before I'd married him, but in treating him like my own personal Superman, I discovered how much of a superhero he actually was. How giving he was. How generous. How kind, caring, and considerate. How passionate. How loving. How genuinely *good*. And whatever wounds had never fully healed from my childhood finally, at long last, formed scar tissue. It was like being able to take a full breath of air for the first time in my life. It was transformative. And it likely would save our marriage, because, at some point, all that withholding would've turned a loving man bitter. On some level I think I'd known that and yet I'd needed my sister to point it out to me and help me change.

Sometimes it's good to have people in your life that know you better than you know yourself.

However, sometimes, when you're faced with the remnants of a late-night poker game, it can be a pain in the keister.

I set to work cleaning up the kitchen, grumbling maybe just a little, but it didn't take me all *that* long. I also dug out some scented candles from the linen closet and set them around the house to disperse the cigar smoke.

By the time I was done, the place looked nice and tidy again, but I was still a mess.

Candice showed up just as I was heading to the shower, and I let her in with an apology. "Sorry," I said. "The boys had poker here last night and it apparently went late enough that nobody cleaned up."

Candice smirked. "Yeah, I know. I got a two a.m. phone call from Brice. Your husband broke out the good scotch and my husband wisely decided to crash here for the night."

"Is that the real reason they weren't at the jail this morning to spring me out of the slammer?"

Candice laughed. "Oh, no. They showed up. Hungover and looking like hell, but they were there."

At that moment a noise from down the hall made us both stiffen. My BFF looked sharply at me and pointed to the corridor leading to the guest rooms, silently asking me if I knew of anyone else in the house.

I shook my head.

Another noise came from the corridor and I gasped and edged closer to Candice. "Someone's in the house!" I whispered.

Candice withdrew a gun from her purse, raising it in a defensive stance as she spoke softly to me. "Stay behind me, Sundance. This could get messy."

Chapter Four

. . .

The second Candice went into her "I'ma kill you, bad guy!" stance, I moved to the credenza just to her left and withdrew my own gun. My BFF's brow rose in surprise. I met her gaze without blinking. Gone were the days when I refused to wield or even hold a gun out of principle. I mean, you have enough encounters with people who want to kill you, and your principles tend to get rearranged.

I checked the chamber on the revolver. It was loaded, and I nodded to Candice and stepped close to her back. If she dropped low, I'd be ready to shoot.

Another sound came from down the hallway and Candice motioned for me to follow her. We walked forward cautiously, sticking to the left of the hallway before stopping at the wall, where Candice and I both flattened our backs for a moment. Candice then peered around the corner and pulled her head back. She made a motion with her hand that she was going to move forward and I nodded.

We rounded the corner and I moved to the other side of the hallway, just behind her with my gun held in front of me, mirroring her stance. We proceeded one slow step at a time.

We stopped just a few feet into the hallway because we both heard the sound of running water. I pointed to the closed door of the bathroom at the far end of the corridor. "Someone's in there!" I whispered. Abruptly the water turned off.

She nodded and moved to my side of the hallway. She then quickly walked to the bathroom and raised her foot. Before I could tell her not to, she gave the door a tremendous kick and it blew open. Steam floated out and I rushed forward to cover Candice, who began yelling, *"Do not move, scumbag!"*

My heart was hammering in my chest and sweat coated my hands, while the gun trembled a little. And then I saw at whom Candice was yelling.

A naked man stood in the doorway, his back to us, his arms raised, and a whole lotta butt crack showing.

A towel was puddled at his feet and his black hair dripped onto his shoulders. The mirror he was standing in front of was completely fogged over, so luckily we didn't have a clear view of the full monty. Candice stepped forward and put the gun right to the back of his head. "Do. Not. Move," she growled.

"Got it," he said.

My brow furrowed.

"Sundance," Candice said to me. "Call the police. I'll hold him here."

I didn't move. Instead, I studied the man's shoulders, which were shaking slightly, but not out of fear. He appeared to be laughing. And then my eyes drifted to the back of the man's head and that black hair. And I caught the sound of his voice.

Candice leaned in a little, pushing the muzzle of the gun into his neck. "Something funny, asshole?" she snarled.

I lowered my gun and shook my head. Candice still hadn't realized who was in my bathroom.

The "intruder's" shoulders began to shake a little harder, and slight snorting sounds came from the effort he was making to quash what I thought might be a howl of laughter. Candice looked back at me as if to ask if I could believe that this guy was actually laughing about having a gun shoved to the back of his skull, and that's when she saw my lowered gun and maybe the smile on my lips.

"What?" she asked me.

"Very funny, Oscar," I said.

Candice's reaction was a bit priceless. She immediately sucked in a breath, pulled her gun back, and yanked Oscar's shoulder so that she could see his face. "Rodriguez?"

He saluted. "Hello, ma'am. Tonight, when you and my boss get together for dinner, maybe you shouldn't mention that you saw me naked today, eh?"

"Gah!" Candice said, turning at once to stalk out of the bathroom, her cheeks decidedly pink.

I covered my mouth to try to hold in a laugh, but some of it leaked out. I also turned my eyes away from Oscar and his bare-butt nakedness, grabbing the handle of the door to pull it closed. "As you were, Agent Rodriguez," I told him.

I attempted to shut the door, but Candice's kick had caused it to come off its hinges a little. The best I could do was tug it partly closed and hurry away down the hall.

I found Candice sitting on the sofa, leaning her elbows on her knees and shaking her head. "Did you know he was here?"

"Nope. He must be a leftover from last night's poker game."

Candice's pink, embarrassed glow had faded completely, and I swore she looked a little pale. "I almost shot him, Sundance."

I rolled my eyes. "Oh, you did not. You had him cornered—I'll give you that—but you weren't about to shoot him."

"But I could have."

"But you didn't."

Candice set her gun on the coffee table, her hands shaking slightly. "I think I've just been up against too many people trying to kill either you or me or both of us. I see an intruder in the house and my first reaction is to shoot first and ask questions later."

I sat down next to Candice and took up her trembling hand. "Hey," I said. "Cassidy, that *isn't* your first reaction. Your *first* reaction is to take the suspect by surprise, disarm him if need be, and send me to call the cavalry. You didn't almost shoot anybody, and you did nothing wrong."

Candice took a deep breath and blew it out. "How's the door?"

I grinned. "Lucky for you, I have a handyman on speed dial."

"Sorry, Abs. I'll pay for the damage."

I waved my hand dismissively. "Don't be ridiculous. The way I see it, it's Dutch's fault for not telling us that Oscar was here. We can dump all of this at his feet and he can pay for the door."

Candice reached forward and lifted a folded piece of paper off the coffee table. It had my name on it, but something told me she'd read it in the moments before I came out to the living room. I opened the letter and it said,

Edgar,

1.   Oscar's in the spare bedroom, sleeping it off. He was the big winner last night, so if he's not awake by noon, feel free to kick his butt out.

2.   Don't worry about the mess in the kitchen, I'll clean up when I get home. (Sorry!)

3. Can I take you to dinner tonight to celebrate getting sprung from jail? ☺

Text me.
Love you.
D

I smiled at the note. "My hubby's pretty cute," I said, setting it aside.

"He has his moments," Candice agreed. "Just wish you'd seen the letter before I got here."

"I was busy cleaning up the kitchen," I said, nudging her in the arm.

She rolled her eyes and chuckled. Just then Oscar came out from the hallway. He was fully clothed at least, in a raggedy T-shirt and baggy cargo shorts that had definitely seen better days. His feet were bare, but he carried his sandals in the crook of his arm, while hefting a gym bag. He offered us a sheepish wave. "Hey," he said shyly. I felt a little bad for him. How embarrassing was it to have not just your coworkers but your bosses' wives walk in on you while you're naked? I resolved not to give him a hard time about it.

"Nice ass," Candice said.

Oscar blushed. "Thanks, Fusco. I'd return the compliment, but I might get shot."

Candice crossed her arms and leaned back against the couch. "That'd be a safe bet."

An awkward silence followed, which I broke by saying, "Well, now that *that's* out of the way, aren't you working today, Oscar?"

He took a seat in a wing chair to put on his sandals. "Nah. I'm off today and all next week. Harrison ordered me to take my vacation time before I lose it."

"Why would you lose it?" I asked.

He shrugged. "Once you accrue too much vacation time, the bureau starts to take it away."

"How much time have you accrued?" Candice asked.

"Twelve weeks."

My brow rose. "Whoa. When's the last time you took a vacation?"

"Three years ago."

I blinked. I got itchy if I went longer than four months without a break. Even if it was just a staycation, I still thought it was smart to take time off from the grind now and then. "Oscar, that's not healthy," I told him.

He shrugged again. "That's what your other half said too."

"So where're you going on your vacation?" I asked.

Oscar blinked. He seemed stumped by my question. "Uh . . . hadn't really thought about it. I'm not much into traveling. I'll probably just stick close to the apartment."

I frowned. My radar had flipped on and I was assessing Oscar's energy. "Dude, not to be blunt, but you need a life."

He smiled. "Thanks for the subtlety."

"I'm not kidding," I insisted. "I told you three months ago to look around for a house or a condo and get out of that dingy apartment, which isn't doing anything for your love life."

Oscar's lids slid down to half-mast, as if he didn't want to hear it, but I'd done an impromptu reading for him a few months back when I'd felt real heartbreak around him, even though he was putting on a good front. When I'd pointed my radar at him, I'd seen that his girlfriend had recently dumped him. It was so clear why too. She'd gotten tired of waiting for him to grow up and take life a little more seriously—I mean, he lived in a one-bedroom apartment close to UT in a neighborhood populated mostly by students, and he drove a beat-up old pickup truck, and his wardrobe left a *lot* to be desired. Mostly, Oscar liked to work, go home, order pizza, and play video games until two in the morning. It was a rut he'd gotten himself stuck in, and one both me and his ex-girlfriend really wanted him to get out of.

So, I'd given him a reading and laid out all the many ways he could rather immediately improve his life. I'd told him in no uncertain terms to get his act together, find a house, buy it, get some new furniture that didn't scream "frat house," furnish said home, and show the girls how grown-up he could be.

I mean, Oscar was a really good-looking guy and he'd been with the bureau since he was in his early twenties. Now in his mid-thirties, he had to be making some great coin, and he was otherwise a very responsible, kind, and decent man. I knew most girls would think him a total catch until he took them home. Then I suspected they'd suddenly remember a cat at their apartment that needed feeding.

"I've been busy," he said in reply to my remark about house hunting.

I glared at him. "You *do* know I've got an inboard lie detector, right?"

Oscar sighed. He knew he wasn't gonna win this fight. "Change is hard for me, Cooper."

Candice was watching our back-and-forth with interest and a little gleam in her eye. "You know," she said casually, "Abby has a pretty great eye for real estate."

I turned to her. "I do?"

She ignored me. "And she's also got a great eye for decorating."

Oscar's brow furrowed and he leaned in. "She does?"

Candice waved her arms around the house as if my living room spoke for itself. I took it all in, and I kinda had to admit, the place did look pretty good, but that was as much my flair as Dutch's. Our styles blended nicely together.

Oscar too was looking around and nodding his head. And then, as if he'd suddenly caught on to exactly what Candice was hinting at, he said, "Cooper, would you help me look for a house?"

"Uh . . . ," I said.

"She's got a really busy week next week," Candice said for me.

Now it was my turn to furrow my brow. What point was she trying to make?

"She's taken on a new case, and all of her spare time is going to be spent chasing down leads."

"Oh," Oscar said, and I swore he looked disappointed.

"Then again," Candice said, as if an idea had suddenly occurred to her, "if she had help chasing down those leads, she'd have more free time to devote to your cause."

I rolled my eyes, but Oscar still looked puzzled. I decided to spell it out for him. "Oscar, if you want to spend your vacation helping me on a cold case I've just taken on, then I'll help you hunt for a house and the furniture to fill it."

He perked right up. "Really?"

"Yes. But I'll also need to take you to a department store. Or maybe the whole mall."

"What for?"

"A new wardrobe, dude. Seriously."

He looked down at himself and grinned. "When you have a body this good, Cooper, you don't need fancy clothes."

I crossed my arms and sat back on the couch, mimicking Candice's pose. "Just out of curiosity, how many dates have you gone on lately?"

His grin faltered. After a pause he said, "Okay, but just a couple of shirts and some shorts. Nothing too crazy."

Candice and I traded a look. "We'll see," was my only promise.

We gave Oscar a lift to the garage next to the bureau offices, as he'd ridden to the poker game the night before with Dutch. Before leaving us, he promised to catch up with me later, after he'd taken another nap. Meanwhile, we girls drove just down the street to our new offices.

Candice and I had been rather unceremoniously kicked out of our last office suite by a jerk of a landlord who had no legal standing to evict us, and even though we'd found awesome new digs not far from our hubbies', it'd still irritated Candice enough to take jerkwad landlord to court. As I'd predicted would happen, at the eleventh hour when it was absolutely clear he'd go to court and lose, he'd offered us a tidy settlement, which had paid for five months' rent at the new place.

Our new building was just off Sixth and Lamar in a hip and trendy section of town about a stone's throw from the original Whole Foods.

We'd signed a three-year lease on the seventh floor of a bright redbrick building with funky lime green trim. Our suite was a corner unit and I'd offered Candice the largest room, which was the actual corner on the east side. The door to her office was all glass, and I had to admit that she presented a fairly striking first impression for our clients, who walked into the entry and looked to their right to see Candice in there, surrounded by floor-to-ceiling windows and sparse but elegant furnishings, seated at a glass desk in a thousand-dollar suit and heels to die for.

Meanwhile I camped out on the west side of the suite in a nearly equally roomy office with great light, a spectacular view, especially at night, and lots of privacy. The best part of the building was the rooftop patio, which had been covered with greenery to help reduce the heat coming off the building, which contributed to nightly temperatures in downtown Austin that, at times, hovered between "Are you freaking kidding me with this heat?" and "*Hell* no."

Candice peeled off to the right and I went to the left as we walked in the door, and I got busy checking my list of clients for the next day and returning e-mails. Candice waved at me about an hour later, indicating she had a meeting with a client. I got bored shortly after she left and on an impulse I got up from my desk and moved to my supply drawer in a credenza behind my desk. Getting out a fresh manila folder, I wrote Skylar's name across it and sat back down in front of the computer. I started with Google, and quickly discovered that Noah Miller's murder trial had been major news covered by every reporter in town. I read every single article, and it took me a while to get through it all, but I had a very good picture of Skylar's background and the arguments presented at trial by the time I was finished.

According to the reports, nine-year-old Noah and his mother had been living in a two-bedroom home in East Austin when one night in early July the police were called to the scene of a homicide at the home.

When police arrived, they found Skylar at her neighbor's house, covered in blood and hysterical. She claimed that she'd been awakened by a sound inside her home, and when she'd gone to investigate, she'd found Noah in his bedroom, on the floor, stabbed multiple times. As she'd collected him in her arms, she'd been attacked by an assailant who'd been hiding in the closet, and she managed to get away from him and run next door for help.

Investigators noted at her trial that Skylar had acted suspiciously at the scene, that her hysteria had seemed "fabricated," and she wasn't consistent about the facts of that evening, leaving out some key details whenever she retold the story during her initial interview with police.

Now, it's been my experience that when you interview someone right after a traumatic event, they go into a mild form of shock, and their memory can get cluttered and jumbled and become a mess. That's one of the reasons that eyewitness testimony has been shown over and over again to be pretty unreliable, but ten years ago the opinion that it couldn't be counted on wasn't nearly as well documented as it is now. Still, it irked me that the investigators had been so keen to point out the flaws in Skylar's initial interviews. Of course she'd be all over the place. She'd just held her murdered son in her arms and been attacked herself by an intruder. But just as my opinion of her innocence was already formed, I suspected that at the time of the trial the investigators' opinion of her guilt was pretty firm.

The investigator on the stand went on to testify that there was no sign of forced entry into the Millers' home, and no other evidence to indicate that an intruder had entered that night. What's more, the kitchen knife that had been used to murder Noah had only her fingerprints on it, and some of those fingerprints were bloody, but others were not. The lab reported that a few of the fingerprints on the blade appeared "older" and a bit "smudged," indicating the knife had come from the family home and had likely been used both before (i.e., in the kitchen as a utility knife) and during the murder.

Witnesses came forward testifying to Skylar's personal struggles with alcohol. Former friends and family lined up to state that Skylar was a fairly peaceful person when she was sober, but when she drank, she was verbally abusive and quick-tempered. Video was introduced at her trial depicting her destroying several hundred dollars' worth of merchandise at a liquor store after being denied service due to obvious signs of intoxication.

Her ex-husband testified that when Noah was just a toddler, he'd come home to find Skylar passed out on the couch while their son wandered the house without supervision. He reported that there were multiple times when Skylar had been neglectful of their son, and after the incident in which he'd witnessed her passed out and Noah unsupervised, he'd left Skylar, filing for divorce and asking for sole custody. He'd been granted that in 1998, just before Skylar went to prison for multiple DWI convictions.

She was out of jail a year later, sober and apparently working to get her life back on track. She had completed an intense stay in rehab, was a nightly regular at her AA meetings, worked two jobs, and went back to court to win supervised visitation time with Noah. She was granted that, then allowed unsupervised time. During that time, Skylar was visited several times by a social worker, who would show up at her door unannounced and interview Noah to make sure he was being well cared for. The social worker then made recommendations to the court, and Skylar's visitation was increased from one night per week to one night, plus every other weekend.

Along the way Skylar completed her twelve steps, sponsored a few other AA members, went back to school, got her two-year degree, and began work as a medical biller. She did well enough to be able to support herself and work from her apartment, even saving up sufficient money to make a down payment on a home in East Austin. Finally, in October 2003 she must've found a *very* sympathetic judge because, in a move that reportedly stunned everyone, she was granted physical custody of Noah and he moved in with her permanently.

A year later, Noah was dead.

In their efforts to paint Skylar as the killer, the prosecution claimed that Skylar had fallen off the wagon and her son had discovered his mother's drinking and probably threatened to tell his father. At the time, Skylar had been receiving a monthly support check from her ex, and it was a pretty good chunk of change. The prosecutor painted the picture of a drunken, abusive mother, who, fearing that a primary source of income was in jeopardy, lashed out at her nine-year-old son in a fit of drunken rage. Grabbing a knife from the kitchen, she'd stabbed Noah to death, then staged the mad dash to her neighbor's house, where she'd invented the story of the intruder to cover up her crime.

The most damning testimony had come from Skylar's own mother, who'd all but nailed her daughter to the cross when she'd testified for the prosecution, stating that she'd worried for Noah's safety from the moment Skylar was given full physical custody. She was quoted in one of the articles I read saying that, all her life, Skylar had made poor choices with the notable exception of her ex-husband, who'd been a wonderful and loving husband and father, but Skylar's drinking and abuse had driven him away, and since then her mother had watched Skylar devolve into a secretive, conniving, mentally unbalanced alcoholic.

Now, it was no secret my own parents and I weren't exactly on speaking terms, but even I couldn't imagine my mother getting up on the witness stand and testifying against me when the death penalty hung in the balance.

The defense's argument was that, since getting out of jail in 2000, Skylar had been a model citizen who'd turned herself around in an effort to win back her life, and custody of her son. Her attorney argued that even though Skylar was receiving enough money from her ex to live on, she hadn't quit work as a medical biller, and often put in extra hours on the job after Noah went to bed. She wasn't a cold-blooded killer, he'd argued. She was a model to struggling addicts everywhere, an example of what you can achieve when you devote yourself to getting help and facing your demons head-on.

In his closing arguments he'd further stated that it was a travesty of justice to charge her with murder—the murder of her son—given how hard she'd worked to get her life back on track. This was a son she loved. Fought for. Devoted all her efforts to. And on a hot, muggy night, he'd been taken away from her in the most heinous way when an unknown assailant had invaded her home and murdered her son in cold blood. Somehow the intruder had left behind no physical evidence—no DNA, no hair samples, no fingerprints, and no footprints anywhere inside the house or out. He'd been careful, her attorney had argued. He'd been good. Practiced even. And, most important, he'd been the one to kill Noah. And he was still out there. The police hadn't been looking for him because they'd been lazy. They'd set their sights on Skylar from day one, and like old dogs with a new bone, they hadn't let go. So the killer, this random, malicious psychopath, was still free while his client was being railroaded for the crime of loving her son enough to take back her life from the brink of ruin.

I frowned as I read the closing statements from Skylar's attorney. It was hard even for me to believe a random stranger had entered the Millers' home, killed an innocent nine-year-old boy, and left no physical evidence of himself behind.

Skylar hadn't testified, and the defense had called precious few character witnesses. Only her neighbors, her AA sponsor, and the social worker who'd monitored her visits with Noah, and had helped her fight for physical custody of him the year before, had been willing to testify on her behalf. Furthermore, her attorney had tried to poke some holes in the prosecution's case, but either he didn't try very hard or his tactics hadn't been very effective, because the jury had deliberated for all of three days and returned with a guilty verdict and a recommendation for life without parole, but the judge had apparently been swayed enough by the prosecution's case to ignore the jury's recommendation, and had ordered that she be put to death.

I read all of this, pages and pages of articles, and at the end of it I sat back in my chair, closed my eyes, and pinched the bridge of my nose. I had a headache forming as the full weight of what I was up against settled onto my shoulders.

"Rough day?"

I jumped and maybe let out a small shriek. "Oh! Oscar, I didn't hear you come in."

He was grinning. "Obviously," he said, taking a seat in one of the chairs across from my desk. "You okay?"

I nodded. "Yeah. It's just this case I'm about to start work on. I knew I was probably facing an uphill battle, but I didn't realize I'd be starting at base camp somewhere in the Himalayas."

"Fill me in?" he asked, taking a seat. I gave him the highlights of what I knew from everything I'd read online, which still took about twenty minutes to tell, and afterward he blew out a breath and said, "You sure can pick 'em, eh, Cooper?"

"You're not kidding."

"How long do we have to work on this case, again?"

"Skylar's appeal was postponed to the nineteenth, so . . . ten days from now."

Oscar shook his head. "Glad we're not pressed for time."

"I told you this was gonna be a tough one."

"You did. Okay, so where did you want to start?"

I sighed. "I was just thinking about that. The case was investigated by Austin PD. Feel like calling any of your buddies down there to ask about it?"

He shrugged and, pulling out a small notebook from his shorts pocket, he started to scribble in it. "Couldn't hurt," he said. "I'll try to get a copy of the murder file. I know a guy in the records room. He usually gets me what I need in exchange for a pizza and a cold six-pack of Tres Equis."

"Awesome," I said, standing up and reaching for my purse. "Meanwhile I'm gonna pay a visit to a friend of mine."

Oscar cocked an eyebrow. "Who?"

"A guy I have to convince owes me a favor."

"Does he?"

"Not a chance."

"Who's the guy and what's the favor?"

"An attorney who defended me last winter when Candice was accused of murder, and the favor I need is for him to drop everything and see if he'll take Skylar's case. Pro bono."

Oscar rose and gave my shoulder a pat. "Good luck, Cooper. You're gonna need it."

"Aww, Oscar. You say the sweetest things."

"Hey, don't forget, you still owe me some house-hunting time."

My radar pinged. "I've got your back, buddy. Not to worry."

We started to walk out together and Oscar said, "You really think you can find me a decent place to live?"

"Yep."

Oscar was silent for a minute and then he said, "I was kinda thinking about getting a cat or something—you know, maybe to have someone greet me at the door when I get home."

"No," I said, with a smirk.

Oscar eyed me quizzically. "No?"

"Your new girlfriend's gonna be allergic to cats, Oscar. You're better off getting a dog. Something small and cuddly. Girls love manly men with little dogs."

He laughed in surprise. "My new girlfriend? Is this anybody I know, Cooper?"

I flashed him a smile. "Not yet, honey. But soon."

"How soon?"

I held up my hand and began to count off on my fingers, "House, furniture, wardrobe, dog, girlfriend."

"In that order?"

"In exactly that order, buddy."

He nodded. "I can live with that."

Chapter Five

• • •

I drove to Calvin Douglas's office, which was on the south side of downtown, not far from my office, just off Fourth Street. On the way I called to ask if he was (a) in and (b) available to see me on short notice. I was told by his very kind secretary that he was both in and available to meet with me.

My lucky day.

After parking in the lot, I hoofed it into Cal's building, a swanky place full of marble and brass in the lobby. Cal's office was up on the second floor, decorated in serious tones of darkest eggplant and forest green. Not my taste but still impressive.

His secretary greeted me warmly and showed me right into Cal's office, which wasn't quite what I was expecting, as I'd never pegged the attorney for a minimalist.

He sat in a fairly small room, behind a desk that seemed severe in both its form and function. The chairs in front of him were simple, made not so much for long visits but for short bursts of billable hours. After I sat down, I knew that most of his clients would start to feel uncomfortable about a half hour in, and be antsy to leave within an hour. I figured that was one way to keep everyone on schedule.

On Cal's desk were a large monitor and an equally impressive mountain of paperwork and manila folders. Behind him were shelves stuffed with law books that looked a bit too pristine to be real—I mean, who even uses law books anymore when everything is online these days? To the left of the room was a large steel filing cabinet, and one picture hung on the wall of a seagull soaring above the waves of a turbulent ocean. A poetically inspiring caption was written underneath.

And that was pretty much it for decor. "So!" Cal said as he sat down after getting up to greet me. "This is a surprise. What brings you by?"

I flashed him my best winning smile. "I need your help."

"With?"

"Well, actually, it's not me who needs your help. See, there's a woman on death row who—"

Cal held up his hand to interrupt me. "Hold it," he said. "Hold it. Are you here about Skylar Miller?"

I blinked. "Uh, yeah. How'd you know?"

Cal pointed to himself. "Dutch called me yesterday to represent you if Schilling didn't let you out of the contempt charge. He then called me a little later and asked if I could pull any strings because they'd locked you up with a death row inmate."

I felt a thread of anger set into my shoulders, remembering the abrupt removal of Skylar from our shared jail. "And did you?"

Cal said, "I made a call to Schilling's clerk. He used to work for me before he took the job with Schilling, and he was willing to extend you a slight favor last night." Cal paused to give me a meaningful look that told me that outing the judge had been a bit of a blessing to the clerk, who was in love with him. I wondered if he truly believed, now that things were out in the open, so to speak, that Schilling would leave his wife for the poor clerk, and I hoped he didn't get his heart broken and lose his job at the same time, because that's what was probably going to happen, and I felt for him.

"Anyway," Cal continued, "he made a few calls and they found a way to keep you isolated from the other prisoners."

I took a moment to breathe deeply. My hubby and Cal had simply made an effort to keep me as safe as possible, but it still irked me that Skylar had been sent away to spend the night at county in isolation when I was fairly certain at Mountain View they kept her in isolation too. She'd had a chance for a bit of respite from that lonely and possibly maddening experience, and the men in my life had taken it away from her unnecessarily. "She wasn't a threat to me," I told him levelly.

Cal sighed. "You talked to her." He said it more as a statement than as a question.

I squinted at him. There was something about the way he was speaking that suggested that he had at least some familiarity with Skylar and her case. "I did," I said. "Have you ever talked to her, Cal?"

He sighed. There was guilt in that sigh. "Twenty years ago I represented her on a vandalism charge and then on her third DWI charge."

My eyes widened. "The one where she served a year in jail?"

He nodded. "She was actually sentenced to four years, but got out after only fourteen months for good behavior and because of overcrowding."

"Still, four years seems kind of harsh for a woman who so obviously needed to be sent to rehab, doesn't it? I mean, I realize it was her third offense, but she didn't crash her car or hurt anybody, did she?"

"No, but back in 'ninety-eight the state wasn't very sympathetic when it came to addicts. The rule back then was punish the offenders and punish them hard. Four years was honestly the best deal I could get her, Abby. The state minimum both then and now is two years for a third offense, and Skylar was smashed when the officer pulled her over—she blew a point one eight. That's a full tenth over the legal limit. She's just damn lucky she didn't get caught with her kid in the car."

"So you know her."

He shrugged. "I *knew* her twenty years ago. I haven't spoken to her since she fired me back in nineteen ninety-eight, right after the judge threw her a four-year sentence."

I tapped the arm of the chair for a moment, letting my intuition flow over Cal's energy. "Do you remember a few months back when I told you that you and I would be working on a case together? A case involving a woman?"

An oblique smile crept onto Cal's lips. "When you did that reading for me at the bureau offices," he said. "I remember almost every single word of it. Including that part. And it'll probably please you to know that all that you predicted did come true—except for that one small part. Last night after your husband called and I started making inquiries, and discovered that Skylar Miller was your cellmate, all the hairs on the back of my neck stood up on end." I said nothing. I wanted to see what Cal was going to conclude from that. "I figured that had to be more than a coincidence, and maybe the powers that be are trying to get a message to me."

"She didn't do it, Cal," I said firmly.

He nodded. "I never thought she did."

We sat in silence for a few beats with that between us. "If we do nothing, she'll lose the appeal," I said softly.

Cal sighed and his shoulders sagged a little as he glanced briefly at the mountain of manila folders to his left. I knew I was asking him to take a holiday from the work that paid his bills to essentially take over Skylar's case and prepare an appeal in just ten days. "I've seen her attorney in court," he said. "He's barely competent."

The ether around Cal shifted and I sat forward, reaching for my purse. "I'm pretty sure I can convince her to fire him and hire you," I said, getting up and turning to leave.

Cal's quiet laughter followed me to the door of his office. "How'd you know I'd be so easily convinced?"

I paused with my hand on the doorknob to look over my shoulder at him. "She's part of your future, Cal. The same way she's part of mine."

His brow furrowed. "Coming in at this late hour is gonna be a nightmare, Abby. Both legally and procedurally."

"I'm aware."

"But you think we can save her?"

I looked past Cal for a moment, staring into space as I felt out the future. "Truthfully? It could go either way. But if we don't join forces and help her, she's got no chance. None at all."

Cal regarded me solemnly. "Sounds like we don't have much of a choice, then."

"Nope."

"Call me after you talk to her."

"Thanks, Cal. Really."

He nodded and I headed out of his office, glancing at my watch as I exited the suite. It was nearly four o'clock, and time was running short both for the day and for Skylar. My next step involved talking to her, which I hoped to do before the end of the day, if I could make it back to my office and my laptop fast enough.

I was already somewhat familiar with the new visitation system Travis County had put in place for its inmates and members of the public. No longer could you actually go to the jail and wait behind Plexiglas to lift a phone and talk to an inmate. Travis County had gone high-tech, implementing a videoconference system that was a whole lot like FaceTime.

I hadn't used the system, but I'd seen it firsthand because all law enforcement personnel had been given a tutorial just a few weeks earlier when it was first coming on line.

Access to video chat with a prisoner came from registering with the county, then filling out a simple online form that asked the name of the prisoner, your relationship to them, etc., etc.

I was already registered as a consultant with the FBI, and that gave me a few extra privileges to boot. I was hoping the special code I'd been given denoting my status would make access to Skylar less of a problem. I doubted that she'd been let out of solitary, which meant that someone (Stern Eyes?) would have to go get her and physically bring her to the videoconference room. Sometimes the COs could give the prisoners in solitary a hard time, and I hoped that Stern Eyes wasn't going to drag her feet bringing Skylar up.

I got back to my office about fifteen minutes after I'd left Cal's, and hopped right online, typing quickly and noting that time wasn't on my side. It'd take a little while to process my request and have it go through the channels, not to mention getting Skylar to the videoconference room in time to talk to her before the system would be shut down at five thirty. She would actually initiate the call on her end, and I waited in my office from four all the way to five nineteen, pacing and eyeing my computer anxiously.

Finally, at five twenty, there was a faint tinny ring from my computer and I rushed to sit down and click to accept the call. The black screen pixelated a bit until it settled onto Skylar's face. She was hovering close to the computer and I could see the dark circles under her eyes the same as the day before; however, today her expression was a bit more curious. "Abby?" she said.

I waved. "Hi, Skylar!" I said. "Thanks for accepting the visit."

She nodded. "I don't get much in the way of visits."

I glanced at the clock again. We had nine minutes. "Listen, I'm gonna make this really fast because we're pressed for time, but I want you to do me a huge favor."

Skylar studied me. Her expression was wary, but also perhaps slightly amused. "What huge favor can I do for you?"

"I want you to trust me."

Her reaction was surprising. She actually laughed. "Trust you?"

"Yes. And I realize you don't know me, Skylar, or have *any* reason to actually trust me, but I am totally sincere here when I tell you that if you don't trust me, I don't think you're going to make it to the day after your appeal."

The humor faded from Skylar's features. "Even if I do trust you, Abby, I'm probably not going to live beyond the nineteenth."

"Skylar," I said, "do you remember what one of your first questions to me was after I told you that I was psychic?"

She seemed to think on that for a second. "I asked you if you could see who broke into my house the night Noah died. I wanted to know who it was that killed my son."

I closed my eyes and nodded. "Exactly." Opening them again, I added, "A guilty woman would've asked me if she'd win her appeal, or how she could win her appeal. Only an innocent woman asks who the real murderer was."

Skylar took that in. "I just want to know before they stick the needle in me, Abby. I want to know who did it, and why."

"I know," I told her, glancing again at the clock. Seven minutes. "Listen, this is the part where trusting me is going to require a pretty big leap of faith, but the way I see it, you don't have a ton of options left, so I'm just gonna say it. I want you to fire your attorney, and then I want you to hire Calvin Douglas."

Skylar blinked and I could see recognition in her eyes. "Calvin Douglas?"

"Yep. And, before you ask, yes, he's the same guy who represented you on the DWI charge."

She rolled her eyes and snorted derisively. "The last time he represented me he got me a four-year sentence."

I stared at her image in the computer without blinking. "I know. And yet, I still want you to hire him."

"Why?"

"Because he's the only chance you've got. Skylar, I've taken a glimpse into your future. It's as bleak as it comes. And your attorney isn't helping you in any way."

Skylar looked away, thinking, and I glanced again at the clock. We had two minutes. I felt a bit desperate, so I added, "I know you think that might be a rash decision, and I know you probably carry a grudge against Cal, but what I think he might be able to buy you is a little time, Skylar. And I need that time to investigate Noah's murder."

Her head turned sharply and she stared hard at me. "*You're* going to investigate?"

I nodded, holding up the official badge the FBI had given me as their consultant. "On occasion, I work for the Feds," I confessed. "And my business partner is a PI. I'm very good, and so is she. And we've also got an agent currently on vacation who's willing to help out."

Her brow furrowed at the rush of words. "Why are you doing this?"

I took a deep breath. What reason could I give that she'd believe? Skylar didn't look like someone who'd been given a whole lot of kindness in her life. I figured the truth was the only thing I had to offer her. "Because I don't believe you did it. And if you didn't do it, then I look at you as any other innocent woman who's about to be murdered. You deserve my very best effort to save your life. It's just what I do, Skylar. And that's the truth."

She studied me for a moment, as if she could read me the way I could read her. And then, she opened her mouth to speak, but at that exact moment my screen flashed with an error message. It was five thirty and the videoconference had been cut off. "Dammit!" I yelled, standing up and glaring hard at my computer screen. For emphasis I pounded my desk a little with my fist. "Dammit, dammit, dammit!" (Ah well, I didn't need that dollar anyway.)

"Bad day?" I heard from the doorway.

I startled. "Oh, hey, Cassidy," I said to Candice, feeling my cheeks flush. "Didn't see you there."

She leaned against the frame, crossed her arms, and adopted an amused expression. "I'll bet."

I took a deep breath and straightened my shirt, still embarrassed for having been caught midtantrum. "How was *your* day, dear?"

Candice chuckled and came into the room to take up a seat across from me. "Better than yours, apparently."

I sat down and shut the laptop. "I was talking to Skylar and our call got cut off."

Candice flicked her wrist to note the time on her watch. "It's after five thirty."

"Yep."

"Is she going to let us help her?"

"Don't know," I said with a sigh. "I gave her a pretty good pitch, though. And I recruited Cal Douglas to represent her, assuming she takes my advice and fires her attorney in the eleventh hour."

"She'd be taking a huge risk, Abby. Her current attorney has probably been working on the case for at least a year or two. Possibly longer."

"Hey," we heard from the door again. Candice and I both looked over and saw Oscar there. "Glad I caught you two."

I glanced down at Oscar's empty hands. "No luck with the records guy?"

Oscar shook his head. "The second I mentioned the name on the file, my buddy handed me back both the pizza and the beer and told me no way. The detective who worked the original case is still around, and he's some kind of big dog at APD and no one's willing to cross him. That means any file with his name on it stays put. Especially that one."

"Shit," I said, then glared at Candice when she arched an eyebrow at me. Opening the drawer to my desk, I lifted out a roll of quarters I kept there for swearing emergencies and slapped it on top of the desk blotter to show her I had the money to cover myself. Turning back to Oscar, I said, "Why would it be 'especially that one'?"

Oscar came into the room and took the seat next to Candice. "Think about it, Cooper. Miller's appeal is in two weeks. No way this close to the finish line does APD want any of what's in that folder leaked out to maybe throw the case open again."

I frowned. "So how do we get a copy of the murder file?"

"Skylar's initial legal team would've kept a copy," Candice said.

"Her original attorney was court appointed," I said, remembering from one of the articles covering the case that Texas didn't use public defenders. Instead it rotated through a list of defense attorneys and appointed cases to whoever was next on the list.

In theory it was a great thing for the accused, because they often got a seasoned attorney well practiced in the art of defense litigation. In practice it had its shortcomings, especially when one of the smaller firms drew a short straw for a big case, because, since there was no money in it for them, they had to continue to work their other cases at the same time, and that meant that they typically put in the least amount of effort necessary to get the court-appointed job done.

I suspected, given what I'd read in the coverage of Skylar's initial trial, that this was exactly what'd happened in her case.

Candice pulled out her phone and said, "Do you remember the name?"

"Whitaker," I said, scrolling through my memory banks. "First name I believe was John."

Both Oscar and I waited while Candice tapped at her phone. She made a face and said, "John Whitaker, the attorney who defended Skylar Miller in the murder of her son, was struck head-on in a collision with a tractor-trailer on Route Three Sixty in the early hours of September second, two thousand eight."

My jaw dropped. "He's *dead*?"

Candice scrolled a little farther down the article before she replied. "Quite," she said with a frown.

"So what happened to his files?" I asked next.

Candice continued to tap at her screen. "He didn't have a law partner," she said. "Which means his practice was probably shut down and the legal files put into storage or destroyed."

"So there's no copy other than the one the cops have of Noah's murder?"

"The attorney handling her appeal should have a copy," Candice said.

It was my turn to grimace. "You mean the one I just asked her to fire?"

Candice rolled her eyes. "You have the best timing. Still, if she requests the file, her old lawyer has to hand it over."

"Right away?" I asked hopefully.

"Well, she is pressed for time," Candice said. "But if she's firing him after he's been fighting for her for a couple of years, then he could drag his feet if he wanted to."

"We need to see what's in that file as soon as possible," I said. Holding up the folder of printouts of the articles I'd looked up, I added, "All I've got is what I printed off from online."

"There's always the county clerk," Oscar volunteered. "They keep a copy of the transcripts, photos, and motions for the judge. We could have them make us a copy."

Both Candice and I groaned. "That'll take longer than Skylar has," I said. It was true. I knew from experience that the typical turn-around time for court docs from old cases was at least two weeks.

"At some point we're going to have to interview the lead detective on the case," Oscar said.

"Who is it?" Candice asked him.

"Ray Dioli."

"Oh, God. Him? That man's a first-class asshole."

"So you know him," I said, stating the obvious.

"Yep. He and I got into it when I went down to APD to give my statement about Dr. Robinowitz."

"Oh, man," I said, remembering Candice telling me about the incident involving the statement she'd had to give APD about the murder of a man from out of town. She'd been scheduled to meet with a Detective Grayson, whom I knew and liked, but Dioli had pulled some weight and he'd interviewed Candice for what should have been nothing more than a courtesy call, just to wrap up the case. In a move that surprised everybody, Dioli had grilled Candice for hours and hours until she'd finally thrown in the towel and called her attorney. It'd taken a couple of added phone calls from the upper echelon of the FBI to the upper echelon of APD to get Dioli to back off. "He's *that* guy?"

"I guess," Oscar said, looking discouraged. Turning to Candice, he said, "He was really that bad?"

"Worse," she told him. "Well, if you guys meet with him, leave my name out of it. I'm pretty sure he won't give you anything if he hears I'm working with you on this."

I sat back in the chair and frowned, trying to think of a solution. "Okay, then. Here's what we'll do. Oscar, call this Detective Dioli and see if he'll meet with us, and in the meantime, I'll put in a call to the office of the lawyer currently representing Skylar and see if I can't convince him that I want to assist with the appeal. I'll tell him that I met Skylar in the county lockup—there for unrelated reasons—and that I volunteered as an investigator to look into her case. Maybe he'll give me a peek at her file out of the goodness of his heart."

Both Candice and Oscar eyed me with unveiled skepticism. "Riiiiight," Candice said. "*That'll* work."

"Got any better ideas?"

Candice pursed her lips. "Not at the moment."

"Thought so," I said, getting up to reach for my purse, as there was nothing more we could do for Skylar at the moment. "So, for now, that's our game plan."

Dutch beat me home from the office, which was unexpected. As I came through the door, I spied him on the couch, wearing boxer shorts and not much else. Oh, except for the single rose clutched in his teeth and the winning smile he was trying to curl around the thorny stem.

I looked at him for a beat, taking it all in. "Cute look."

Dutch took out the rose and slid off the couch to get down on one knee. Offering me the flower, he said, "Abby Cooper, will you accept this rose?"

"Depends on where you're taking me to dinner," I told him. "But here's a hint: I like steak and red wine and lots of ambience."

"Texas Roadhouse?"

I frowned, refusing to take the rose. "*Romantic* ambience."

Dutch swept his arms down toward the boxers. "What do you call *this*?"

"A poor attempt to get out of taking me to dinner because you're horny, tired, and hungover and you'd rather stay in, eat leftovers, and bonk the night away."

His grin widened. "It's like you know me."

I crossed my arms and began tapping my foot. Dutch got up, laid the rose gently on my arms, kissed the top of my head, and said, "I'll get dressed and call Gino. He should be able to reserve us a quiet booth in the corner."

"Smart man," I told him, swatting his bum for good measure.

Dutch paused before heading around the kitchen to our master bedroom to say, "And, Abs? Thanks for cleaning up the kitchen. I came home after lunch to grab a file I forgot, and saw that you'd taken care of it and you didn't even give me any flak about the poker game last night."

"You've been working hard, honey. I think you and the guys needed a night to blow off some steam."

Dutch nodded and the look he gave me expressed more than words how much he appreciated the small gesture. "Have I told you lately that I love being married to you?"

"Every day, babe," I told him. Dutch wasn't one to hold

back on whispering sweet nothings to me, something I adored him for.

"Yeah, well, I stopped off on my way home to get you a little something to show you how much I appreciate all you do for me," he said, with a mischievous grin.

That got my attention. "What kind of little something?"

My hubby bounced his eyebrows. "It's on the island. See for yourself."

I'm not ashamed to say I threw aside my purse and keys and dashed madly into the kitchen. Dutch tended to spoil me rotten when it came to gift giving. Visions of gourmet chocolates wafted through my mind. Or maybe something fun like tickets to the theater.

When I got to the central island in our grand kitchen, I came up short. Like really short. Dutch chuckled softly as he continued on past me toward the bedroom. My breath quickened as I crept closer to the small box, neatly wrapped with silver paper and a gorgeous bow.

Lifting the box, I shook it a little. Something vibrated ever so slightly from inside. At that point curiosity got the better of me and I tore open the wrapping paper. The Apple icon revealed itself to me from an otherwise unmarked shiny white box. I gave in to a little gasp and lifted the lid. "Holy *freakballs!*"

The sudden sound of the shower being turned on was Dutch's way of saying that he knew he'd done good.

For a moment all I could do was stare at the brand-new Apple Watch Edition, which had JUST come on the market and was priced waaaaay beyond even the current tally of my swear jar.

I love, love, love gadgets, especially shiny gold gadgets that are the IT accessory must-have on everyone's list. Lifting the watch out of the box, I slipped it on my wrist and admired it. Then I shrugged out of my clothes and slid into the shower, where there was perhaps even more slipping and sliding . . . (eyebrow bouncy, bouncy).

Later, after I'd shown Dutch my "appreciation" for his thoughtful gift, we lounged on the bed and I said, "Maybe we should skip the restaurant."

He hugged me to his chest and said, "Yeah?"

I rolled over slightly and admired him while resting on my elbows. Such a beautiful man was my husband, with light blond hair, midnight blue eyes, a square manly jaw, and the chiseled body of a guy who takes exceptional care of himself. "Yeah."

"You hungry?"

"I am."

"Pizza or Thai?"

"Thai."

Dutch reached for the phone and ordered us the usual—two pad Thais with extra chopped peanuts—and we headed out to the living room to await the delivery guy. While we waited, Dutch got up to feed Eggy and Tuttle, and as he was in the kitchen preparing their dinners, I got my watch working. "Hey!" I shouted to him. "You can make a phone call on this!"

"I know," Dutch said.

"And if you got one, I could send you my heartbeat!" I called, even more excited as I played with the watch.

"Yep."

And then a thought entered my mind and my wrist fell to my lap. "You already got one, didn't you?"

I heard Dutch clear his throat. "Is that the delivery guy?"

Narrowing my eyes at his profile, I got up and walked over to him. "Show me."

He sighed. "Top drawer of my dresser," he admitted.

"Seriously?"

Dutch set the doggy bowls on the floor and turned to me. "That heartbeat thing is freaking cool, Edgar. I thought it'd be nice to let you know when I'm thinking about you."

I tapped my temple. "I *already* know when you're thinking about me." Dutch and I had a rather pronounced telepathic connection. Or at least I always knew when he was about to call or text.

"Yeah, but this is more romantic," he said.

I glared at him.

"Why are you mad, dollface?"

"Because I thought you got me a gift out of appreciation. Not because you wanted an excuse to buy yourself a new gadget."

Dutch sighed before putting his hands on my shoulders and eyeing me square. "I *did* buy you a gift out of love and appreciation for the wonderful wife you are, and because I'm happy and more in love with you than ever. And while I was buying you this gift, the saleswoman showed me all the cool features that can be shared between two watches, and she won me over with the heartbeat thing."

Damn. He wasn't lying. My irritation was unwarranted. Still, it irked me. Just then our doorbell dinged and Dutch said, "Ah. Saved by the bell." He then kissed me on the cheek and hurried to the door.

I let the pups out as Dutch brought dinner into the kitchen and began to plate it. "Fine," I said. "But next time you want to be thoughtful, maybe don't be *so* thoughtful, okay?"

My hubby grinned. "Deal."

We headed to the dining room and sat down for dinner and I had to move some of Dutch's files aside to make room. "These should go in the study," I told him, lifting the stack to a chair.

"Those are for you," he said.

"Huh?"

"The other victims in the case against Corzo," Dutch reminded me.

I sighed. I'd almost forgotten about Corzo. "I've been through Wendy McLain and Donna Andrews's files before, honey. I'm not sure what I'll be able to find."

Dutch tucked into his food. "It doesn't have to be a big lead like the one you pulled out for us on Misty's case," he said. "Even a small thing can lead to something bigger. Right now, we've got nothing. We're at the wall. No leads, no clue how to nail him, so just think about finding something small for us, and maybe while we're looking into it, we'll find something bigger. Corzo was careful—I'll give the son of a bitch that—but the evidence we found at Misty's crime scene proves he's not infallible."

I eyed the stack moodily. "I'll look at them later."

Dutch nodded. "So, tell me, how was the rest of your stay in county?"

I twirled some noodles on the end of my fork. "Solitary," I said, and watched his face for a reaction.

He moved his own noodles around a bit. "No trouble, though?"

"Nope. It's hard to get into trouble when you're the only one in the cell."

Dutch continued to shove his dinner around on his plate. I could tell he knew I was irked that he'd made the call to Cal. "I was just looking out for you, Edgar."

"I know. But I'm not sure I needed it."

Dutch finally lifted his gaze to me. "She's on death row for a reason. She's dangerous and they *never* should've put you two in the same cell together."

He'd said that a tad forcefully and, while I could understand his wanting to protect me, it still irritated me that he (a) thought I couldn't take care of myself and (b) didn't think I was a good judge of character. "See, that's where you're wrong, cowboy," I said levelly. "Skylar Miller is neither dangerous nor deserving of the needle."

"I looked her up," Dutch said, without a hint of apology. "Abby, she killed her son. Her young son. Brutally. You gotta be pretty cold-blooded to kill your own flesh and blood like that."

"She didn't kill her son," I said firmly.

"Well, that's not what a jury of her peers said."

"I know. Which is why I'm helping her. She was railroaded and that conviction is a total injustice."

Dutch dropped his fork. "Wait . . . you're *helping* her? What does *that* mean?"

"I'm going to look into Noah's murder, and I'm going to try to save Skylar."

Dutch stared at me rather incredulously. "Isn't she on her last appeal?"

"Yes."

"Which she'll probably lose."

I nodded.

"You know that Texas usually executes their death row inmates within hours of losing their last appeal, right?"

"I'm aware of the time constraints."

"Why are you getting mad?"

"Why are *you* getting mad?"

"Because I love you and I don't want to see you get involved in a case you can't win."

I glared at him. "Way to be supportive, Dutch, and also, way to trust my intuition! I mean it's fine to trust me when I'm looking in on one of *your* cases, but heaven forbid I should want to point my radar at a miscarriage of justice for a change."

Dutch closed his eyes, took a deep breath, which he let out slowly. When he opened his eyes again, his whole demeanor had changed. "You're right. I'm sorry. I do trust you. It's just . . . I read a few of the articles about her online, Abby. The evidence against her speaks for itself."

"I read those same articles, honey, and I know it looks bad, but my gut says she didn't do it, and it also says that I need to help her. I mean, I know it sounds crazy, but I don't think that it was a coincidence that I was paired up with her in that jail. I think that maybe her son is attempting to manipulate things a little from the other side."

Dutch cocked his head. "Her son?"

I nodded, taking another bite of my dinner. "I can't explain it other than when I first met Skylar, there was an energy around her, one that I couldn't readily identify, and I was struck by the sudden urge to help her. I'm no medium, but sometimes spirits from the other side communicate with me in more subtle ways; they'll sort of point something out that I need to pay attention to, or they'll make me do something that feels a bit impulsive. I don't think that after meeting Skylar I could turn my back on her. I just feel like I've *got* to help her."

Using air quotes, Dutch said, "Yes, but what does 'helping' her mean?"

"Well, it means recruiting Candice and Oscar to do a little in-vestigative work into Noah's murder."

"Oscar's on vacation," Dutch said.

"Forced vacation," I corrected.

"Abby," my husband replied with that note of irritation creep-ing into his tone again. "I told Oscar to take the week off to go hang out on a beach somewhere, not work on another investiga-tion."

"Oh, please," I said with a dismissive wave. "Oscar has no idea how to take time off. Hanging out on the beach alone somewhere is the equivalent to him of sitting inside a dungeon with nary a video game in sight." Dutch folded his arms and lowered his brow, so I added, "Listen, in exchange for helping me on this case, I'm going to help Oscar find a house."

"A house?"

"Yeah. He needs to get out of that crappy, run-down apartment of his. After that, I'm going to help him pick out some furniture, update his wardrobe, find a dog, and get a girlfriend."

Dutch suddenly let out a deep laugh. "A total makeover, huh?"

I nodded. "The man is a disaster. I've let it go on for far too long. And I can't help him if he's on the beach somewhere."

"He helps you, you fix his whole life."

I pointed at my hubby. "Exactly."

"Poor bastard."

"I know. He barely saw it coming."

Dutch studied me for a moment and then he said, "What's in it for Candice?"

"My undying gratitude."

"So . . . not much."

I pointed again to him and took a long tug on my beer. "Bingo."

"Who else are you recruiting?"

I set the beer bottle down with a flourish. "Cal Douglas."

His brow rose. "Really?"

"Yep. It was a busy day."

"So you've got your team together. Need my help with anything?"

"You're volunteering?"

"I figure I need to before you recruit the rest of North America."

I lifted my beer in a mock toast. "Ha. Ha. Ha-ha."

"Seriously, do you need my help?"

I gave that some thought. "No, but thank you. I believe we've got it covered. At least for the moment. Besides, you guys have your hands full with the Corzo case."

"True," Dutch said with a sigh, pushing aside his plate. "I still can't believe that bastard walked yesterday."

"You guys have a tail on him, though, right?" I asked as a jolt of alarm went through me.

"We do. But we've got to be careful. Corzo's attorney already sent us a letter saying that any obvious signs of a tail on his client would be seen as harassment."

"That guy's a total scumball."

"Yeah, but he's also a good lawyer, and we'll need to be careful. I've got Cox on Corzo tonight, and Wilson, Biggs, and Sutkowitz in rotation. Nobody likes the duty, but it's better than seeing another girl get murdered."

I focused my radar on what Dutch had said. "He'll kill again if we don't stop him," I said. "And if we don't bring new charges soon, he'll move to another town in another state, where it'll be easier to get away with it."

Dutch got up and collected his plate, then motioned to mine and I nodded that he could take it. "If that's the case, then I'll clean up if you'll look through the files. But remember that anything you find can't be traced back to you. Otherwise, Matt's not going to take it into court."

"In other words, I've got to find something obscure and make it look obvious?"

Dutch winked at me. "Exactly."

I sighed and lifted the first file. "Just the way I want to spend my Friday night."

A moment later Dutch set a second beer down next to me. "Thanks, babe. We owe you."

I waved absently and opened the file, bracing myself for the task at hand. "Okay, Corzo. You might have been careful, but you'll need more than that with me on your case." And with that, I got to work.

Chapter Six

· · ·

I had vague memories of Dutch carrying me to bed sometime in the middle of the night. Right around one a.m. I'd nodded off, collapsing onto a pile of crime-scene photos and witness statements.

But my sleep had been restless and fitful, filled with horrible images of dead women, lying prone and strangled, staring sightlessly up into the camera capturing their last, frozen expressions. When I finally woke up around seven, I felt like I'd gotten very little rest.

Sitting up in bed, I blinked blearily and heard rustling out in the kitchen. "Dutch?" I called. My voice was hoarse and my throat felt a little raw.

He appeared in the doorway. "Morning," he said, coming forward to sit on the bed next to me and offer me up a cup of coffee, heavy on the cream.

I took a sip and closed my eyes. There is nothing like that first sip of really good coffee, is there? "You are a god and I shall worship you forever."

He chuckled. "My wife thinks I'm a god. Life is good."

"I was talking to the coffee."

He frowned. "Life is less good."

"Should I remind you that you got lucky last night, and if you play your cards right, you'll probably get lucky again today?"

"Oh, yeah? Which cards will make it a sure thing?"

"Breakfast cards. Breakfast cards that involve bacon, eggs, and perhaps a muffin of some kind."

"And will I be getting lucky before or after these breakfast cards get laid out on the table?"

I took another sip of coffee. God love him, he'd put a bit of nutmeg into the mix. Setting the cup aside, I wrapped my legs around him. "Now's good."

After I'd again demonstrated my appreciation for him (and he for me—winning!), Dutch set out to make us breakfast. I followed him to the kitchen and warmed up the coffee in the microwave. No sooner had I sat down than there was a knock on the door. Dutch and I both looked at each other, then at the clock, then at the door. "You expecting anyone?" he asked me.

"Nope. You?"

"Nope," he said with a little irritation. Glancing at the clock on the stove, he added, "It's seven forty-five in the morning. Who the hell knocks on the door before eight a.m. on a Saturday?"

The knock came again. Dutch looked at me expectantly and I groaned, sliding out of the chair to go answer the door. Covering myself with the silk robe I'd shambled into, I opened the door a crack and peered out. "Hey," Oscar said.

I blinked. "Dude. Do you know what time it is?"

Oscar lifted his wrist and stared at his watch. "Seven forty-three." He then looked back at me as if expecting me to be grateful for the info.

"What are you doing here?"

Oscar held up his phone. "I drove by this house this morning. It had a For Sale sign."

I stared at the image, then back up to Oscar. "And?"

"And it's in my neighborhood. Maybe I should get it."

"Oh, for the love of God," I sighed, opening the door all the way and waving him inside.

Dutch leaned out from the kitchen and eyed Oscar with a mixture of curiosity and annoyance. "Good morning, sir," Oscar said with a slight wave.

"Rodriguez," Dutch replied. "You're here. In my home. On a Saturday. Before eight."

Oscar nodded, but then he sort of seemed to get it when he took in my robe and Dutch's pajama bottoms and T-shirt attire. The agent's cheeks reddened. "Uh . . . sorry. Did I get you guys up?"

I smiled sweetly at Oscar. "No, honey. We got each other up."

Dutch ducked his chin to hide a smile and turned back to making breakfast, while Oscar's face flushed even more. Clearing his throat, he said, "Maybe I should come back later?"

I waved a hand at him. "Oh, forget it. You're here now. Dutch can throw a few more eggs and sausages on. You might as well join us for breakfast. Now, come with me to the study. I'm feeling good about our chances of finding you the perfect home."

Leading Oscar to the study, which was off the dining room, I felt my radar practically singing to me. Sometimes I'll feel so strongly about something that it almost seems like a memory that I'm recalling with great clarity. In my mind's eye when I'd told Oscar that he needed to buy a new place, I'd seen a simple bungalow of white stucco, with a prominent A-line roof, and a small but tidy yard. I'd also had a feeling that the home was farther east than where Dutch and I lived, and south of downtown, so after hopping on Zillow, I scrolled over the area I felt drawn to and within ten minutes I'd actually found *that* house.

When I clicked on the address, the house came up for us and Oscar leaned in to peer at the pictures. "Oscar," I told him with a flourish, "welcome to your new home."

"Huh," he said.

I blinked. "Don't blow me away with your enthusiasm."

"It's kinda big, don't you think?"

"It's eighteen hundred square feet. That's hardly 'big.'"

"But it's three bedrooms. Cooper, what am I gonna do with three bedrooms?"

I held up my hand and ticked off on my fingers. "Master bedroom, home office, guest bedroom slash extra storage." When he still looked unconvinced, I read the description out loud. "'Hardwood floors, granite countertops, new AC and furnace, separate shower and garden tub in master bath.' Honey, this house is awesome! And look, it just came on the market yesterday! If we call the Realtor after breakfast, I'll bet we can get you in for a showing today!"

Oscar frowned, clicking through more photos. "I don't know . . . ," he mused.

I sighed and threw up my hands. Pointing to the screen, I said, "I'm not sure how to break it to you, buddy, but *that's* your new home."

And then Oscar stopped clicking and he said, "Whoa."

"What's 'whoa'?"

He went back a photo. "There's a pool."

I smiled. "And it's a nice pool at that."

"And a hot tub."

I pointed again to the screen, this time to the list of features. "And it's wired for sound throughout, even out to the hot tub."

Oscar took out his phone, his fingers practically shaking with excitement. "What's the number to call?"

I chuckled and covered his phone with my hand. "You can't call *now*."

"Why not?"

"Because it's just past eight a.m. on a Saturday morning. Seriously, if you were my client, I'd kill you if you called me that early."

"Then when can I call?"

I closed the window to Zillow and pulled up my personal e-mail account. From there I typed in the name of a client who was also a real estate agent, and after finding her e-mail address, I sent her a quick note asking her to call me as soon as she got the message, as I had an eager client ready to make an offer on a house very, very soon.

Next I turned to Oscar and said, "Have you already applied for a mortgage?"

Oscar blinked. "Uh, no. I was sorta gonna pay cash."

It was my turn to blink. "You were sorta . . . gonna . . . what?"

"It's only two hundred thousand, right?"

"You have two hundred thousand dollars *saved*? Like . . . in a checking account?"

Oscar shrugged. "Well, yeah. My rent's only five hundred a month, Cooper. My car's ten years old and I bought it for cash back then too. Most of my paycheck stays in the bank."

Just then Dutch stepped into the doorway. "Breakfast is on," he said. Then he must have caught my expression. "What's wrong?"

I stood there for a sec, slack-jawed, and looked from Dutch to Oscar, then back again. "He's got two hundred grand in his checking account," I said. "He's gonna pay for his new house in *cash*."

Dutch's eyes widened. "Good job, Oscar."

"Thank you, sir," Oscar said, with a bit of both embarrassment and pride.

Dutch nodded. "Eggs are getting cold," he said. The man brooked no argument about getting to the table to eat a hot meal.

Oscar waited for me to lead the way and all I could do was shake my head. On the way to the dining room, we passed the large pickle jar that was half-full of shiny quarters, its other half full with various bills and pieces of paper with "I.O.U." scrawled across the surface. That jar accounted for much of my savings.

Dutch seemed to read my body language as I passed the jar because he said, "Maybe this time next year you'll have sworn your way to paying off our mortgage."

I stiffened, but Oscar made a choking sound and when I looked at him over my shoulder, he was covering his mouth to hide the smile and added a forced cough.

"Wiseass," I growled, narrowing my eyes at Dutch.

He was having himself a pretty good chuckle. Just for that, I wasn't going to do the dishes.

Halfway through breakfast Oscar got a call. He looked at the display and excused himself from the table to take it in the living room. I frowned as he left because I knew he wasn't the type to take a call in the middle of the breakfast his boss had just prepared unless it was something important.

Across the table from me, Dutch didn't say anything, but I could tell he thought the same thing. We ate in silence for a few moments before he pointed to the stack of files he'd brought home for me to look through. "Did you get anything?"

I shook my head. "Nothing off Wendy McLain's murder, but I still haven't finished with Donna Andrews's file."

Dutch sighed. "Damn," he muttered.

I stabbed at a bit of hash brown with my fork. I wanted very much to give Dutch a lead that he could act on, but I'd scoured Wendy McLain's file for anything I could find that might link her murder back to Corzo. So far, I'd come up with bupkes. The small dent I'd made in Donna Andrews's folder wasn't leaving me too optimistic either. "I'm trying, honey," I told him.

"I know, doll," he said, reaching out to give my hand a squeeze. "I know."

Oscar came back to the table, looking like he had news. "What's up?" I asked as he took his seat and put his napkin back in his lap.

"That was the lead detective on Skylar's case—Ray Dioli. He finally returned my call. I told him what we wanted, and he shut me right down."

"Shit!" I swore, then glared angrily at the swear jar across the room. I was gonna go broke at this rate.

"Wait," Oscar said. "You didn't let me finish. After he told me no way, he asked me who I was working for, and I told him that I was freelancing for you, and then he changed his whole tune."

I blinked. "Changed his tune? What does that mean?"

Oscar lifted one shoulder in a slight shrug, and I took in the rather amused quirk to his lips. "He's heard of you."

I blinked some more. "Heard of me?"

"Yep. Said his kid came to see you a few months ago. Do you remember reading a Chris Dioli?"

I searched my memory banks. For a long time, most of my clients were women, but for about the past year or so, I'd been getting more and more men, so some guy from a few months ago was not much to go on. "No," I said.

"Well, I guess you hit it out of the park for Dioli's kid, Cooper, because he's now a huge fan. A lot of stuff you predicted for the kid has already happened, and you even told him to tell his dad to lay off the sodium to cut down on his hypertension. You also told him that his dad needed to do something to lower his blood pressure, or he'd be cutting his life expectancy short. Turns out Dioli had had a doctor's appointment the very same day his kid came to see you, *and* at the same time, and while you were telling his kid about his hypertension, his doctor was saying the *exact* same thing to Ray."

"Huh," I said. Even though I've been predicting the futures of my clients for almost a decade now, I'm still surprised by how accurate the stuff that feels like it just rolls off my tongue can be.

"Anyway," Oscar continued, "after I told him I was working with you because you'd taken an interest in the case, he changed his mind. He'd like to meet with us."

I cocked my head at him, sensing Oscar was holding back something. "He'd *like* to meet with us, or he's *agreed* to meet with us?"

Oscar took a bigger interest in his food. "Uh, he sort of asked me if it was gonna be just me, or me and you, and when I said it was the two of us, he was happy."

I squinted suspiciously at the agent. "Happy? Why was he *happy*, Oscar?"

Oscar cleared his throat and refused to look at me. Shoveling a sizable portion of eggs into his mouth, he mumbled, "He'd like to get your opinion on something."

"A case?" I guessed, feeling my shoulders set with irritation.

Oscar shrugged. "I guess. He wasn't really specific."

I glared at Oscar, but Dutch said, "What can it hurt, Edgar? You look into his case and he lets you look into his."

I pointed to the stack of files to my left. "I've already got a full caseload, babe."

"So you make up the terms before Dioli can rope you into another investigation. Tell him that in exchange for your first impressions, you'll need a copy of the file on Skylar Miller. Once he agrees, spend a little time with him on his case, collect your copy of the murder file, and leave."

I tapped my finger on the table. "Yeah, okay. I guess that's a good compromise. Oscar, when did Dioli want to meet?"

"I told him we'd see him in half an hour. And that was five minutes ago." Oscar then paused to look me over while I gaped at him. "Cooper, you might want to shower first."

I rushed through a very quick shower and got dressed in light-weight capris and a loose-fitting tank. The low overnight had been eighty degrees, and when Oscar and I rolled up to the APD sub-station in separate cars, my phone said it was already ninety-two. As I parked my car next to Oscar's, my phone rang, and I saw that it was Bonnie, my client the Realtor. I got out of the car and held up a finger to Oscar as he waited for me to walk with him into the building. I chatted quickly with Bonnie and made arrangements for her to meet Oscar at the house we'd found online at eleven. "You're not coming?" Oscar asked, the second I was off the phone with Bonnie.

"I have clients starting at ten thirty, which is why I insisted we take separate cars. I barely have time to meet with Dioli."

He frowned but nodded, and I followed him inside the building, which was air-conditioned to a comfortable degree rather than the frigid temps Dutch and his crew kept the bureau offices.

Making our way upstairs to the second floor, we inquired about Detective Dioli with the duty officer and we were on our way to sit in the chairs in the small lobby when we heard someone call, "Hey" behind us.

My first impression of Dioli was that he resembled a lot of the cops on APD's force, who all seemed to have come from the same genetic stock—thick in the shoulders and neck, a bit of a belly, face of a bulldog, and completely bald. I offered him a perfunctory smile and hoped he wasn't also thick in the head.

He waved us over to walk with him and we followed obediently past several empty cubicles to the back of a room lit with harsh fluorescents. We stopped behind him at a smallish round table with three chairs.

I noticed that Dioli had dressed casually in jeans and a black T, and I thought he might be off duty but getting in a little extra paperwork time over the weekend.

In the center of the table were two thick stacks of folders. Before we sat down, the detective turned to face us with outstretched hand. "Ray Dioli," he said. "It's nice to finally meet you, Miss Cooper. I've heard a lot about you."

I took his hand and shook it. "It's 'Mrs.' now, and please call me Abby, Ray. It's nice to meet you too." Dioli then shook Oscar's hand and we all sat down.

Leaning forward to rest his elbows on the table, Dioli said, "Agent Rodriguez said you're interested in the Skylar Miller appeal?"

"Yes," I said without any elaboration.

Dioli looked me square in the eye, as if attempting to read me the way he knew I could read him. "You think she'll win the appeal?"

"No."

Dioli nodded. "Good," he said with no small measure of bitterness.

I worked hard to keep my expression neutral. "You're convinced she did it?"

He held my gaze again. "Without a shadow of a doubt. She did it. She butchered that little boy."

I took in both his conviction and his statement before I asked my next question. "Can you tell me about the case?" I knew I could bargain for the file, but I thought that since Dioli had been the lead detective, he'd be the best person to give me the highlights of how he came to make the case against Skylar.

Dioli tapped his index finger on the table and chewed on the inside of his cheek, as if considering my request. "Yeah, I can tell you all about it, but I'd like something in return."

"Of course," I said easily. "I'm always happy to assist the APD."

Ray chuckled. "Yeah, so I hear." Even though his comment held no malice, I knew by it that he must've heard about the times I'd butted heads with those in APD. "I had your partner down here a couple of months ago."

"She says you gave her a rough time." I probably shouldn't have baited him, but where Candice was concerned, my inner protective tiger came out.

Dioli shrugged as if it was no big deal. "Her husband's a Fed," he said.

"As is mine."

"Yeah, but you weren't filmed shooting a guy in a parking garage. I worked that scene. It was ugly. Anyway, I had to push her and see if there were any holes in her story. I wouldn't be a good cop if I didn't."

I took a deep breath and was aware that Oscar was sitting quietly in his chair, his gaze roving back and forth between us. "I guess that's fair," I told Dioli. "She doesn't seem to harbor any hard feelings at least."

He chuckled again, like he thought me a nice little white liar. "So! About our bargain. I tell you about Skylar Miller, and in exchange I'd like your thoughts on a case that we're having a hell of a tough time cracking and, due to the lack of any solid leads, is about to get put on ice."

"I agree to your terms except with one added request."

"Which is?"

"I'd like a copy of Noah's murder file."

Dioli narrowed his eyes at me . . . suspicious. "Why?"

"I'm writing a book," I said easily. Wow, that lie had just totally rolled right off my tongue. Maybe I'd need another jar for those.

"You're writing a book?" the detective asked me, as if my answer didn't quite make sense to him.

"Yes."

"You're a psychic—why would you want to write a book about a murder you didn't help solve?"

"Color me adventurous."

Dioli chuckled again. I hoped it was a good thing that he found me amusing at least. "You working for Miller?" he asked me, suddenly losing all sense of humor and narrowing those eyes again.

"No." Holding up a pinkie, I added, "Pinkie swear."

Dioli glanced at Oscar as if to get his take, but Oscar merely offered him a mildly polite blank stare. Finally Dioli sat back and said, "Okay, but if I'm gonna make you a copy of the file, then I want your word that you're not working for Skylar Miller or any of these liberal groups trying to get death row inmates out of the needle."

"You have it, Detective. I assure you, my interest in Miller's case is personal. I'm advancing my own agenda here. That's it."

At last, he nodded and said, "Okay. I'll make you a copy of the file."

"Awesome, and I'll give you my impressions on this case of yours."

Dioli stuck out his hand again. "Deal." We shook on it and then he started telling me about the murder of Noah Miller, and bless Oscar, he subtly set his phone down to record Dioli in a way that only I saw. "It was a big case that took up two years of my life, so I remember it like the back of my hand," he began. "The call came into dispatch at two thirty-eight a.m. At first it was reported as a burglary in progress. Unis were dispatched to the scene, and as they went through clearing the house, they saw bloody footprints leading out from the back bedroom. The house had only two bedrooms, both off the hallway leading from the living room.

"Anyway, they went into the back bedroom, found Noah on the floor, checked for a pulse, found none, and called me. I was on duty that night with my partner, Jay Perkins. He retired three years later, and then a heart attack took him on the fifth hole of a golf course. . . ." Dioli stopped speaking and he seemed to need a moment to find his voice again. He must've really loved his old partner, because I swear his eyes were a bit shiny right then.

After clearing his voice, he said, "Jay was the best damn detective I ever worked with. Taught me a lot, that guy. Anyway, the two of us got dispatched to the scene and were given the scoop from the unis. They were keeping clear of the house until we had a chance to process and take pictures, and they were keeping a close eye on the mom, who I first saw sitting on the curb, rocking like a crazy person back and forth while one of the neighbors, Mrs. Mulgrew, sat with her.

"Jay went inside to check that the scene was secure while I went over to interview Skylar. Now, at first Skylar seemed pretty out of it. I tried to get her attention, but she was feigning shock pretty good. She was somewhat unresponsive and shaking all over. I finally got it out of her that she'd woken up to a noise, but she couldn't remember what the noise was. She said she'd gotten out of bed and gone to check on her son, and found him on the floor next to the bed, facedown. She said she thought he might've fallen out of bed and she was trying to lift him back into it when she realized that he was wet. She says she thought he might've wet the bed, but then she felt something sharp on her hand, and it cut her. She felt around some more and said that she then realized that Noah was bleeding, and he'd been stabbed with a knife, and then all of the sudden she's hit by something from behind and gets shoved to the floor. She tells me she struggles with someone in the room, manages to get away, and goes running out of the house to the neighbors'."

So far the story Dioli told didn't seem that implausible, other than the fact that someone had murdered a young boy in cold blood. With as much violence and hate as I've seen and experienced in my life, I've never understood how anyone could mentally get to a point where they could hurt or murder a child. It's beyond my ability to fully comprehend. And yet, the news was full of reports of predators more than willing to do just that. Even the idea of a parent killing his or her child wasn't nearly as shocking as it'd been a decade ago. To my mind, it was still somewhat unfathomable. Causing harm to someone else's child was a despicable thing. Causing it to your own made you a particular kind of monster, and as much as I heard Dioli's derisive tone whenever he mentioned Skylar's name, I just couldn't see her as that brand of monster.

"After taking Skylar's statement," Dioli went on, "I spoke briefly with the neighbors, who corroborated her account from the time she came over to bang on their door and scream for help. From that point forward they said that she was so hysterical they couldn't make sense of anything she was saying, but they saw her nightgown was bloody and Noah wasn't with her, so they called nine-one-one right away."

"Did you ask them what they thought of Miller's behavior?" Oscar asked.

"Yeah, but later. They've always supported Skylar. They believed her story."

"At what point did you begin to suspect her story wasn't true, Ray?" I asked.

"Pretty early on," he said. "Jay met me outside after I got through interviewing the Mulgrews and he told me there were some things I needed to see. He took me into the house and showed me the hallway leading to the bedrooms. There was a single set of bloody footprints leading away from Noah's room, and we suspected those were Skylar's because they were small and slender—like a female's—and you could also tell they were made by bare feet."

"Why was that suspicious?" I asked. "If Skylar told you that she went into her son's room to check on him, wouldn't it be the case that she would've likely tracked some of the blood from his room into the hallway?"

"It would. But that's not why it was suspicious. What was suspicious was that the hall had been recently vacuumed. We could see the prints of the uni who went into the house in response to the burglary in progress. When you get that kind of a call and you're in the process of clearing the house, you hug the wall, and we could see his footsteps doing exactly that." The memory of Candice and me inching our way along the wall in my own home when we didn't know it was Oscar in my bathroom flashed through my mind.

"The footsteps of the uni went down the hall to the far right," Dioli continued, "and came back on the far left. But other than his footprints and Skylar's, there were no other tracks in that house."

"Could the assailant have gone out the window?"

"Nope. Shut tight, free of blood, and the screen was in place.

All the windows in the house were like that, pristine and showing no sign of forced entry. What's more, Jay took me around the outside of the house and we couldn't find a single footprint, scuff mark, or broken blade of grass. And neither could the crime-tech guys."

"I'm assuming there was no other sign of forced entry," I said, recalling one of the articles I'd read had highlighted that detail.

"None," Dioli said. "The front door was left open from when Skylar went out, but she'd unlocked that herself. Hell, she told me she'd done that on her way out the door, because I'd asked her if her front door had been locked.

"What's more, there wasn't a single hair, fingerprint, DNA fragment, or scrap of other physical evidence left by this supposed intruder. We could account for every single speck of physical evidence in Noah's bedroom as belonging to him or his mom. If there was an intruder in that room, he wore a hazmat suit."

I frowned. Something felt a little off to me about that statement, but I didn't think I wanted to question the detective. Instead, I'd pay close attention to the file notes on the physical evidence collected.

"Did she ever confess?" I asked.

Dioli shook his head. "Nope. We grilled her all the rest of that night and through the middle of the afternoon the next day, but she stuck to the story. Fourteen hours we went at her, and she finally asked for a lawyer. Once we couldn't talk to her anymore, we started interviewing everyone in her life." Dioli paused to shake his head, like he was remembering something tragic. "I tell you, that poor kid Noah was put through the wringer before she finally went nuts and killed him."

I leaned forward. "Tell me."

"Well, Skylar married pretty young. She and her ex were high school sweethearts, and Skylar got pregnant at nineteen and the kids got married. Anyway, Noah comes along and Skylar's still kind of a kid herself. She's upset that all her friends are out having fun and she's got a baby at home, so she starts dumping the kid on her mom and heading out to party.

"Pretty soon she's a full-blown alcoholic and she spends three months in a rehab center and comes home to be the good little wife. She was back in rehab six months later. Then a year after that."

That surprised me. "Rehab is pretty expensive," I said. "How'd two twenty-something kids with a baby afford multiple stays?"

"Chris Miller—her ex—he comes from big money. His folks told me they always suspected Skylar got herself pregnant to trap Chris, and, in the beginning, they wondered privately if Noah was even his."

"Was he?" I asked, not knowing if they'd do a DNA match postmortem if that was a question.

"He was Chris's son," Dioli confessed. "The parents had done their own DNA test right after Noah was born without ever telling Skylar, and we also did one just to cover our bases. Noah was Chris's kid. Anyway, Chris and Skylar get along about as well as you'd expect. They both cheated on each other, and Skylar was given to disappearing for days or weeks on end. She'd just leave Noah with her mother and trot out the door and they wouldn't see her for a while. Then she'd show up drunk off her ass.

"Chris finally threw in the towel when he found her passed out on the couch, leaving Noah unsupervised, and a day later she got arrested for her third DWI."

"You'd think he would've thrown in the towel long before then," I said. I couldn't imagine being in that kind of toxic relationship, especially when I had a young son to think about.

"Chris had opened up his own business and he was working long hours, so he put dealing with her on the back burner until it became apparent that she couldn't be left alone with Noah. He convinced his mother-in-law to move in and provide child care after Skylar got arrested. Mrs. Wagner—Skylar's mother—had had enough of Skylar's shit too. She helped Chris get full custody."

"Wow," I said. Across from me Oscar grimaced. "Skylar must not have been happy."

"Nope. We think that might have been some of the motivation for murdering Noah."

"How would that be motivation?" I asked.

"If you interview Chris, you'll understand. That guy lived for his son. We had to do the notification the day after the murder, and I've never seen a man so gutted. He said that his phone had rung in the middle of the night, but he'd been too tired to answer it, and when we came by, he ran to get his phone and showed us that Noah had called him in the middle of the night. There was no message, but it fit with the time of the murder."

"He called his dad?" I asked. That detail had been left out of the articles I'd read.

"He did," Dioli said. "We think he woke up, saw his mom was about to attack him, grabbed the phone, and hit redial. The call was only two seconds in length, so she must've hung it up before the call could connect and Noah could cry out for help.

"Noah had a phone in his room?" I asked next. Not only was it a bit unusual for a nine-year-old to have a phone in his room, but the phone call itself felt important to my radar.

"Noah had talked to his dad right before bed," Dioli said. "He probably never put it back before falling asleep."

"Anyway, it was one of the most gut-wrenching notifications

I've ever done. You had to see it, I guess. Chris blamed himself for not answering the call, and for losing custody of Noah in the first place. At the time, I had a son only a little older than Noah, so it hit me pretty hard too."

"No wonder you worked so hard on the case," I said. It made sense then why Dioli had been so determined to nail someone for Noah's murder.

"Yeah. The case was too close to home," he admitted. "Anyway, we think Skylar fell off the wagon soon after Noah moved back in with her, and we also think that Noah caught her in the act. Chris said that he got the first call from Noah the night of the murder at around nine p.m., and he recalled that his son told him he needed to talk to him in private. He said he tried to get Noah to tell him what was so important, but he says that Noah wouldn't talk about it with his mom in the house. At the time, Chris just thought Skylar was being a little strict with Noah or something. Later, he figured that Skylar might've been listening in on the call, and she knew that Noah was planning to tell Chris about the drinking. Skylar was getting a pretty good child-support check every month, and she knew she'd lose custody if she was caught drinking again, which was also a violation of her parole. Knowing her free ride was over, she killed Noah to get her revenge against Chris."

"Against Chris for what?" I asked. "Divorcing her?"

Dioli shook his head. "No. For getting her thrown in jail in the first place. Chris was the one who called the cops on Skylar the day she was pulled over for her third DWI."

"Wow. That's some tough love," Oscar said.

Dioli snorted. "No love, just tough," he said.

I shifted in my chair. Not only did the motive Dioli offered as Skylar's reason for killing Noah seem seriously flawed, if not out-

and-out ridiculous, the picture Dioli was painting of Skylar just didn't jibe with the woman I'd met in jail. I mean, the Skylar I'd seen had been beaten down by a terribly tragic life. She hadn't seemed defiant, or rebellious, or even feisty. She'd seemed exactly the opposite, in fact, someone who'd been pummeled by life, and there wasn't much left in her except for the tiny acts of kindness she could manage to scrounge out of her current existence to re-mind herself of her own humanity.

And yet, the more Dioli spoke of her past, the more I knew that if I'd known Skylar fifteen years ago, I'd likely look at her with a whole lot less sympathy, and that made me wonder if Dioli's ver-sion of who Skylar was wasn't somehow skewed and profoundly biased.

Based on the facts Dioli had presented, it was easy to see how he could've been so convinced that Skylar was guilty.

He continued to tell us about the case, and a bit about the trial, until I glanced at my watch and said, "Ray, I'm so sorry to inter-rupt, but I have clients in twenty minutes and I've got to get to the office. Can I come back later today to pick up the file and the one you'd like me to look at for you?"

Dioli pulled his head back in surprise. "Oh, you gotta go?"

I nodded. "Sorry. I have clients today."

"Uh, okay. Yeah. But I'm only gonna stay here long enough to copy the files."

"I can wait," Oscar said pleasantly. I smiled gratefully at him.

"I guess that could work," Dioli said. "The file I'm giving you is a murder I worked on eight months ago. Girl found in Zilker Park. We eventually identified her as a recent UT graduate. She'd been here on a scholarship from Vietnam. Kept to herself and lived alone. Her parents didn't even know she'd been missing."

I winced. Another dead girl. Sometimes I hated my consulting job. "I promise to look at it later on today, Ray. I'll call you tomorrow if I can give you any info."

"Great," he said. "And if you give me any leads, I've got a few other cases I could use your thoughts on."

Although the detective's acceptance of my particular talent was refreshing, I wondered if he realized I didn't work for free. Still, I decided to hold my tongue until after I got my hands on Noah's murder file.

"Let's make sure I can give you something on this first one," I said, standing up to thrust my hand forward to shake Dioli's and thus control my exit. "It was truly a pleasure, Ray. Thank you again for taking time out of your weekend to talk to us."

"Sure," Ray said. I could tell he was a little thrown by my sudden departure.

"Until we meet again," I said, pumping his hand one last time before winking at Oscar and hurrying away.

As I exited the building, all that Dioli had told us about Skylar settled firmly on my shoulders like the weight of a thousand pounds. There didn't seem to be any doubt in the detective's mind that Skylar had been lying through her teeth about the intruder. He was certain she was guilty.

Getting in my car, I mentally began to gather a list of things I'd need to get to the truth. "First things first," I muttered as I looked behind me to pull out of the slot. "Skylar Miller, you and I are gonna have another little chat."

Chapter Seven

. . .

I read for five clients nearly back-to-back and by the time I was done, I felt numb with fatigue.

Most people don't realize how much effort it takes to give a reading. For the record, it's a buttload. I know it looks like we psychic types are just chatting away happily, merely having a conversation with our clients, but really we're expending lots of our own energy assessing your energy, filtering out distractions, searching for solutions, trying to home in on the most accurate interpretation of what we're sensing. It's work. A lot of work.

Anyway, after closing up shop, I headed home and found Oscar once again in my living room. "Hey, Cooper," he said, looking about as peppy as I felt.

"Oscar," I said, plopping down on the couch next to him right before Eggy and Tuttle assaulted me with kisses and wriggling bodies. "Where's my hubby?"

Oscar motioned toward the study. "In there working on his private security gig."

Dutch and his best friend, Milo, ran a personal security business, which Milo managed on the people end and Dutch managed on the numbers end. "Ugh. He'll be working on spreadsheets all weekend," I said. One weekend a month my husband devoted all of his time to making sure D&M Security made a tidy profit. It always did, but mostly because Dutch ran a tight ship and knew his way around the tax code better than most accountants.

Setting Tuttle in my lap while Eggy curled himself up next to me, I glanced again at Oscar and said, "You look like you had a day. What happened?"

"Someone else bought the house," he said.

I shook my head. "What? How can that be?"

"Dunno, Cooper. I met your Realtor, she took me through the house, I really liked it, like a lot, and I told her I wanted it. She made a call and the other Realtor said the sellers had just accepted another offer."

Tired as I was, I sent out my radar to assess the situation. "Hang on," I said, digging out my phone and calling Bonnie. She answered right away. "Abby! So great to hear from you. Oh, that Oscar Rodriguez is such a cutie! Thank you so much for referring him to me. I'm not going to stop until I find him the perfect house. I mean, I know he must be disappointed to lose out on the one today, but I told him there were plenty of other listings, and I'm working on a whole batch right now."

Bonnie had said all of that in a single breath. It was exhausting just to listen to, but I liked Bonnie because she had such wonderfully high energy and she worked extremely hard for her clients. "Yeah, about that, Bonnie. What's the deal on the house from today?"

"Oh, you know how it is. Terrific listing in a great area for the right price, they go fast, Abby, especially when they're within a decent commute to downtown. I guess a couple from the listing agency went through it last night and they made their offer this morning right after we got to the house."

"Can you call their Realtor back and let them know that you have a backup offer should their deal fall through?"

There was a pause, then, "I can. Absolutely. But maybe I should warn you that, according to the seller's agent, the other couple have excellent credit and they're going through a terrific lender."

"Oscar's offer would be a cash deal, Bonnie."

I heard her suck in a little breath. In real estate there's nothing better than a cash deal. Quick, painless, no appraisal, no mortgage insurance, no lender contingencies to deal with, just money for keys. "He didn't tell me that," she said.

I slid a glance sideways to Oscar. Newbies. "Yeah, this will be his first purchase. You know how it goes. Anyway, I'm going to hand my phone to him and you two can discuss offer price. I have a very strong feeling the deal the sellers have on the table is gonna fall through. Maybe it won't appraise. Maybe their lender will find some other flaw, but this is going to be Oscar's house."

She practically squeaked with excitement and I handed the phone over to Oscar; then I got up to give him some privacy. He'd of course heard my entire conversation, so he knew my thoughts, and while he worked out a deal, I headed in search of my husband. "Hey," I said, looking into the study.

Dutch sat at the desk, squinting at the screen, with his fingers poking the keyboard like someone who nudges a bug to see if it's dead. He blinked and rubbed his eyes as I came into the room. "Hey, yourself. How was the day?"

"Long. Yours?"

"About the same. Oscar still here?"

"He is."

"He's been waiting for you since three."

"Sorry, honey." I knew Dutch liked to have the house to himself sometimes.

"It's fine," Dutch assured me, but I could tell it kinda wasn't. "He brought you those two files," he added, motioning with his chin to the right side of the desk. One was a lot thicker than the other.

I sighed. "Skylar Miller and the case Dioli wants me to dig into."

Dutch's mouth set in a frown. "I thought you were going to give your impressions to him at the meeting?"

"He took too long telling us about Noah Miller's murder, and I had a full list of clients to get to."

Dutch's frown deepened. "You're working a lot, dollface. Think you might be taking on too much?"

"Yep."

His frown split into a grin. "Well, as long as you're pacing yourself."

I sighed. "When it rains, it pours."

"What's Dioli's case?"

"A former UT student here on a student visa from Vietnam, found in Zilker Park a week after she went missing."

Dutch nodded. "Yeah, I heard about that one on the news a while back. Tough case from what I heard."

"All the cold ones are tough, honey."

"Did Dioli give you the rundown on Skylar Miller?"

"He did, and from what he told me, I've got a straight uphill battle."

"Without a lot of time," Dutch reminded me.

I closed my eyes and inhaled deeply. "Yes. Without much time, which means I need to work through being tired and soldier on. You gonna be okay for dinner on your own?" I asked, getting up.

"You're leaving?" Dutch asked.

"Yeah. There're a few things I need to check out. Something

about the crime scene is really bothering me, and I feel like I want to go there and feel it out."

"You're not going alone, are you?"

I moved around the desk to kiss him on the cheek. "No, honey. I'll take Oscar."

He squeezed my arm. "Okay," he said. "Call me if you're gonna be out past ten."

I promised I would and headed away to find Oscar and recruit him for some gumshoeing.

Forty minutes later we were each nibbling on some fast food and staring at a tiny house in an adorable secluded community just off Highway 183 on Austin's east side. "Nice neighborhood," I said with a bit of surprise.

"Yeah, given the area, this is a pretty cool little sub," Oscar said, craning his neck to look at the surrounding houses. "You think there're any for sale in this hood?"

I cut him a look. "Will you stop? I told you, you're getting that other house. Have a little faith, would ya?"

"Sorry, Cooper, but when the Realtor says the sellers have already accepted another offer, I'm sort of inclined to move on."

"Trust," I said, a bit distracted by the small house at the end of the cul-de-sac. "I wonder if anybody's home."

"Only one way to find out," Oscar said. Getting out of the car, he approached the house and I hustled out to follow behind him. After knocking, we waited and were rewarded with the sound of an elderly woman who asked, "Who is it?" through the door.

Oscar identified himself as an agent with the FBI and when she opened the door, he flashed her his badge and said immediately, "I'm very sorry to disturb you, ma'am, and I don't want you to be alarmed. My associate and I aren't here on official business, and if you want us to leave, we will immediately. However, we're here investigating a cold case from a decade ago, and we were hoping that we might look around your property, simply to get a feel for what might have occurred here in two thousand and four."

The woman blinked her eyes rapidly, as if she couldn't quite keep up with Oscar's speech. She was a cute old lady. I'd put her roughly in her seventies with short curly white hair; big, round, pink-framed glasses; and a mouth that fell perpetually open. "What happened here a decade ago?" she asked him.

I spoke up. "A young boy died, ma'am. We're simply trying to get a feel for how it might've happened."

The old woman put a hand to her chest and said, "Oh, my. How old was he?"

"Nine, ma'am," I answered.

She paled and turned slightly sideways to peer back into her home. Then she turned back to me and said, "He died in the back bedroom, didn't he?"

Wow. The old lady had just shocked me and, judging by the look on Oscar's face, she'd shocked him too. "Yes, ma'am," I said. "How did you know?"

She shuddered. "I've lived here two years," she said. "I love the house, but that back bedroom creeps me out. I won't go in there unless I have to, and I always keep the door closed. Ever since I moved in I've felt something awful happened in there, but I never knew it was the death of a little boy."

"I'm sorry if we've upset you by telling you that," I said, and I truly was. I wondered if she was a renter instead of the owner. Realtors in Texas were required to inform their clients of any deaths that occurred on the property, but landlords were excluded from needing to provide such info.

"It's fine," she said with a wave of her hand. Then she looked at us a bit expectantly. "What did you two want to do, just look around?"

"We would be very much obliged," I told her, crossing my fingers that she'd say yes.

"Well, I wasn't expecting company, but I suppose it'll be all right." She stepped back to allow us inside and, upon stepping over the threshold, I immediately felt the presence of the violence that had taken place in the house—even from a decade ago.

Some acts are so monstrously despicable that the atmosphere soaks them up like a dry sponge, and it stays like that for a very long time. The more horrible the act, the more the atmosphere is stained with the imprint. I felt it like a heavy weight on my chest and it was a bit difficult to breathe, but when I glanced at Oscar, he seemed to be totally unaware of any change. I figured the old lady who'd let us in fell somewhere in the middle of the spectrum of sensitivities. She was able to live in the house as long as she didn't venture down the hall to the back bedroom. I'd be lucky to make it an hour in the place without needing to leave.

While I did my best to buffer myself against the energetic assault, the woman introduced herself as Molly Cummins. "I'm sorry for the mess," she said, her cheeks glowing pink as we followed her forward into the living room.

I looked around and thought she had no reason to be embarrassed. The place was neat as a pin except for a quilt on the sofa that was slightly askew—as if Molly had been cuddled under it before our knock on her door had disturbed her. The TV was on and blaring rather loudly, but I could still pick out the hum of an air-conditioning unit outside whirring to keep the house cool. I shivered both for the cool temp in the house and the atmosphere. "Can I offer you some iced tea?" she asked politely.

"None for me, thank you," I said right away. I didn't want to take advantage of the sweet woman's hospitality.

"I'd love a glass," Oscar said, and followed her into the kitchen. I was about to frown at him when he turned to wink at me over his shoulder and motion for me to go down the hall and check out the back bedroom. I suddenly realized that he was allowing me some undisturbed time to scope out the house psychically.

"Thank you," I mouthed to him, and headed down a hallway on my immediate left, which obviously led to the bedrooms. On the way, I passed a bathroom, also on the left, and adjacent to the bathroom was a narrow door, which I opened and discovered led to a broom closet. Across from the bathroom on the right-hand side of the hallway was the open door to a bedroom. I paused for a moment and peered into the room, which was obviously Molly's master bedroom. It was maybe twelve by twelve, fairly small, especially for a home I guessed to be less than twenty years old. Pulling out my phone, I took several photos of the room, making a note of where Molly had her bed positioned against the far wall between two windows; then I turned back to the hallway and snapped another photo of the distance between the master bedroom and the guest room at the end of the hall. Looking down, I saw that the carpet seemed fairly new—it was a light shade of tan and not well-worn or stained. I stared at it, imagining Skylar running down the hallway in her bare and bloody feet, and I turned to look back behind me. The hallway was maybe fifteen feet if that. If she was running, she'd take, what? Five actual steps?

It bothered me greatly that Dioli and his partner hadn't come across other footprints in the hallway and I wondered how late in the day the hallway had actually been vacuumed the night Noah was murdered. Had Skylar vacuumed right before going to bed? That seemed an odd thing to do, even for a neat freak, but maybe not. When I thought about it, I'd vacuumed a rug or two after nine p.m.

From the kitchen I could hear Molly and Oscar chatting away.

Molly was telling him that she sold her home after she retired, and didn't know if she wanted to stay in Austin, so she decided to rent the house for a year, which had now turned into two.

There was a part of me that wished I could abandon my next task and go hang out with them in the kitchen, but I knew that I couldn't. We'd come this far, and Molly had been incredibly kind to allow us to enter and snoop around her home as it was. Most people wouldn't have allowed us past the welcome mat.

With a sigh I turned back and proceeded down the hallway, pausing at the closed door of the back bedroom. Another shudder went through me. I swear I could feel a sense of malice as a left-over by-product of the night Noah was killed.

I opened the door and stepped inside. The room was bare except for a large antique dresser and one lone floor lamp. I flipped on the overhead light and surveyed the room.

It was powder blue with the same tan carpet from the hallway. The trim and the closet door were white. The blinds were off-white, and I could barely breathe.

Still, I pushed myself to stand there and feel the energy of the space. I wanted to sense the flow of the crime, even though I knew it'd be almost as bad as witnessing it.

I closed my eyes and tried to brace myself again, but it was like an assault on all my psychic senses. The attack had been brutal, and without mercy. I had a very real impression that Noah had felt an intense amount of pain before he died, and I shuddered in addition to the shivering I was already experiencing.

I opened my eyes and pulled a manila folder out of my purse. Taking a deep breath, I opened the folder and stared at the photo of Noah's room as it had been on that night back in 2004. Stepping to the side, I looked from the photo to the two windows on the far wall. Noah's twin bed had been positioned on that wall, between the windows like in his mother's room. In the photo, his bedspread and sheets were a tangle, and the angle of the photograph had captured only his bare feet sticking out past the bed on the floor.

The rest of the scene and the images recording it were a bit too horrible to describe, and I found that I'd been unable to look at them more than once, which was why I hadn't brought them along with me from the file I'd left in the car. I'd carried only three of the photos with me into the house: this one, the one showing Skylar's bloody footprints in the hallway, and the one of her bedroom, just to get a feel for how her room had looked at the time.

Taking another deep breath, I moved two steps forward, toward the windows, and looked back and forth from the photo to the windows a few times. Then I stepped all the way to one of the windows and pulled up the blind to reveal the actual panes.

I looked back and forth between the photo and the window a few more times; then I pulled up on the bottom sash. It came up easily. I pushed lightly on the screen and it fell out. Just like that. It simply fell out of the window and into the backyard. "Shit!" I hissed. (I'd worry about the swear jar later.)

"Pssst!" I heard behind me, and I jumped. Sliding the window back down quickly, I turned and adopted a friendly smile. Oscar stood in the doorway, eyeing me curiously. "You okay, Cooper?"

"Uh . . . yeah. I am. Okay."

"You sure?"

I moved away from the window a little. "Yes. Positive. Would you mind running through a scenario with me, though?"

"Sure," he said. "What're you thinking?"

I got out the photo of Noah's room and pointed to his bed. "See how the sheets are all rumpled and twisted around? He slept like most kids do, full of movement, but what's weird is that if he were pulled out of bed by his mother and stabbed, wouldn't we see the sheets tugged to one side?"

Oscar nodded. "I'm with you," he said.

I then pointed at the pile of sheets at the bottom of the bed. "Instead of being pulled to one side, his sheets are pushed down toward the end of the bed." I handed him the file and moved to about where the middle of Noah's bed would have been, then got down on the floor and lay down on my back. "Instead of being dragged out of bed, Noah's sheets look like he was awake right before he was attacked, and that he'd gotten out of bed himself." I then sat up, pulled my knees up, and pushed them down to mime how Noah would've sat up in bed, pulled up his knees, and shoved the covers down toward the end of the bed with his feet. Then I mimed getting up out of bed to stand next to the window.

"Makes sense," Oscar said, looking from me to the photo.

"Now," I said, heading back toward Oscar. "I glanced at the ME's report on the way over here, and he indicates that Noah was stabbed from behind, right?"

"Yep," Oscar said. "I read the file."

"You be the assailant and I'll be Noah," I said, turning away from him. I felt Oscar come up behind me and wind his left arm around my shoulders, pulling me into him; then he moved his right fist up high out in front of me before arcing it down toward my chest. He did it fast and his fist bumped gently but firmly against my sternum, and I couldn't suppress a shudder as my intuition practically shrieked when it connected with the real act of murder from ten years earlier.

Oscar let go of me immediately. "Sorry, Cooper, you okay?"

I squared my shoulders and turned around to show him no harm, no foul. "Yeah. Fine. Just the energy in this room is awful."

Oscar looked pained. He was as seasoned an investigator as they came, but I knew he abhorred violence against women and children most especially. Sometimes that granite cop exterior cracked a little and I saw the real Oscar, the teddy bear. I put my hand out and rubbed his arm. "Really. I'm okay," I assured him. He nodded and I got back to the macabre work of going through the events that'd happened in that room. "Now, from what I saw of the other crime-scene photos, it looks like the attack began when Noah was facing the wall and not the window, but at some point the killer turned him a little and that's how blood got on the back wall, right?"

Oscar nodded.

"And there was no interruption in the spatter pattern on those two walls, meaning that the ME's report was probably accurate. Noah was stabbed facing away from his assailant."

"True," Oscar agreed.

"So the murderer didn't want to look at him when he killed him."

"Or it was easier to control him that way. No arms or legs to block the attack."

"Yeah, that's true," I said. "And yet, a stabbing is so personal, Oscar. I mean, it's one of the cruelest ways to kill someone. There was rage in that attack. Real rage, and I wonder what fueled it."

"Maybe Skylar knows," Oscar suggested.

I shook my head. "I'm not convinced. One of the reasons Dioli thinks she's guilty is that she was covered in her son's blood when she fled to the neighbors." Stepping around behind Oscar, I reached up and assumed the position of the assailant, making him Noah, and pivoting him toward the wall. "But if she stabbed him like this," I said, miming the attack, "then how did she get all that blood on her? Isn't it more likely that her version of what happened is the truth?" For emphasis I moved back several steps to the door as if I were entering it, then walked forward and crouched down as I continued to explain. "She comes in the door, finds him on the floor in the dark, begins to pick him up, he rolls limply forward into her arms, and her clothing gets stained that way."

Oscar nodded. "I'm with you," he said.

"And," I added, "as she realizes something's wrong, she lays him back down on the ground and begins to feel around him, encountering the sharp blade of the knife and cutting her hand. She probably picked up the knife at that point just to see what the heck had sliced her palm, and all the while her mind, which is still trying to catch up from having just been in a deep sleep, is starting to put it together." Pointing to the corner of the room, I said, "At that point, the assailant, who's still in the room, maybe hiding in that corner, attacks her. . . ." I stood up and pretended to get pushed to the side violently. "They struggle, she somehow manages to get away, and he heads out the window."

Oscar frowned. "You had me right up to the point where he heads out the window. If there was some other assailant in the room and that's the way he got out, then for sure there'd be a bloody fingerprint on the windowsill. I mean, I can see how he'd avoid getting blood on his clothing, but not on his hands."

"Not if he was wearing gloves, Oscar, which maybe he took off right before he went out the window. That also would be backed up by the fact that they only found Skylar's prints on the knife. Whoever handled it could've been wearing gloves. And when he made his escape, he could've taken off the gloves, and dove out the window. I mean, look at them," I said, moving over to stand sideways next to the windows. "They're low enough where he could've just picked up his leg and shimmied out on his butt." I mimed that for Oscar. "He probably never even had to touch the sill with his bare hands."

"That's a whole lotta careful planning for this crime," Oscar observed.

"Exactly," I said. I totally agreed with him. I felt strongly someone had worked very hard to make it look like Skylar had murdered her son, but who and why were the big questions. "There's just one more thing I need to check out and then I'd like to get a look in Molly's backyard. Do you think she'd let us?"

"Let's hope so. You gotta put her screen back in the window."

I glared at him as I stepped past him and into the hall. Backtracking my way to Molly's bedroom, I sifted through my folder and pulled out the photo of how Skylar's room had looked the night of the murder.

Holding up the photo, I saw that the image had been captured from the doorway. It showed Skylar's bed, fairly unruffled except that one corner of her bedspread had been thrown back and there was still a small dent in her pillow. Otherwise the room was neat and orderly, nothing out of place.

I squinted at the image to study it more closely. On the nightstand was a framed photograph. The image was fuzzy, but I could make it out because I'd seen the photo within the frame before. It'd been in the back of Skylar's book back at county, the one of Noah and her at his ninth birthday party.

Turning to Oscar, I said, "Let's look at the backyard."

We went quietly to the living room and Molly sat on the sofa, the quilt laid back over her legs. "Are you finished?" she asked us.

"Almost, ma'am. Would it be all right if we did a simple walkabout around the perimeter of your house, starting in your backyard?"

She cocked her head. "You don't think you'll find any evidence of that boy's murder from ten years ago, do you?"

"No, ma'am," I confessed. "I'm just trying to get a feel for the house itself. I promise not to disturb a thing."

"Well, all right, then," she said, getting up to walk to the sliding glass door that led to the backyard. Undoing the latch, she said, "Please watch out for my mountain laurels. They're young and fragile and I'm still nursing them along."

"Yes, ma'am," Oscar and I both said as we stepped back out into the hot summer night.

It was going on eight o'clock but still plenty light out. Oscar and I stepped carefully around Molly's plants, which were set in a row along the house, but about two feet away, so we were able to walk the edge without a lot of trouble. "The grass grows right up to the edge of the house," I said, more to myself than to Oscar.

He heard me and said, "Didn't Dioli say that they didn't find any footprints along the exterior?"

"He did." I wondered if Oscar was thinking the same thing I was.

"How would he know that if there was grass here? Footprints wouldn't have been evident."

Playing devil's advocate, I said, "Maybe the lawn is new."

Oscar bent down and began poking at the edge of the lawn. "This is Saint Augustine," he said. "Toughest grass there is. It grows deep roots if given enough time and water. Molly's got an in-ground sprinkler system, looks to be at least a decade old." Oscar then looked up at the folder in my hand. "You got a photo of the backyard from 'oh-four in there?"

I shook my head. "It's in the car. I only took three of the crime-scene pics with me."

Oscar stood and rubbed his hands together to shake off the dirt. He then walked with me over to the bedroom window with the screen that I'd knocked to the ground. "So what's the deal with the screen?" he asked me.

I bent to pick it up and studied it. It was dirty as all get-out, and older. I was betting it was the original. I tucked it into place in the window as easily as I'd knocked it out. "I tapped it and it fell out," I said to him. "And look at how loose it is."

Oscar stepped forward and studied the screen. "It's about an eighth of an inch off," he said. "It'll stay put as long as you don't knock it."

Oscar then took out a small pocketknife from his cargo shorts and flipped up the blade. He inserted it between the rim of the screen and the window and angled the knife away from the window. The screen came out with barely any effort.

"If this is the original screen," I said, "then an intruder could've easily popped out the screen, opened the window, and gotten into Noah's room."

Oscar nodded but said nothing as he replaced the screen, then moved over to the other window and tried to do the same thing with his knife to that screen. It didn't budge. "It would've had to be this window," he said, coming over to tap the loose screen. And then he leaned forward and studied all the other screens along the back of the house one by one before turning back to me. "They're all the same as far as wear and tear. Frames are all identical colors. I'd bet they were all manufactured and installed at the same time."

"Like when the house was built?"

Oscar stepped back from the house and studied it and the surrounding yard. "I'll bet you this place was only a year or two old when Miller and her son moved in. It might've even been brand-new."

"It's younger than I would've guessed," I said, moving over to him to look at the house too.

"Texas can be hard on a house," he said. "The heat in the summer can bake the youth right out of it. The real clue is that tree," he said, pointing across the yard to an oak tree that was just a smidge past small and headed to medium size. "That guy can't be more than fifteen years old, which means he probably got planted when he was four or five."

"Why is that important?" I asked, thinking anyone in the past ten years could've planted that young tree.

"All the trees in the hood are about that size," he said. "I'll bet the builder gave everybody two trees for their landscaping package and you could have them in the front or the back, or one in the front and one in the back."

My gaze traveled over the fenced-in yard to the neighbor's yard, where a similar-sized tree stood. And then down a few more houses to another tree, also about the same size. As far down as I could look, in fact, I couldn't find a much bigger tree, and then I remembered pulling up to the house and the smallish-sized oak tree in the front yard.

I jotted a note to myself on the cover of the manila folder. "Skylar bought this house right before she moved Noah in. I can ask her if she bought it brand-new."

I then opened the folder so I could show Oscar what I'd noticed from the photo of Skylar's bedroom. "Oscar," I said. "Look at this and tell me what you see."

He edged close to me and peered over my shoulder. After studying the image for a few seconds, he said, "Awful tidy room for a woman who's fallen off the wagon."

I pointed to him, pleased that he'd picked up on it so quickly. "Bingo. I mean, look at her room. Everything is neat and orderly. Alcoholics aren't neat. They're slobs." I knew this from personal experience, actually. "So if she'd fallen off the wagon, wouldn't there be signs of her alcoholism in the house? I mean, the fact that the hallway was vacuumed and the house was neat as a pin, especially her room, should've been a sign that she was still abstaining."

"There was also no sign of alcohol on her breath when Dioli interviewed her," Oscar said.

I looked sharply at him. "How do you know that?"

"I asked him after you left. His theory for her motive seemed pretty lame, so I asked him if he'd seen any empty bottles in the kitchen or if he'd smelled any booze on her, and he said no, that she'd been careful and had planned ahead of time to make it look like she was still running sober."

"Right," I said, rolling my eyes. Focusing back on the photo, I said, "Look at the bed. Notice anything?"

Oscar squinted. "No," he said, shaking his head. "What am I missing?"

I pointed to the bedcovers. "See how the whole bedspread is perfectly smooth and flat, except for this section where Skylar obviously slept—the covers here have been folded over."

Oscar continued to study the photo. "Cooper, I'm still not seeing anything weird. She had a neat room and she had a neat bed. What's throwing you off about it?"

"Well, it tells me two things: The first is that Skylar is a deep sleeper. At least she was on the night her son was murdered. I mean, you can see that she did actually lay her head down on the pillow long enough that it left an impression, and the same thing with the sheets, right? She was in bed and sleeping when Noah was attacked, so if she's in a deep enough sleep not to have kicked the covers around, I'm thinking she was in a deep enough sleep to not have heard the beginning of Noah's attack.

"Then there's the covers themselves, especially this section that's been thrown back over to reveal the sheets. If you're fast asleep and you hear a noise loud enough to startle you awake, and you think maybe your son's in trouble, you're going to throw back the covers hastily. Like, whip them off you to get out of bed, right?"

Oscar's brow rose and he began to nod. "Yeah, Cooper, you're right. They do look thrown over."

"Exactly. The other thing that's bothering me is this," I said, pulling out the photo of the hallway with its one set of bloody footprints, and a lighter set of prints walking the edge of the hallway toward the back bedroom, and then away from it on the other side of the hallway. "I see a total of three sets of footprints here, and I'm wondering why I don't see four."

Oscar's brow dipped low again. "Assuming it was an intruder who killed Noah," Oscar said, "he could've gone out the window and covered his tracks by closing the window and popping the screen back on."

"I'm not talking about the killer's exit," I said. "I'm talking about the knife. The CSI report says that knife came from her kitchen, right?"

"Yeah, it did. So?"

"So, if we're to believe Dioli's version of how it went down, Noah calls his dad, tells him he has a big secret. Skylar overhears this, assumes he's about to rat her out, and she waits until two thirty in the morning to go into Noah's room and murder him. So when did she grab the knife?"

"Before she vacuumed," Oscar said.

I shook my head. "I'm not buying it. According to Dioli, Skylar starts drinking again; then she overhears Noah on the phone to his dad; then she cleans the place all nice and tidy-like, making sure to grab the knife before she vacuums the hallway, and stows the murder weapon somewhere in her room. Then she waits in bed under the covers without moving more than an inch until two thirty in the morning, when she stages it to look as if she was startled out of bed, rushes into Noah's room with the knife, kills him in a fit of rage that she's somehow managed to keep perfectly contained for the previous five and a half hours, and flees the scene, covered in her son's blood, tracking the only footprints down the hallway away from the scene. What about *any* of that makes *any* kind of sense?"

Oscar glanced at the window with the loose screen. "Yeah, but, Cooper, the knife only had *her* prints on it, old prints and ones made during the murder. I mean, if she didn't grab the knife from her kitchen before she vacuumed the hallway, who did?"

"Someone who knew where to look for a weapon in her kitchen. I mean, we have no idea when the knife was taken, only that it was by someone who was familiar enough with Skylar and her belongings to know where to locate it. And this same someone also knew that screen could be pried loose. And he also knew which bedroom her son slept in."

Oscar stared at the house for a long moment, and I could practically see the wheels in his head turning. "But why?" he said at last. "Why kill the kid, Abby? I mean, you gotta be a special kind of monster to do that to a nine-year-old boy."

"I agree," I said, feeling a well of anger curl up around my insides. "And that's why, no matter what happens to Skylar, we're not gonna stop until we hunt his ass down and make him pay."

Chapter Eight

· · ·

Oscar dropped me back at the house a little after nine. I found Dutch spoon-deep into a bowl of ice cream in front of the TV. After dropping a five note into the swear jar (it'd been a long day and I might've taken some liberties), I sat down next to him and leaned my head on his shoulder. "Hey, beautiful," he said to me, kissing my forehead. His lips were pleasantly cool from the ice cream. "Tough night?"

"You could say that."

"What happened?"

"Oscar and I went to the crime scene and met this sweet old lady who lives there now. She let us look around the place and in doing that, we became convinced that Skylar didn't murder her son."

"Really?" Dutch asked, his deep baritone going up an octave. "Oscar's convinced?"

I smirked. "Heaven forbid you should be surprised that *I* was convinced too."

"I thought you were already convinced."

"No. I was just ninety-nine percent sure. Now I'm one hundred percent sure."

"What put it over the line?"

I sat up and pulled the folder back out of my purse. I went over the contents in detail with him, telling him what we'd found at the scene and comparing it with the photos taken. "Even though we have no physical evidence of an intruder, I'm still convinced that there was one."

"You're right," he said once I'd finished. "We don't always find physical evidence tying an intruder to a crime scene. Think about the hard time we're having finding anything on Corzo."

I nodded. Yeah, it was more the rule than the exception to not find a killer's physical evidence at a crime scene these days. Too many psychopaths were big fans of the CSI shows.

"The knife is the tough part," Dutch said. "Everything else you're describing would fit an intruder except for the fact that the murder weapon came from the home, and there were no signs of forced entry and no signs that the intruder used the hallway to access the knife from the kitchen."

"But what if it was taken in advance of the crime?" I said to him. "What if someone who knew Skylar took the knife without her knowledge and brought it back to the scene when he decided to commit the murder?"

Dutch scratched the back of his head absently. "That's one elaborate plan there, Edgar. I mean, stabbing someone is a highly personal crime. And to stab a little kid, you gotta be one hell of an evil son of a bitch."

"You gotta be the worst kind of evil son of a bitch," I agreed, feeling a white-hot anger burn inside me. "And one that I'm gonna hunt down and hold accountable."

Dutch turned his head to consider me for a moment. "Be careful on this one, dollface. If this guy really did kill a little kid and framed the mother for it, he'd think nothing of doing you in."

I smiled confidently. "I've got Oscar *and* Candice on this one, cowboy. Let this asshole *try* to get past that posse."

Dutch hugged me and kissed my cheek. "And yet, I'm still worried."

"Shocker," I said.

"In my defense, I'll point out that, on several prior occasions, you've managed to get into trouble even while in the company of Candice and Oscar."

I cocked an eyebrow at him. "And on a few other occasions I've also managed to get into trouble with *you* as my chaperone."

Dutch made a face. "Noted," he said. Then he appeared thoughtful. "You know what I wonder?"

"What a great girl like me is doing with a worrywart like you?"

That won me a smile. "That, and if it's truer that you find trouble or trouble finds you?"

I hugged him. "It's not me. I never go looking for trouble."

Dutch pointed to my legs. "Hey, liar, liar, I think your pants are on fire."

The next morning I was up crazy early. I had a lot on my mind and hadn't slept well, so around four a.m. I got up, crept out of bed and into the kitchen, where I huddled over the kitchen table with a cup of coffee and the grisly pictures of Noah Miller's crime scene.

Something about the photos in the file was bugging me, but I really couldn't put my finger on it, until I got to a group of photos taken of the back wall, where Noah's bed was.

There was a series of photos showing the blood spatter, and I tried not to think too much about the actual pattern dotting the walls, until I looked at one photo in particular. It was my *Eureka!* moment.

Hurrying through the kitchen and into our bedroom, I found

Dutch on his stomach, snoring softly while hugging my pillow. I debated with myself for a solid minute about waking him up before I shook his shoulder. "What's happening?" he said, jerking to a sitting position and looking around blearily.

"I need help," I said.

Dutch shot out of bed. Grabbing the gun he kept on his nightstand, he held it up with his right hand, and shoved me behind him with his left. "Intruder?" he said quickly. "In the house? Did you see him? Is he armed?"

"Uh, cowboy?"

"Yeah?"

"How about you ask questions first this one time, okay?"

Dutch turned his head to look over his shoulder at me. "No intruder?"

"Nope."

"Are you okay?"

"Ducky."

Dutch blinked and glanced at the clock. "It's four forty-five in the morning, Edgar."

I offered him my biggest, most apologetic smile. "There's coffee."

Dutch made an indelicate irritated sound and moved to put his gun in his shoulder holster, which hung from the bathroom door. Yawning, he got back into bed, curled around my pillow, and pretended to ignore me.

"I'll make you breakfast," I sang.

He turned his head away from me.

"And I'll even do the dishes," I sang some more.

"Edgar?"

"Yes, oh love of my life?"

"Remind me later to call Cal and ask him for the name of a good divorce attorney."

"I will if you'll help me," I said sweetly.

With a giant sigh Dutch pushed himself up to a sitting position again and switched on the bedside light. With drooping shoulders he said, "What is it that can't possibly wait three hours on a Sunday?"

I offered him the photo I'd pulled from Skylar's folder.

"What's this?" he asked, with a yawn.

"It's a photo taken from Noah Miller's murder scene."

"It's a wall," he said, eyeing the photo with no small amount of impatience.

"Yes."

"There's blood spatter," he said.

"Yes."

And then he dipped his chin a little to look a bit more carefully at the image. "And a void on the curtain."

"And on the window," I said, moving over to one of our windows. Undoing the latch, I lifted the sash all the way up and took the curtain and shoved it up between the screen and the top pane to show him visually what I thought had happened. "The screen in that window is about an eighth of an inch too small to fit securely. It falls out with just a little prying. I think an intruder popped the screen, opened the window, and then maybe the wind pulled the curtain out, leaving a void right there." For emphasis I made a hand motion around the left-hand portion of the wall where the curtain obscured the wall. "That's how the blood spatter avoided staining the curtain and the window, but got the wall and the windowsill and everything else in that area."

"Could Skylar have had the window open while she killed Noah, then shut it after the deed was done?" he asked, rubbing his eyes to get the sleep out.

"No."

"I like how you take the time to consider the scenario," he said.

"Actually, I have considered it, but I rejected it for three reasons. First, it makes absolutely no sense for Skylar to claim that an intruder killed her son, then shut the window to make it look like the intruder came in from . . . where? The front door? Or the sliding glass door? Neither of which had any obvious signs of forced entry. No way.

"Second, what about the screen? It had to have been out for the curtain to have been pulled through and avoid the blood spatter, so how did it fall out, then get put back in? She couldn't have reached over the windowsill to get at it, because there'd be blood all over the sill from her clothes, and she couldn't have gone down the hall and outside to the backyard to put it back in, because there's only one set of bloody footprints down the hallway, and they turn toward the front door, not the back.

"And third, look at the curtain, Dutch. There aren't any bloody fingerprints on it. If Skylar had pulled the curtain back through, somehow managed to replace the screen, and then shut the window to boot, where are all the bloody fingerprints? And yet, photos of Skylar at the scene show her hands smeared with blood. Did she kill Noah, wash her hands, pull in the curtain, replace the screen, shut the window, and then get her hands bloody again? It makes no sense."

Dutch looked at me, blinking a little. "I stand corrected. You have considered it. Carefully."

I came to sit down on the bed in front of him. "So, tell me something, Agent Rivers. If this here photo raises such huge red flags for you and me, then why didn't it raise any red flags for either the detectives working the scene or Skylar's defense team?"

Dutch shrugged. "You know how circumstantial cases go, Abby. Once an investigation focuses on a suspect, anything that doesn't fit the scenario becomes invisible or nothing but a distraction. We can never explain every single bit of circumstantial evidence at a scene. We go with a preponderance of the evidence to help us point the way to the killer, and I gotta be honest here, babe. . . . If I'd walked in on that scene with that little guy in the bedroom butchered like that and only one set of bloody footprints leading out from the bedroom, and his mother covered in her son's blood with a knife from her kitchen with only her prints on it, I can't say that I would've gone a different way than Dioli."

I frowned at my husband and lifted the photo out of his hands. "Yes, you would've, Dutch. You would've because not only are you a great detective, but it took you all of five seconds to pick out a discrepancy in one photo of the crime scene. And you did that half-asleep! These guys ignored a major piece of evidence because it was more work to go look for an unsub than it was to arrest the traumatized mother at the scene. That's not overlooking evidence because there's so much more in favor of another scenario—that's ignoring the elephant in the room because you're too fricking lazy to get off the couch."

Dutch sighed. "I don't think it was laziness, doll," he said gently. "I think that whenever you have the violent murder of a child, there's a hell of a lot of pressure from up the ladder to solve the crime as fast as you can. And their scenario made sense to a jury, and to two appeals courts, who found Skylar Miller guilty, and then upheld that conviction."

"And because of their shoddy investigation, an innocent woman could get the needle," I said angrily.

Dutch put a hand on my shoulder. "Sometimes, innocent people become victims of the system."

I patted Dutch's hand and got up off the bed. "I know. But it still sucks."

"Agreed. But now Skylar's got the best advocate I can think of in her corner, and if you take that photo and your argument to Cal, maybe he can use it to get the appeals court to give her a new trial."

My brow lifted. "You think?"

"Worth a shot."

I glanced at the clock. It was now only a little past five a.m. "It's probably way too early to call Cal, right?"

Dutch chuckled. "I think it's too early to be awake period," he said, sliding back down on the bed and wrapping himself around my pillow again. "Wake me in two hours for that coffee and breakfast you promised me."

Three and a half hours later I called Dutch's cell. "Rivers," he said, his voice froggy with sleep.

"Hi, sweetheart. Listen, coffee and breakfast are in the kitchen, for you. I'm at the office waiting on Candice."

"You left?"

"Yes."

"You're not having breakfast with me?"

"No."

There was a pause (in which I detected no small amount of disappointment), then, "Okay. Call me later to let me know when you'll be home and what you'd like for dinner."

"Will do!" I said cheerfully, then hung up.

"You made Dutch breakfast?" Candice asked, sauntering into my office to drape herself elegantly into a chair.

" 'Made' is a rather loose term here," I said. "But, yeah." I'd set a package of powdered doughnuts on the kitchen table and a mug for the coffee that I'd prepared myself a few hours earlier next to the box. The coffeemaker had probably turned itself off by now, and the brew was likely to be cold, but when I'd promised Dutch coffee and breakfast, he hadn't demanded that it be anything specific, so technically I figured I could get away with the bare minimum, especially since I had far more important things to do.

"Is Oscar joining us?" Candice asked.

I shook my head. "His niece's *quinceañera* is today, so he won't be able to join us till later if at all."

"Ah," she said, crossing her legs and getting comfortable. "Then fill me in, Sundance."

I talked for the next hour, taking Candice carefully through everything that Oscar and I had discovered at Skylar's old house, and then I showed her the photo of the blood-spatter void on the curtain and she took the photo and studied it closely without saying a word. At last she whispered, "Holy shit, Sundance. She's innocent."

A small weight that I hadn't known was even there lifted from my shoulders. It was one thing to convince others of my gut feelings, but when Candice got on board, it felt like charging into battle alongside Joan of Arc. "She is," I agreed. "And if we don't move quickly, she'll die for the murder of her child." I couldn't imagine a worse injustice.

Candice pursed her lips and tapped the desk with her index finger. Her usual "I'm thinking" pose. "We'll need to cover multiple fronts on this," she said, her eyes unfocused as I knew she'd be rolling through a list of bases to cover in her mind. "First, when was the last time you spoke to Skylar?"

"Friday. I tried to reach her again yesterday on my lunch break, but she'd used up her two video calls for the week. I was told the next time I could videoconference her is tomorrow."

Candice cocked her head. "Besides you, who else did she talk to?"

"Don't know. Maybe her lawyer?"

Candice nodded. "To fire him?"

"Let's hope so."

"So we're in a holding pattern on the legal front until Skylar retains Cal, is that right?"

I sighed. "We are."

"Okay, well, that might not be a bad thing. The way I see it, we'll need a whole lot more proof than just this one photo and the other oddities in the circumstantial case that Dioli missed or flat out ignored."

I squirmed in my chair. "You don't think what we've got so far is enough?"

Candice shook her head. "It might've been enough at the very first appeal, Abby, and it definitely would've been enough if Skylar's defense counsel had done his job initially, but at this stage, I gotta tell you, it's a long shot. This isn't *new* evidence—it's a spin on *old* evidence. Evidence already presented and argued upon at trial. I doubt the appeals court is going to buy the argument that just because the old evidence could be interpreted a different way, they should grant Skylar a new trial.

"In other words, once you reach the Texas Supreme Court stage, you're at the Hail Mary point, and you gotta have some *very* compelling evidence in hand, new evidence, or they're gonna let you fry."

I gulped. "We've only got nine days left, Candice. What can we possibly dig up that wasn't already presented at her first trial in time to save her?"

"Don't know," she admitted. "That's why we're going to treat this case like it's a brand-new investigation. We're gonna look into Skylar's life and find out who else could've done it. And I also think we need to accept here and now that Skylar had some sort of connection to the killer. An acquaintance, someone posing as her friend, an old enemy . . . someone who had a score to settle against her. No way was the crime committed by a random stranger. Noah's murder was far too personal."

I pointed to the thick file on my desk. "In her initial statement to Dioli she swore for fourteen straight hours that she had no idea who could've invaded her home and killed Noah."

"And maybe that's all true," Candice said. "Or maybe she's had ten years to think about it, and maybe all that time sparked a suspicion."

I frowned, thinking back to the brief time I'd spent with her in the cell. "I'm not so sure—and by that, I will totally agree with you that it was someone familiar with Skylar, because there was a hint of that in the ether around her when I was first pointing my radar at Noah's killer—but when we spoke that first time in our cell, Candice, Skylar asked me if I could tell her who killed Noah. That's not something you ask if you've formed any kind of opinion. If she'd asked me if so-and-so had done it, then I'd agree with you, over the years she would've formed a suspicion about who it could've been, but when I as much as said to her that she knew the killer, she stared at me in genuine confusion. I really don't think she knows who did it."

"Well, then we're gonna look at who was close to Skylar and maybe had something against her or her son."

I laid my head back against my chair. The world was a darker place than I liked to imagine it. "Who could've had anything against a nine-year-old bad enough to murder him in cold blood?"

"I don't know, Sundance. But in order to find out who the real murderer is, we need suspects. Someone knew how to get into that house and where that knife was. And if you're right, and the knife was taken before Skylar vacuumed that hallway, that means he had access to the kitchen, either when Skylar and Noah weren't home or when they were."

"You think it could've had something to do with her history?" I asked.

"You mean the fact that she was an alcoholic?" Candice said. I nodded. "Possibly. Addicts like company, and if Skylar had overcome her addictions, maybe someone wasn't too happy about that. Hell, maybe she even owed somebody money and they were pissed that she wasn't paying up. We won't really be able to isolate a motive until we look at a few people in her life that had means and opportunity."

"How do we start if we can't talk to Skylar until tomorrow?"

"We start with this," Candice said, opening up the file to the statement Skylar had given to the police. "And we ask Dioli about who else he might've considered for the murder besides Skylar. While we're at it, we also ask him about that window."

"When you say 'we,' do you mean 'we' as in 'you and me,' or 'we' as in 'just me'?"

"You and me," she said. "I'm not gonna let that asshole intimidate me again. Plus, we already have the murder file. If he gets defensive, then so be it."

I sat back and chewed on my lip for a minute. "He wanted me to look into a case for him. That's how I got the file."

"What case?"

"Murdered girl here on a student visa. Found in Zilker Park about eight months ago. Dioli's got no leads and due to the amount of decomp at the time the girl was found, the medical examiner isn't even one hundred percent positive of a cause of death, so they're labeling it suspicious, but Dioli seems pretty convinced it was murder."

"What're your thoughts?" she asked me as I fell silent, thinking.

"I think Dioli is likely to be more cooperative with us if I can give him a lead on the girl found in the park."

"Do you have the file?"

I reached down for my bag and pulled it up. I'd stuck the file in there absently, and thank God I had. Opening it, I sorted through the notes and pictures. Candice leaned forward to peer at the file and I saw her make a face as one of the close-ups of the body slipped out. "Sweet Jesus," she hissed, looking away.

"I know," I said, trying hard to ignore the photo. Finally I located Dioli's notes, which were just a summation of the crime scene and all the leads they'd followed up on. I scanned the pages and as I did so, I clicked on my radar, allowing my sixth sense to travel over the file and seek out a clue, like a dog hunting for a scent. I closed my eyes to concentrate for a moment, and then I opened them again and reread Dioli's notes.

One sentence stood out. I took up a pen from the side of my desk and circled it. Then I lifted my phone and dialed the number that Dioli had left me on the front cover of the file. "Hey," I said when he answered. "It's Abby Cooper. I have a lead for you to follow up on for the murder of Tuyen Pham. When can we meet?"

"We have to meet?" he asked.

"Yep," I said, without explanation. There was no way I was going to give up any information over the phone and lose my advantage.

Dioli didn't answer me right away. Maybe he smelled a trap, but at last he gave me an address and told me to meet him there at eleven. I hung up with him and pointed to Candice. "Let's roll."

"He's meeting us now?" she asked, getting to her feet.

"Nope. In an hour. I figure that'll give us just enough time for coffee and a pastry."

"I love how your stomach dictates our schedule," she said with some mirth.

"Hey, if I'm distracted by hunger pangs, my radar isn't as effective."

"Oh, well, then," she said dramatically, "by all means, let's make haste to the pastry counter!"

An hour later we arrived at a bar that had definitely peaked sometime about three decades ago and since then had been gathering serious speed on its downhill decline. "Charming," I said, popping the last of my Danish into my mouth before getting out of Candice's car.

Candice smirked and led the way to the wooden door. She had to pull pretty hard to get it to open, and we walked into the dim interior, alive with the sound of pool balls smacking against one another, country music wafting from a pretty crappy sound system, and the smell of stale beer and cigarette smoke, which assaulted my nose. "And the charm continues," I whispered while we scanned the faces of the patrons for Dioli.

A whistle cut through the din of pool balls and background music and Candice and I turned to see Dioli waving at us from a barstool. Candice's shoulders stiffened slightly, but she walked purposefully forward, and I was right at her side. We got to Dioli and he eyed her without a hint of malice or suspicion. "Miss Fusco," he said curtly.

"It's Mrs.," she corrected. "As in Mrs. Harrison, Detective. You remember my husband, don't you? Special Agent in Charge Harrison."

Dioli didn't even blink. He simply flashed her a toothy smile and said, "Hell of a guy. Met him when he came to rescue you from my clutches." And then he laughed like he thought that was really funny.

Candice stared him down and for a second I wondered if she was going to clock him. "Thanks for agreeing to meet with us," I said to Dioli, hoping to remind everybody why we were there.

He continued to smile at Candice like he was enjoying rattling her cage, and God bless my bestie, because she seemed to realize it, and with two deep breaths I saw her rein in her temper and pull out a stool to sit down on. Waving at the barkeep, she ordered us a round of beers. Once everybody had a cold one in front of them, I pulled out the file on Tuyen and opened it to the notes I'd scribbled under his notes at the bottom of the page. "She was definitely murdered," I said. Closing my eyes, I put my hand to my throat and added, "I think she was strangled. And I'm sure you've already guessed that she was sexually assaulted too."

"That's what we assumed," Dioli said, a skeptical glint in his eye. "The ME said the hyoid was intact, though."

Dioli was referring to the small bone in the throat that often snapped as a result of strangulation. "I figured as much, but sometimes it doesn't break," I said, stating something that the three of us most certainly well knew.

Dioli continued to look skeptically at me, and I could tell he was disappointed by what I was offering. Little did he know that I was just getting started. "Your suspect is a male, of course, and I'm definitely leaning toward light skin. I think he's Caucasian, not Asian. I also believe he's connected to Tuyen's work and not the school. From your notes I see that you looked deeply into her peers at UT and even into her professors, but I feel strongly that her killer wasn't connected to the school. Again, I feel there was a definite connection between them through her work."

Dioli scratched absently at his shoulder. "She worked part time at a dry cleaner's," he said. "We checked the owner and the two other staff members, who're also all Asian, by the way. Not a parking ticket between them."

I pushed the file back at him. "Don't know what to tell you, Ray. The killer is connected to her work. Go back and interview everyone again. Someone knows something. There's a clue there." He continued to sort of look at me blankly, so I offered him a hint. "Did you check out the customers at the dry cleaner's?"

Dioli barked out a laugh. "Yeah, we checked out the customers. All three thousand six hundred of them. Took us six months."

"And?" I asked when he paused.

"And we found the usual mix of mostly law-abiding citizens mixed with some guys with minor criminal offenses, and three with what I'd call questionable criminal credits, but all those guys alibied out for the night Pham disappeared."

I frowned. My intuition was insisting that Dioli had missed something. "No other red flags?"

"Nope," he said, clearly disappointed by my intuitive prowess as a crime fighter.

Then Dioli offered me a one-shoulder shrug and said, "I was hoping you were gonna get a hit off of Pham's lab partner."

"Her lab partner?"

"Yeah. A research student named Len Chen Cheng. No, wait, maybe it was Len Cheng Chen. They mix their names up over there, so I don't remember which way is right, but he went by Len as a first name. Anyway, we heard through the vine that he and Pham shared a lab, and they didn't get along. Might've been a cultural thing, her being from Vietnam, and him being from China, but either way there were witness reports of arguments for lab time. Pham was the better student, and Cheng's alibi was paper-thin. Supposedly he was home alone at the time of Pham's disappearance, and similar to Pham, he was kind of a loner. We like him for the crime, but we've been having a hard time coming up with any evidence to nail him."

I sighed. "That's because there is none, Detective. He didn't do it."

Dioli took a defensive posture. "How do you know?"

I pointed to my forehead. "My intuition says no way. There's something at the dry cleaner's. The murderer has a connection there."

Dioli gave me a rather challenging look. "How about I get you the list of customers and you can pick a name out of that haystack?"

I crossed my arms. "No problem."

Candice coughed into her hand. Clearly she didn't think the idea of me poring over a list of three thousand customers was an effective use of my time. But I also had to consider that while I was doing Dioli's job for him, maybe he'd be a little more open with the info we needed to clear Skylar.

"I'll get you the list Monday," Dioli said, his demeanor somewhat dismissive.

"Awesome," I said. Then, before he could tell us to buzz off until Monday, I pulled out my notes from Skylar's file. "Now that we've gotten that out of the way, mind if I ask you a few questions about Skylar Miller's file?"

Dioli raised his beer and took a lazy sip. "Ask away," he said.

From my purse I got out the photo of the window with the void on the curtain. "Can I ask you how you guys were able to explain this void?" I asked, pointing specifically to the white area around the curtain.

Dioli arched a skeptical eyebrow. "Sure. We determined it was caused by Skylar Miller as she was stabbing her son. She blocked the curtain from the spray."

I nodded, as I'd sort of expected Dioli to say something like that. "See, I was thinking the same thing, but then I saw this photo," I said, digging again in my purse and pulling out the next photo of the wall with the blood-spatter pattern that otherwise would've been on the curtain. "See how the spatter is intact from the middle of the window all the way to the far left? There's no break in it. Which tells me that Skylar couldn't have been standing there when she stabbed Noah. The void was only present on the curtain."

Dioli shrugged, and turned his gaze away from me to the TV above the bar. It was obvious that he knew about the spatter pattern and hadn't been able to convince himself of the explanation he'd just offered me. "The curtain could've been up on the bed," he said. "Out of the way of the spatter at the time of the stabbing."

I considered the photo again, and the distance from the curtain to the bed. "See, now, that'd make sense, except for the fact that in this picture . . ." I dug into my purse again and riffled through the photos I'd been over a dozen times. Finding the one I needed, I pulled it out and laid it on the bar. ". . . it shows the bedspread had some blood spatter on it too. And there's no void where the curtain would've fallen, and no spatter on the curtain."

Dioli turned to me again and his brow furrowed while his eyes glinted with suspicion. "Why are you so interested in the curtain?" he asked.

"Because I can't explain it," I told him. "And I don't like it when I can't explain things like this. I need to offer the readers of my book a good explanation, Detective. Something reasonable that will firmly lay the blame at Skylar Miller's feet. This is a loose end, and I'm seeing some problems with it."

"You can leave that part out of the book," Dioli offered. "No harm, no foul."

I wanted to push back at him, but decided that it might arouse his suspicions and he'd shut down on me, so instead I simply nodded and put the photos away. "Good advice," I said. "Now, can I ask you if you ever considered anyone else besides Skylar for the murder?"

Instead of answering me, Dioli propped one elbow up on the bar and cupped the side of his head with his index finger and his thumb. "Why?"

"Because the readers are going to expect that I've looked at and dismissed other suspects in the case in favor of Skylar."

Dioli gave me that lopsided shrug again. "We did look into other people," he said. "Miller kept questionable company, so we looked."

Next to me I saw Candice lay her phone facedown on the bar. I had a feeling she'd hit the Record button. "Who specifically did you look at, Ray?"

"A couple of Miller's exes, and her pimp."

I blinked. "Her what?"

"Her pimp," he said, clearly enjoying the fact that he got to share that fact with me. "Before her trial for the DWI charge, she was let out on bond, which Chris put up for her, maybe because he felt a little guilty that he'd called the unis on her for driving drunk. So, he'd gotten her out of jail, but he'd had it with her drinking and wouldn't let her live in the house. She found *work* on the streets and spent four months in the company of a guy known for running girls."

I felt a pang of sadness in the center of my chest. I wondered how desperately addicted you'd have to be to resort to that, and silently whispered my thanks to the powers that be that I'd never been hit with the addictions that'd possessed so many members of my family, including my father, an uncle, two aunts, and a few cousins. "So," I said, trying to get over my shock at Skylar's checkered past. "About this pimp . . ."

"Guy by the name of Rico DeLaria," Ray said. "Nice guy, if you like slime buckets."

I scribbled down the name. "I'm assuming you interviewed him?"

"Yeah. Once we caught up to him. He's pretty slippery. He didn't have much of an alibi, but there didn't seem to be a motive. At least not one as good as the one we had on Skylar."

"You mean the whole being cut off from child-support payments," I said.

"Yeah," Dioli said. "I mean, along with jail, she'd spent time on the street. I doubted she wanted to go back to that life."

Candice leaned in. "But wouldn't killing her son bring about that end anyway? Killing off Noah meant no more child support, which, according to the argument made by the prosecution, was her only reason for keeping Noah around in the first place."

Dioli adopted a sly smile. "You guys don't know about the trust, do you?"

"Trust? What trust?" I asked.

Dioli polished off his beer and motioned to the bartender for another before he explained. "Chris Miller's parents were loaded," he began. "When Noah was born, they set up a two-million-dollar trust in his name. The trust went through a few changes over the years, and the one that was the most interesting was set in place not long before Noah was murdered, but I'm getting ahead of myself. The trust itself had some very specific rules attached to it. The first rule was that it could only be accessed by his legal custodial guardian when Noah turned sixteen."

"Legal custodial guardian?" I asked. "It actually said 'custodial'?"

Dioli nodded. "Not long into the investigation, we learned about the trust. Grant Miller, Noah's grandfather, was dying of bone cancer, and his wife, Lynette, was in the first stages of Alzheimer's. I got to meet with Grant only the one time, and I asked him about the trust, and he said that they'd never have chosen Skylar for a daughter-in-law, but he said that he'd been impressed with how she'd turned her life around, so he and his wife amended the trust to reflect that should she continue to provide a good and loving environment for Noah in the coming years, then she could also be trusted with his money.

"Grant explained to me that she wouldn't just be able to write herself a blank check—the trust would have the oversight of a bank officer and an attorney, and Skylar would be required to submit to random drug and alcohol testing from the time that Noah was sixteen all the way until he was twenty-one, so in order to access the money, she had to be clean and sober."

"I still don't see how that's a motive if she couldn't have access to the trust until Noah turned sixteen," I said. "He'd have to have been alive for her to get any money, right?"

Dioli's eyes sparkled. "Nope," he said. "The trust had a provision that—and I memorized it, so I can quote it—'if Noah dies before he reaches the age of twenty-one, and it is deemed that his death is in no way caused by any negligence, purposeful neglect, or act on the part of his legal custodial guardian, then all monetary funds available within the trust shall revert back to his heirs,' and at the end of all this other legal mumbo jumbo it lists Skylar Miller, specifically, as one of Noah's heirs."

"Wouldn't it also have named Chris?" Candice asked, mirroring my thoughts.

"Yeah, and it did," Dioli said. "But he didn't need the money. He inherited everything after his parents died. Two million bucks was chump change compared to what I heard his folks were worth."

"Who else did the trust name as heirs?" I asked, hoping for a creepy cousin or long-lost uncle.

"Just Skylar, Chris, Grant, and Lynette."

"So," I said, trying to figure out Dioli's argument, "what you're saying is that Skylar murdered Noah and claimed it was an intruder so that she could get ahold of the money?"

"Yes."

"Why wasn't that argument presented at trial?" Candice asked.

"Grant Miller had passed away by the time the trial rolled around two years later, and Lynette's mental state was questionable at best by then. The DA didn't want to make things too complicated, and they didn't want Skylar's attorney dragging Lynette Miller into court as a rebuttal witness. There was also the minor issue that they'd sent Skylar a copy of the trust's provisions along with a notice she needed to sign saying that she agreed to the terms, including the drug and alcohol testing, and she never returned the signed agreement, so there was no way to prove that she'd actually read the trust. But come on, she read it. So in the end we stuck with the motive that she'd fallen off the wagon, and killed Noah because she was worried he'd rat on her and she'd have her child support cut off and get sent back to prison for the violation of her parole."

I scowled. The prosecution's argument sounded even flimsier the second time I heard it from Dioli. "It still seems a little far-fetched, Ray."

"Hey, when it comes to money and an addict, Abby, it's been my experience that they'll try anything to get their hands on it. Especially when they're looking at a million bucks."

Another pang of sadness went through me. As a recovering alcoholic, Skylar had never had a chance with this judgmental detective. "Was there anybody else you looked at for Noah's murder?" I asked, wanting to move off the subject of motive and back onto other possible suspects.

"Yeah," Dioli said, adopting a bored expression. "We looked at a guy named Connor Lapkus for about a minute. Skylar and he dated right after rehab. Turns out she owed him some money but not enough to kill a little kid over, only a couple of grand. Anyway, he alibied out. He owns a machine shop off Lamar, and four of his homies say he was with them the night of the murder."

"Could they be lying?"

"Sure," Dioli said. "But it's still a better alibi than Skylar's. You get placed at a crime scene covered in the victim's blood and leaving a trail of bloody footprints down a hallway, with your prints on the murder weapon, and any other digging we do is simply to arm the prosecution should your lame-ass defense attorney try to interject reasonable doubt."

I nodded like I totally agreed with Dioli, even though a big part of me wanted to punch him in the nose. "So, just Rico DeLaria and Connor Lapkus," I said. "Nobody else in Skylar's life could've had a checkered past?"

"The only other guy we did a background check on was her neighbor down the street. A guy by the name of John Thomas, who's a registered sex offender. Turns out he liked little boys about Noah's age, and he spent a dime up in Dallas before moving in with his mother in Miller's neighborhood. He didn't have much of an alibi either: claims he was playing video games all night. He was introduced as a possible suspect by the defense at the trial, but he's a guy who, since he's been out, has met every single probationary protocol, and there were no witnesses that ever saw him and Noah within a hundred feet of each other. Plus, nothing in his past indicated any use of violence. The defense tried to bring him forward as a possible suspect, but the jury dismissed him outright. After we presented all of our evidence, there was no room for them to doubt our story. Skylar did it. It was a slam dunk, really."

Getting up from the barstool, I left a twenty on the bar and said, "Thank you, Ray. I appreciate the time."

Candice got up too, and as we were turning to leave, Dioli called after me, "I'll have that list of names for you on Monday."

I waved a hand over my shoulder and didn't look back. I was kind of sure that if I did, I'd give in to the urge to go back up to Dioli, and punch him in the nose.

Chapter Nine

. . .

We drove away from the bar and toward the city in silence. Mostly because I was fuming. It wasn't as much that I thought Dioli was a bad guy as I thought he was a narrow-minded, pig-headed, chauvinistic son of a bitch who'd run roughshod over a woman reeling from the murder of her young son. He'd seen those bloody footprints in the hallway, and he'd made up his mind then and there. That was the one thing he couldn't get over. Those damn bloody footprints and no sign of forced entry in the house. He'd ruled out an intruder within a few hours of being at the crime scene.

It galled me that such a seasoned detective could be so closed-minded, or so cold about sending a woman to the needle, given the very shaky holes in his circumstantial case. He'd flat out ignored huge inconsistencies in his theory, and done only a cursory job of investigating other suspects.

"Goddamn him," I muttered. (My purse was full of quarters. I could splurge.)

"Yep," Candice agreed. She seemed just as angry. "Still, we have some people to look into."

"But hardly any time to look into them," I groused.

Candice was quiet for a moment and then she said, "Well, we've been under the gun before, and we've always managed to work with what we have. So we can spend time getting good and mad, or we can get going on finding out who really murdered Noah."

I took a deep breath and blew it out nice and slow. "Who do we start with?"

"I like Rico," she said. "Mostly 'cause I know where he hangs out."

"You do?"

"Yep. For a pretty sizable fee, he slipped me some info on one of my missing persons cases. Teenage runaway. Rico's info led me right to her."

"I gotta admit that I'm surprised you know a guy like him."

Candice's expression was wry. "Sometimes, Sundance, when you walk the mean streets, you gotta get your shoes a little dirty." Taking an exit for Highway 360, we traveled south all the way past the west side of the city and continued on to Lamar Boulevard. Candice followed Lamar southbound, finally taking a turn into a pretty shoddy-looking apartment complex.

I scowled. "Why do scuzzballs always live in the worst places?"

"Makes them feel at home," Candice said, taking her gun out of the glove box to remove the clip and replace it with another full one, also from the glove box. Sliding back the barrel to arm the gun, she tucked it into the back of her jeans, pulled her shirt out of her pants to cover it, and motioned for us to get out.

We crossed the parking lot and I followed Candice up an outside staircase to the second floor. She paused in front of one door, then seemed to reconsider and moved down to one next to that. Knocking, she and I waited on the landing, me staring uncomfortably around, and Candice looking like she was about to visit with an old friend. The door opened a crack and a guy with black hair and lots of stubble peered blearily out. "Yeah?"

"Rico!" Candice said, like they were best buds. "How you doin', guy?"

"Who the fuck're you?"

Ah. Rico was what we in the trade liked to call a "romantic." Candice didn't answer; instead she stood there appearing incredulous with her arms outstretched like she couldn't wait to hug DeLaria.

He considered her from head to toe before he finally edged the door all the way open. "Lady, I don't know you," he said, crossing his arms and leaning against the doorframe.

Candice tapped her head. "Oh, right!" she said. Then she added a laugh and turned slightly to me to say, "Maybe this'll refresh your memory." And then, quick as a flash, Candice rounded back to face forward and punched DeLaria right in the nose, much like I'd wanted to do to Dioli.

Rico's head snapped back and his knees buckled, causing him to stagger back into the apartment. Candice shook her hand a little and followed him inside. Shocked down to my socks, I stood there mutely for a second before I shrugged and headed in too.

"What the hell?!" DeLaria shouted, holding both hands over his nose as a little blood dribbled down between his fingers. "You fucking bitch!"

Candice offered him a crocodile smile and kicked him in the nads. DeLaria emitted a squeak high-pitched enough to put little girls to shame and sank to the ground, doubling over and rolling onto his side, one hand holding his nose, the other covering his nethers.

Candice stepped forward to push her heel at his shoulder and lay him flat on his back. There wasn't even a hint of mercy in her eyes. "Candice," I whispered, afraid she'd already pushed this too far.

She ignored me. Reaching down, she hauled DeLaria up by the collar and got into his face. "I found the girl you ruined, you son of a bitch," she said. "She was seventeen when you two met—her on the street, scared, hungry, cold, and naive, and you a wolf in sheep's clothing. You wasted no time recruiting her into your little ring, and when she started to fall apart, you fed her drugs until she wasn't even a shadow of her former self, you gutless, heartless piece of shit. Oh, yeah, for a price you tipped me off about where I could find her, but only because she wasn't any good to you anymore." Candice then shook DeLaria hard and his head bobbled on his neck and blood came out of his nose more earnestly.

I'll admit that I was sickened by the scene. Putting a hand on Candice's shoulder, I tried to interject a little reason into the situation. "Candice," I said. "Please."

But she refused to let go of Rico. With strength that belied her thin frame, she hauled him halfway off the floor by his shirt and spat, "She's tried to kill herself three times since I got her home, Rico. *Three times!*"

Rico's trembling hands came up to grip Candice's arms. He was starting to recover from the blows she'd dealt him, and he was maybe a good dose of adrenaline away from becoming a real problem.

Well, maybe a problem for anyone who wasn't my BFF. With a snarl she let go of him and he fell back to the floor with a thud. Before he could get up again, Candice drew her gun out from the back of her waistband and pointed it right at his head. "Something you should know, DeLaria. Stacey's dad has a few bucks. The last time he called to tell me that they'd just barely gotten his little girl to the hospital in time to save her life, he asked me how much it'd cost him to put you down. I named my price, and he didn't even flinch."

I was sweating buckets as Candice talked, and not just from the heat snaking its way into the apartment. What bothered me was that my lie detector hadn't gone off as Candice spoke about the girl's father offering her money to kill DeLaria. Nor when she told him she'd named the price. I knew Candice better than anyone else in the world, even her husband, which meant that I knew exactly what she was capable of. Hence I was shaking in my boots.

Candice lowered the gun a little closer to DeLaria's face. "So here's how this is gonna play out, Rico," she said softly. "I'm going to ask you a series of questions, and you're gonna answer them honestly. If you fail to answer them honestly, my friend over there—who's a human lie detector—is gonna let me know that you're a big fat fibber, and I'm going leave this apartment a *much* wealthier woman."

I wasn't the only one shaking now. DeLaria was visibly trembling and his face took on a shade of white so severe, if he stopped moving, he could've been mistaken for a corpse. I wanted to say something to defuse the tension in the room, but Candice seemed to be right on the edge, and I was afraid anything I said or did would tip her over. The best that I could hope for was that DeLaria cooperated fully, but then, even if he didn't, I had no intention of ever admitting to Candice that he was lying.

Still, when DeLaria's desperate gaze traveled to me, I crossed my arms and cocked my head slightly, just to let him know that he'd better play along all nice-like. "Whad do you wanna knowd?" Rico asked, his speech hampered by the severe swelling to his nose.

"Skylar Miller," she said. "Remember her?"

DeLaria's eyes darted to me and I cocked an eyebrow. He looked back at Candice and nodded his head subtly.

"Good, Rico," Candice said, the gun in her hand never wavering from her deadly aim at his head. "Did you murder her son?"

Rico blinked and he even pulled his chin back in surprise. "Wah? Naw! Naw! I swear! I dinnit!"

Candice glared hard at Rico. "Sundance?"

"He's not lying," I said, so relieved that he'd been honest, because I was fairly certain that if Rico had lied about that, Candice would've seen through him and I didn't know if she'd be able to hold back from pulling the trigger. Hell, I would've been tempted to put him down if I knew he'd killed Noah in the manner the young boy was murdered.

"Do you know who did?" she asked Rico next.

He shook his head. "Naw! Naw, I swear!"

Candice stood there without saying anything further, and into the silence I said, "Again, he's telling the truth."

Candice then said, "Rico, you just admitted that you don't think Skylar murdered her kid. What do you know that the cops don't?"

Rico gulped. "I don't. I mean, not for sure," he said. "But my girls, they're in the know, you know?"

"Start talking," Candice said, the gun moving a fraction closer to Rico's fast-swelling nose.

"One a my girls said the judge on the case was on the take. Someone wanted her to hang, man."

"Who?" Candice demanded.

"I don't know, man!" Rico insisted, shaking in fear; it was pretty obvious he was telling the truth about that.

Candice inhaled deeply, absorbing what he'd said. She knew, like I did, that the judge had imposed the death sentence above the jury's recommendation that Skylar serve life in prison without parole.

In other words, the jury had been convinced by the evidence that Skylar had murdered her son, but something about the case had bothered them enough not to go for the death penalty. Maybe there was something about the prosecution's case that didn't quite add up. Or maybe the jury had enough members on it that simply couldn't believe a mother would murder her beautiful boy in that manner. And I understood that. It was too abhorrent to even imagine.

Still, even knowing about a possible bribe didn't get us closer to identifying the real killer. But then something in Rico's energy got my attention and I said, "What aren't you telling us, Rico?"

His posture stiffened and his eyes darted once again to me. I glared hard at him, now even more convinced that he was hiding something. Candice leaned forward menacingly with the gun and his hand came off his privates to splay in front of his face. "Wait! Wait, wait, wait!"

"Better start talking," I advised him. "Candice looks like she's getting tired holding back that trigger finger."

"It was just something I heard!"

I made a "get on with it" motion with my hand. "Which was?"

Rico took a steadying breath. "One o' my homies who got popped around the same time that Sky's sentence was handed down, he overheard another inmate say that Sky got what was comin' to her. Said she'd disrespected him or somethin', and she was payin' for it. He said the guy said it like he'd had a hand in it or somethin'."

A chill went through me. "What was he in for, do you know?"

Rico began to shake his head, but then he seemed to remember something and said, "B and E. Pretty sure that's what Wayne said it was."

Another chill went through me. "What was his name?" I asked.

Rico shook his head. "Don't know." Candice growled impatiently and Rico added, "I swear! I don't know his name. He was just some guy in the holding cell with one of my bros."

"Where do we find this bro, yo?" Candice asked in a tone that wasn't at all friendly.

"He works at Rounders on Sixth."

"He working today?" Candice pressed.

"Uh, yeah, I think so," Rico said with more than a little enthusiasm. He wanted us to go, and bad.

"What's he look like?" I asked. We'd want to pick him out prior to asking for him.

Rico put his hand a little above his head. "He's an inch or two taller than me. Brown hair. Goatee. Looks a little like Ethan Hawke."

Candice shifted her gaze ever so slightly to me. "Sundance?"

"He's telling the truth."

Candice stepped back two paces and eased off pointing the gun at DeLaria's face. "Okay. We'll hit up Rounders. In the meantime, guess what you're gonna do, Rico?"

He audibly gulped. "What?" he asked meekly.

"You're gonna get out of the recruiting business and take up another profession. Something that doesn't involve ruining young runaways."

Rico blinked at her. He was obviously still scared, but seemed reluctant to give up the life of being a scuzzball. Candice pointed the gun back at his face and took the two steps forward again. He held up both hands in surrender and yelled, "Okay! Okay! Don't kill me, man! I'll give up pimping!"

But Candice wavered. She seemed to study him for a very long time before she said, "I don't believe you, Rico." And then she pulled the trigger.

The gun made a loud pop and I jumped and Rico screamed. It took me a sec to realize that she hadn't actually shot him, but I worried about where the bullet had gone. If there was anyone in the downstairs apartment, she could've killed them. Candice put the gun back into the waistband of her jeans and coolly said, "That's your final warning, you son of a bitch. If I *ever* catch you running girls in this town again, I'm going to cash in that offer from Stacey's father. You *get* me?"

Rico was curled into a ball, quivering, sweating, and actually crying. "I won't, I won't, I won't, I won't!" he said, weeping in earnest now. It was terrible to witness, but I had little sympathy for him. He'd brought it upon himself.

Candice made a subtle motion with her chin and I eased backward away from DeLaria to the door, holding it open for her as she backed out of the room too. Once we were safely in the car again and Candice had started it up, I said, "What the hell was that about?"

"What do you mean?" she said casually.

"Candice, I love you," I began, "but if you ever shoot at an unarmed man in my presence again, I may have to quit you." Seeing her behave like that had seriously unsettled me. She'd turned into someone else up there, and I didn't want any part of it.

Candice chuckled warmly before reaching behind her to pull out her gun and hand it to me. "Check the clip, Sundance," she said.

Frowning at her, I took the gun and stared at the clip, which was filled with odd-looking bullets. Popping one out, I examined it. It felt lighter than normal and nothing like the hollow points Candice typically shot with. "What the hell are these?"

"Blanks. I keep a clip of them when I really need to get info out of someone. They're super effective without all the mess."

I sagged in my seat. "Oh, thank God! For a minute there I thought you'd done lost your mind."

Candice nodded absently. "It was a good thing I had the blank clip," she said. "Stacey was this really sweet kid before Rico got hold of her. That fucker murdered who she could've been. And I'm sure there're many more girls out there like her working for that asshole."

"You weren't kidding about the offer from her dad, were you?"

Candice fiddled with the radio and refused to answer the question, which I was actually thankful for. I knew enough disturbing things. I sure didn't need to add another to the list.

We got to Rounders and headed inside. As it happened, I was a little hungry, so Candice and I got a table and settled in to peruse the menu and subtly observe the employees. Midway through my perusal Candice cleared her throat to get my attention. Pulling my gaze away from a bacon/mango/chestnut pesto concoction, I looked up and saw her motioning with her chin toward the kitchen staff, visible behind a counter at the back of the narrow restaurant. A guy had just joined the crew, probably in his mid to late thirties, a little taller than Rico had been during the short time I'd seen him standing.

Height. Check.

Brown hair. Check.

Goatee. Check.

Looked a bit like Ethan Hawke. Check and check.

"Wayne!" I called, waving to him, all friendly-like.

His head turned and he eyed me with interest, and a few of the other guys nudged him and I could see them ask, "Who's that?"

Wayne kept his gaze on me and shrugged off the other guys,

moseying out from around the counter and wiping his hands on his white apron. He approached with the practiced steps of a guy who's used to convincing girls to go home with him. He had no interest in life beyond conquering his next piece of ass. I hated guys like Wayne. And I'm a little ashamed to admit that I'd dated more than my fair share of them before I'd met Dutch. Right before he got to our table, I sent up a silent prayer of gratitude to the powers that be that I was lucky enough to share my bed with the real deal, and not some poser like Wayne.

Still, I kept my smile wide and my eyes blinky and Wayne closed in with a dipped chin and a slight grin. "Hey, baby," he said, like we were old friends. "Where you been?"

I giggled. He had no idea who I was, but he was playing it like he recognized me from some tryst we'd had and was pleased I'd stopped by. "Oh, here, there, you know," I said, patting the seat next to me.

Wayne sat down and tipped an imaginary hat at Candice. "Who's your friend?" he said, that interest sparking fresh volts as he took in Candice's gorgeous face.

She extended a hand. "Candy," she said, with a hint of a Southern accent. Casting me a sideways glance, she added, "Sundance, you didn't tell me Wayne was so hot."

Wayne chuckled and sat back in the chair, full of confidence. I knew he figured there was no way he wasn't getting lucky tonight. "Oh, shush," I said to her. "I told you he looked like Ethan Hawke!"

Wayne nodded, as if he got that particular comparison a lot. "I get that a lot," he said. (See?)

Candice reached over and fiddled with her purse for a moment and I said, "So, Wayne, I was wondering if you could settle a bet Candy and I have going on."

"A bet?" he said, his eyes glinting with mild curiosity. Then he laughed as if he already knew what we'd bet on. "Commando, baby, don't you remember?"

I laughed wickedly and shoved at his shoulder. "No, not that! Something much juicier."

Wayne wrapped an arm across my shoulders. I bore it mostly because of what I was about to say next. "What's the bet, baby?" he asked.

I smiled really wide at Candice. She was enjoying this too. "Well," I said, turning back to whisper softly to Wayne. "I bet my friend Candy that she'd need two shots to take your balls off, and she swears that the gun she has trained on your crotch right now would only require one bullet."

Wayne stared at me, his eyes getting bigger by the moment as my smile became less forced and more sinister. And then he leaned carefully back and eyed the napkin-wrapped bundle in Candice's right hand. There was no mistaking from his angle what it was. "What the hell is this?" he said, lifting his arm away from me.

"Relax," I told him. When he looked like he was about to bolt out of the chair, I put a hand on his arm and said, "I mean it, Wayne. Candy has a hair trigger. Just ask your buddy Rico."

Sweat coated Wayne's forehead and he looked around the restaurant to see if anyone else was paying attention to us. Nobody was. Even the kitchen crew had lost interest. "Listen," he said, his voice quavering, "I never made you any promises, baby. I mean, I'm sorry if you wanted something more, but I'm not the settling-down kind of guy."

I made a face and waved a hand at him. "Dude, first off, eww. Second off . . . *eww*! We didn't sleep together and you'd never have a chance with me or with my BFF over there anyway."

She nodded congenially. "That's true," she said.

"Then what the hell?" he whispered.

"We need some intel," I said. "The sooner you tell us what we want to know, the sooner Candy puts her gun away and you get back to slinging pizzas for nine bucks an hour."

Wayne wiped his brow. "I don't know anything!" he whispered harshly.

"Oh, but we believe that you do," I countered. "Now, let's test you for honesty. Did you ever know a woman named Skylar Miller?"

Wayne's eyes blinked furiously. "Sky? What the hell she got to do with this?"

"So you did know her," I said.

"Duh," he said. "She was my ex."

My brows arched. "She was?"

"Yeah, man. Only woman I ever loved, if you gotta know. They don't make 'em better than Sky."

"What happened between the two of you?" I asked, my intuition buzzing a little.

He shrugged. "She wanted to get her kid back, and her social worker told her the odds were better if she ditched me, 'cause I had a record."

"Really?" I said. Wayne nodded. My eyes narrowed. "Did you hold a grudge against her, Wayne? For dumping you?"

"Grudge? Naw, man. Well, maybe a little in the beginning, but when you saw her with the kid, well, you sorta got it, you know? Nobody was ever gonna be more important to her than Noah, and even I knew I wasn't ever gonna be a good influence for him, so it sucked for a while but whatev. Plenty of bitches still left in the pond."

Candice and I traded looks. Hers asked me if I suspected Wayne as the killer. Mine said that I didn't think his energy was trying to hide anything, but I couldn't be sure. Then Candice said, "Rico told us that you heard somebody at county brag about killing Noah."

Wayne pulled his head back a little, surprised by her statement. "Bragged about killing Noah?" he repeated. And then he seemed to understand. "Naw, man, it wasn't like that. It was just some guy from the holding cells where they put all the new prisoners together—you know, like ten of us to one big cell until they can process us through?"

Candice and I both nodded, and Wayne continued. "Anyway, I had a homey in there with me, and he asked me about Sky, 'cause he'd heard she was on trial and he knew we'd gone together. I guess this other guy was listening, because he starts to butt in, you know, like it's his business too, or something, and says that he was glad she was getting what was coming to her. That pissed me the hell off, you know? So I got into it with him, and he said that she'd disrespected him in front of the kid, and he made sure she got what was coming to her. I popped him and started asking him what he meant by that and then the COs pulled me off him before I could get anything else outta him. We were separated after that and I was processed to another section of the prison. Never saw him again."

"When was this?" Candice asked.

Wayne stared down at his hands. "About eight years ago. Right after the jury found Sky guilty."

"Why didn't you go to the police with what this guy said to you?" I demanded. Candice shot me a warning look because my voice had risen a little, and I cleared my throat as two people at a nearby table glanced our way.

Wayne said, "I *did* go to them. I told my parole officer that there was a guy in lockup the cops needed to look at, and he got me in touch with this detective at APD. When I told him what'd happened in lockup, you know what he said to me?"

"What?" Candice and I both asked.

"He wanted to know where *I* was the night Noah was killed." Wayne shook his head in disgust. "Asshole. If I'd pushed it, he would've gotten me on conspiracy 'cause of my history with Sky."

I felt white-hot anger burn into the center of my chest, positive that Wayne had spoken to Ray Dioli, that lazy, smug son of a bitch. (I was gonna owe my swear jar another five spot by the end of the day.)

"He really told you that?" Candice asked Wayne.

Wayne shrugged. "Something like that. He said he didn't need me coming around after the verdict was announced to try to make trouble for the case."

"What was the name of the inmate?" I asked, thinking I'd take the issue up with Dioli later.

Wayne shook his head. "I don't know his real name. He told everybody to call him Slip."

"Slip?" I said. "What the hell kind of a nickname is that?"

"He said he got it from being able to slip in and out of a house without being seen. The guy was in for B and E, so I guess he wasn't as slippery as he thought."

Candice lifted the hand covered by the napkin above the table-top and as Wayne jumped, she removed the napkin to reveal nothing more dangerous than an elegant Montblanc pen. Casually she then reached inside her purse for a small notebook and made herself a note. Wayne stared at her hand for a long time before he shook his head, got up, and muttered, "Bitches."

I smiled and waved daintily at him. "Thanks for all your help, Wayne. Tell Rico we appreciate his help too."

He glared at me and said, "Y'all might not want to eat here. You never know what could fall into your food."

My smile widened. "We had no intention of eating here, honey. Now off you go."

Wayne looked like he didn't much like being dismissed, but then a guy in a short-sleeved dress shirt and khakis came out from the back and glared hard when he saw Wayne out from behind the counter. Our delightful host walked stiffly away and Candice and I wasted no time leaving a five-dollar tip for the waitress who'd brought us waters. Before we headed out, Candice paused to whisper something to the manager, he said something softly back to her, and she smiled and motioned for us to leave.

"Did you rat him out?" I asked as we walked to the car.

"Nah," she said. "I just asked the manager for his last name. It's Babson."

"What a corny last name for a poser," I said.

"Word," she agreed.

I looked a little sadly at Rounders as we drove away. I'd lied to Wayne. I'd have eaten there. The pizza had smelled amazeballs, and I mean, a pizza with mango plus bacon plus chestnut pesto plus my add-on of extra bacon? Srsly.

"Where to now?" I asked Candice with a sigh.

"Well, judging by the way you're drooling out the window at the restaurant we just left, I thought I'd take you for something to eat before we head back to the office, so I can try to find out who Wayne's cellmate was that was spouting off about Skylar getting what she deserved."

"How're you gonna do that?"

Candice stopped at the red and half turned to me as she answered, "I've got a new database that allows me to search for someone using their nickname. I've never had to use it until now."

"It's freaky how many resources you have."

She turned back to the wheel as the light flicked to green. "Stick with me, kid, and you may learn a trick or two."

We ate lunch at a place called the Steeping Room—an absolute favorite of mine, which is odd given the fact that it pretty much serves nothing but healthy (wonderfully flavorful) food. By the time we left, I was feeling full, happy, and antioxidanted.

After another short drive, Candice pulled into a slot in the parking garage next to our building, and I waddled after her while she headed to the front doors of our office. As it happens, this was quite fortunate, because it allowed me to see Rico DeLaria spring from the alley next to our building, intent on stabbing Candice with a very big knife. *"Candice!"* I screamed.

Her response was poetry in motion. Without even flinching, she dropped down into a crouch, spun, and thrust her leg out at the same time, striking Rico midcalf. There was a sickening popping sound and he stumbled. Trying hard to stay erect, he grimaced through the pain but didn't recover himself enough before Candice vaulted up from her crouched position to karate kick him square in the chest. He shot backward, straight off his feet, with an "Oomph!" and landed flat on his back with an awful-sounding smack. My BFF then stomped on the hand holding the knife before dropping to one knee right on top of him, causing yet another series of cracking sounds from DeLaria's ribs. Candice finished her dance by jamming her palm into his nose. No crunching sound this time because DeLaria's nose was already broken.

To say that Candice had effectively disarmed and disabled DeLaria was like saying the atom bomb had had a little kick to it. In the three to four seconds that she'd been in motion, I'd maybe managed to blink and drop my jaw. Am I a good backup sidekick or what?

Not even breathing heavy, she flipped Rico over and pulled his hands up behind him to then pin them there with her knee. The only sign that she'd done anything strenuous was the little puffing sound she made to blow her bangs out of her eyes as she glanced at me over her shoulder. "Sundance?"

"Yeah?"

"How about calling nine-one-one for me?"

I nodded dully but found that I was shaking almost too much to hold the phone. I mean, it's not often your BFF gets jumped by a knife-wielding criminal, or that she then deals with his punk ass more effectively than Batman. Still, after a few tries I managed to tap the right numbers on the screen and call for backup.

The police arrived as a small crowd gathered. Lucky for us, there were three witnesses who saw the whole thing. They all vouched for Candice's side of the story, but were perhaps not really necessary given the fact that DeLaria wasn't exactly able to articulate anything more than, *"Owwwwwwwwwwwwww!"*

No one on the scene had a single ounce of sympathy for him. When an APD officer asked Candice if she knew DeLaria, she said that she'd been by his apartment earlier in the day to question him about his connection to a missing runaway, but that DeLaria had declined to answer any of her inquiries. She made our earlier encounter with him sound like nothing more than a polite social visit.

I nodded my head and corroborated her statement. After what DeLaria pulled, I'd swear to it on a Bible if I had to. Principles be damned. Had I not been ten paces behind Candice, she'd be dead, and maybe me along with her.

After the police had shoved DeLaria into a cop car, and we were told we could go, a black sedan pulled up to a halt next to us and Candice's husband jumped out of the car. He ran straight to her and caught her up in a hug, and it was only then that I noticed how distraught he looked.

"Hey, babe," Candice said, hugging him back. "I'm okay. It's okay."

Brice held her without speaking for another pronounced moment and then he let her go, but only enough to grip her shoulders and study her critically. "One of my APD contacts told me you'd been involved in a stabbing," he said. "They didn't have any more details than that. Just that your name popped up in connection to a guy with a knife and the address of the attack."

"I'm fine," she said calmly.

"She is," I assured him.

His gaze shifted to me. "You'd better call Dutch before he hears about it from one of his sources."

I blanched. Our husbands could be a weensy bit protective of us, even though we'd proved over, and over . . . and maybe over, and over, and over, and over, again that we could take care of ourselves. Hmmm, maybe we'd proved it a few too many times for them to trust our luck?

Before I could whip out my phone again, however, another car came along to pull up next to us. This time Oscar jumped out and rushed around to us. "Are they okay?" he asked Brice.

"We're fine," I assured him.

Still, Oscar waited for Brice to nod his head before letting go of his tense posture. Turning to me, he said, "You'd better call Rivers, Cooper. He's gonna freak out if he hears what I heard."

"What'd you hear?" I asked.

"That you and Candice had been stabbed."

"Uh-oh," I muttered. I managed to get my cell up to chest level so I could call Dutch, when we heard a siren barreling toward us, followed by a horn making an additional bloody racket, and the screeching of tires. With a sigh, I pocketed the cell. "He already got the call," I said as more screeching of tires sounded and the siren reverberated back and forth against the tall buildings all around us.

Dutch's car rounded the corner like Steve McQueen's Mustang, sliding and screeching wide to somewhat right itself before barreling at eleventy miles an hour down the street right for us.

I sighed again. Oooh, boy. Dutch pounced on the brakes and the car made even more of a racket as it screeched to a stop in the middle of the street—light box in the rear window still emitting flashing red neon. My husband got out of the car faster than a speeding bullet and looked ready to tackle Titans. His fists were bound up, his shoulders were hunched, and his expression was downright lethal.

"Hi, sweetie!" I called, adding a wave when he didn't seem to see me.

In an instant that whole testosterone-induced posture relaxed, and the granite, "I'ma kill anyone who messes with my woman!" look on his face vanished. He inhaled deeply and crossed the space between us in a few quick steps. Catching me up just like Brice had done to Candice, he held on to me until it got good and embarrassing, and then he sighed into my hair and said, "You're gonna make me an old man before my time, you know that?"

I kissed his cheek and said, "This time, it totally wasn't my fault. Someone at APD got it all wrong."

Dutch let go of the embrace but held tight to my hand. "So what happened?" he asked, in a way that said I better not leave anything out.

"Nothing!" I said, knowing full well that if I admitted to the fact that DeLaria had tried to kill Candice because we'd pushed him to answer our questions about Skylar, Dutch would have a

Steve McQueen–sized cow. "Just some random guy tried to mug Candice."

Dutch's eyes narrowed.

"Okay, so maybe he wasn't so random."

Pressing his lips together, Dutch turned to Candice and said, "Will you please tell me what happened?"

Her gaze went from Dutch, to Brice, to Oscar—who were all staring at her like she'd really better spill the beans—and then back to me. I shrugged. If we didn't tell them, they'd just get a copy of the police report. "Upstairs," she said, and led the way toward the front doors to our building.

Once we were seated comfortably in her office suite, Candice patiently and methodically explained almost all that'd led up to the attack from DeLaria. This was actually a good thing because it caught Oscar up to date and allowed Dutch and Brice to see that I wasn't chasing a silly theory—Skylar really was innocent.

"So why did DeLaria jump you?" Brice asked. Candice miiiiiight have left out the part about pointing a gun at the scumball and shooting blanks at him.

"Dunno," Candice said. "Maybe because he didn't like being told to give up his business and get the hell out of town."

"Did you threaten him?" Brice pressed.

"Only a little," she said with a wink and a coy smile.

Brice sighed and looked at Dutch like, "Can you believe her?" He looked back like, "Dude, I got my own set of worries sitting in the chair next to me."

At least Oscar was focused on the right part of the story. "You're gonna try to track down this guy Slip?"

Candice nodded. "Yes. That's why we were headed back here. I was going to use the new database update and see what it'd toss out."

"Cool. As a backup, I'll see if I can't trace Wayne through county prison records and see who was in with him."

"He was in holding, remember?" Candice told him. "It'll be tough to trace Slip that way."

"Only so many new inmates come in at any given time," Oscar said. "The pool might not be as big as we think, and I can also narrow it with the B and E, if that's really what landed this Slip inside at that time."

Brice stood up and said, "Well, it looks like you're okay and you have things well in hand." Turning to Dutch, he said, "Beer?"

Dutch rose. "Thought you'd never ask." Kissing me on the head, he added, "You. Be careful." And then he pointed to Candice and said, "You too." Last he looked at Oscar and said, "You're in charge of keeping them safe, Rodriguez. And yeah, I know you're off the clock, but I'm still ordering you to watch out for them."

Oscar gave him a firm nod. "Yes, sir."

After Dutch and Brice left, and Candice and Oscar got to work trying to find this Slip character, I headed to my office and called Cal. To my surprise, he took my call, which I gave him credit for, as it was four o'clock on a Sunday. "Did you hear?" he asked when he answered the line.

My brow furrowed. "Hear? I was calling to update you."

"Oh," he said. "You go first, then."

My radar pinged. "Well, mine's kind of long, and it feels like you've got news, so why don't you go first?"

"Okay," he said. "It's official. Skylar fired her attorney and hired me."

I sat forward. "She did? Really?"

"Yeah. I had my first meeting with her today at county. She seems freakishly calm about firing her attorney of six years nine days before her final appeal. Her demeanor wasn't anything like I thought it'd be."

That made me sad. "She doesn't think she'll win the appeal," I said. "I think she's afraid to hope, but it also shows me that she was willing to trust me, which suggests that she hasn't completely given up yet."

Cal sighed. "I gotta tell you, Abby, this is one uphill battle we're facing. After reviewing the case a little more since Friday, I was tempted to call you and tell you that I wasn't going to offer to represent her."

"What?" I said, shocked and a little angry at the admission. "Why?"

"Because I don't want to put Skylar in an even worse position facing that appellate court than she's already in. Switching attorneys this late in the game is a real gamble. It could easily backfire on us."

I felt out the ether and shook my head. "No, Cal, this was the right move. You've just got to trust me on this. We are Skylar's only hope, and even though I'll agree with you that the odds are against us, we're all the fighting chance she's got."

"Yeah, okay," he relented. "I'll trust you. So what is it you've got for me?"

I spent the next hour laying out everything that we'd discovered in just two days of investigating. When I was done, Cal said, "Damn. Abby, if all of us had been on Skylar's team eight or nine years ago, no way would she have been found guilty. In fact, I doubt this would've gone to trial. Unfortunately, even though you're currently digging up some really compelling evidence to create reasonable doubt, unless you get something closer to a confession, it's not going to be enough."

"But, Cal," I complained, "I mean, *come on*! How could even an appellate court ignore the inconsistencies in the evidence and the fact that we have a witness that'll state that he overheard another guy practically confess to the crime?"

"Easy," Cal said. "The defense had a chance to drill down on that evidence at the first trial, and even at the first appeal, and they didn't do it. I'm going to argue like crazy that Skylar's representation committed gross negligence for not arguing the points you brought up, but I can tell you with certainty that the appellate court has been there, and heard that, a thousand times or more. It's the standard argument, and they don't tend to fall for it. So I need more, Abby. A lot more. And soon."

"Okay," I relented. "We'll keep working it. Maybe we'll get lucky and find this guy Slip."

"Even if you do find him, you're going to have to get him to confess," Cal warned. "Skylar would need nothing short of that to sway the appellate court."

I bit my lip. "And if we don't get a confession but continue to find good evidence that it was someone else? Then what, Cal?"

"Then we'll lose the appeal," he said bluntly. "But we'll have something to take to the Board of Pardons."

"Board of what, now?"

"The Texas Board of Pardons and Paroles. It decides clemency cases."

"What about the governor?"

"He got taken out of the equation years ago," Cal said. "It's part of the reason why Texas executes such a high percentage of its death row inmates. There're no politics with the board. No pressure from the public. They just make the decision and go home."

I gulped. "How often do they grant pardons?"

Cal was silent for a beat. "There's always a first time."

"Oh, God," I said, feeling the wind go right out of my sails.

"Hey," he said. "There *is* always a first time, Abby. And just because they have an abysmal record for granting pardons doesn't mean we shouldn't try."

I nodded, but there was now a knot the size of a grapefruit in the pit of my stomach. Cal continued to try to reassure me by saying, "This race isn't over. Not by a long shot. You keep working your investigative end, and bring me any new evidence, no matter how minor, okay? I'll keep working on amending the brief that was submitted to the court on behalf of Skylar's former attorney. He left a lot of holes in it that I'm going to need to fill, and the more I pack in there for them to look at, the better. So don't give up. Not yet."

"Yeah, okay," I said, feeling suddenly weary. "Thanks, Cal."

"You're welcome. Oh, and one more thing, I registered your name as part of Skylar's legal defense team with the prison, so if you need to talk to Skylar, you should be able to set up a time on the visitors' video system as early as tomorrow."

"Awesome," I said. "That'll be a big help. Thanks."

After hanging up with Cal, I spent the better part of the late afternoon writing out notes about Skylar's case on three-by-five cards. Doing this sometimes helped me draw certain random clues together. Of every clue we'd uncovered so far, the one about Slip felt the most urgent. We needed to find this guy, and fast. And then, if we could prove that he'd been the one to crawl into Noah's window and murder him, we needed to get him to confess to that, and I doubted he'd be swayed by the argument that a woman's life was held in the balance. If he'd truly murdered Noah as revenge for some slight—which I couldn't really wrap my head around—then seeing Skylar take the fall for his crime was the ultimate revenge.

Putting the cards down on the desk, I began to arrange them

in random patterns, hoping something would trigger another valuable connection or clue. I kept feeling like we didn't have the whole story. My eye fell on Detective Ray Dioli's card, and that burning anger welled up into my chest again. I hate bullies. Truly detest them, and the more I learned about Dioli and all the evidence he'd overlooked in Skylar's case, the bigger a bully he became. Somewhat blinded by the fumes of that anger, I picked up my office phone and called his cell. He answered with a gruff, "Dioli."

"Detective? This is Abby Cooper."

"You can't get enough of old Ray today, can you, Abby?"

I smirked. He thought he was *so* charming. Asshat. Still, it wouldn't pay me to come out all guns-a-blazing right off the bat. "Sorry to bug you yet again on your weekend, but I'm wondering if you could close the loop on something for me."

"What's that?"

"Well, we had an interesting conversation with a guy named Wayne Babson today. Do you by any chance remember him?"

Dioli was quiet for a moment, and then he said, "No. Name doesn't ring a bell."

My lie detector didn't exactly go off, but it suggested that Dioli thought the name might be familiar, even though he couldn't quite place it.

I thought I'd help jog his memory. "He used to date Skylar," I told him. "But they stopped seeing each other shortly before she won back custody of Noah. Anyway, in a somewhat strange coincidence, Babson says that he got popped for something back in 'oh-five, and while he was in holding at county, another inmate there seemed to have intimate knowledge of Noah's murder. Babson claims that it so alarmed him that he talked to his parole officer, who then put him in touch with a detective on the case, and I was wondering if maybe it was you that he'd spoken to?"

Another pause and then Dioli said, "Nope. Wasn't me."

My lie detector went off. Which meant that Dioli had suppressed evidence that Babson had been in contact with him. Unless Wayne's old parole officer had made a special note of it, we'd be hard-pressed to introduce it to the appellate court as evidence that the APD had purposely hidden some evidence, which I was beginning to think it absolutely had.

I was careful to keep my voice light. "Okay, thanks, Ray. I don't think I'll include the incident in the book, but I just wanted to make sure I'm covering the whole story."

"Uh-huh," he said. I doubted he believed me, and I got the distinct impression he was pretty much done helping me with Skylar's case.

"I'll call you if I get any other hits on Pham's case," I said, still trying to remain in his good graces, although why I wasn't sure.

"You don't need to worry about that anymore," he said cryptically. "We're all set on that."

And then he hung up. Abruptly. Not even a good-bye kiss. How would I ever get over it?

With an eye roll, I got back to work sorting through the three-by-five cards. Candice poked her head into my office around six o'clock, looking tired and frustrated. "No luck?" I asked.

She shook her head. "Not really. I got a few hits on some names that're close, but no one who was in holding at county at the same time as Wayne. Still, I'm gonna track down those leads just to make sure."

I motioned to the door with my chin. Oscar had been working on his laptop in Candice's office when I came into mine. "I take it Oscar didn't have any luck either?"

Candice stretched and yawned. "Not yet, but he promised to work it tomorrow. He left about ten minutes ago and said he'd be in touch tomorrow morning."

I gathered up the three-by-five cards into a neat stack and stood up. "Okay," I said. "We'll hit it again tomorrow. Let's call it a night."

Chapter Ten

. . .

Monday morning I was back at the office. There was a sense of urgency that went beyond simply knowing that Skylar's life depended on us figuring out who murdered Noah in the next few days. I felt so strongly that there was something more going on, a bigger picture to put it all into context, and I knew that I'd continue to flounder around until I had a chance to talk to Skylar. To that end, I filled out the required online application for a video visitation and impatiently sat back and waited for it to be approved.

About an hour after sending the form, I received notification that the visit had been approved and that I would be able to speak with Skylar at ten a.m. I spent the hour waiting for the visit by going about the painstaking business of creating a list of the e-mail addresses of all my clients whose sessions I'd previously recorded. Matt had instructed me that if I ever wanted to contribute to another federal case again, I'd better get my clients in a row by sending them an amended terms of agreement, which flatly stated that the e-mail copy of the recording of our session together counted as approval for the actual recording of said session, and that they merely needed to check the little box marked "Agree" at the bottom of the e-mail and send it back to me to make it all legal-like.

This was no small task. I had almost four thousand clients. And while Matt had assured me that I probably didn't need all of them to reply to the amended agreement, I quite likely needed about seventy percent to get on board.

I figured it was going to take me at least a solid month to reach out to them all and beg them to simply click the little check box at the bottom of the e-mail. "Stupid Stephanie Snitch," I muttered as I squinted at my computer screen. I would never understand why some women could be so aggressively catty to other women. The small child in me was hurt that she'd betrayed my trust when all I'd wanted to do was give her an experience that made her feel good and took away her worries. I'd wanted the best for her, and she'd made an effort to sully my name, and of course get a serial killer off on a technicality. She'd done that just to get some attention. That part alone was unforgivable.

And that gave me an uncomfortable reminder that I had to call Director Gaston at some point and let him know that I'd hit a dead end with the other girls that Corzo had murdered. After poring over the files of the other two victims the night before, it was clear to me, intuitively speaking, that there was nothing new to be gleaned. I couldn't even offer him a new angle to pursue.

I stared into space for a minute as that weight settled firmly onto my shoulders. So much about the week ahead held the potential to absolutely cripple me emotionally, because these weren't just cases to me. When I used my radar to help solve a case, a little piece of me went into it. A piece I never got back. The fact that I could contribute helped offset the loss of that energy. But if I wasn't going to bring home a win on any of the three cases I was currently working, then what was the freaking point?

I closed my eyes and sat back in my chair, trying to remember that it mattered that I was fighting the good fight. That there were plenty of times when I'd helped to put someone seriously dangerous behind bars. That the judgment of others didn't matter; only that of the people who loved me and fought alongside me counted.

Still, I couldn't quite convince myself.

Opening my eyes, I looked at the clock. I had fifteen minutes to go. Sitting up, I reached for the phone and made the call. "Gaston," he answered before the third ring.

"Director," I said. "It's Abby Cooper."

"Good morning, Abigail," he said, his voice crisp and clipped. He was all business this morning. "Did you manage to find something for us?"

I bit my lip. "Sir, I'm very sorry. Truly. But I went over the files several times and nothing there indicates that there's anything left to discover. At least not that I can pull out of the ether."

Gaston seemed to take that in before he said, "Very well, Abigail. I'm sure you tried your best. We'll just have to continue to press on with the investigation on our own."

I felt a pang. His words were right, but I could practically hear the disappointment in his voice. I'd failed him. "Maybe we'll have some luck with the fourth victim," I said. And then realized that I'd spoken without even thinking about it. In fact, what I'd just said had sprung from my mouth as if someone else had said it.

"What did you say?" Gaston asked, leaping on the statement.

I shook my head a little. Where the hell had that come from? But I already knew. Sometimes my radar acts a bit like a case of Tourette's. Stuff sort of falls out of my mouth without any forethought, and it's those times when what comes out tends to be the most truthful and predictive. "The fourth victim," I said, almost whispering it. "There's a fourth victim out there, but either we haven't found her or her case hasn't been connected to Corzo yet."

"We've done extensive searches within our shared databases, Abigail. No other cases were similar enough to suspect Corzo was responsible."

"He changed his method," I said, knowing that was true. "He's altered the way he disposes of his victims. I don't think he leaves them in plain sight, or poses them anymore. He's hiding them now."

"So you believe there's another woman's body still out there?"

I focused on that question, but my radar was a little iffy on the answer. "I can't say for sure, Director, but there is a sense that we will connect these dots, and that as clever as Corzo thinks he is to change things up on us, he's actually messed up royally. He's left us a giant clue, and we only need to look out for this fourth victim to figure it out."

And then Gaston asked me something that sent a slight chill up my spine. "You believe that Corzo has already killed this fourth victim, correct? This isn't a woman he intends to kill or has targeted?"

I tapped my finger on the desk. "No. No, it feels like she's already dead. However, Corzo definitely plans to kill again. I hate to say this, but I think he murdered this woman while we were trying to put a case together against him for the murder of the other three. I think it was done within the past year."

I heard Gaston sigh. "We turned our focus away from him a few times in the past twelve months," he admitted. "Other, more pressing cases needed our attention."

Gaston didn't have to say it, but I knew of two cases in particular that'd taken our attention away from Corzo, one involving Candice, and another involving a different serial killer who liked to blow things up. Literally.

Still, I had a sneaking suspicion that Corzo's fourth victim had been murdered during the time of the bomber, when we'd all been seriously distracted. (And some of us more than others.)

"We should look at missing persons reports from mid-October of last year through early November," I said to Gaston. "Sometime during that stretch I think Corzo struck."

"I'll get everybody on it," Gaston promised. "Thanks for the call."

I set the receiver down in the cradle of my desk phone with a satisfied sigh. Sometimes, it felt really great to have a little extra advantage over the bad guys, and my radar had often proved to be the thing that they couldn't quite circumvent.

My smug satisfaction lasted all of two seconds, because Candice came into my office carrying a newspaper and slapped it down on my desk. "Dioli's an asshole," she proclaimed.

I glanced at the clock before looking at the paper. I had three minutes before Skylar's video visit. Enough time to get good and bothered. Eyeing the paper, I read the headline, *UT Research Student Arrested for Lab Partner's Murder.*

"Son of a *bitch*!" I yelled, taking up the paper to glare at it murderously. "I *told* that son of a bitch Dioli that Cheng didn't do it!"

"He's choosing to ignore you," Candice deadpanned.

"How can he even do this?" I demanded, still staring hard at the paper. "I mean, he's got nothing! Nothing on this kid!"

"Read the article," Candice said. "He's got a threatening e-mail from Cheng to Pham that was written on a friend's computer, almost as if Cheng didn't want it traced back to him."

"Oh, bullshit," I spat, and threw the paper into the trash can.

"He's got squat and he knows it. I'll bet he's trying to get a confession out of him as we speak! And this poor kid is an exchange student from China, where the police can torture a confession right out of you. I'll bet Cheng's not even aware he can ask for a lawyer and stop the interrogation."

Candice seemed to light up at that statement. "I'll bet you're absolutely right," she said to me, turning on her heel to head out of my office.

"Hey!" I said. "Candice? Where're you going?"

"To make a call," she replied from somewhere deeper in the suite.

"But I've got Skylar coming up for a video chat in thirty seconds!" I yelled.

Candice said something, but I couldn't take it in, and in the next moment my computer made a ringing sound. I hit the space bar, and the screen jumped to life, pixelating for a moment before filling with the image of Skylar Miller.

I waved at her and tried to shrug off my irritation with Dioli. "Hi, Skylar," I said. "Thanks for taking my call."

Skylar's face held very little expression. It wasn't that her features were flat and withdrawn, more that she put no energy into visually expressing what she was feeling. It gave her an intensely serene aspect, and I will admit that it made me a bit self-conscious. "Cal said you were still intent on working the case," she said. It was less a question and more a statement of fact.

"Yes. We've got some promising leads."

Skylar nodded and her serene expression never wavered. It made it difficult to tell if she believed me. "I'm assuming you want to hear my side of the story," she said.

"Yes," I said, and moved my mouse over to an icon I had on my desktop. Clicking it, I said, "Skylar, I've just hit the Record button on my computer. I'd like to record this discussion if that's okay with you?"

"That's okay with me," she said.

I made a motion for her to continue and she rested her hands on the desk where the monitor was presumably mounted. "Noah and I had had a busy week," she began. "I bought my house from a builder who'd painted everything vanilla, which is so boring to live with, and Noah was really excited about the idea of painting the house. I was on a pretty limited budget, but I knew a guy at Home Depot who let me pick through all the paint that got returned from other customers, and it was practically free. Anyway, Noah was an amazing little helper. He picked up painting really fast, and we cranked out the whole house in about a week. I also found a duvet and sheet set for him at the thrift store that was still in its original packaging, and you should've seen the look on his face when I brought it home. He thought I'd actually splurged on him."

For the first time I saw the same sweet melancholy in Skylar's eyes that'd been present at my first encounter with her. Her gaze was far away and there was such a heartbreaking soulful sadness that I felt my own eyes mist a little. She continued. "That day—his last day—Noah and I made a few final touch-ups to the paint job, then picked up all the drop cloths, brushes, and paint cans and stored them in the garage. I would've just left the place somewhat picked up and headed for the couch, but my son wanted the house to be perfect, so we spent an hour vacuuming, and dusting, and mopping, until it was neat as a pin.

"After that, we ordered pizza and watched a movie together. Noah called his dad to say good night, and I took a shower. Then I ordered him into the tub and he got ready for bed. I'll admit that I was so beat from that week that I went to bed at the same time he did."

"What time was that?" I interrupted.

"Around nine," she said. "I got Noah tucked in; then I vacu-umed the hallway just so the house would be absolutely perfect when we woke up the next morning, and turned in. I think I was asleep before my head hit the pillow."

Skylar paused for the briefest moment and for the first time the mask of serenity faltered, and her mouth curled down as her lower lip gave a tiny tremor. She blinked, and recovered herself, but I'd seen the flash of gut-wrenching heartbreak across her face. That instant display of vulnerability and truth was enough to convince me that I was right to believe in her.

"I woke up sometime in the middle of the night. I don't re-member what woke me. Maybe Noah cried out. Maybe the mur-derer made some noise. Whatever it was I can't be sure, but I do remember sitting straight up in bed and feeling like something was off, even though I couldn't say what. And then I heard some-thing from Noah's room."

"What?" I asked.

Skylar shook her head. "A thump, or a bump. Something like furniture being knocked against the wall. I figured that Noah was having a bad dream and maybe he'd fallen out of bed. So I went down the hall and his door was closed. I remember think-ing that was so weird, because Noah never wanted his door closed. We had a small night-light plugged into the outlet in the bathroom, and he liked that he could see it from his bed. Any-way, when I opened his door, I saw him on the floor next to the bed. I thought he was sleeping and I even laughed a little. . . ." Skylar's voice broke off for a second. Another flash of heartbreak washed over her face, but it was also gone in a moment. She cleared her throat and continued. "I thought he'd slept right through falling out of bed," she said. "I went over to him, got my arms underneath him, and that's when I felt how wet he was.

My first thought was that he'd wet himself, but as I was trying to lift him, my hand got sliced on something and I jerked my right arm back in a reflex. That's when Noah made this . . . this . . . sound."

I didn't want to ask, but I knew I had to. "What kind of sound, Skylar?"

She closed her eyes and shook her head. "It was like a gurgle," she said. "But also a sigh. I think it was his very last breath. He breathed it in my arms, but I was pulling away from him in that moment, reacting to the cut on my hand."

I bit my lip. Man. To live with that had to be killing her. "I'm sure in that moment, Skylar, he wasn't aware of much besides maybe that his mom was there."

She didn't look at me, and I knew that what I'd said was probably a little lame, but it was also perhaps . . . just perhaps . . . the truth.

She inhaled a deep breath and continued with her story. "After I sliced open my hand, I was sort of starting to add things up in my head. The synapses were firing and I began to realize that Noah wasn't asleep, that he'd been hurt, and he hadn't wet himself, it was blood on my hand, and then I saw that the window was open, and it was all clicking so fast, but it felt almost slow, and then I realized that Noah wasn't breathing. I put my hand back under him to feel his chest, and it was warm and wet, and I put everything together in that one instant."

Skylar's eyes met mine. The mask of serenity was gone and her face registered something horribly haunted, pained, and terrible to witness. She dropped her chin and it was a moment more before she was able to speak.

"I think I must have screamed," she said quietly. "But I can't quite remember if I did. I know that when I replay that moment back in my mind, I'm screaming my head off, but the truth is, I can't be sure that I did. I do remember trying to lift him into my arms again, but he was totally limp, and slippery, and I couldn't manage it for a second. And that's when there was a noise from behind me. I think it must've come from the closet."

"What kind of a noise?" I asked. I knew it might seem like minutiae to her, but no detail was too small to leave out.

She shook her head. "A rustling, maybe? And then the door creaked a little, and that was another one of those instant knowings. I knew my son had been stabbed and that the person who did it was still in the room."

"What'd you do?" I asked.

She stared at me and the pain had returned tenfold to her eyes. I felt she was on the cusp of confessing something to me. Something she felt deep regret over. I waited and offered her a nod to let her know it was okay. "There was an instant before the intruder came out of the closet," she said, her voice quavering, "where I could choose to take an extra few seconds to pick up Noah and try to run, or I could leave him and go for help."

Oh, God. Oh, God, poor Skylar. This poor, poor woman. "You ran," I said when she fell silent with her shame.

She dropped her chin again. "Yes."

"And that's the *only* reason you're alive, Skylar."

She didn't lift her gaze, but she did reply, "What good was it in the end, Abby? I should've stayed with my son. I should've died with him. That way, I'd never go to my grave accused of murdering him. And we'd be together."

"True," I said. "But something tells me Noah never would've wanted it to end up like that. He would've wanted you to run. To get help. To fight for the truth."

Skylar shook her head, her curly blond hair falling forward to cover her face. "He's up there all alone," she said, lifting her chin. "So I'm not going to fight too hard, Abby. I'll give you this chance, but I'm not praying for a reprieve or anything."

Whoo, boy. "Understood," I told her. Then I began to ask her a few questions, mostly about what Dioli had documented in the file. "You escaped the house," I began, "running down the hallway and out the front door."

"Yes. The intruder came out of the closet and lunged at me, but I was already running for the door. I felt him grab my shoulder, but I managed to get out of his grasp and keep going."

I jotted myself a note. "And you never saw his face?"

She shook her head. "No. It happened way too fast and the room was dark."

"But at some point while you were in the room you noticed the window was open."

"Yes."

"How did you notice it? I mean, if the room was dark, then how did you know the window was open?"

Skylar thought for a moment. "I heard the wind and felt the breeze," she said.

I nodded. If she'd been faking her answers, she would've gone for some visible clue, like that she'd been able to see the curtain fluttering by the light given off from the night-light in the bathroom. To give me what she heard and not what she saw meant she was remembering, not creating.

I wrote myself a note and moved on to my next question. "At any point did the killer say anything to you?"

Skylar shook her head. "No."

"Did you notice anything about him, like his height, or his weight, or even if he was wearing cologne?"

Skylar stared off for a moment, then turned her attention back to me and said, "No. He was just a shadow. A shape. The boogey-man who came into my home and murdered my son."

"Okay," I said, accepting that if there was anything else she could think of, she'd tell me. "Let's talk about the knife."

Skylar shifted uncomfortably in her chair, but I pretended to ignore it. "The police say it came from your kitchen—"

"It did," she admitted.

"You're positive?"

She nodded. "They showed me that knife a dozen times, Abby. It was my knife. It came from my kitchen drawer."

"A lot of kitchen knives look alike, though," I said.

She shook her head. "That knife was part of a culinary set that'd been a wedding present from my dad. In our divorce, Chris had actually been fairly generous. He'd not only given me my fair share of the household assets, but he'd also given up all of the wedding presents we'd gotten to complete the kitchen, because, between us, I'd always been the cook. Anyway, once I was out of jail, I'd furnished the house with my half of the belongings from the divorce, and it'd worked out perfectly because my house had been so small that I hadn't needed much.

"So that's how I know that the knife came from my kitchen. I wish it hadn't, but I have to be honest at this point—it did. It was my knife. It even had my fingerprints on the handle—the ones not smeared in Noah's blood. That part of the prosecution's case is ironclad, and I know it. So, somehow the killer managed to get into my house without any obvious signs of forced entry, take the knife from the drawer, then sneak back out and climb through Noah's window to murder him, again without any sign of forced entry."

"Could Noah's window have been unlocked?" I asked, remembering how easily the screen popped out.

"No way," she said. "Never. Noah knew never to open his window at night, and I always kept them locked. The area to the east of our sub was a little sketchy, and neither of us took that lightly."

"Okay," I said, trying to think up my next question. "Back to the knife, did you maybe notice it missing in the days leading up to the attack?"

"No," she said. "It hadn't been. I remember using it that night to cut up vegetables for a salad to go with our pizza."

"So the killer got it out of the sink?" I asked, trying to figure out how the killer had first come by the knife.

Skylar rubbed her temples. "No," she said. "He got it from the drawer. I washed the knife and put it away right before the pizza got there."

And then an idea occurred to me. "Skylar, was there anything about the pizza delivery guy that maybe struck you as odd?"

"It wasn't a guy, Abby. It was a sixteen- or seventeen-year-old girl."

"Ah," I said. "So, let me just ask you straight out. Do you have *any* idea who would want to murder your son?"

"No. No one. Noah was the sweetest boy you'd ever meet. He was kind. He loved animals. He was polite. He'd strike up a conversation with anyone, and he'd help anyone too. He was a loving, caring, sweet, sweet boy."

"I believe you," I said. "But now let me ask you a tougher question. Do you know anybody who might've wanted to hurt you by killing your son?"

Skylar sighed. "That's something I've had to ask myself a thousand times since that night," she said. "I mean, until I quit drinking, I was a total mess, and I probably did make some enemies, but I just can't picture anyone I know hating me enough to murder Noah. I'd been clean and sober for almost four years by that time.

Who would hold a grudge that long before acting? If they'd wanted to hurt me, they could've done it at any given time when I was struggling to get it together, living in some dicey neighborhoods. I was an easy mark until I started working the program. It doesn't make sense that someone would pass up so many opportunities to hurt me if that was their goal."

I jotted a few more notes before I went to my next question. "Skylar, my associate and I met with a man you used to date. Wayne Babson. Remember him?"

Her brow furrowed. "Wayne? He's still in town? How'd you find him?"

I looked her steady in the eyes. "Through Rico DeLaria."

Her breath caught. "Oh," she said, and a flush tinged her cheeks. "So you heard about that, huh?"

"Yes. And I'm not judging, Skylar, please believe me. But Rico's a pretty dangerous guy. He attacked my partner with a knife yesterday, as a matter of fact."

Skylar's eyes widened. "Is she okay?"

"She's ducky. He's in the hospital because he brought a knife to a kung fu fight."

Skylar pursed her lips and there was the barest hint of mirth there. "Sounds like your associate can take care of herself."

"She can. And sometimes she also takes care of me." I glanced up for a moment and saw Candice leaning against the doorframe with her arms crossed over her chest, and an amused smile on her lips. "Anyway, we met briefly with Wayne, and he says that shortly before the verdict came in against you, he was approached by a man serving time for breaking and entering. This man went by the name of Slip, and he may have known you."

Skylar's brow dipped again. "I've never heard of a guy named Slip."

My radar said she wasn't lying. "He suggested to Wayne that he felt you had disrespected him in front of your son and that he might've gotten even by teaching you a lesson. Can you think of any stranger you might have somehow offended while your son was with you right around the time he was murdered? Maybe it was another driver you cut off. Or maybe it was a rude shopper at the grocery store. Anyone come to mind?"

In an instant Skylar's face became deathly pale and she laid her hands flat on the desk as if her equilibrium was compromised. "Oh, my God," she said. "The guy at Home Depot!"

"What guy at Home Depot?"

Skylar was breathing hard and she'd started to sweat a little. It looked like she was having a panic attack. "Oh, my God!" she whispered. "Oh, my God!"

Candice came fully into the room and around the desk to peer at the computer screen. "Skylar?" she said in a loud firm voice. "I'm Candice Fusco, Abby's associate. Listen to me. I'm going to start counting from one to four over and over, and you need to breathe in time to my counting. Can you do that?"

Skylar's eyes were wide and panicked. She was gripping the table, and barely seemed to hear Candice. My BFF began counting, somewhat rapidly at first until she was sure she was keeping up with Skylar's inhalations; then Candice slowed the pace bit by bit until it was at a calm, even rhythm. "Better?" Candice asked.

Skylar nodded. "Yes . . . thank . . . you."

"Feel up to telling us about this guy at Home Depot?"

Skylar looked sick. She was pale and there was an almost greenish pallor to her face. "Noah and I had gone to Home Depot one morning to get some paint supplies," she said. "While I was talking to my friend at the store who was hooking us up with free paint, Noah wandered off. I was panicked when I realized he wasn't next to me, and ran up and down the aisles looking for him. I finally found him in the tool section talking to some guy, and the guy had his hand on Noah's shoulder, leading him along the aisle. I was so scared about having lost sight of Noah and then seeing this total stranger with his hand on my son. . . ."

"What happened?" I asked when Skylar fell silent.

"I freaked out," she said. "I ran up to them and yanked Noah away, and then I told the man to never, *ever* go near my son again and we left the store immediately."

"What was this guy's reaction?" Candice asked.

Skylar closed her eyes as if trying to recall the memory. "He just stood there, and stared at us like he was totally shocked. He was taller than me, but I don't think he was close to six feet. Maybe five-nine or five-ten, and he had white hair, like almost albino white, but I don't think he was actually albino. His skin wasn't that pale that you see on true albinos."

I wondered if the little guy had said anything that might help us track this man down, like maybe where he worked or lived. "What did Noah say about the encounter?" I asked.

Skylar sat back in her chair and shook her head, as if she still couldn't believe it was the man she'd encountered that morning. "Not much. When we were in the car and driving home, Noah got upset, of course, because he was alarmed by my reaction, but I talked to him all the way home about how he knew to never talk to or go with a stranger. It was a really hard thing for my son to grasp because he never met a stranger. To him, everybody was a friend just waiting to be introduced. He was so trusting.

"So, after I drilled it into his head that he could never, ever do something like that again, I didn't bring it up anymore, because I was afraid that if I continued to harp on it, Noah would become fearful enough of people that he wouldn't go to an adult if ever he needed help. It was a fine line I needed to walk with him."

"Was there a chance this guy from Home Depot could've followed you home?" Candice asked Skylar.

She simply shrugged. "It never occurred to me that he would," she said. "He'd been pushing a cart full of hardware supplies while he talked to Noah, so I never really thought about him following us out. I think I just figured he'd take his stuff to the register and check out and by the time he got out of the store, we'd be long gone."

She paused for a moment and shook her head again, her eyes pinched with remorse and regret. "While I was yelling at him, he looked shocked, but also a bit ashamed, like he'd realized as I was yelling at him what he'd done wrong and was sorry, but he never spoke a word to me. It's why I never thought of him as the person who broke into my home. In the days afterward, I'd actually felt a little bad that I'd yelled at him like that, because maybe he'd just been being friendly to Noah, but at the time, I'd been so alarmed to see my son walking with a total stranger who had his hand on my Noah that I'd lost my cool. Like I said, we rushed out of the store, and once I turned away, I was so focused on Noah that I didn't really look behind me to see if he was nearby, so if he wanted to abandon his cart and follow us, he probably could have."

Candice and I exchanged a look. I *knew* that's exactly what this guy had done. Candice turned back to Skylar and asked, "Did you by any chance report the incident on the way out? Or do you remember if anyone took note of what was going on and approached him?"

Skylar's shoulders sagged and she shook her head. "No," she said. "I mean, I'm sure some heads turned, but no one asked us about it before we left the store."

"What about your buddy behind the paint counter?" I asked. "Did he see anything?"

"I don't know," Skylar said. "He knew I went looking for Noah, but he didn't mention anything to me about it a few days later when we went back for those same supplies. I doubt he was even aware that anything had happened."

"Still, it might be a good thing to check out," Candice said. "Can you give us his name?"

Skylar sighed. "I knew him through AA," she said. "We're supposed to keep each other's identity secret."

"Skylar," Candice said firmly. "Your life is hanging in the balance. I think we can bend the rules just this one time."

"Okay," she said. "His name is Allen Lambrecht."

"Do you know if he still works at Home Depot?" Candice asked next.

"I don't," Skylar said. "It's the one on Fifty-first and I-Thirty-five."

Candice jotted herself a note. Then she gazed at Skylar for another minute and said, "Being so overtly friendly to a total stranger's kid isn't something our culture allows anymore." I could tell she was trying to get Skylar to see that she'd been absolutely right in calling out this guy at the hardware store. "He had to know that he was being inappropriate, Skylar, and you weren't wrong to suspect he might've had an ulterior motive in befriending your son. Your mom instincts kicked in, and nothing you did was wrong."

Still, Skylar appeared anguished, as if the full weight of that past action as the catalyst for what'd happened to her son was coming home to rest firmly on her shoulders. She seemed to shrink before our very eyes, and she wouldn't look into the camera of the video screen. That worried me.

"Skylar," Candice said softly.

"It was me," she whispered. "I was the cause."

Candice and I both stared hard at her. There was nothing more we could say. I had several more questions I wanted to ask her, but a warning light on the screen told us that we only had five minutes left and Skylar was now sinking into herself, drowning in a pool of guilt. I knew we were pressed for time, but she simply didn't look able to continue further questioning. At least not until we'd given her a little time to absorb this new possibility of the guy from Home Depot being the killer. "Okay," I said. "Candice and I are gonna follow up on this new lead and give you some space. But do me a favor. Think back if you can to the days following that incident and see if Noah maybe dropped a hint about this guy from HD. A name or what he did for a living might actually help us track him down."

"He was a welder," Skylar said suddenly, her eyes finally lifting to us again.

Candice and I both leaned forward a little toward the screen. "A welder?"

"Yes. Yes, I'm sure that's what Noah told me when I asked him why he'd walked away from me with a stranger. He said that the guy wasn't a stranger, he was a welder, and he knew a lot about tools."

Candice arched an eyebrow at me. "That's a great lead," she said. "One we can follow."

Skylar nodded absently. She was beyond our ability to reach and I hated that she was suffering her son's murder in a whole new and terrible way.

After signing off with Skylar, Candice and I called Oscar. He landed in our office twenty minutes later and we brought him up to speed. "Okay," he said, writing himself a note in a small notebook. "We have a description, an occupation, and if he was employed, he'd have to have a welding certificate issued by the Texas Department of Transportation."

"TxDOT?" I asked, using the acronym, which sounded out like "Tex-dot." "Really? They cover welders?"

"They cover a lot of things," Oscar said, "including a welder's certification. Unless he's no longer licensed, or welding without one, which would make it hard to get a job, then I should be able to narrow it down to at least a list of possibles."

"Would they issue an accompanying photo ID?" Candice asked him.

Oscar shook his head. "Doubtful. But they'll have a list of names of certified welders active in two thousand four. I'll do a search on any with criminal records, and cross-reference any of those hits with driver's license photos, and maybe we'll get lucky."

"How long will that take?" I asked.

Oscar shrugged a shoulder. "Don't know. Depends on how quickly TxDOT gives me the list."

"Ugh," I said. "We'll be waiting forever. Nothing in government moves with any efficiency."

Oscar got up. "Let me make a few calls," he said. "I might be able to get it expedited."

"It'd be a whole lot faster if you could use your FBI credentials," Candice observed. Oscar was a guy who didn't break the rules, and Candice knew he'd never even hint that we needed the list to assist with an FBI investigation.

"Probably," he agreed. "But that's not an option for us. If Gaston caught wind that I was using my badge to get info for a private case, he'd hand me my ass and put me on desk duty for the next six months."

I wanted to protest, but I knew Oscar was right. We wouldn't get around the rules with this one. "Thanks, Oscar," I said. "See what you can do."

He got up, saluted us, and headed out.

Candice eyed her watch. "Feel like a road trip?"

"Home Depot?"

"Yep."

"Let's roll."

Chapter Eleven

. . .

Traffic was light, given that it was that freaky hour between rush hour and lunch, and we managed to make it to the Depot a bit before noon. As I got out of the car, I took a look around at our location. Pointing to the east, I said, "Skylar lived about four miles that way."

"Which means this guy she confronted could've lived or worked close to here at the time," Candice said.

"Easy access," I agreed. "Might help Oscar narrow his scope even more."

Candice produced her cell and typed rapidly on it. "Done," she said, then motioned with her chin toward the entrance.

We could've gone directly to customer service to inquire about Allen, but Candice suggested we use a softer approach by meandering over to the paint section. I knew it was a long shot to find him still working there after ten years, but Lady Luck had been with us so far on this case; maybe she'd hang with us for one more swing at bat. "Hey there," Candice said to the guy behind the paint counter. He wore his paint-speckled orange apron over a blue T-shirt and jeans. In black ink above his right breast was the name *Casey.* "Is Allen working today?" Candice asked him.

Casey nodded, adding a pleasant smile. "He's on break. I'm here, though. What can I do for you?"

Home Depot people. So friendly. Candice slid closer to the counter and offered Casey her most sweet-as-a-little-lamb smile. "Would it be possible to page him? He gave me some painting advice last week about this tricky glaze effect for my living room, and I think I goofed. It's not turning out like I thought it would."

Casey suddenly seemed unsure. "We're not supposed to call employees off break," he said, apologetically. "See, we only get about forty-five minutes in a ten-hour shift, and Allen likes to take his smoke breaks when he can."

"Oh," Candice said, sounding surprised. "I had no idea. I'll definitely wait. When did he go on break?"

Casey glanced at his watch. "You just missed him. He left about two minutes ago. He should be back in fifteen minutes or so."

"Perfect," Candice said, offering him another sweet smile. "We'll be over in electrical and come back in twenty. Thanks, Casey."

With that, Candice took my arm and we walked toward the back of the store. "What are we getting in electrical?" I asked.

"Nothing. But I figure that section of the store faces the highway, and it's probably the part of the parking lot least likely to have customers park, and also likely to be the place where employees are allowed to take their smoke breaks."

"Ah," I said, marveling at my clever friend. "Your powers of deduction never cease to amaze me."

Candice slid her gaze to me. "This ain't my first rodeo, Sundance."

We found an exit out into the rear section of the parking lot, and sure enough there were two guys there wearing orange aprons and inhaling lots of cancer. I flipped my radar on as we approached, and the older guy on the right was already showing the first hints of black disease in his lungs. My guess was he'd be dead in five years.

The pair watched us approach but said nothing until we were standing in front of them. I decided to take the lead, as I was still sorting through Allen's energy intuitively, and had a pretty good guess as to how to engage him. "Hey, there," I said, pointing to the older man on the right. The name on his apron gave him away. "We're looking to talk to Allen Lambrecht. Are you by any chance him?"

Allen eyed me curiously. "You need help with something in paint?"

"No, sir," I said, pulling out my FBI consulting badge. "And I'm sorry to bother you on your break, but we have a personal matter to discuss with you."

Allen leaned forward and studied my ID; then he seemed to get a bit nervous. The man next to him cleared his throat and stubbed out his cigarette in the tall ashtray set up for the employees. I was glad to see that he didn't just throw the butt on the ground, as most of Texas was still in a drought and wildfires were a constant threat. "I should head in," he said, before shuffling off.

Allen too stubbed out his cigarette. "What's this about?" he asked in a mild tone. I knew I'd caught him off guard, but there was no avoiding that.

"We need your help," I said plainly. "My associate and I are working on Skylar Miller's final appeal. Do you remember Skylar?"

Allen's brow shot up and he looked both relieved and surprised. "Of course I remember her," he said. "Hard to forget Sky. You're trying to clear her name?"

"We are," Candice told him.

He shook his head. "I never was convinced she killed her boy.

She loved that little guy. Hell, she would've jumped in front of a train for him. I couldn't believe it when they arrested her. I mean, you never really know someone, but I'd been in the program with Sky for five years. She was my buddy, and I'd never once seen her lose her temper. Not even when everyone was against her as she was fighting for custody. She put in the time and the work and did everything the program called for and everything her social worker told her to. She was a good kid."

"We've drawn much the same conclusion," I told him. "In investigating the case, we've come to believe that there was someone else responsible. We've even narrowed it down to a possible suspect, which is why we wanted to come talk to you."

Allen suddenly broke into a sweat again and he held his hands up in an "I'm innocent!" motion. "Hey," he said defensively. "I had nothing to do with that."

I cocked my head. "Of course you didn't. But we think you might have had a glimpse of the man who did."

Allen lowered his palms and pointed to himself. "Me?"

Candice said, "Skylar told us this morning about an incident here at this store when she came with her son to pick up some paint supplies and visit with you. There was a point at which Noah wandered away from her. Do you remember that?"

Allen nodded. "Yeah," he said. "She found him talking to that guy in tools."

My eyes widened. "You saw that?"

He nodded again. "I did. And once she gave him a piece of her mind, I went over and told him to leave the store or I'd alert my manager. The guy was creepy, and the way he had his arm around Noah made me think he shouldn't be around kids."

"Did you tell your manager about it?"

Allen's face flushed. "Uh, no. I just told the guy to leave, and followed him to the exit. Then I watched the door for a little while to make sure he didn't come back."

I held my emotions carefully in check. Inadvertently, Allen had sent this predator right after Skylar and her son. Whoever this Slip character was, he'd probably been seething with rage not only from being yelled at by Skylar, but also for being thrown out of the store. "And you never told Skylar that you'd confronted this man?" I asked.

He shook his head. "She seemed really upset by the whole thing, and she'd left her paint and all her brushes behind, so when she came back in, I didn't want to remind her about it. I just pretended nothing happened."

Allen's face was creased with worry, and I knew his brain was starting to put two and two together. "You were a good friend to her," I said.

Still, he asked me, "Do you think that guy followed her? I mean, do you think he was the one who killed Noah?"

"We're not sure at this point," Candice told him. "We're only following a lead."

Allen wiped his face with a shaky hand, and he reached inside his apron for his smokes. Lighting one up, he said, "I can describe him if you need me to."

"About five-nine, very blond hair, light-colored eyes?" I asked.

Allen nodded. "That's him."

"Anything else about him you can remember?" Candice asked.

Allen thought about that for a minute before he nodded. "Yeah, he had burns on his arms," he added, tilting his forearm to indicate the inside portion of the man's arms.

"Any tattoos or other physical quirks?" Candice asked, writing in her notebook.

Allen thought for another second. "None that I remember."

"The burns on his arms help," Candice told him. The poor guy looked so sincere, like he really wanted to help us, even though both Candice and I knew the burns had probably come from his welding jobs. "Did you ever see him again in the store?" she asked next. "Or catch a glimpse of him in the area?"

Allen shook his head. "Naw. And I would've remembered. That guy was bad news. I kept an eye out for him for a while after that."

"Do you remember what time of day this all took place?" Candice asked.

Allen rubbed at his chin. "Pretty sure it was morning, but not too early. Maybe between nine and noon? I remember taking a break from watching the door to go take my lunch, which has always been scheduled at one o'clock, so I'm pretty sure that nine-to-noon window was the time frame."

"Did you ever connect the incident with what happened to Noah?" I asked. Some people have really good intuition, and I wondered if after he'd heard the news of Noah's murder, Allen's own radar had maybe kicked in.

He looked down at the ground. "I didn't," he said. "I mean, I think I was kind of in shock. I just couldn't believe it, you know? I went to Noah's funeral, and they'd arrested Sky by then. I visited her in jail right after and told her how beautiful the ceremony was and how many people came. She was sorta destroyed by the whole thing. Catatonic even. I don't even know if she remembers me visiting her."

My lips pressed together. The injustice that'd been done to this poor woman filled me with a deep and seething anger. "That was nice of you to visit her," I told him.

"I was the only one who did," he said bitterly. "Not even her mom showed up to support her. And her ex . . . man. I never told

Sky this, but at the funeral the guy was in a rage. He cursed her in front of the entire congregation. Swore he'd get even with her for murdering his son, and I guess he did, because the judge gave Sky the death penalty. I have a friend in the program—I guess you know that's how we met, right?"

Candice and I both nodded. "She told us," I said. "But she didn't want to. She wanted to keep you anonymous."

"No, it's okay," he said. "I would've wanted her to send you guys to me. Anyway, I have another friend in the program who's high up in the court system, and he said there was a rumor that the presiding judge had been unduly influenced by the Millers' money."

I scowled. "We heard that too."

Allen was thoughtful for a moment before he said, "Do you think you can save her?"

I wanted to say yes. Man, did I want to say yes. But my intuition was still laying even odds on whether we'd be able to save Skylar from the needle. "We're going to do everything we can," I promised.

Allen sighed. "I should go visit her," he said. "I haven't seen her in eight years. Since they moved her to Mountain View."

"She's back at county," I told him. "You can sign up for a video visit through their Web site. They don't allow in-person visits anymore, but if you don't have Wi-Fi, you can go to the jail and they'll set you up in a room with a monitor."

Allen's eyes widened. "Technology," he said. "Stealing a little piece of your soul one megabyte at a time."

"True that," I told him. The new video system was very efficient, and probably terrific for those people who couldn't make the drive to county, but also ridiculously impersonal. Sometimes, inmates and their families needed that extra dose of physical reassurance that a window of Plexiglas could provide and a computer monitor just couldn't.

Candice suddenly seemed to get an idea. "Speaking of video systems, Allen, do you think there's any way there might be a recording of the incident involving Skylar and this guy you threw out of the store from back then?"

Allen's brow lifted. "You know," he said, "there might be. The store is packed with security cameras because the company gets a lot of accident claims and people walk out of here all the time with stuff they don't pay for. I know that the feed is sent to headquarters in Atlanta, and they hold it for ten years or so until the statute of limitations runs out. You might get lucky and get a copy, but you'd be right under the wire, 'cause it's been almost exactly a decade."

"Do you remember the approximate date?" Candice asked, her voice excited.

Allen rubbed the stubble on his chin with his hand. "Well, let's see. It was about two weeks before Noah was murdered, which would've made it mid-June, and I think it was a Tuesday, Wednesday, or Thursday shift, because back then they had me on that rotation, and I know we weren't busy that day, so it couldn't have been a Saturday—and it probably wasn't a Thursday either, 'cause the closer we get to the weekend, the busier we get, plus inventory comes in on Thursday and I don't remember being busy with that."

Candice had her phone out and was scrolling through it. "Could it have been the fifteenth, sixteenth, or seventeenth of June two thousand four?"

Allen nodded. "Or the week before. I'm pretty sure it was two weeks before Noah was murdered, but I'm not positive."

Candice pocketed her phone. "Thanks, Allen. We'll check it out. You've been a really big help."

We left Allen and headed back inside the Depot. Candice then approached the customer service desk and inquired about a contact to their headquarters, flashing her badge and letting the girl behind the desk know this was a matter of some urgency.

Ten minutes later the manager had helped us navigate the complicated world of HD headquarters, and we had the name of the director of IT, who could assist us with obtaining a copy of the video, and confirmation that HD held on to store surveillance footage for exactly ten years. The director was out when we called, but Candice left him an urgent message, along with her credentials as a consultant to the FBI and a private investigator in Austin. I thought it very clever that she kept dropping the whole "consultant with the Federal Bureau of Investigation . . ." line. It opened doors, and at the moment I wasn't too worried about getting into trouble using the street cred.

When we finally piled back into Candice's car, I felt a measure of satisfaction and tense excitement. "Man! If we could get that tape, Candice? That would be a game changer!"

"Don't get your hopes up yet, Sundance," she warned.

"Why not?"

"Because we don't have the tape yet and because we'll have to sift through hours and hours of video to find the two minutes we're looking for. Plus, once we find that section, who's to say there'll be anything usable on it? Surveillance footage captured by cameras from ten years ago isn't like it is today. It's grainy and fuzzy and barely passes for acceptable by current standards. And even if it's crystal clear, it's not like we have a name to match it. Or, for that matter, any way to convince the appellate court that what's on the tape is motive for murder."

I crossed my arms and frowned at Candice. "If I was a parade, you would be rain."

She smirked. "I'm just saying that it's too early to get your hopes up. We need a name more than anything else, and the longer we spend trying to find it, the closer we get to our deadline."

"Still, it backs up the theory that there was an encounter that could've motivated someone to take revenge on Skylar," I said.

"True. But what I don't like is that this guy waited two, possibly three weeks to get even with her. I mean, by then he should've cooled down, right?"

"Not really," I said. "Maybe it took a little while to fester. Maybe it took him some time to come up with a plan."

"I'll give you that," Candice said, "but I'm not sure that the appellate court would see it that way. They might view the encounter, wonder the same thing I did, and decide that a crime so heinous would be driven by passion, not cool calculation. Noah wasn't just murdered—he was butchered, and that's not the action of a guy who sits back and waits for an opportunity. Plus, I have to question one thing that keeps really bothering me."

"The knife," I said, knowing that's what she was going to say. It was bothering me too.

"Yep. How the hell did this guy break into the house without waking anybody, or leaving signs of forced entry behind, walk into the kitchen, get the knife from the drawer, head *back out* of the house to the backyard and the window leading to Noah's room, open the window, crawl in without Noah waking up to scream his head off, then, after Skylar fled the room, calmly slip back out the window, close it without leaving a single smudge, *and* put the screen back in? It makes *no* damn sense."

I sighed. She was absolutely right. Much as I tried to make sense of this guy's motive and method, I couldn't. "Only one way to find out how it actually went down," I said.

Candice started the car and began to back out of the space. "What's that?"

"We talk to Slip and get him to tell us," I said.

Candice let out a little laugh. "Love your enthusiasm, Sundance."

"It's how I get through the day," I said.

We headed back to the office, making a detour for a smoothie before we got back to work and checked in with Oscar and brought him up to speed on our progress. He had nothing new to report, unfortunately.

As Candice talked to Oscar on speakerphone, I kept thinking about poor Noah and his life cut so short. I remembered the words Skylar had used to describe her son. That he was outgoing, personable, and kind to humans and animals. He certainly hadn't deserved his fate, and I felt so much sorrow that such a bright light had been so brutally snuffed out.

"You okay?" Candice asked me, and I realized I'd been staring off into space and that she'd hung up with Oscar.

"Yeah. Just thinking about Noah. Seemed like a great little kid, you know?"

"He did," she agreed.

I poked at my super-healthy smoothie with my straw (Candice's idea) and said, "It makes me curious, actually, about whether he mentioned this guy Slip to anyone else."

"What do you mean?"

"Well," I said, sorting through the thought as I spoke. My intuition was buzzing with something, and I needed to talk to work it through. "I can see why he wouldn't have mentioned Slip to his mom after the encounter at Home Depot. I mean, he probably didn't want to upset her again, but what if he'd mentioned it to someone else, like a teacher?"

"It was the summer, remember?" Candice said. "School was out for the year."

"Oh," I said, "that's right." *Buzz, buzz, buzz,* my intuition chimed. Something was there, so I pushed a little more at the line of thought. "But maybe," I said next, "he brought it up with someone else. Like, isn't that the kind of thing you confess to your grandma?" As I said that, I felt a light tingling in my abdomen. I was on to something.

"Maybe," Candice agreed, squinting at me. "You look like you want to go ask her about it."

"I do."

"Intuition buzzing?"

I grinned. "It's like you *know* me."

Candice got up from her chair. "No time like the present," she said. "Give me ten minutes to find Skylar's mom's name and address and we'll roll."

I drove while Candice navigated, or, more accurately, I drove and reacted to Candice's infrequent pointing while she spoke on the phone to various clients and made a second attempt to reach our IT contact at Home Depot headquarters.

Eventually, we pulled onto Westlake Drive, which is a section of town where the houses are ginormous and the property tax bracket is likely in the mid–five figures. I started to feel a little self-conscious driving my fairly new hybrid SUV when every other car that passed me cost more than the entire sum of my college education. At last we pulled up to a grand gray masonry estate (there was no other word for it) and peered down the long drive.

"Skylar's mom lives *here*?"

Candice read the address on the side of one of the pylons at the edge of the drive and said, "The estate belongs to an A. Hudson and, judging by the address I pulled up for Faith Wagner, I think she lives in the guesthouse."

"Where's the guesthouse?"

Candice pointed down the drive to a small pond. On the edge of the pond was a cottage constructed of the same gray masonry as the main house.

"Do you think we can just head up the driveway and park?" I whispered.

"Unless you want to walk from here," Candice said, motioning impatiently with her hand for me to turn into the drive.

"But what if they come out?" I said, still hesitating. Big money intimidates me. And I admit this even though my own sister could probably afford a place like this. Maybe two or three places like this.

"Just freaking drive," Candice said impatiently.

I gripped the wheel and turned onto the estate, creeping down the driveway like I did it every day and being careful not to look toward the main house. I parked next to a gold-colored Volvo and we got out. I kept my keys out just in case a SWAT team of security burst out of the house to chase us off the property, but no one appeared from the main house and I let Candice lead us down the slight hill to the guesthouse.

On the way Candice looped the lanyard holding her FBI ID around her neck and I did the same.

As we stopped on the front step, we heard music from inside. Piano music. Bad piano music. Candice knocked and the music stopped. A moment later the door was opened and a woman in her mid to late sixties, bearing a strong resemblance to Skylar, minus the curly blond hair, stood there peering at us over bright red reading glasses. She was smartly dressed in a steel blue silk blouse and a camel skirt with matching flat-heeled shoes. "Yes?"

Candice tilted the badge hanging from her neck toward the woman and said, "Mrs. Wagner?"

She blinked a few times as she looked from Candice to the badge, then over to me, and down at my badge. "Yes?" she said. "What's this about?"

I couldn't help noticing that Skylar's mother had broken out in a sheen of sweat, and I wondered, what was up with *that*?

Candice introduced us and said, "We'd like to ask you a few questions about your grandson, if we could?"

Mrs. Wagner's lips pressed down in a hard line. "I don't have a grandson," she said, anger erupting in her eyes. Again, I wondered at her reaction.

"I'm so sorry," Candice said, trying to appease her. "I didn't mean to upset you. It's just that we've been investigating Noah Miller's murder, and we've turned up some compelling evidence that we're following up on."

Mrs. Wagner's hands balled into fists. "My *daughter* murdered my grandson, Ms. Fusco. A crime for which she is going to pay the ultimate penalty. I see no reason why you would want to dredge up the most horrible incident of my life now, when it's already too late to alter the outcome."

"Mrs. Wagner," I said gently, trying to get a feel for her energy, "I know you're alarmed by our sudden arrival on your front step, but we've been investigating the murder of your grandson, operating under the premise that your daughter committed the crime, only to discover that there are several inconsistencies in the evidence presented at court that blow giant holes through that theory. All we want is the truth, ma'am. And we believe you could hold vital information." When Skylar's mother continued to stare angrily at me, I added, "Ma'am. What if Skylar *didn't* do it? Wouldn't that be worth discovering before it's too late?"

She let out a breath and shook her head. "My daughter is a master manipulator, Ms. Cooper. You've obviously talked to her, and she's convinced you that she's innocent."

"No," Candice was quick to say. "We examined the evidence, ma'am, and *that* alone was enough to convince us."

"What evidence?" she demanded.

I found it really unsettling that a mother could be so cold and callous toward her own daughter. Then again, my own mother was cut from much the same cloth as this woman. "We think there really was an intruder that night," Candice said patiently. "And we have multiple witnesses that suggest he might've been out to hurt your daughter *and* her son. We're currently waiting on video surveillance, in fact, to confirm that he threatened her."

Candice was fibbing a lot here, but I didn't care. We had to get past the ice wall this woman was putting up if we were going to find out if Noah had spoken to her about Slip.

For her part, Mrs. Wagner seemed to mull that all over. Finally she said, "I don't know how I can help. I certainly never witnessed my daughter or my grandson being threatened."

"We know," I said. "But maybe Noah talked to you about a particular incident that took place at a Home Depot about two weeks before he was murdered?"

Mrs. Wagner's eyes widened slightly in a flash of recognition, but she seemed to catch herself, and then her features smoothed out, as if she were suddenly the most calm and reasonable person you'd ever want to meet. "I don't recall any such conversation," she said.

My radar detector went off like a tornado warning siren. "I see," I said, narrowing my own eyes. I wanted her to read my disbelief. She started sweating again. "So he never told you about the guy in the hardware store? The welder who knew all about tools?"

"No," she said, a bit too quickly.

I glanced at Candice and shook my head, again not even trying to hide my disbelief. "Mrs. Wagner," Candice tried. "You *do* know that your daughter will quite likely be put to death next week, right? And that will happen because she's been unjustly convicted of the crime of murdering her own son."

"It's in the court's hands," she said, turning up her palms as if there weren't anything to be done about it.

"All right, then," Candice said.

My best friend turned to leave, but anger got the better of me and I stepped threateningly close to Skylar's mother. "I don't know what you're hiding, Faith Wagner, but I sure as hell intend to find out. And when I clear your daughter of the charges, I'm going to make sure that she knows her own mother was willing to let her die rather than offer us one simple kernel of truth."

I then looked her up and down to show her she wasn't all that, and turned to go, marching right past a gaping Candice on the way.

"Well, that went well," Candice said as we got in the car. Mrs. Wagner was still glaring hard at us and I was tempted to flip her the bird, but held myself in check. Barely. And only because she wasn't worth the quarter.

Her attitude was just a bit too close to home for me, so I settled for squealing backward out of the space to turn the car and screeching the tires on the tidy concrete as we zipped out of the drive.

"Why do you think she won't cooperate?" Candice asked after a bit of protracted silence (during which I fumed and mentally doubled the amount in my swear jar).

"There are two reasons why people usually withhold information," I said angrily. "The first is because they think it'll get them in trouble. The second is because they have something to gain by keeping whatever it is a secret."

"Which one do you think it is with Wagner?"

I shrugged. "Possibly both. She was awfully nervous when we started flashing our badges. That tells me she's broken the law. Her energy reads as a cold, calculating narcissist, so it wouldn't surprise me that she's working some angle that puts her just this side of what's legal. Also, the way her features smoothed out—I mean, did you *see* that? It was practiced. Once she regained her composure, she fell into the act of portraying herself as some sort of exemplary citizen. And the joke is that any idiot can see right through her!"

"You're getting a little worked up, Sundance," Candice said, eyeing the road nervously. "Maybe I should drive?"

I ignored her. "What really sticks in my craw is that she got up there on that witness stand and testified *against* Skylar. She had to have known that her testimony could've swayed the outcome! I mean, the prosecution was asking for the death penalty! But what Wagner doesn't get, what she is truly too dense to understand, is that juries can see right through shit like that. They probably looked at Skylar and thought, yeah, this woman murdered her son, but no wonder she's a little off. I mean, have you seen *the mother*?"

"Sundance?"

"What?" I snapped. I was so angry, and in the back of my mind I knew I wasn't just mad at Faith Wagner, which made me even *more* mad.

"You're drifting in and out of the lane and if you get any closer to the car in front of you, I will have to crawl into the backseat just to get some legroom."

I took a deep breath and exhaled slowly while easing off the gas pedal. "Sorry."

"Totally okay," Candice assured me, like she fully understood exactly where all that pent-up anger came from. And I knew for a fact she did.

After a while of more quiet (which I spent breathing deeply and obeying every rule of the road), I said, "Where to?"

Before answering, Candice rummaged around in her purse, pulled up her notes, flipped through the pages, and finally rattled off an address. "Head back toward Lamar," she instructed. "I'll let you know how far down it is."

"What's the address?" I asked.

"Central office for the Department of Social Services. We have an appointment to meet with Diane Pickett."

My memory keyed in on the last name from one of the articles I'd read covering Skylar's trial. "Skylar's social worker?" I guessed.

"Yep. She's still working in that capacity."

"Wow," I said. "I would've thought that Skylar's verdict would've been political suicide for Pickett."

"I'm sure it wasn't pretty," Candice said. When a social worker was involved in the case of a dead kid, he or she always got some of the blame. "Still, she's still there, and she's willing to meet with us."

"When did you contact her?"

"I sent her an e-mail this morning. She just replied back."

"That's some nice timing," I mused.

"We've had a bit of that on our side this whole case—have you noticed?"

I smiled sideways. "It's like someone up there doesn't want Skylar to die for the wrongful conviction of her son's murder."

"Yep," Candice agreed.

We got to Pickett's office about fifteen minutes later and walked up two flights of stairs (the elevator was out) to come through the doors into a sea of misery. The place was filled with people, almost exclusively women and children. Not one smile among them. Beyond the front waiting area was a vast room of short cubicles, all of them rather similar: occupied by women, each sitting in front of a computer at a desk with enough paper and files stacked on top to threaten its stability. Next to each casually dressed social worker was another woman outfitted modestly and, almost as a rule, at least two to three children gathered around her. Kids outnumbered the adults in here three to one.

Candice and I sort of stiffened as we came through the door in our spiffy professional wear with designer purses and full stomachs. All eyes turned to us. Judgments likely followed.

Candice stepped forward to a small reception area, where most newcomers were prompted to take a number from a red ticket dispenser by the door. Candice leaned forward, displayed her badge, and whispered something to the woman behind the desk, who then nodded, picked up her phone, dialed, and motioned for Candice to head back to the waiting area.

We didn't sit down, even though there were a few empty chairs. I think we were too ashamed. There's nothing like staring poverty and hardship in the face to make you think about how good you have it, and how little you've been appreciating it. The watch Dutch had given me just the other day felt heavy on my wrist, and I covered it with my palm self-consciously.

We stood like that, not speaking, for about a half hour before a woman in her mid to late fifties, with gray shoulder-length hair, round features, and a pleasant smile, came out from the area behind the counter and headed straight for us. "Candice?" she asked me. I pointed to my left, and the woman I assumed was Diane Pickett swiveled slightly to greet my partner.

"Thank you for seeing us, Diane," Candice said, extending her hand.

Diane took it and offered us a warm smile. After I was introduced, Diane said, "Would you mind if we talked on the go? I only get a half hour for lunch and it'll be better if I don't cut into my time on the clock."

"Of course," Candice said quickly. No way did either of us want to take Diane's time away from the people who really needed her.

We went out the door and down the stairs, and as we only had a half hour to talk, Candice got right to it. "As I said in my e-mail, we're working on Skylar Miller's appeal, and we'd like to get your take on a few things, if we could."

"That poor girl," Diane said. "I've been watching the news, waiting for any word on the appeal. Does she have a chance?"

"There's always a chance," Candice said.

"I still have nightmares about it," Diane said. "In this line of work you always wonder if you could've done something to prevent harm to a child, but I've gone over and over and over every single one of my interactions with Noah and Skylar, and there was never a hint of anything but love and affection between them. She was a good mother. She was. Hell, she was a good *person*."

"We think so too," I said.

Diane beamed at me. Her loyalty to Skylar was apparent. "How can I help?" she asked as we came out into the bright sunshine and heat of the day.

"We're curious about a few things," Candice said. "First, I know you had regular meetings with Noah and Skylar, correct?"

"Once a month plus the odd surprise visit to the home," she told me. "It was part of the terms of Skylar's custody agreement and her parole."

"Did you by any chance talk to Noah in the two weeks prior to his murder?" I asked, hoping that maybe Noah had mentioned something about Slip to her.

"No," she said sadly. "Skylar and Noah were scheduled to see me the week after. She'd been doing so good with him too."

"Can you talk a little about your history with her?" I asked. I felt intuitively that Diane had information for us that we'd need, somehow.

"Sure," she said, pointing down the street to the sign of a deli. "We're heading there, by the way." We adjusted our pace slightly to a less hurried walk and Diane told us about Skylar. "She was assigned to me right out of jail," she said. "The first thing she said to me at our introductory meeting was that she wanted to get her son back. I told her she'd never get him back. I mean, I wanted to be honest with her. Her ex-husband came from money; she'd spent the last fourteen months in jail. . . . I told her she'd be lucky to get supervised visitation, and she didn't even blink. She said that if all she ever got was supervised visitation, then she'd take it as the chance to show Noah just how much he meant to her."

"Pretty awesome attitude," Candice said.

Diane nodded. "That was Skylar. She did everything I and the court asked her. She went through the twelve steps, got her medal, took it slow with Noah, got to know him and let him know her, and they bonded. Most of the women I work with truly love their children, but Skylar and Noah were especially close. They seemed to understand each other in a way that was so beautiful to watch. She was so patient with him, so fascinated by how his mind worked, what he came up with, how he looked at life."

"What was Chris like?" I asked.

"Chris Miller?" Diane said. She seemed to think about her answer before giving it. "He lived for that boy too. He just couldn't stand Skylar. I think he was worried that she'd end up back on the bottle, and he didn't want to see his son heartbroken. He fought really hard against her gaining any kind of physical custody, and in the end, it backfired on him.

"When they went to court to revisit custody, he and his dad

came in with their high-powered attorney and they basically stunk up the court with their derision for all that Skylar had done to get her life back, and the judge didn't like it."

"The judge granted Skylar custody out of spite?" I asked.

Diane laughed. "No. But she had a choice of shared physical custody or solely granting it to Skylar, and after hearing from Noah, well, she made the right choice."

"Noah didn't get on with his dad?" I asked.

"Oh, no, he loved his dad. He just really didn't like his grand-mother. Skylar's mom was babysitting Noah while Chris was at work, and Chris worked long hours."

"We just came from Faith Wagner's house," Candice told her. "She's a real piece of work."

"Oh, then you caught her on a good day?" Diane chuckled as we arrived at the deli and got in line. "Faith never gave anybody the warm fuzzies."

We stepped forward to the counter and ordered our sand-wiches, were given a number, and took a seat at a table to wait for our lunch.

"How did Chris take the judge's decision?" I asked while we sipped on our drinks.

"He seemed upset but not as upset as his father. Grant Miller threw a fit in the courtroom, yelled at the judge, and nearly got his butt tossed in jail for contempt. He couldn't believe the deci-sion, and you could tell he wasn't a guy who liked to lose. He even yelled at Chris like it was his fault. That guy was a piece of work too."

"Wait," I said, making room for the delivery of our sandwiches. "We heard that Grant and his wife were pleased by Skylar's turn-around and even offered to have Skylar put on a trust he'd set up for his grandson."

"Oh, that," Diane said. "That came almost a year after she got custody. I think it was Skylar. She didn't let Grant's outburst in court get to her, and she told me that she'd been in contact with the Millers through e-mail in the days after the custody hearing, promising them that anytime they wanted to visit with Noah, they could. She didn't want anything to change about Noah's life except to provide him with the constant love he deserved from a repentant mother.

"The tactic worked. The Millers calmed down, saw their grandson whenever they wanted, and actually grew to respect Skylar's efforts to make something of herself. When she got accepted into UT's undergrad physical therapy program, which is no easy program to get into, mind you, they actually sent her a laptop."

"She was headed to UT?" I asked. That was new information.

"She was," Diane said sadly. "She'd wanted to specialize in pediatric therapy—helping kids recover from injury or genetic limitations was what she dreamed about doing. She never got there, obviously. Anyway, along with the laptop, Skylar told me they'd also sent her the paperwork on the trust as their way of letting her know that they were supporting her as their grandson's mother and primary caregiver. What they didn't understand was that she didn't want anything to do with their money. They'd used it to try to control her in the past, and she didn't want that type of relationship with them, so she ignored it. I think the fact that she never signed it was the sole reason it wasn't used against her in court, not that it mattered. In my opinion, the jury found her guilty the moment they heard she was once an addict."

I finished my sandwich and sighed. It was all so sad. How were we going to overcome all that'd been taken away from Skylar? "Can I ask you something personal, Diane?" I said.

"Depends on what it is," she replied, but she smiled in a way that told me she was teasing.

"How did you avoid the political fallout from Skylar's conviction?"

All the humor in her smile drained away. "It was bad," she said. "For a lot of years it was bad. My job was somewhat protected by the union, but that didn't stop my boss from doing everything she could to get me to select out, as they say. I was assigned the worst cases in the worst areas, but I hung in there because of Skylar. I *knew* she hadn't murdered Noah. And because I'd helped her get her life back in the days up until it was ripped away from her, I also knew I'd made a difference to her and to Noah, and if in those days she hadn't quit, I didn't think I could either. Still, I've often found it so odd that, because of my relationship to Skylar Miller, I've been both lifted up and pulled under, but I'll never let myself drown. Like Dory, I'm just going to keep swimming."

We let Diane get back to work and headed back to the office. Candice wanted to check in with the guy at Home Depot's headquarters and she also commented that she wanted to check into Faith Wagner's income tax records.

When I asked her why, she replied, "It's like you said: She's either hiding something or has something to gain, and I think you're right that it could be both."

I pulled up to the curb to let Candice out at our office, and before she got out, I told her that I had something of my own to check out. "What's that?" she asked.

"It's not anything to do with Skylar," I assured her. "It's for the case I got from Dioli. I still can't believe that idiot had Cheng arrested. I want to swing by the dry cleaner's before they close and check the place out with my radar."

"You want company for that?" Candice asked me.

"Nah. I'm not gonna ask any questions. I'm just gonna go there, take some clothes in, posing as a customer, and feel out the ether."

"You have clothes to take to the dry cleaner?"

I threw a thumb toward the backseat. "Dutch's shirts. I was supposed to take them in for him two weeks ago, but I've been forgetting. Poor guy keeps looking for his favorite blue shirt and I keep lying and telling him I don't know where it is."

Candice twisted to look into the backseat and said, "Being married to you is a real picnic, ain't it, Sundance?"

I offered her my most winning smile. "The good times just keep on rollin'."

Chapter Twelve

．．．

After dropping Candice off, I headed north and west to the address of the dry cleaner's I'd lifted from the file on Tuyen Pham. I wasn't at all sure what I'd find, but my intuition was sending me there, either because I'd pick up a valuable clue or because Dutch was about to finally figure out that I'd been driving around with his dirty shirts in the back of my car for two weeks. My crew—the spirit guides tasked with looking out for me—were all about keeping my marriage intact.

The dry cleaning business itself was a pleasant enough looking place: a stand-alone building with parking in the rear and a cute dark green facade with a window box full of flowers and a little bench outside. The presentation gave it a homey look.

Most dry-cleaning places I'd been to were far more utilitarian, and I was just a teensy bit thrown by the fact that the outer appearance of this one was so charming. I think I might've been expecting something more sinister.

Still, I shrugged it off, got out all of Dutch's shirts (dropped one or two on the ground while I was at it), and headed down the long drive toward the front door. As I rounded the corner to go inside, I came to an abrupt halt. Heading in just in front of me was none other than Don Corzo, carrying a toolbox and wearing a blue work shirt.

He smiled pleasantly at me as he pushed open the door, and I gasped as I recognized him. "Holy shit!" I squeaked. (No way does swearing at the sight of a serial killer cost me a quarter.)

Corzo suddenly paused midway through the door.

I gripped Dutch's laundry.

Corzo dipped his head back out to give me another look.

I put two and two, and two, and two, together, which in my crazy math world added up to four dead girls.

Corzo's eyes narrowed.

I stood there frozen, still adding, dividing, and multiplying, all synapses firing at once as questions with obvious answers bulleted through my mind. Hadn't I read in Wendy McLain's file that she'd once lived above a dry cleaner's? And hadn't one of the photos of Donna Andrews's murder scene been in the parking lot of a strip mall with a dry cleaner's in the background? Didn't the air-conditioning units at most dry cleaning places run continuously because of the heat produced by the dryers? They'd break down a lot, wouldn't they?

Corzo began to ease back out of the doorway.

My head pivoted as if turned by an unseen force to look across the street. The restaurant where Misty Hartnet had worked as a waitress was in plain sight three blocks down.

Out of the corner of my eye I saw Corzo take a slow step in my direction.

Turning my attention back, I looked at the storefront I stood in front of. Tuyen Pham had worked here. Tuyen Pham had been strangled and left in a park, just like the other three girls, only her body had been hidden, because, knowing we were onto him, her killer had changed up his pattern.

Corzo took another slow step toward me.

I stared at him.

He inched forward.

I blinked. And blinked again.

He bared his teeth. He knew I knew. And then he dropped his toolbox, raised his hands, and lunged.

I threw all of Dutch's shirts in his face. Corzo's outstretched arms blocked the laundry, but some of the shirts landed over his head. Instead of running, I took a page out of the self-defense course Candice had been teaching me and reached forward to grab Corzo's collar, simultaneously sticking my leg out and pulling him forcefully forward while twisting my upper body to the side.

His legs tripped over mine and he and the laundry went sprawling to the ground. I then let out a war cry and pounced on his back, jamming my hand into the back of his head and driving his face onto the concrete. The expletive he'd been in the middle of uttering was cut short by a pretty sickening crunch. And still I didn't let up. Driving my knee into his left shoulder, I yanked at his right arm, twisted it behind his back, then switched knees and pulled his left arm back.

It was over in about five seconds.

Also, that's about how long it took to have Agent Cox come to my rescue. "Jesus!" he shouted as he got close enough to help me secure Corzo's hands. "I saw the whole thing!"

The folks inside the dry cleaner's also came pouring out to see what was happening. "We saw it!" one of the women said to Cox. "We saw him try to attack her! And she took that sucker *down*!"

Cox grinned at me. "At least we'll get him on assault," he said to me.

I winked at him. "Nope, Agent Cox, you'll book him on at least one count of *murder*!"

Cox's brow arched. "You know something I don't?"

"He murdered Tuyen Pham. APD has been investigating her case for about eight months. I've got a copy of the murder file in my car, and if you look into it, you'll find some evidence linking Corzo to her murder, but I'm not sure what, and I can't direct you any more than that."

Cox's grin widened as he yanked a dizzy and bloody Corzo to his feet. "That's okay, Cooper. I trust you."

Coming from Cox, that was kind of a big deal.

As it turned out, however, I was absolutely right. Cox and the rest of the Austin bureau descended on the evidence collected by APD in Pham's murder like a group of ninjas. By ten o'clock they had the ultimate prize. The medical examiner had discovered a bit of duct tape on Pham's wrists. As it happened, under a microscope, the slightly frayed ends of the duct tape from Tuyen's wrist had *exactly* matched the slightly frayed ends of a roll discovered in Corzo's trunk. It was found stuffed under the spare tire, in a plastic bag containing a black ski mask, black leather gloves, rope, and directions to Stephanie Snitch's apartment.

I just knew he'd taken a shine to her during the trial.

And, according to a receipt produced by the dry cleaning store's owner, two days before Tuyen had disappeared, Corzo had come to repair the overworked air conditioner.

After giving my statement, I'd gotten the heck out of there; I didn't want to taint the case for trial. As it stood, Corzo's attorney was going to have a hard time explaining why his client had attacked me completely unprovoked.

"How'd it go?" I asked when Dutch came through the door around midnight.

He shuffled over to me, looking exhausted but also a bit elated. "We've got him solid for Tuyen Pham. The duct tape alone could nail him, but we also had our crime lab sift through the trash bags collected from where Pham's body was found, and you'll never guess what they found."

A white flower blossomed in my mind's eye. "The white carnation?" I asked. It was a trademark of Corzo's, and I was surprised that he'd been dumb enough to leave it near Pham's body. But then, he was an arrogant son of a bitch.

Dutch pointed a finger gun at me. "Bingo," he said. "I'm not surprised APD missed it," he added. "By the time they found the body, the flower had dried up and wasn't recognizable amid the other flora."

"That'll connect him to the other three girls," I said, with a satisfied smile.

"It will, but we also have a link that's even stronger in the Misty Hartnet case. As you know, she was found with duct tape residue on both wrists, and Oscar says he swears one of the trash bags we collected from the scene had a bit of tape in it. He's having the crime guys request it from storage and go back to look for the duct tape in the morning."

"I thought Oscar was on vacation."

"He heard we nabbed Corzo for attacking you and came down to help us process the evidence we yanked from APD on Pham."

Dutch then laid out the rest of the incriminating evidence found on Corzo, including the stuff found in his trunk, the map to Stephanie Snitch's house, and a photo of Tuyen coming out of the dry cleaner's, which was taped under the liner in the back of his trunk along with a photo of my friend Stephanie. "I don't know where he hid all that stuff when we checked his vehicle six months ago, but he's pretty stupid to be carrying it around, knowing we were on to him," Dutch said.

"He got cocky," I said, feeling it in my gut. "After the mistrial, he figured he was untouchable. Add to that the news story that Len Chen Cheng was arrested by APD for Pham's murder, and he probably would've been on his way to Stephanie Snitch's house within the week."

Dutch rubbed his eyes. "We called her, you know."

"You did?"

My hubby yawned. "Yeah. Wanted her to know just in case Corzo has a sidekick we haven't heard about."

"He doesn't," I said. I'd felt out Corzo's energy so many times that I was certain he worked alone.

"Yeah, well, maybe we also wanted to rub it in a little. She cost us our first case, and we wanted her to know she'd been marked as a target by the very serial killer she'd helped to walk."

"Ah. How'd she take it?"

"Not well."

"Shocker."

"We're all still reeling down at the bureau."

I chuckled and shook my head. "The bitch."

"That'll cost you a quarter," Dutch kidded, wrapping an arm around me.

"Worth it."

"Yeah, I know," he said, leaning over to nuzzle my neck. "Which is why I'll sponsor it. In fact, if you search my pocket, I'm pretty sure you'll find a roll of quarters. Or I'm just happy to see you."

As it turned out, Dutch was very, *very* happy to see me. We spent the night cuddled together, enjoying the high of putting another bad guy behind bars.

The next day Oscar called me before I'd even finished my coffee to say, "The buyers' financing on that house fell through!"

"Quelle surprise," I said flatly.

"We're going to submit my offer this morning."

"Drop your price by five grand, Oscar," I said to him. "No, wait. Drop it by ten."

"But Bonnie told me in this market, it might be smarter to offer close to asking."

"See, now, that's why I sent you to Bonnie, because she's smart and she knows her stuff. But as I'm currently sitting here, feeling out the ether, I can see that your offer is a smidge high and you can safely drop it by five grand and still have it snatched up. Trust me, honey. You'll get it."

"Thanks, Cooper," Oscar said, excitement in his voice. "I'll call you back!"

"Of that I'm sure," I said, stifling a yawn as I hung up with him. A sound rumbled out from the bathroom. Dutch was in the shower. Singing. Which he often did after showing me his roll of quarters. It'd be sweet if my adorable husband could carry a tune. Ah well. He had other "attributes."

While I was wistfully thinking on those very attributes, there came a knock at our front door. I cinched up my robe and padded out through the living room to answer it. Candice stood there looking so put together it made you want to hate her. "*Why* do you *always* have to look so gorgeous?" I said, blocking her way into my home.

She arched an eyebrow. "It's a gift?"

I grunted and stepped aside. "It's not fair, ya know."

"Life never is, honey." Candice gave my arm a gentle squeeze as she crossed the threshold.

I poured her a cup of coffee and told her all about my encounter with Corzo. She'd no doubt heard it from Brice, but she still wanted to hear it from me too.

"Brice was the one on the call to Snitch," Candice confided

when I was done. "He flat out told her she should apologize to you, because you'd pretty much saved her life."

"Really?" I said. "Brice actually said that?"

"He did."

"What'd she say?"

"That she'd think about it."

I rolled my eyes. Hell would freeze before I ever got an apology from Stephanie Snitch. Which was fine, because if she apologized, then I'd have to accept it, and I sorta liked being mad at her.

Changing the subject, I said, "Did you come over here to tell me that? Or is there something else you can update me on? Like maybe the video footage from Home Depot came in?"

Candice lifted her mug in a silent toast. "That radar of yours never quits, does it?"

"Not on a case like this. How many hours of footage is there to go over?"

"Three cameras from three different angles covering paint and tools for roughly a five-hour period from eight a.m. to one p.m. for six days brings it to roughly ninety hours of footage."

"Wait, I thought Allen said it was between nine and noon?"

"He did. I added an hour on each end to be thorough, and I requested the footage from June fifteenth, sixteenth, and seventeenth of two thousand four, and the week before, just to cover our bases. I figure we can start with the week of the fifteenth, and if we have to go back a week, at least we'll have the footage."

I groaned. "That's still gonna take us forever."

"You can fast-forward through a lot of it," she said.

"Wait, *I* can fast-forward through it? What about you?"

"I'm still working on figuring out what Faith Wagner is hiding."

"Turn up anything interesting?"

"Mostly I'm turning up nothing, which is the most interesting thing of all."

"Why is turning up nothing interesting?" I asked, refilling Candice's cup from the carafe on the table.

"Because she's living pretty high on the hog for someone whose tax returns suggest she couldn't afford more than a cheap one-room studio."

"So how is she paying the rent?" I said, getting where Candice was headed. "Benefactor?"

"That's my thinking."

"Landlord?" I asked next, remembering the great big house next door to Faith Wagner's cottage.

"Alicia Hudson," Candice said. I assumed she'd had time the day before to at least figure that much out. "She's worth big bucks. Big. But what her connection to Faith is, I can't figure out. Skylar's dad passed away in early two thousand. He'd divorced Faith years before, and didn't leave her any money as far as I could tell. She married three more times, and was most recently divorced in two thousand six. What's interesting about the timing is that she filed for divorce from husband number four the day after her daughter was convicted of murdering Noah."

"Interesting," I agreed. "But what does it mean?"

"Don't know. Yet. Anyway, from what I can tell, she's never worked. She just keeps marrying these guys and they keep divorcing her, which is no surprise, because, well, we've met her and found her company to be as delightful as they likely did."

"Word," I said, holding out my fist. Candice bumped it with hers.

"I have a theory, but I can't prove it," she said next.

"What's the theory?"

"I think that Chris is giving her money."

"Didn't she live with him at some point?" I asked.

"She did," Candice said. "She lived with her ex-son-in-law on and off in between husbands from 'ninety-eight through two thousand three. When Chris lost physical custody of Noah, he sure didn't need her hanging around, so she moved in with the next guy she married and got divorced from in 'oh-six."

"Did she maybe get some money from any of her divorces?" I asked, trying to piece together the threads.

Candice made a puffing sound. "Not enough to live on. In my check through public records, she was awarded a total of a hundred grand."

"That's not chump change," I argued.

"Over the past twenty-five years?" Candice countered.

"Oh," I said. "I stand corrected."

"Yeah. So, other than a monthly five-hundred-dollar stipend from Skylar's father's pension, she's earning no income that I can find."

"So what's she living off of?"

"I think Chris is keeping her afloat."

"For what reason, though?"

Candice shrugged a shoulder. "He's got big money and she did him a favor."

"What favor?"

"She sent her daughter to the needle for murdering his son."

"You think he put her up to her testimony against Skylar?"

Candice tapped the table. "I do. I mean, if you think your ex had killed your kid after taking him away, wouldn't you want a little revenge?"

I thought on that. "Didn't Allen say that Chris had been going off about Skylar at Noah's funeral?"

"He did," Candice said.

"Okay, so how does knowing any of this help Skylar's appeal?"

"It shows prejudice and perjury," Candice said. "And it might help to show the appellate court, at the very least, that the death sentence imposed by the presiding judge was a little harsh, given that Skylar's mother was enticed to lie on the witness stand as an act of revenge on the part of Noah's father. It might not be enough to get Skylar a new trial, but if it saves her life, it'll also buy us time."

I frowned. "That sounds like a long shot."

"All we've got left are long shots, Sundance."

"Okay, so what do we do? Go see Chris?"

Candice smiled in that way that said she was way ahead of me. "I already called Oscar. He's heading there after he stops off at his Realtor's to sign his papers."

"We're not going?"

"If you were Chris Miller, an angry white man who's had his whole world taken down by a woman, who would you rather talk to? Us? Or Oscar?"

"That sounds like a rhetorical question."

Candice pointed her finger at me and made a clicking sound with her tongue.

At that moment Dutch came out, wearing only a towel around his waist and a glistening sheen from the shower. Candice pretended to avert her eyes while subtly sneaking peeks at my hubby's exquisite physique.

"Morning!" he said, grabbing a cup from the cupboard.

"Uh . . . good morning," Candice said, dipping her chin.

"Hey, honey," I said, enjoying his appearance very much.

Dutch poured himself a cup of coffee from the carafe, winked at me, and headed back to the bathroom to finish his morning ablutions.

There was a moment of silence before Candice let out a low whistle. "Abigail Cooper, you are one *lucky* bitch."

That made me laugh and laugh.

Several hours later she and I were at the office. I had been fast-forwarding video from one of the cameras pointed to the tool section for what felt like hours. So far I'd fast-forwarded through June 15 and June 16, and I was well on my way to finishing up with June 17 when the time stamp was approaching ten thirty a.m. and suddenly, two individuals, one tall, one short, waddled forward into view. I sat up and smacked the Pause button, freezing the screen. "Holy shit!" I shouted. (Swearing during moments of crime-solving exuberance shouldn't cost me a quarter.)

The inner office intercom on my phone beeped. "You find something?"

"I've got them!" I called, rewinding the tape a little and hitting Play. Candice clicked off and a moment later I heard her heels in the hallway. "Look," I said, pivoting my laptop slightly so she could see.

The image on the screen was a bit fuzzy, but even so, it was clear enough to see a man with white hair and a blond boy walking alongside the tools lining the wall, while he pushed a cart a little ahead of him. The man paused at each tool, pointed to it, and said something to the boy. At one point, the boy spoke and the man reacted as if he was having a hearty laugh. He leaned back and held his sides, and then he put his arm on one of the young man's shoulders. At that moment Skylar Miller appeared in the video. She came charging up the aisle like a mama bear, grabbed Noah's arm, tugged him from the man's grasp, and put her son behind her protectively. She then appeared to be yelling at the man, wagging her finger, until she must've had her say, because she then turned, picked up her son, and hurried away.

I almost stopped the tape at that point, but Candice, who must've read my mind, said, "Let it keep going." We watched the next few seconds and they revealed the man walking down the aisle in the same direction Skylar had gone and peering around the corner. At that moment another figure came into view. Allen. He tapped the guy on the shoulder, got up close and personal to him, and then pointed toward the exit.

The man walked away with his shoulders hunched and his stride angry.

"Bingo," Candice said. Reaching for my sticky-note pad and a pen, she wrote down the time stamp on the video and said, "Come with me and bring the laptop."

I followed behind her and we went back to her office, where she picked up her desk phone and, after checking something on her cell, dialed from the landline. Just a moment later she said, "Hi Gary, it's Candice Fusco from Austin. Listen, that tape you sent us showed us exactly what we were looking for. Thank you so much, but I'm wondering if I could ask you for some additional footage?" There was a pause, then, "Awesome. The footage we need would be from the parking area facing the northwest corner of the lot closest to the exit. And the time stamp would be Thursday, June seventeenth, two thousand four, at approximately ten twenty-eight a.m. Fifteen minutes of footage around that time should be perfect."

There was another pause; then Candice said, "You're the best, Gary. I really appreciate it."

Once she hung up, I said, "That throaty voice you use when you ask for information really turns the boys on, doesn't it?"

She chuckled. "Whatever gets me the info, Sundance."

"Heartbreaker," I mocked.

"It should take about ten minutes," she replied, ignoring me.

"I'm assuming we're trying to see if Skylar was followed out of the parking lot?"

"We are," she said, taking a seat. "And while we wait, let's check in with Oscar."

I took a seat. I'd been so focused on the footage, I'd forgotten all about him. Candice called him on her cell and had the phone on speaker when he answered. "Fuscoooo!" he said, clearly in a good mood. "I was just about to call you."

Candice and I traded smirks. Sure he was. "Abby's here," she told him. "What've you got?"

"Chris Miller wouldn't say much, other than he hopes that Skylar feels the sting of that needle and that she burns in hell."

"Nice guy," I sneered. "Is he taken?"

Oscar ignored me. "He totally blames her for Noah's murder. According to him, Noah would've grown up, gone to college, and lived a great life if only his mom hadn't won custody. He also blames the system, which he says was set up to award custody unfairly to the mother. Even if—and these are his words—'she's a crack-pipe-smoking whore.'"

"Did he mean Skylar?" I asked. "Did she do crack?"

"I think it was more a general statement," Oscar told me. "He was pretty worked up."

"Okay, so he's still convinced she did it," Candice said.

"Oh, yeah."

"Did you ask him about Faith?" Candice said next. "Is he supporting her?"

"He clammed right up when I brought that up."

"Interesting," Candice and I said together.

Oscar laughed. "My guess, he's supporting her, but he's being careful about it because, like you said, Candice, if we found out there was some sort of an agreement between them, it could be used to help Skylar's appeal."

I looked at Candice. "You gotta dig and find the money trail," I told her, feeling a sense of urgency about it.

"Did he say anything else?" I asked, hoping that maybe Oscar had asked him if Chris remembered talking to Noah about the man in Home Depot. I doubted that Chris would tell us if he had, but maybe he'd slip up and say something offhand that would help us.

"Nope. The second I asked him if he was supporting his ex-mother-in-law, he told me to get out of his office and go talk to his attorney."

"Well, that's telling," Candice said. And then she filled him in on the videotape.

"Wow," he said, and then he started to say something else, but he cut off midword and instead said, "That's Bonnie. Can I catch up with you guys later?"

"Sure!" I told him. "And congratulations on the new house!" I knew it was preemptive, but I wanted to be the first to say it. My radar said Bonnie had good news.

Candice's e-mail pinged at that moment and she pulled her laptop forward and clicked to download the footage. Then she clicked on the screen again and swiveled her computer so I could see.

We watched in silence for a few minutes until all of a sudden we saw Skylar appear from the exit and walk over to a nearby station wagon, still holding on to Noah, who appeared to be crying. She spent a few moments soothing him next to the car, and in those moments another figure appeared. "There!" I said, pointing to the lower right-hand corner.

"Yep," Candice agreed.

We watched the guy who called himself Slip move over to a

beat-up pickup a row away and climb in. He sat there, not moving, the whole time Skylar was consoling Noah, putting him into his booster, and buckling him in. She then got into the driver's side and a moment later had pulled out of the space to turn the car to the right and drive up the aisle. A half beat later, Slip had also backed out of his space, turned his car to the right, and drove up his aisle, where he waited for Skylar to pass him; then he turned right and drove after her.

"It was him," I said. "It really was!"

Candice didn't say anything. Instead she rewound the tape, and used her fingers on the keypad to enlarge the image. "Holy Lady Luck!" she said when the image had finished pixelating.

"I can see letters!" I yelled, excited by what was on the screen.

"Is that a *P* or an *R*?" she asked me.

I squinted. *"R,"* I said. "R, W, three . . . or is that a five?"

"Three, I think," Candice said.

I squinted and pushed my face closer to the screen. "I think that's a six and maybe a one?"

"And the last letter is *F*."

"Or *E*," I said.

Candice wrote down several of the letter-and-number combos that the plate might contain, and then she said, "What do you think for make and model of the truck?"

"It's a little small," I said. "I don't think it's an F-one-fifty."

"No way is it an F-one-fifty," she agreed. "Maybe a Chevrolet? They made some smaller-model trucks in the early two thousands."

"Yeah, but that thing looks pretty beat-up. My guess is that it's from the nineties."

Candice jotted herself a note. "I'll do some digging. Now how about the color?"

The footage from the parking area surveillance camera had been in black-and-white. The truck appeared to be of a dark color, but whether it was dark blue, dark green, black, or charcoal, I had no idea. "My guess is that it's navy blue," I said. "I mean, that's a pretty popular color among truck owners."

Candice nodded and wrote that down. I saw that she added black, gray, and brown to the mix, just for good measure. "How long do you think it'll take us to find this truck?"

Candice sat back and pulled her laptop toward her on the desk. "Don't know. But the sooner you let me get cracking on searching for it, the sooner we'll find it."

I saluted her and headed back to my own office, where I promptly called Oscar, who was just about at our office. "So, are you a new homeowner?"

He chuckled. "I am, Cooper."

"Told ya!"

"I close a week after the inspection, assuming the property doesn't have anything big wrong with it."

"It's fine," I assured him.

"I need to go furniture shopping!" he said suddenly.

"Tonight," I promised him. I figured we could do some major damage to his credit cards sometime after five. And, along the way, I was also going to make him swing by a department store so that he could stop looking like a bum on his days off. "First, I need you to come and take a look at the feed we got off the parking lot surveillance video from Home Depot. Slip gets into a truck and looks to be following Skylar and Noah out of the lot. We can see most of the plate, but the make and model of the truck are what's throwing us."

"I'll be there in an hour," he assured me. "I have to head to the bank, and then to Bonnie's office to drop off the check for my earnest money."

I felt anxious. "Get here as soon as you can," I told him.

"You okay?" he said, obviously detecting the impatient tone in my voice.

"I feel like we're running out of time, Oscar."

"Don't worry, Cooper," he said confidently. "Between Candice and me, we'll track this guy down in time."

I heard his words and waited to feel the lightness in my mid-section, which was a surefire way of knowing that what he said would come true. But there was no lightness. Just a subtle flatness that worried me for the rest of the day.

Chapter Thirteen

. . .

It took us two more days to find Slip. Two long, frustrating, irritating, annoying days to finally, *finally* get the right license number on the right make, right model truck in the right color for the right year.

Oscar came up a total bust on the welding-license angle, even going back several years and trying to match a criminal record for B and E to a welder registered with TxDOT. The search was a complete waste of time.

"He must've worked off the grid," Oscar concluded.

"Who would've hired him?"

"Probably cheap builders who were taking advantage of the big construction boom from two thousand two to two thousand seven," Oscar said. "Or he could've faked a certificate."

"If he was breaking and entering, he probably wouldn't have thought twice about creating a fake license," I said.

"Nope."

All our hopes rested on Candice, who worked hard on finding a match to the grainy image of the license plate from the surveillance footage at Home Depot. For the record, finding something like that isn't like it is on TV, where you just press a button and the computer whirs through a million bits of information per second and then blammo! You've got your bad guy!

The way that particular technique works is that you have to enter all the parts you think you got right, and the computer spits out a series of possible matches. In our case that was a few thousand trucks, and we kept trying to narrow our search by eliminating possible matches. In other words, we'd painstakingly select a combination of what the most likely matches might be, like, for example, a black 1992 Mazda pickup with a plate that began RW3, and plug that into the computer to see if it would narrow the choices down to something less than a hundred, but it was like trying to find a needle in a haystack.

After three days of endless effort to get everything to match, we finally found the truck, which was a 1995 GMC Sierra in navy blue with the license tag BW5 36L, and in 2004 it'd been registered to one Doug Gallagher.

We all wanted to celebrate, except that when we pulled up Doug Gallagher's driver's license, it showed an old man with greasy silver hair and at least four chins. "Dammit!" I swore, leaning over Candice's shoulder to look closely at the license.

No one called me out for swearing, because both Oscar and Candice had used the f-bomb. F trumps D every time.

I rubbed my tired eyes and looked again at the spreadsheet we'd been keeping to narrow each successive search. "Where did we go wrong?"

"We didn't," Candice said, her shoulders slumped. We were all exhausted. It was going on ten o'clock and we'd been at it—off and on—since that morning.

"So how come that's not the guy from Home Depot?" I snapped. Did I mention I get grouchy when I don't eat, sleep, or rest after a full day of clients and searching through databases until my head hurts?

Candice wisely ignored my snippy attitude. "I can think of a few reasons," she said. "Either the truck was stolen, borrowed, or sold without the title ever being transferred, or this guy could be a relative."

I let out a bitter sigh. "He doesn't look anything like the description of our suspect."

Oscar reached for a piece of paper and a pen and he wrote down Gallagher's information. "I'll swing by this guy's place in the morning," he said. "Feel him out for info. In the meantime, you two should go home and get some rest. You both look exhausted."

It was Candice's turn to sigh. "Yeah, okay," she said, closing the lid to her laptop. "Come on, Sundance. I'll walk you down to your car."

I stared at both of them in disbelief. I mean, I was crazy tired, but it was freaking Thursday. Thursday! Skylar's final appeal was the following Tuesday and the Hail Mary of passes we'd thrown trying to save her had just gone wildly out-of-bounds. (Impressed by my football metaphor, ain'tcha?)

"There's got to be something more we can do!" I protested. And then, quite unexpectedly, my eyes began to well up and a tear slid down my cheek.

"Abby," Candice said gently, reaching out to take hold of my hand. "Honey, we're doing the best we can. You know we are. But like I told you when we first started this case, you get too attached to the outcome, and, honey, you can't do this with Skylar. The odds are too long here."

More tears leaked down my cheeks. "Candice, we can't just let her die!"

"We're not letting anybody die," she said, rubbing my arm, while Oscar handed me a tissue. "We're all gonna fight to the bitter end, honey. If we go down, it won't be because we didn't give it our all. But there's only so much we can do in a given day. So let's get you home, put you to bed, and fight again tomorrow, okay?"

I bit my lip and tried to stop the floodgates. The image of Doug Gallagher came up in my mind and I couldn't help but feel that we'd wasted nearly three whole days chasing a ghost.

"Maybe this guy will know something," Oscar coaxed. "Maybe he'll point us in the right direction."

I took an unsteady breath and wiped at my cheeks with the tissue. "I'm going with you tomorrow, Oscar."

He studied me. "You sure?"

"I am."

"Okay, Cooper. I'll pick you up here at nine a.m."

"And I'll do a few more searches," Candice added. "I mean, maybe there's another make and model truck that we haven't thought of yet that could fit that description."

I sighed heavily again. "No," I told her. "Don't bother. My gut says it's the right truck." What my gut didn't tell me was why it was registered to the wrong guy.

"Well, okay, then!" Candice said, her voice a bit too enthused. "See? Progress. We haven't hit a dead end yet, Sundance. And this ain't over."

"Yeah, okay," I muttered, getting up from the chair and moving toward the door with my two companions. "Tomorrow, then."

As I came through my front door, I found Dutch on the couch, watching baseball. "Hey, beautiful," he said.

"Hey," I said without an ounce of enthusiasm. Scooping up Tuttle, who'd roused herself from the doggy bed to jump about at my feet, I moved over to the couch and plopped down. Tuttle took that opportunity to cover me in kisses, and then Eggy had to get into the act, and before I knew it, the pups were in some kind of kissing competition and I was laughing.

Sometimes there's nothing better for a bad day than a pair of sweet pups to remind you that you're loved. When I finally got them to settle back down in the doggy beds, I looked up and found Dutch standing over me, holding a bowl. "Eat," he said.

I took the bowl. He'd made his famous spaghetti carbonara. It smelled and tasted like heaven. I ate a few bites and Dutch sat beside me, quietly watching the game. "I'm worried about you," he finally said.

I snorted. "That's nothing new."

"True. But I think you're pushing yourself too much on this case, Edgar."

I ate another two bites before answering him. "I can't look away from this one, Dutch. Skylar Miller is innocent. She is. And if someone doesn't do something, she's gonna die next Tuesday."

"Cal could win the appeal."

"Pigs could also fly." Nothing in the ether had changed about the direction of the appeal. It still felt like Skylar was going to lose, which meant we wouldn't have enough evidence to provide the appellate court with the reasonable conclusion that she might actually be innocent. That's what kept driving me. "It's like I've told you," I said to Dutch. "The future isn't set. It's fluid, but there are some things, some distinct points, within the context of the future that have a certainty to them. Some events simply feel inevitable to me. Most don't, thank God, which means we can alter the future to our advantage when we need to, but there are some things that simply feel like they're headed to a specific destined conclusion, and the only way to alter them is to find the one thing, the one variable, that might alter things."

"The appellate court's decision is going to be nay, eh?" Dutch asked.

"Yes. Skylar and Cal are going to lose."

"So why try so hard?" Dutch said. "I mean, Edgar, if it's inevitable, why are you trying so hard to change it? Why are you killing yourself when you can't win?"

"Because I don't know that I can't win, babe."

"I'm confused."

I thought about how to explain it. "It's like I'm chasing after this speeding train, and this speeding train is headed to a certain destination, and I know I want to beat the train so I can throw a switch and alter the course of the track, but I haven't found the shortcut yet that's going to let me beat the train."

"So you think you can alter the outcome of the appellate court's decision?"

"No, I don't know if I can, but knowing that I might not be able to doesn't mean that I won't find a way if I keep at it. If I keep trying. If we can just find this guy from Home Depot and arrest his ass and bring him in—"

"Whoa, whoa, whoa," Dutch said, twisting on the couch to face me. "Edgar, how are you going to arrest this guy if you find him?"

I blinked. "What do you mean, how am I going to arrest him? I'll have Oscar slap the cuffs on him and bring him in."

"On what charge?"

I looked at him like he was stupid. "Murder."

"Whose?" he said, ignoring the level look I was giving him.

"Noah Mill—" My voice cut off because it suddenly dawned on me that we wouldn't be arresting anybody for Noah's murder, because as far as law enforcement was concerned, that case was solved, closed, and the murderer was about to hang for the crime. "Aw, son of a . . ."

The rest of that sentence cost me a buck fifty, but I didn't really care because if we couldn't bring this Slip guy in for questioning, then he didn't have to talk to us. We had no jurisdiction, no cause, and no case. I set down the bowl of pasta and leaned forward to put my face in my hands. I thought the worst thing that could happen was that we wouldn't be able to find Slip before the appellate hearing. But it wasn't. The worst thing that could happen was that we would find Slip and he'd refuse to say boo to us, and we'd have to let him go without so much as a "We know you did it."

"What're we gonna do?" I moaned.

Dutch put a hand on my back. "Listen," he said. "This guy from the Home Depot store has a criminal record, right?"

"We think so, yeah."

"Then I'm pretty sure that if you're diligent, you can find some kind of parole violation. Assuming he's on parole."

I felt a tingle of lightness in my abdomen and my head snapped up. Grabbing Dutch by the face, I pulled him forward and kissed him passionately. "You are the best husband *ever*!"

He grinned. "Just remember that the next time you get mad at me."

I stroked his cheek. "If I forget, I'm pretty sure you'll remind me."

"What are good husbands for?"

The next morning I was at the office promptly at eight forty-five and Oscar showed up a few minutes late. My radar pinged the moment he walked through my office door wearing his new duds. I felt good news surrounded him. "Look at you," I said, giving him an appreciative up-down.

Oscar puffed his chest out a little. "This is where I remind you that you're a married woman, Cooper."

My smile widened. And then I noticed something on his new shirt. Leaning forward, I saw that it was hair. Dog hair. "Dude," I said, swiping my hand across his shirt to help clean it off. "What's with all the hair?"

Oscar offered me a big ol' cheesy grin. "I went by the new house last night, just to look at it before heading home. The sellers don't live there anymore—they've already moved—so it's not as creepy as you might think. Anyway, I parked at the curb and was sort of just taking in my new place when this woman walks by carrying this white, matted mutt. We got to talking and she said that she was house-sitting for a couple two doors down, and the dog she tells me was a stray from the neighborhood that she's been setting out food for and trying to coax it to trust her so that she could rescue him. She said he finally let her get close enough to grab him, and that she was thinking about taking him to a rescue shelter in the morning.

"Anyway, she starts to ask me if I like dogs, like she might want me to take him, and swear to God, Cooper, what you said to me about getting a dog pops into my head, so before you know it, the little guy's in my car and I'm taking him home, giving him a bath and a big cut of my steak dinner. He cleans up really good, see?" he said, showing me a picture of an adorable little white and tan pup with big brown eyes and perky little ter-rier ears.

I started to laugh. "Oh, Oscar," I said. "He's adorable!"

"Yeah. He's really sweet. I named him Amigo."

"I love it. But you should take him to a vet as soon as you can. Get him checked for heartworm and see if he has a chip."

"I dropped him off about ten minutes ago," Oscar said. "That's why I'm late. They're gonna call me after the vet sees him. I hope he doesn't belong to anybody. I really want to keep him."

And then my radar pinged again. "Did you get her number?" I asked.

Oscar actually blushed. "Whose?"

"The house sitter."

"Uh . . . ," Oscar said. "Not yet. She's there for another week, she told me. She was really cute, though. Think I should ask her out?"

I rolled my eyes. "I *know* you should ask her out." Grabbing my purse, I motioned for us to go.

As we were headed out, Oscar said, "You know, Cooper, I've been around you for a couple of years, and your radar is always really cool to watch in action, but when you point that thing at me, I gotta tell you, it freaks me out how you can just lay out my life like that."

"Yeah?" I said, taking that as a compliment.

"Yeah," he said. "I mean, house, furniture, wardrobe, dog, and maybe a girlfriend. That's the order you told me it would happen, and bam, bam, bam. It's all coming true."

I gave him a heavy-lidded look and took a partial quote out of Candice's book. "You ain't my first rodeo, pardner."

Oscar chuckled. "Yeah, yeah. Anyway, let's go see an old geezer about a truck."

The drive to the address on the driver's license of Doug Gallagher was a bit long. It took us south, well out of Austin proper and into a more rural section of town. We finally pulled up in front of a run-down old house on a fairly sizable plot of land. I let Oscar take the lead as we headed cautiously up to the house. I noticed that my colleague had slipped his badge to his belt, despite what he'd told Candice about not presenting himself as FBI during our investigation. I figured he'd gotten it out because he finally realized what a desperate situation we were in.

Oscar knocked on the door and I stood off to one side. We waited for a bit, and heard some rustling sounds from inside. At last the door was opened by a squat, fat old man wearing nothing more than his tighty-whities.

I averted my eyes. Immediately.

"What?" the old man demanded.

Oscar put a hand on his badge, a subtle yet perfectly clear move to indicate to the old man that he was acting in an official capacity. "Good morning, sir," Oscar said. "Sorry to bother you at an early hour, but I'm looking for Mr. Doug Gallagher."

"Who wants to know?" the old man rasped. His voice was high and reedy. It grated on the nerves as badly as Edith Bunker's. I figured I'd be able to stand it for about ten minutes. Tops.

Oscar introduced us and said that we were looking into a cold case involving a truck matching the description of one registered to him back in 2004.

"My truck?" the old man said, giving himself away. Not that we had any doubts, of course. He matched the photo on his driver's license very well, except for the no-clothes thing. "What kind of trouble that old truck got itself into?"

I had the distinct impression the old man was fishing for information that had less to do with the truck and more with a certain someone he knew who attracted trouble and had maybe borrowed the truck.

Oscar didn't miss a beat. "A series of B and Es, sir. I mean, a series of breaking and enterings."

"I know what B and E stands for, sonny," the old man snapped, working his jaw like he had a bad tooth. Or five. "I don't have that truck anymore, though," he said. "It finally broke down five years ago. We junked it."

"We?" I asked. The old man had given himself away again.

"I," he corrected.

Oscar said, "We don't believe you had anything to do with the series of B and Es, sir. We have surveillance footage of someone else using your truck as a getaway car. But if you know this individual, and won't tell us who it is, then you could be arrested for obstruction."

The old man scowled at Oscar. "You gonna arrest me, then arrest me. I got nothin' to say to you."

I decided to step in. "Sir, I know that coming here and asking you these questions must be upsetting to you, and I'm so sorry." Gallagher turned his watery blue eyes to me and looked me up and down, settling his gaze about midchest. "I also think you might want to protect the young man you lent the truck to, but, sir, the case we're investigating involves the murder of a young boy."

At the mention of this, the old man's gaze snapped up from my chest and he stared at me in shock. "What did you say?"

"A young boy was murdered," I repeated. "And your truck was involved."

Gallagher swore under his breath and twisted his body away from us so that we couldn't see him curse some more. "That son of a bitch," he said. "No-account, lazy, no-good son of a bitch!"

While Gallagher wasn't looking, I bounced my eyebrows at Oscar. I had a feeling we were about to get lucky. "I wasn't in on it," he said when he turned back to me. "I only loaned him the truck."

"Who, sir?" Oscar said.

I held my breath. *Please, oh please, oh please!* I prayed.

"My nephew," he said at last. "Dennis Gallagher. But everybody calls him Denny."

I exhaled. *Yes!*

Oscar wrote down the name in his notebook. "Do you know where Dennis is right now, sir?"

"Probably at work, if he hasn't gotten fired again."

"Where does he work?" I asked.

"He's on a construction crew for Mason Builders. They got a subdivision going up in Buda. You can probably find him there."

"Excellent, sir," Oscar said, extending his hand to shake the old man's.

I shook it too, but in that moment I seriously could have hugged him, tighty-whities and all. It was the first big break we'd had.

"If you wouldn't mind keeping this conversation to yourself," Oscar said to Doug. "We'd appreciate that too." His meaning was clear; he was hoping the old man wouldn't tip off Dennis.

Gallagher waved a hand dismissively. "I want nothin' more to do with that sorry piece of ass," he said. "Kid owes me three grand from five years ago when he skipped his hearing and I lost the bond. He ain't never gonna pay up."

I tried not to let my mounting excitement show. If Gallagher had indeed skipped a hearing five years earlier, it was highly likely he was still on parole, especially given the fact that he'd been in county almost a decade ago for additional crimes. I wanted to thank him for being a repeat offender and making our work of confronting him legitimately so much easier.

Oscar nodded at the old man like he understood exactly how no-account nephews could be. "Thank you, sir," he said. "And sorry to disturb you."

As we turned to leave, Gallagher took one small step forward, as if he had additional information for us. "He told me he never hurt that little kid," he said. "I swear I believed him."

I pressed my lips together to keep from screaming. If only this guy had come forward ten years ago when Skylar was living through the nightmare of the murder of her son and the subsequent arrest and trial, an ordeal so horrible it was a wonder she survived it, he could have spared her and many others so much pain.

Oscar's features became flat. I knew the statement made him angry as well. "Okay, sir," he said.

Gallagher stuck out his chin as if emphasizing that he'd said something true, then turned to head back into the house.

We didn't even wait for the door to close before we were hurrying for the car. We had no time to lose, as we both knew that, at the moment, Doug Gallagher might be willing to cooperate with us by not calling his nephew to warn him about our impending visit, but blood was always thicker than water, and it was best not to let too much time go by before the old man could have second thoughts about keeping his trap shut.

After looking up the location of the construction on Mason Builders' Web site, Oscar drove fast, but not Candice fast, which meant that at the end of the ride I didn't want to leap from the car and kiss the ground, but was still mildly carsick.

We got out of the car and I hung up the phone with Candice. She'd looked into Dennis Gallagher's record, and he had one as long as your arm. Three B and Es, one arrest for possession, and a DWI—the guy was a poster child for bad news getting badder.

His last time in the clink had been five years earlier, and he'd gotten out three years ago. He was currently still on parole. Good news just kept getting gooder.

Oscar and I met at the front of the car and looked around at the dusty terrain dotted by pickup trucks and men wearing construction hats putting up dozens of homes, each in different stages of completion.

We stood side by side for a minute, surveying the scene. "What's the game plan?" I asked.

"We confront him, provoke him, and get him on a parole violation," Oscar replied. Simple. Easy. If only it would go that way.

I nodded in agreement and Oscar motioned for me to follow him. I took it that he also wanted to take the lead when we confronted Dennis. We walked with purpose toward a large trailer set at the front of the group of houses that looked to be the most complete, and Oscar didn't even hesitate to open the door and step inside.

As he and I walked into the trailer, two men, bent over blueprints, looked up in surprise. "Can I help you?" the first guy asked. He was a round man with sagging pants and the red face of someone who's spent too much time in the sun.

Oscar introduced himself as Agent Rodriguez of the Austin FBI, and asked after Dennis Gallagher.

The two men looked startled. "He in some kind of trouble?" the round man asked.

"I'm not at liberty to say, sir. However, I can inform you that if Dennis is doing any welding work on your site, he doesn't currently have a certificate from TxDOT to operate as a welder."

The two men exchanged a look, and the other guy—taller and leaner than the first—said, "I told you I wanted that guy off my crew."

The round man appeared to smolder at both the rebuke and the information. "Let me call him over here," he said, lifting out his cell.

Oscar took a step forward, not to threaten him, but simply to get his attention, and said, "If you would do us a favor and not mention that we're here asking about him, I would appreciate it, sir."

"Will do," the round man said. We waited quietly while the call was made. It was short and to the point, and we all stood around for a few minutes until the door opened and in walked the spitting image of the guy who Skylar had described to us.

Dennis Gallagher was about five-nine, with white blond hair, and piercing blue eyes. His skin wasn't very tan for someone who worked all day in the sun, and I suspected he used liberal amounts of sunscreen to keep from frying up like a raisin.

He also wore a long-sleeved shirt, which was customary with construction crews in the summer in Texas, as it actually kept them cooler. He looked nervous and fidgety when he entered, which was good, because it said he was a guy with things to hide, even from his employers.

"Hey, boss," he said as he entered. "What's up?"

Instead of answering him, the round guy looked at us and said, "We'll leave you to it." He and the other guy then walked to the door, but on their way out, the round guy added, "And, Dennis, after they get done talkin' to you, you can collect your last pay-check. You're fired."

Dennis's head was swiveling back and forth between us and his bosses and he seemed to be trying to take in all the bad news at once. He muttered some faint half-word protests, but nothing co-herent came out as the two men exited, leaving us alone with a child killer.

"Hey, there, Dennis," Oscar said, as if they were old buds.

"Who the hell are you?" he demanded. But it was a weak de-mand, filled with quivering tones and shaking vocal cords.

"Justice," Oscar told him, and I saw his hands clench into fists. Uh-oh.

Dennis seemed to have the same thought because he pivoted quickly and laid a palm on the door handle, but Oscar was much faster, and he sprang forward and threw the weight of his body against the door, while he shouted, "Look out, Cooper! He's got a weapon!"

I dove to the floor, even though I hadn't seen a gun, and covered my head with my hands. Nearby I heard the sounds of a struggle, and perhaps a fist or two connecting with flesh, followed by grunts of pain. And then Dennis's face was level with mine, but squished into the thin carpet.

I uncovered my head and sat up. Oscar had Dennis's hands drawn up behind his back and was snapping them into handcuffs. He then fished through Dennis's pockets, and pulled up a pocketknife, which he tossed to the floor at my feet. "Threatening an FBI agent with a weapon is a federal offense, Dennis," Oscar said loudly.

He then hauled the man up to his feet and pushed him toward the door. He paused in front of it and gave me a meaningful look, then eyed the knife on the floor. I somehow managed to recover from the shock of what'd just gone down, and picked up the knife by the ends, depositing it into my purse before ambling forward to open the door so that Oscar could shove Dennis out and down the steps. Standing very close to the door were the same guys from inside the trailer. They watched us with open mouths and hustled to get out of the way while Oscar forced Dennis to walk in front of him. "Gentlemen," my companion said with a nod as he passed by.

"Thank you for your help," I added as I followed Oscar. They sort of half nodded to us as we left.

Hustling ahead, I got the passenger door of the car open for Dennis, and Oscar did that whole move of pivoting Dennis to stand with his back against the opening, then put a hand on top of his head to basically jackknife him into the car.

"I didn't *do* anything!" Dennis yelled as Oscar closed the door in his face.

Oscar held out his hand and I dug around in my purse to lay the knife in his palm. "Beg to differ with you, buddy," he said, wiggling the closed pocketknife at him through the window.

It was hard, but I managed to quell any protests about what was going down right in front of me. Oscar played by the rules. He *never* broke them. So to see him doing this, to see him basically setting Dennis up, was big, and the fact that somewhere along the way a switch had been thrown that allowed him to compromise his principles like this bothered me.

And to clarify, I wasn't at all upset by the fact that we'd be able to prosecute Gallagher under the false pretense, and hopefully get him to confess to Noah's murder. Hell, I'd place my hand on that Bible and swear before God and man that Dennis Gallagher had produced a knife and had threatened us the second we'd introduced ourselves, and I'd do it without hesitation because the guy had murdered a sweet, innocent little boy, and he was about to play a part in the murder of that boy's mother. If lying about what'd gone down in the trailer was what it took to save her, then I'd do it.

No, what bothered me was what breaking the rules would do to Oscar's conscience. He was a decent, hardworking, honest agent, and I worried that this one incident could be a slippery slope.

Now was probably not the time to talk about it, however, and I settled for hopping in the front seat as Oscar slid in next to me and we headed out.

For most of the forty minutes back to downtown, Dennis yelled, swore, and threw a pretty good hissy fit, demanding to know what he'd done wrong. Where we were taking him. Who we were. Why we were kidnapping him. He lectured us on his civil rights. On the Constitution. On being innocent until proven guilty. He threatened to sue us. To have our badges taken away. To have *us* thrown in jail. He said he knew people. Important people. People who knew people.

For all of the ride back, Oscar said not one single word. I took his lead and kept my trap shut too, but it was disconcerting to have a guy handcuffed in the backseat making such threats when I knew we were the ones currently skirting a fine line with the law.

At last we'd parked in the underground garage of the bureau's downtown office and Oscar yanked Dennis out of the car and pushed him along up the stairs to the office.

As we came through the door, it was interesting. Every person in the large open room stopped talking and looked up. The place got eerily quiet except for Dennis, who started yelling up a really great storm, making his performance in the car look like a modest dress rehearsal.

Dutch came forward out of his office and edged over next to me. "Hey, Edgar," he said quietly. "How's it going?"

"Oh, you know . . ."

"The usual?"

"Yeah. Just another Friday."

"Good, good," he said. Then he motioned with his chin toward Oscar and the prisoner. "What's the story?"

"He's the guy who killed Noah Miller," I said. And then my conscience got the better of me and I carefully added, "And when we confronted him at his work, Oscar believes he threatened us with a pocketknife he carried in his back pocket, which is clearly a direct violation of his parole."

Dutch eyed me with narrowed eyes before turning that same look on Oscar. I couldn't tell if there was disapproval there or acceptance. "I see," he said, his tone giving no further clue as to how he felt about what I'd pretty much revealed.

"It's our only chance to question him about Noah," I said quickly, before he could demand that Oscar cut Dennis loose.

Dutch waved an arm toward the pair just down the aisle from us. "Then by all means."

I blew out a breath and hurried after Oscar, who was turning right toward the only interrogation room we had. (Ours was mostly a cold-case bureau.)

By the time I caught up to them, Oscar had Dennis shoved into a chair. He then made eye contact with me, nodded toward one of the other chairs on the opposite side of the table, and took a seat right across from Dennis.

I slid in next to Oscar and waited for him to begin. Oscar started by clicking on the microphone in the center of the table, took out a small card from his shirt pocket, and began to read Dennis his Miranda rights. Dennis glared hard at him. "What the hell, man?" he said when Oscar was done. "I didn't do nothin'!"

"Oh, but you did, Slip. Didn't you?"

Dennis had gotten himself good and worked up with all that yelling in the car, being handcuffed and hauled off to the bureau offices, and for all of the time since I'd met him, his face had been flushed and sweaty.

The second Oscar called him "Slip," Dennis's face drained of color, and I swear most of the sweat all but evaporated from his skin.

"Naw, man," he said. "Naw. That ain't me, okay?"

"No?" Oscar asked him as he stared him down. "We heard that's what you liked to call yourself, bro. Slip. You slip in and out of homes before anyone knows you're there, right, Slip?"

"Stop callin' me that," Dennis said.

"Why, Slip? You afraid that name might be associated with something you don't want to be known for?"

"Dude, I mean it," Dennis said. "Stop callin' me that."

Oscar shrugged, like maybe he would, maybe he wouldn't. Dennis squirmed in his chair. Some of the color had returned to his cheeks, and I seriously thought he was going to start freaking out again. Especially if Oscar called him Slip one more time.

My radar had been all over Dennis since we'd sat down. I expected to see certain things in his energy, but it was more what I didn't see that puzzled me. So I reached out and put a hand on Oscar's arm, and said, "Dennis, you know we've got you for a parole violation, right?"

"Aw, man! I use that knife for work! And you know it!"

"Oh, I'm not talking about the knife, honey," I said. "I'm talking about the fact that you haven't obtained certification from TxDOT for a welder's license, and you've never applied for one. Which means you forged one. Which means you're guilty of fraud. A direct violation of your parole, and a probable misdemeanor at best."

Dennis swallowed audibly. "I needed a job, man!" he shouted. "And they won't let you get a license if you've got a record!"

"Ah," I said. "Yeah, that is a conundrum."

"A con what?"

"Problem. But see, that's not even the biggest issue we have with you. The biggest issue we have is that we've recently come across some really interesting surveillance video of you stalking a woman and her young son."

Again the flush vanished from Dennis's face. He stared at me with big wide eyes.

"You were driving your uncle's truck that day. You went to Home Depot. You met a young man named Noah. You put your arm around him—something that even eleven years ago was completely inappropriate—and when his mother confronted you and told you to stay away from her son, you made your way out of the store, waited for her to leave the parking lot, and followed her home." The next ten seconds were totally silent. You could've heard a pin drop. Dennis seemed to be barely breathing, except that his lower lip began to tremble a little. "Didn't you?" I asked softly. He pressed his lips together to still the trembling and refused to answer. "You did, Dennis. You sure did. How long did you stalk the mother? How many nights did you drive by and check out the neighborhood so that you could slip in from the open field behind the sub, creep into her backyard, head over to her son's window, and—"

"Lawyer," Dennis said, cutting me off. "Now."

I opened my mouth to ask him if he'd want to reconsider bringing a lawyer into the mix, or if he might like to cooperate, but I didn't even get a sound out before he leaned forward toward the microphone and said, "This is Dennis Gallagher. I'm being held by the FBI. My civil rights are being . . . uh . . . inpinged upon, and I want my fucking lawyer—right now."

Chapter Fourteen

· · ·

We came out of the interrogation room after moving a phone onto the table so Dennis could make his stupid call. Oscar didn't seem rattled, but I was. Big-time. A lawyer would never let Dennis talk. Our last chance for Skylar seemed to be going up in smoke. "I shouldn't have pushed him," I said. "I should've eased into that whole thing more gently, or maybe I just should've let you take the lead and talk. God, I blew it!"

"Hey," Oscar said, putting a steadying hand on my shoulder. "Cooper, you handled that great. Really. I mean, did you see his lip quivering? I thought he was gonna start bawling like a little baby."

"What good does it do us if he clams up, Oscar? We had one chance at this, and I totally blew it."

Dutch appeared in the small hallway off the interrogation room and said, "How'd it go?"

Oscar thumbed toward the door. "He's calling his lawyer."

My husband grunted. "Did he give up anything useful before he lawyered up?"

I shook my head, but Oscar nodded. "The second we talked

about a connection to Noah Miller, he almost broke. There's something there," he said. "And it looks like guilt has been eating away at him for the last ten years."

"His lawyer's never gonna let him admit to anything," I said.

Dutch walked forward. "What else do we have him on?"

Oscar looked Dutch in the eye when he said, "We've got him on attempted assault of a federal officer, and forgery, which isn't federal, but it'll still count against him."

Dutch rubbed his chin. "Well, that's something," he said. "The attempted assault on a Fed is the thing that could put him away for life. It'd be a third strike for him, right?"

"Oh, yeah," Oscar confirmed. "He's facing twenty to life, mandatory."

"Let's hope we don't have to enforce that," Dutch said.

Oscar was quiet for a moment, and then he said, "Yes, sir."

I stared at the floor and Dutch shifted subtly on his feet to move a little closer to me. "I'll call Matt. Get him down here to talk him into leaning on Dennis's attorney. We can hold him on the assault charge and hope he wants to cut a deal. I don't know if Matt is gonna want to make a deal for information involving a state case that's already been adjudicated, but we just handed him a major win on the Corzo case, so he might be willing to do us this favor."

"Thanks, honey," I said to Dutch.

He reached out and took my hand. "We'll figure this out, Edgar," he said. "Don't lose hope."

Matt showed up before Dennis's lawyer, about the same time Candice did, and Dutch, Oscar, Candice, myself, and Matt all gathered in the conference room to discuss the case.

About midway through, Brice also joined us, and other than a nod to his wife, he didn't interrupt as he took his chair and sat quietly while I finished telling Matt about Skylar and Noah Miller.

It took a bit of time to go through it all, but I made my argument by laying out all that Oscar, Candice, and I had discovered in just a week of investigating the case, displaying the photos from the crime scene, and the photos Oscar and I had taken, and Candice had even brought along her laptop showing the video of Dennis following Skylar from the Home Depot parking lot.

I ended by telling Matt that when we'd confronted Doug Gallagher—Dennis's uncle—he'd confessed that Dennis had mentioned to him that he'd "never hurt that kid."

"What else could that be but a confession?" I asked rhetorically.

Everyone in the room wore somber expressions, and Matt appeared to be intrigued but also a bit reserved. "So, let me get this straight," he said. "You want me to press Gallagher's attorney into making a deal on the federal charge if he'll confess to murdering the little kid?"

"No," I said quickly. "We just want him to tell us if he followed Skylar from the Home Depot parking lot. There's no way he'll confess to murdering Noah. I'm sure of that. But if we can get him talking and go on the record about that day, then we can present him as an alternate suspect that the APD refused to investigate. And we can have Wayne Babson give us his witness statement about Gallagher's confession to him at county, and that he'd gone and told Dioli about Gallagher, and that Dioli refused to even look into it."

"Still," Matt said. "You're asking me to push for information on a case where we have absolutely *no* jurisdiction. A case that has already been adjudicated, and where the defendant was found guilty at trial and at all of her appeals thus far. You really want me to play with that kind of fire?"

"Yes," Candice, Oscar, and I all said at once.

"Yes," Dutch said after a moment. I looked at him and hoped he could read the gratitude in my eyes.

"Yes," said Brice after another pause. That caught me by surprise. I hadn't expected Brice to block our efforts, but I certainly hadn't expected him to help sway Matt to work with us.

Matt seemed surprised too. "Really, Brice?" he asked. "You want your neck on the line here too?"

"The woman's innocent, Matt," Brice said. "I've reviewed the case and the new evidence these three have uncovered. I'm convinced."

My heart rate ticked up and I was filled with a sense of pride to be working for a man like Brice Harrison, who was as principled and decent a man as my husband.

Matt shook his head. "You realize that if we push this, APD and the Travis County prosecutor's office are bound to get royally pissed off."

Brice turned his palms up. *"Que sera, sera."*

Matt stared hard at Brice. "You need to really think on this, my friend," he said. "You guys are a fairly small division. Dallas, Houston, and San Antonio have triple the guys you have and APD knows that you're fairly small-time. APD also outnumbers you by at least a hundred to one. If you get a case that you need APD's assist on, they could make life hard for you."

Brice leaned forward and put his elbows on the table. "Matt," he said firmly. "If the woman wasn't down to her last appeal before being put to death, I might not push this, but she didn't do it. And the guy who murdered her little kid and somehow managed to frame her is currently sitting in our interrogation room just waiting for the clock to run out. No way am I gonna let that happen without a fight. No way."

I was so moved by Brice's declaration to stand by us that I

wanted to get up out of my seat and go hug him. But that would've been totally inappropriate. Not to mention unprofessional. Yep. Really not the time, nor the place.

"Aww, to hell with it," I said, getting up from my chair to walk over and briefly hug my boss. He sat there very stiffly for a minute before he gave three pats to my back and said, "Okay, okay, Cooper. Now go sit down."

I wiped a tear, cleared my throat, and headed back to my chair. Candice reached out and took my hand, giving it a big squeeze. "Ya big softy," she whispered with a wink.

And you know what? I think my little emotional display did something to convince Matt, because when I again looked up hopefully to him, he nodded at me. "I guess I owe you one for finally giving us Corzo," he said. "You really pulled that case out of the crapper, Cooper. So, fine. I'll go to bat for you on this, but if we walk in there on the federal assault charge and you even *flinch*, Gallagher's attorney is gonna smell blood in the water, and all leverage you have to motivate Dennis to confess his sins is gonna go down the toilet."

"Yes, sir," Oscar said without batting an eye.

I settled for really vigorous nodding.

Matt stood up then. "Okay. Let's play ball."

Dennis's attorney arrived close to five o'clock. He'd kept us all waiting for several hours and the second he walked in, I swear my skin crawled.

He looked like one of those slick TV attorneys who make their reputation and fortune chasing ambulances. His tan looked fake. His teeth were definitely fake. And I had my suspicions about the mound of hair at the top of his head too. He introduced himself as Jeffrey Bachman. "Not Jeff," he said to us, as if we might dare be tempted by the abbreviated moniker. "Jeff*rey*."

He could've skipped driving that point home. I'm pretty sure the only name we'd use to address him going forward was also two syllables of the "douche" and "bag" variety.

"Now, where is my client?" he demanded.

Oscar showed him to the interrogation room, where we'd made sure to make Dennis quite comfortable with a few bags of chips from the vending machine, a candy bar, and an extra-large slush from Sonic. We'd also made sure to deny him bathroom privileges for the past two hours, ever since it became obvious that his attorney was taking his sweet-ass time.

I had a feeling that Dennis and Jeffrey weren't gonna spend their time together making idle chitchat.

Sure enough, ten minutes later the door opened again and Mr. Douche Bag announced that his client had to use the men's room.

"Sorry," Oscar said, thumbing over his shoulder to the restrooms just down the hall. "They're working on the plumbing. Bathrooms are out of order."

Jeff's eyes narrowed. He was on to us. "Then I must insist that he be allowed to use the building's restroom."

Oscar made a face. "Yeah, sorry about that too, sir. Maintenance has the water turned off in the whole building. You can check if you want. There's a public restroom out the main door and down the hall on the left."

We'd put up an OUT OF ORDER sign and turned off the water leading to that toilet mere minutes before good ol' Jeff had arrived.

Bachman glared at Oscar before turning his steely eyes to me. And that might have been because I was having to work really hard to hide a smile. Clearing my throat, I said, "You know, the sooner we can all sit down to chat, the sooner we'd be inclined to walk your client down to the local gas station, if he's really that bad off."

Jeff checked his watch. "Fine," he said. "Where's your guy?"

"Matt Hayes," I said, referring to our assigned federal prosecutor. "He should be here any second. . . ." I made a point of looking at my watch. "I mean, he was here earlier when we were all waiting for you, but then he had to leave. Hopefully traffic won't be too tied up and he can get back here soon."

There was a noise from inside the interrogation room, and if I had to guess, I'd say that Dennis's bladder might be ready to explode.

Jeff squared his shoulders and said, "While we wait for Hayes, why don't you take my client to that gas station?"

"We could," I said, looking at Oscar and nodding at him in our well-rehearsed scenario.

"But we won't," Oscar said, right on cue. And then we both smiled at Jeffrey and headed out to the front of the office to wait on Matt. (Who was actually down the hall using another public restroom.)

About five minutes later, Matt came in, and became all smiles and confidence when he heard whom Gallagher had hired. "Let's move this along," he said. Oscar and I followed him around the corner.

As we rounded into the hallway again, I saw Candice duck into the conference room. We'd set up a camera system from there to monitor and record the conversation, and I knew that Dutch and Brice would head in as well now that Matt was here and we could begin the negotiations.

Matt knocked once and held the door for us as we filed in. Dennis was hunched forward, as if he was extremely uncomfortable, and judging by the slight shadow at the bottom of his slush cup, indicating he'd drained most of it, I could only imagine.

I took my seat across from him and flipped on the old radar. Matt sat next to me, and Oscar was on the other side. "You guys can't keep me here like this without letting me go to the bathroom!" Dennis yelled. "This is freaking torture! It's cruel and unusual punishment!"

Matt set his hands on the table and laced his fingers together. "I'm sorry, Mr. Gallagher, but the facilities are out of order at the moment. I'm sure we can locate a working restroom for you just as soon as we have a short discussion about the charges you're currently facing."

Dennis's face turned crimson. "I told you I didn't do anything!" Pointing to Oscar, he screamed, *"He's freaking lying!"*

Oscar rolled his eyes convincingly. Matt said, "And yet, this is a federal agent with a sterling reputation. And he has a witness to back him up." Motioning to me, he said, "Miss Cooper? You were there, correct?"

"Yep," I said. "I saw the whole thing."

Dennis kicked at the floor in frustration. "They're *lying*!" he yelled again. "I got a kid now, man! A kid! I'm clean! I don't make trouble no more! I keep my nose clean and I go to my parole officer every freaking week!"

My radar pinged with an odd thought. So odd that I tilted my head as I tried to sort it out. Meanwhile, Je*ff*rey said, "Do you have video of this supposed attack on your agent, Mr. Hayes?"

Matt smiled. "We don't need video, Mr. Bachman. I've got the testimony of an agent with thirteen years of experience and a sterling reputation along with the eyewitness testimony of one of the FBI's most trusted consultants. You, on the other hand, have the word of a convicted felon. A man with a rap sheet as long as my arm, and a man who had recently forged a certificate of license for welding by the Texas Department of Transportation. An offense that, even without the assault charge, could clearly land him back in jail."

"Not by your office," Bachman snapped. "What's your angle here, Hayes? Seriously, why is the FBI rooting around in a state welding-license forgery?"

Matt sat back and crossed his arms. Jeffrey had just played right into his hands. "We're actually not interested in the forgery," he said, staring intently at Dennis. "We're interested in a miscarriage of justice. And you know *exactly* what I'm talking about, Mr. Gallagher."

Bachman's brow furrowed and he looked to his client, whose face had once again gone crimson. A tense silence filled the room and the only sound was the squeak of Dennis's chair as he squirmed in it. At last Bachman, who'd read every subtle sign, said, "Even if my client knew what you were hinting at, I don't. So how about we cut through the bullshit and you tell us what you want to know."

Almost imperceptibly, Matt moved his chin toward me. "We want to know about Skylar Miller," I said directly to Dennis. "We want to know why you told Wayne Babson that you'd gotten even with her. That you'd made sure she'd gotten what she deserved."

Dennis squirmed again. "I wish I'd never said that," he said quietly, his face going crimson yet again, but this time . . . this time the blush was different. If I was a bettin' woman (which I am), I'd say it was rooted in shame.

And that gave me a little encouragement. I leaned forward and said, "Isn't it time, Dennis? Isn't it time to tell the truth and get this burden off your chest?"

He glared at me, but his eyes glazed with mist. I pressed on.

"She doesn't deserve what's happening to her. She's going to *die* on Tuesday for a crime you and I both know she didn't commit. Come on, man. You can't let that happen, can you?"

Dennis's lower lip began to quiver, and indecision wavered in his gaze. And then, his asshole attorney put a hand on his shoulder and said, "Don't say a word, Dennis. Not one word."

I wanted to murder that son of a bitch attorney, but I settled for giving him a look that could freeze molten lava. "I'd like to confer with my client," Bachman said, pointedly turning his head away from me.

Clenching my hands into frustrated fists, I started to get up, but then Matt began speaking. "Of course, counselor," he said. "But before we leave, I'd like to say the following to your client. Dennis, either way you're going to spend the rest of your life in jail. I *will* convict you on the assaulting-a-federal-officer charge, and I *will* get the state to prosecute you on the forgery charge. You'll serve twenty years for the federal charge, and if I can make it stick, given your record, I'll push for another ten on the other. But it'll be spent in federal prison as far away as I can ship you. Lewisburg, PA, for instance, where the average guy like you doesn't tend to see the end of his sentence if he's got no homies to protect him. I'll make sure you're nice and cozy there. Additionally, you'll never see your kid again. Unless your baby mama is willing to drive all the way up to Pennsylvania every weekend, your kid's gonna grow up not knowing you. And I mean that."

Matt paused for a dramatic moment while Gallagher absorbed what he'd said. And then Matt continued. "All we want is information. We want to know what happened the night Noah Miller died, Dennis. And in exchange for that information, we're willing to talk to the DA and convince her to take the death penalty off the table and keep your worthless ass local. You'll still spend the rest of your miserable life in jail, but at least you'll get to see your kid grow up. So think about it. Hard."

With that, Matt got up and Oscar and I followed. The door banged behind us, and I couldn't help but feel that it'd been the final thing to bring the message home to Gallagher that he'd spend the rest of his life in a small cramped room, waiting for permission to use the bathroom.

Fifteen minutes later, the lot of us, including Candice, Dutch, Brice, Oscar, myself, and Matt, were standing around, shuffling our feet, waiting to see if Dennis would take the bait.

Bachman walked right up to Matt and began laying out the terms. "First," he said, "you'll let my client relieve himself. Second, he'll tell you what he saw in exchange for immunity. Third—"

"No," Matt cut him off. "No way would I *ever* promise immunity on the murder of a little kid."

"My client didn't do it, Hayes," Jeffrey said.

"Your client is a *liar*, Bachman," Matt replied. "No deal."

Bachman played with his tie casually. "Fine. Then Skylar Miller dies."

"We have enough evidence to implicate him to the appellate court," Matt argued. "And enough evidence to take the case to the DA."

Bachman made a *phhht* sound. "On the highly improbable assumption that you have enough evidence to overturn the first verdict for Skylar Miller, and on the even more highly improbable case that she'll get a new trial and be acquitted, do you really think the DA is going to want to charge my client and try this case again when I'll argue—convincingly—that my client had nothing to do with the murder and even the state was certain that his own mother did it? I believe it would be the very *definition* of reasonable doubt."

"Okay," Matt said coolly. "Then your client spends twenty

years in a federal prison in upstate PA. You wanna call my bluff, counselor? Call it."

Bachman's lips pressed together and he turned on his heel and walked back to the interrogation room. Meanwhile my heart was threatening to pound its way right out of my chest. I almost couldn't handle all this back-and-forth. What if Gallagher decided to take his chances in court on the assault charge? I'd have to lie. I'd have to perjure myself. And while I was totally willing to do that when we'd first arrested Gallagher, something was niggling at me in the ether. Something I didn't really want to look at.

Five minutes later, Bachman came back out and over to us again. "I will insist on the following," he said. "One, you allow my client to relieve himself. Two, you take the federal assault charge off the table. Three, you give him immunity on the forgery charge. Four, you and the DA agree not to prosecute him for obstruction. In exchange for that, he will tell you exactly what he knows."

My brow furrowed. "Obstruction? Why is he worried about an obstruction charge?"

Bachman turned his mud brown eyes to me. "To learn about that, you guys *and* the DA are going to have to agree to the terms."

"No," said Matt. "I'm not gonna tell the DA what she can and can't prosecute."

"Then we have no deal," Bachman said. "The DA has to agree not to prosecute my client or we'll take our chances in court." I could tell by the fire in his eyes that he wasn't going to back down on that point.

Matt was leaning against a desk, his arms folded over his chest as was his usual posture, but something about him had changed subtly, and it made me think that he was a tiny bit less sure of things now that Bachman had laid out the terms. His gaze flicked to me in silent question, and I scanned the ether, searching it for an answer. Again a tiny thought came to my mind, but it was so odd, and so weird, that it sort of stumped me. Still, Matt was waiting on me, and I gave him a nod. We had nothing left to either play or lose.

"Okay, counselor, you can tell your client we have a deal." I let go of the breath I'd been holding and Matt motioned to Oscar and added, "Agent Rodriguez, would you please escort Gallagher to the men's room?"

"Yes, sir," Oscar said, and moved off with Bachman.

The minute they were out of earshot, Matt motioned me over to one of the corner cubicles and pointed to a chair. I took it and looked at him expectantly. "I think we just hit an impasse," he said.

"What? Why?"

Matt lifted his chin in the direction of the interrogation room. "Bachman wants the DA to sign off on immunity for Gallagher, and I don't think she'll agree to help us, especially since we're after information about what happened the night Noah Miller was murdered."

And then it fully dawned on me. He was absolutely right. No way would the DA agree to help us on a case her office had pursued all the way to the state's supreme court. She'd fight tooth and nail to uphold the conviction against Skylar Miller, and there was no way to get her cooperation without looping her in as to why we needed her help. It was a classic Catch-22.

"Do you have any leverage, Matt?" I asked. I knew that oftentimes the U.S. attorney and the district attorney coordinated efforts and helped each other out.

"Some," he said. "But, Abby, I gotta be honest with you. I

know Rosemary. She's smart, she's tough, she's fair, but she's also protective as hell of her office. She's not going to agree to this, mostly out of principle and precedent."

I felt all my hopes begin to swirl around the drain. We were so close. So close to finding out the truth, and yet the Tuesday deadline was looming ever closer. We had to work fast in order to get any testimony out of Gallagher that might help us, and that meant that if the DA stalled or didn't agree to the terms, we were as good as dead in the water.

And so was Skylar.

"Please try, Matt," I begged. "Give it everything you can, okay?"

"I will, Abby. But I just want to caution you about the outcome. We may not be able to interrogate Gallagher in time."

I felt my lower lip tremble, but I swallowed hard and managed to say, "Okay. Then that'll have to be good enough. Thanks, Matt."

He squeezed my shoulder and headed away, probably to try to get ahold of the district attorney. I sat by myself for a while, staring out the window, until I felt someone sit down next to me. "Hey," I said to Candice.

"There's still time," she told me. Obviously she'd been made aware of the deal and its obstacles.

I felt a sinking feeling in the pit of my stomach. In my heart of hearts I knew we didn't have enough to do what we needed to do. A tear slid down my cheek and I brushed it away, annoyed by its presence. "How did we come so close and not be able to help?" I said out loud.

"Abby," Candice said. "We're not out of time yet. Matt might be able to bring the DA around."

I turned in my chair to face her. "No, he won't. It's over, Candice. We lost."

She frowned at me. "So you're giving up? Just like that?"

I lowered my chin. Ashamed and angry, but also defeated. "I don't know what else to do."

Candice stood. I could feel her own anger wafting out at me. "Why don't you call Skylar and let her know you've given up and she should get her affairs in order?" With that, she left me.

I knew that Candice wasn't mad at me—it was more that she was trying to make a point: She didn't want me to give up. She wanted me to use my intuition to find another way to help Skylar, but for the life of me I couldn't. Except for the one tiny question that kept bobbing around in my mind.

I swiveled the chair around and faced the room, which was now mostly empty except for Candice, Dutch, Brice, Oscar, and Matt, who appeared to be just wrapping up a call. By the look on his face, we could all guess how it'd gone. Still, his gaze found me first, and he shook his head. The DA wasn't going to help us.

I got up to walk over to him and the others and as I neared, I heard him tell them what the DA had said. "She wouldn't budge," he said. "The second I told her that Dennis Gallagher might have information about what happened to Noah Miller on the night he was murdered, she shut the door on any assistance she'd be willing to offer."

"Even though she wasn't in office when the conviction came down?" Dutch asked.

"Yep," Matt said. "And I'd expect nothing less of her. As a DA, you've gotta back your predecessor or spend your time as a prosecutor retrying cases. No way is she willing to step into that hornet's nest."

"So we're dead in the water," Dutch said, using the exact verbiage I'd thought of earlier.

"Effectively," Matt told him.

"Isn't there anything you can do, Matt?" Candice asked. "Maybe talk to Bachman about renegotiating the terms?"

Matt sighed. He looked tired, and no wonder, it was going on nine o'clock on Friday night and I knew he'd had a long week with the Corzo case. "I can try," he said. "But I doubt it'll amount to much."

"Can I go with you?" I asked.

Everyone looked at me in surprise. "Uh, sure, Abby," Matt said after a bit.

He led the way toward the interrogation room, where Bachman and Gallagher were waiting to see if we had a deal. We entered the room and found the pair eating carryout that Oscar had gotten for them, mostly as a show of goodwill for coming to some agreement on terms.

After we'd both taken a seat, Bachman wiped his hands on his napkin and said, "So? What's the word?"

"The DA won't go for it," Matt said.

Bachman didn't seem surprised. In fact, I almost thought he looked pleased, but Gallagher's reaction was puzzling. He looked downright disappointed. "Well, then," Bachman said, wrapping up what was left of his burger. "I'll be off, then. Dennis, I'll be back at your bond hearing Monday morning. If you—"

"Dennis," I said, interrupting the counselor. "Can I ask you a question that has nothing to do with any of this?"

Gallagher's eyes widened, and he blinked at me, then looked to his attorney. Bachman was staring at me as if he couldn't believe how rude I'd been to interrupt him. I ignored him and kept my focus on Gallagher. "Please, Dennis? Just one simple question, and if you don't want to answer it, then I'll totally respect it."

"What's the question?" he asked.

"You mentioned that you had a kid," I said, my radar humming. "It's a boy, isn't it?"

Dennis paled ever so slightly, but he nodded his head.

"I'm guessing he's about two years old," I said, careful to make that sound like a statement and not a question.

Dennis nodded again. "He's twenty-two months."

"Can I please ask, what's his name?"

Dennis's complexion drained of all color, which was the oddest of reactions, and it made Matt lean forward a little, and even Bachman cocked his head quizzically. "Why you want to know?" Gallagher asked me, his voice hitching a little with nerves.

I made sure not to blink as I answered him. "Because everything else rests on it."

In my peripheral vision I saw Matt's brow furrow and Bachman seemed impatient to be on his way, annoyed with us for engaging in idle chitchat, but Dennis held my gaze and his posture suggested that he understood exactly what I meant. "Noah," he said in a croaky whisper. "His name is Noah."

And there it was. I sat back in my chair and stared at him. Nothing he could've said would've stunned me more except for the fact that my own intuition had practically begged me to ask the question, which had been a huge hint in and of itself. But the answer still uprooted everything I thought I knew about Dennis Gallagher and what'd happened the night Noah Miller had been murdered.

Still, when I thought about it, I could understand perfectly why Dennis's attorney was insisting we get the DA on board with immunity over prosecuting Gallagher for obstruction. In this case it would've been a felony, and that would've sent Dennis away on his third strike for life.

"Is that it?" Bachman asked me, once again fiddling with the leftovers of his dinner.

I ignored him yet again. Leaning forward to rest my elbows

on the table, I said, "I'm going to honor my word, Dennis, and I'm not going to ask you a single question more, but I am going to say this: I know you were there that night. I know you saw who came out of that window. And I know you covered the killer's tracks. Why? I can't say. Maybe you peeked in the window, saw Noah dead on the floor, and freaked out, closing the window and putting the screen back out of panic. Maybe you saw Skylar run out of the house and developed a plan on the fly to make sure the police suspected her, to get back at her for yelling at you in the store, or maybe, maybe the killer saw you after he went back out the window and threatened to kill you if you ever told anybody. Whatever way it was, Dennis, Skylar's going to die on Tuesday."

As I spoke, Gallagher's face went from pale to ashen. I could see Bachman's mouth open to say something, so I rushed on before he could get a word in edgewise. "Noah's death might not have been your fault, Dennis, although I know you feel guilty. You and Noah bonded at that Home Depot. The name you gave your only son shows how guilty you still feel about Noah's murder, but it wasn't your fault he died. That rests solely with the killer. But if Skylar Miller is put to death for a crime she didn't commit, a crime you witnessed and helped to cover up, then her death rests solely on your shoulders. And if that happens, Dennis, if that actually comes to pass, then I will spend the rest of my life—*the rest of my life*—making sure you're never out of jail long enough to father a daughter you can name Skylar."

With that, I got up and walked out of the room.

Chapter Fifteen

• • •

Candice met me in the hallway. "What the hell just happened?" she asked.

"He's not our killer," I said.

She grabbed my shoulder when I kept moving. "What do you mean he's not our killer? Sundance, if he's not the guy, then who the hell is?"

I rubbed my temples. All the adrenaline and anxiety and stress were starting to catch up with me. "I don't know, Candice," I admitted. "But Dennis does."

Candice stared at me, confusion and frustration causing small lines to form around her eyes. "Okay," she said at last. "How do we get him to tell us?"

"We lock him up for the weekend and let him think about it, and hope he does the right thing come Monday morning."

"That'll be cutting it really close," she said.

"It will. But his attorney's not gonna let him say a word tonight, and we can't ask him anything without the attorney present, so unless Dennis comes to us, he's a dead end."

"So . . . what?" Candice asked me. "We just give up until Monday?"

I shook my head. "We give up only on tonight. I'm exhausted and my radar is also exhausted and I need some rest before I face a full list of clients tomorrow. After that, I'm gonna review every inch of Skylar's murder file and pray to God I can find something else in there to give to Cal."

Candice sighed. All of a sudden she looked exhausted too. "Okay," she said. "Okay."

Dutch drove me home and put me to bed. I could barely form words—I was so beat. The next morning he drove me to the office, where the first thing I did was make a request for a video visit with Skylar for four p.m., and that meant that I couldn't go over the time limit with my last client, but I managed okay, and right after she left, I rushed to my office and clicked the screen until I was staring at Skylar.

"Hey there," I said when she came into view. She looked thin and stressed. The Zen face she'd worn every time I'd seen her had vanished, and what remained was a very slight woman in personal agony. I realized when I saw her that she'd taken the news that the stranger in the Home Depot could've been the one to have murdered her son a lot harder than I'd thought she would. "First of all," I said to her, "I need to tell you that we tracked down the guy from the Home Depot. He's currently in custody."

Skylar's mouth fell open and she seemed to sag with relief. "You got him?" she asked me. "The man who murdered Noah? You really got him?"

I scooted forward a little, wanting to be closer to the screen. "No," I said frankly. "And by that, I mean we have the man in custody, but, Skylar, I don't think he murdered your son. But I do believe he was there that night."

She squinted. "I don't understand."

I explained the path that had led to finding Dennis Gallagher, careful to leave out the fact that he hadn't actually tried to attack us, and left it that we'd merely arrested him for a violation of his parole. An infraction that we could prosecute on a federal level if we pursued it. "But that isn't likely," I said to her. I wanted to be frank, and there was no way I was going to let Oscar perjure himself when I was convinced that Dennis wasn't the one who killed Noah. "So the best we can do is let him sit in jail over the weekend and hope that his conscience gets the best of him."

"Why don't you think he's the man who murdered my son?" she asked me.

"Because he's recently become a father," I said. "And he named his son Noah."

Skylar put a hand to her mouth. "He did?"

"Yes. And I know that doesn't exactly clear him of the crime, but trust me when I tell you that a man capable of murdering a little boy isn't going to name his own son after the victim. It's a thing he'd want to put out of his mind, not remember every single time he looks at his little boy."

"But you said you also think he was there that night," she said.

"I'm intuitively positive he was there," I said. "But either he was with the killer as an accomplice to a B and E, and things got out of hand, or he came into the scene as the killer was sneaking out of the house, and he covered it up for some reason, although what that is, I'm not yet sure. That's what he's still feeling guilty over. Covering up the crime. And why he named his son after yours. A part of him is trying to make it up to Noah by being a better example to his son."

"That's a lot of conjecture," she said to me, and I could see she wasn't convinced by my logic.

"It is," I told her. "But it's also backed up by a finely honed psychic sense that I'm absolutely on the right track."

Skylar rubbed her arms as if she was cold. "So we still don't know who murdered my son?"

"No. It could've been someone Dennis knew, or it could've been someone from your past, or it could've been some random stranger, but I told you the day we met that I thought it was someone you knew."

Skylar turned her head to look away from me. The guilt crept back into her expression. "But who? Who from my life would want to hurt my son?"

"Do you think Rico could've done it?" I asked, and then I reminded her about how Rico had come after Candice with a knife.

Skylar bit her lip. "I don't know, Abby. I mean, obviously Rico's capable of violence, but we hadn't seen each other in over two years, so why would he suddenly want to hurt me?"

"I'm not sure," I said. "How about Wayne Babson?"

Skylar immediately shook her head. "No," she said. "Wayne was always great with Noah. He liked him a lot. And Noah liked him. It's just that Wayne had a record, and when I was fighting to get some of my custody rights back, Wayne's record got in the way. He took it really well, and I swear we ended things as friends."

"Okay," I said, hating that I was even going to ask my next question. "Do you think your mother could've been capable of it?"

Skylar didn't react like I thought she would. I expected her to gasp anew and maybe even get a little angry, but she shocked me by replying, "I've often wondered that myself."

"She just seems awfully motivated to have you face the needle."

"Oh, she'd like nothing better than to see me dead," she said bitterly. "I have a feeling that the minute I'm carted off to potter's field, she'll make a bid for the part of Noah's trust that would've gone to me."

I felt like there was more to the story, so I pressed Skylar a little. "Has she always been like that?"

"A narcissist with psychopathic tendencies? Definitely. She took my ex-husband's side in the divorce too. It ended up being just the motivation I needed to get sober, actually. Once I found out that she was caring for Noah while Chris was at work, I got serious about getting my act together. I couldn't stand the thought of her raising him. I mean, she raised me and look how that turned out."

She then seemed to catch herself, and she eyed me in that way that all adults who grow up with an abusive parent look at other people—as if we're waiting for the judgment and doubt to come down on us like a hammer. "We have a lot in common," I told her, and offered her a sympathetic smile. "Truly."

She relaxed a little. "Most people don't understand."

"Which is a good thing when you think about it," I said. "Candice and I believe she struck a deal with Chris that in exchange for her testimony against you, he'd take care of her once the guilty verdict came in. She's currently living in the guest cottage on an estate."

Skylar nodded. "I figured they'd come to some agreement. She sat next to Chris throughout the trial and when her turn came, Mother was a little intense on the witness stand. She's good at the theatrics. Whose estate is she living on?"

"An estate off Westlake Drive. I think, if I remember correctly, the owner was an Alicia Hudson."

Skylar made a face. "Chris's godmother," she said. "She was Lynette's closest friend and like an aunt to Chris."

My brow shot up. "Ooooh, Skylar, I think you might've just given us something usable." I then explained that if we could show the appellate court that there had been some sort of an agreement between Faith and Chris to trade her testimony for his taking care of her, we might be able to get the death sentence reduced to life in prison, which would buy us time.

Skylar didn't seem to be so excited by the idea. Maybe because she'd been in jail long enough to know how the system worked. "Abby," she said, "the appellate court isn't going to just take our word for it that my mother and Chris had an arrangement. There has to be proof."

"I know, I know," I told her. "And we're working on that."

Skylar seemed skeptical. "You'll need a confession," she said. "And neither my mother nor Chris is ever going to give you that."

"But what about Mrs. Hudson?" I asked.

"Alicia? Good luck finding her, Abby. The woman spends most of her time out of the country."

"Okay," I said, taking that in. Every road kept leading to a barricade. It was frustrating as hell. "Is there anybody else you can think of, Skylar, whom you might've thought of over the years as the killer? Anybody with a grudge against you, maybe? Another ex-boyfriend? Someone in rehab? Even someone who could've taken an unwanted interest in you in your AA meetings?"

Skylar put her fingers up to her temples and closed her eyes. "There was a guy in one of the AA groups who was interested in me," she said. "I only know his first name. It was Kyle. He asked me out a couple of times, but I always said no. I wasn't interested in dating. I just wanted to focus on Noah and get him through the summer and the next trial date."

My ears perked up. "What trial date?"

Skylar shook her head. "The next custody trial date. We had one scheduled for the end of July."

"But I thought custody had already been decided."

Skylar sighed tiredly. "It was, but only on a probationary period. Given my track record, the judge thought it was best to take it three months at a time. She looped Noah in for his opinion on where he wanted to be and how well I was doing, which kept me honest. She really valued his input, which made her a great judge, in my opinion. And I gotta say that Noah took that responsibility seriously. He was always telling me that he couldn't lie to the judge, so I had to try my best." Skylar's gaze was far away for a moment and there was the ghost of a smile on her face, and then it vanished.

I felt something stir in the ether. "And they used that against you at the murder trial," I said.

Skylar nodded. "Chris claimed that Noah had hinted to him that night on the phone that he'd caught me drinking and that he was going to tell the judge about it at the end of the month. There was no way to defend myself against the lie. The minute he said that, I lost the trial."

I cocked my head. "What *did* they talk about that night, Skylar?"

She shrugged. "I don't know. Chris called to talk to him about his day and I headed into the shower. I always gave Noah his privacy when it came to his nightly phone call with his dad. I suspect they talked about going to the Astros game. Chris was going to take Noah that weekend."

"Did Noah love baseball?" I asked. It wasn't an important question, but I suspected that Skylar missed being able to talk about her son to anyone who wouldn't automatically judge her.

Her ghost of a smile returned, and while it didn't quite touch her eyes, it did give her face a pleasing lift. "He did. Chris played college ball, and Grant played in the majors back in the seventies. Noah was so proud of that. His prized possession was a baseball signed by Nolan Ryan that his granddad had given him for his last birthday. He used to tap it before bed every night, like a good-luck charm."

The yellow warning light illuminated above the video visitor's window and I knew that our time was about up. "Okay, Skylar, thank you so much. We'll keep working on our end. Just try not to lose hope."

She looked me in the eye and sighed sadly. "You say that like I had any hope to begin with, Abby."

The yellow light began to flash and a moment later the screen went black.

I spent that night with Skylar's file laid out on the dining room table. Dutch sat next to me and we went through it piece by piece. While he sorted through all the witness statements, I spent my time laying out all the photos of the crime scene. At some point Dutch got up, shuffled off to the kitchen, and came back with a couple of beers. Setting one down in front of me, he clinked the neck with his and said, "Take a break, Edgar."

I sighed and lifted the beer in silent toast to him. "Thanks, honey," I said, indulging in a nice long sip. "I keep feeling like I'm missing something."

Dutch peered over my shoulder at the spread on the table. "Seems to me you've already pulled out a whole lot for Cal to work with so far," he said.

I rubbed my eyes, and the images danced around in my mind. There was something I was missing. Something important, I just knew it. And then my lids flew up and I began to scramble through the photos. "Holy crap!" I said, pulling one of them forward.

"What?" Dutch asked, hovering closer as I showed him the photo taken outside Skylar's house. It captured the image of her, wrapped in a blanket, her hands and the bottom of her shirt covered in blood. Behind her was a couple. The woman was plump with scraggly gray hair and the man next to her was tall, heavyset, and he wore a baseball cap. An Astros cap.

"Hold on, hold on, hold on," I said, shuffling through the photos again until I came up with one photo showing blood spatter on the wall and dresser across from the bed. "Oh . . . my . . . God!" I gasped when I saw the image.

"Edgar," Dutch said. "What are you seeing?"

I pointed to a small round disk on the dresser. "What do you suppose that is?" I asked Dutch.

He frowned. "Looks like a stand for a baseball," he said. I could've hugged him.

"Exactly!" I shouted. Then I lifted the photo of Skylar with the couple. I guessed from the witness statements that they were her neighbors, Doreen and Ted Mulgrew. Holding it up to show Dutch, I said, "Skylar told me that Noah's prize possession was a signed baseball by Nolan Ryan. She said he used to tap it for good luck every night before he went to bed. But look," I said, handing him that photo and grabbing for the other one. "In this picture it's missing. And . . . ," I added, searching through the other photos for one showing Noah's nightstand, "it's not here either."

"Someone took it," Dutch said.

"The *killer* took it," I said, and then tapped the photo of the Mulgrews. "I'm guessing an Astros fan took it."

Dutch scratched his head. "Yeah, but, Abs, didn't Skylar go running over to the Mulgrews right after the attack? I mean, if your theory is right, how did Mulgrew go from murdering Noah, attacking Skylar, to answering his door when she started pounding on it?"

I held up a finger. "But he *didn't* answer the door, Dutch! His wife did!" I got up and moved down the table to the witness statement I wanted, fished around in the stack, and came up with it. Bringing it back, I handed it to Dutch. "See? Doreen answered the door. She says that she had to holler to her husband to call nine-one-one while she tried to tend to Skylar."

"Wouldn't she have known if her husband was home or not?"

I sighed in frustration. My theory was wild, for sure, but I could imagine a scenario where Ted Mulgrew attacked Skylar, and the second she raced out of the room, he grabbed the baseball—or maybe he already had it—and dove out of the window, running over to his own backyard, which was right next door, and maybe he headed in through his own back door just as his wife was answering Skylar's knock. Maybe Doreen didn't realize her husband wasn't in the house at the time. I said all this to Dutch. "I mean, it's possible that in the confusion of being awakened in the middle of the night by incessant knocking, Doreen didn't notice her husband was gone. Maybe she was so focused on Skylar, bloody and hysterical at her door, that she didn't take note of where her husband was."

"That's a bit of a leap," Dutch said.

I sat down and thought through the theory a little more. "But it's possible, Dutch. Someone who knew intimate details about Skylar's house and could gain access to it broke in and murdered her son. Maybe Mulgrew got into Noah's room because he was after the Nolan Ryan baseball. I mean, what's something like that worth, anyway?"

"Depending on the year and the game, probably anywhere between three hundred bucks and a thousand."

"So it'd be valuable," I said.

"Somewhat," Dutch said. "But I don't know that I believe it'd be worth killing over."

"But what if Noah woke up as Mulgrew was taking his most prized possession?" I argued. "Seriously, Dutch, what if Mulgrew panicked and stabbed Noah to shut him up?"

Dutch's expression told me he wasn't buying it. "I suppose it's possible, but I don't know that I'd hang my hat on it."

I took the picture of the Mulgrews from him. "Yeah, well, I don't think we can afford to leave any stone unturned here. I'm gonna have Candice check out Ted Mulgrew and I'm gonna ask Oscar to come with me to interview him."

Dutch reached out and rubbed the back of my neck. I hadn't realized how tense I'd been until his magic fingers began working on the muscles there. "Okay, Sherlock, but for now let's call it a night."

I purred under the massage. "Keep doing that and I'll offer you every penny currently in the swear jar."

He chuckled. "I'd rather have the IOUs. They gotta be worth double what's in the jar."

"Triple," I confessed. "But who's counting?"

The next morning I was on the phone with Candice and Oscar. Both of them listened to my argument, but neither of them expressed much enthusiasm for my theory. Basically they both mirrored Dutch's rebuttal; the timing didn't really seem to fit. "I'll admit that it's possible, Sundance," Candice said after I kept pushing the theory. "But it still doesn't explain the missing footprints from the hallway."

"He went out the window, Candice," I said with a little irritation.

"On his way out? Possibly. But what about on his way in?"

"Again, the window," I said, and then realized what I'd missed.

"Okay, then why aren't there footprints in the hallway from when he went to get the knife from the kitchen?" she asked. "That's the thing that's really bothering me about this whole case. We need a plausible reason why the killer would've entered the home from the front door, taken the knife, avoided the hallway, retraced his steps out of the house, and headed out and around to the back of the house to climb in through Noah's window."

I sighed. "I haven't figured that part out yet. But that doesn't mean Mulgrew didn't take the knife at some earlier point. Like maybe he was invited in for some lemonade or something and he snatched it then."

"Didn't Skylar say that she'd used the knife earlier that night?" Oscar asked.

"She did, but I've been thinking about that," I said. "Maybe Skylar only *thought* she used the same knife to cut up the salad she'd had for dinner. Maybe she'd used another knife and simply got confused. I mean, that knife was a part of a set. There had to be other knives she could've used and the shock of her son's murder sort of scrambled her memories a little."

Candice and Oscar were both silent for a bit before Candice said, "That is actually a more possible scenario. I've been doing lots of research on eyewitness testimony, and it's common for people to replace certain objects in a memory with other familiar objects. The shock of her son's murder definitely could've scrambled Skylar's recollection."

"The timing for Mulgrew to have done it is still too tight for me," Oscar said. "And he's only wearing an Astros hat in the photo, Cooper. It doesn't mean he was involved. Plenty of people are Astros fans."

"More so some years than others," Candice muttered, with a smile in her voice.

"True," Oscar said. "If they ever win a game again, I'll get back to rooting for them."

"Can we keep this on point?" I snapped. I really wanted to interview Mulgrew, and didn't appreciate the idle chitchat about the freaking Astros' winning/losing average.

"Sorry," Candice and Oscar said together. "Okay, Abs," Candice said. "I'll look into Mulgrew's background, while you and Oscar go interview him."

"Thank you," I said, relieved I'd have company when I went to talk to Skylar's neighbors.

"Pick you up in twenty," Oscar said.

Oscar met me at the door, and I was armed with my argument and the two photos I wanted to throw in Mulgrew's face when I accused him of murder. I was convinced I was on to something, and I had a frantic passion to make this theory stick. In the back of my mind I knew without a doubt that much of what was fueling me was a sense of desperation, because time for Skylar was definitely running out. We had very little to offer Cal for the appeal, and his warning to me from the day before when I'd brought him up to speed, that we would need nothing short of a confession from either the actual murderer or Chris and Faith Wagner about their arrangement, was what was fueling my efforts to push the line.

The trip to Skylar's old neighborhood was unencumbered by traffic. Not much moves in Austin on a lazy Sunday morning and I felt a little bad about snapping at Oscar on the phone, so I asked him how Amigo was doing.

"Oh, man," he said, with a sweet smile and a shake of his head. "That pup is so damn cute. No heartworm or parasites, which is great, and the vet thinks he's only about a year old. We both also think he belonged to somebody, because he walks well on a leash, knows sit, stay, and shake, and he's obviously housebroken. There wasn't a microchip, though, and a search of local Web sites for lost dogs didn't come up with a hit. I'll keep looking to see if I can reunite him with his owner, but, like I told you before, I really hope I get to keep him."

I leaned back in the seat and relaxed the tense set to my shoulders. The positive changes in Oscar's life were such a nice little respite from the awful business of Noah's murder and Skylar's impending execution. "Amigo's yours, buddy. It was meant to be."

"You sure?" he asked, sliding a sideways glance at me. "I really like him, Cooper, and I don't want to get my hopes up if some little old lady from South Austin pops up to claim him."

I tapped my temple to let him know my radar had already looked into it. "You'll have no such bad luck, honey. The pup is yours for keeps."

Oscar's grin widened. I think he was happier about Amigo than he was about the new house or the prospect of getting a girlfriend.

When we arrived at Skylar's old neighborhood, Oscar parked across the street from her house and we got out and surveyed the house to the right, as there was nothing but a drainage field on the left. The Mulgrew residence was bigger than her home, but not by much. At least not in outward appearances.

I noted that the gate leading to Skylar's old backyard was within a few feet of the gate leading to the Mulgrews'. "See?" I said, pointing to the gate. "He could've ducked through the backyard and into his own yard without anybody being the wiser."

Oscar nodded, but his expression remained skeptical. "You want to take the lead? Or me?"

"Me," I said, marching forward to the front door. I checked my watch before ringing the bell. It was ten a.m. Not too early, not too late for a Sunday. I hoped.

It took a minute, but we eventually did hear footsteps shuffling behind the door. They came to a stop and I smiled brightly at the peephole. After another slight hesitation, the door opened and a round-shaped woman in a big baggy purple T-shirt stood there. "Yes?" she asked.

I glanced quickly at the photo in my hand. She'd aged quite a bit in ten years, but she still looked enough like the woman in the photograph for me to be certain we'd come to the right place. "Mrs. Mulgrew?" I said, pulling on the lanyard with my ID, and offering it out in front of me so that she could read it. "My name is Abigail Cooper, and this is my associate Oscar Rodriguez. I know it's early, and a Sunday, but we're doing some investigative work on behalf of Skylar Miller, and I was wondering if I could ask you a question or two."

She pulled the door open a little more so that she could inspect my ID. Oscar offered up his badge and photo ID too, just to make it official (unofficially speaking, of course . . . ahem).

"Sure," she said, folding her hands over her middle. She appeared eager to talk to us, and I breathed a sigh of relief.

I dove right in. "I know that Skylar came to your house the night of Noah's murder," I said, trying to be discreet as I peered around her into the house to see if her husband was perhaps inside.

"Oh, yes," she said, shaking her head as if the memory was a terrible one to recall. "Poor Skylar. Poor Noah. What an awful thing that happened to them. You know, I told my husband that we needed to move, because I didn't want to be in a neighborhood where you could get murdered in your sleep, but he said no, so I ordered an alarm for the house, and then of course we found out that Skylar was the one who killed Noah, and he made me cancel the alarm."

I squinted at her. She was giving me a lot of information. "So, you believe that Skylar murdered Noah?"

Doreen Mulgrew made a face, as if she couldn't quite decide. "I mean," she said, "we lived next door to them for only a year, and she seemed really nice, but like, didn't Jeffrey Dahmer's neighbors say they thought he was really nice too?"

"I'm sure they did," I said. "But you still seem to have some doubts."

Doreen sighed heavily. "I just can't account for it," she said. "Every time we saw them together, Skylar was hugging Noah or he was hugging her. They seemed to really love each other. And at his birthday party . . . he was just so happy and outgoing, you know? You could tell that kid didn't have a worry in the world, which just didn't fit with what they were saying about Skylar. My mom drank, and I don't ever remember a day I wasn't scared or worried for her."

I remembered the photo of Noah and Skylar from his last birthday party. They had indeed both seemed so happy. "So you were at Noah's ninth birthday party?"

"We were," she said.

"Do you remember who else was there?" I asked, more to keep the conversation going while I assessed her energy.

"Well, let me think," she said, tapping her lip. "Skylar invited us, I'm sure, only because so few people showed up. There aren't many kids in this neighborhood, and other than us and the neighbors from up the street—the Barclays, who moved out about six years ago—that was it for the neighborhood. Noah's grampy and grammy were there at the start of the party, but they had to leave because Mr. Miller had to go get his chemo treatment, and then later Noah's dad came but just for a minute to drop off Noah's present. He wouldn't even stay for cake, even though I baked it myself and told him it was homemade. Kind of looked down his nose at the house and all of us too. The grandparents were also a little snooty to us, but I found out at the trial that they were loaded, so it figured. Anyway, it was kind of a sad party, but Noah didn't seem to mind. He was the happiest kid you ever met. His grampy had given him a baseball signed by a real famous player and he carried that thing around like it was his prize possession. He was so cute! And, I'll be honest, I don't even like kids very much, but I liked Noah. And, to be even more honest, I liked Skylar. She—"

"Dory?" came a voice from the back of the house. "Who's here?"

I leaned to the side a little to see around her, but her form was blocking the hallway. "Just some people asking about Noah," she called back.

"Are they reporters?" he said, and I could hear a note of eagerness in his voice.

"No, Ted," she said. "Go back to your ESPN." Then she turned to me and said, "If you were reporters, he'd be all over you to give his opinion. That man loves to talk." She laughed and nudged me as she said it, and I chuckled right along. Mostly at the irony.

"So," I said, trying to get the conversation back on track, "the night of the murder, you and your husband were sound asleep and you heard, what? Screams?"

Doreen shook her head. "No," she said. "I heard this pounding, like, bam, bam, bam, bam!" She took a moment to demonstrate on her own door how loud it had been. "Woke me out of a dead sleep," she continued. "I jumped out of bed, heart racing, and ran to the door, thinking there was a fire or something."

I held up a finger. "Wait, *you* ran to the door? Your husband didn't go with you?"

She laughed. "Ted couldn't run if his life depended on it."

I didn't get the inference, but I said, "Ah," and pretended to make a note on the small pad of paper I'd brought with me. "So you left him in the bedroom, and rushed to the door."

She appeared thoughtful for a moment, and said, "No. No, he was asleep on the couch. I remember because when I opened the door and found Skylar standing there all bloody and hysterical, I had to yell a few times for him to come to the door and help me."

"Does your husband often sleep on the couch?" Oscar asked.

"Sometimes," Doreen said, and then she cast suspicious eyes at him. "Why?"

Oscar offered her a sheepish smile and a little white lie. "I snore. My wife keeps telling me to move to the couch, but it's not very comfortable."

"So, Ted would've been at the rear of the house, I assume?" I asked.

"Yes," she said.

"And he didn't hear anything unusual coming from the Millers' backyard?" I asked.

"Naw," she said. "He was fast asleep until I started yelling for him."

"Are you sure, Doreen? Maybe he heard something and went back to sleep?" I asked the question because I wanted to see if maybe they'd had a conversation about it, which I wanted to believe had been Ted's cover story. That he'd been fast asleep on the couch when really he'd been sneaking back in from the yard.

"Well, you can ask him yourself," Doreen said, turning to yell for her husband.

While she was calling to him, I shuffled the photo of Ted in his Astros hat to the top of my pad of paper. I wanted to push him a little on my theory to see how he reacted. When I looked up, Doreen was stepping to the side a bit farther than I would've guessed she'd need to, and then I saw why. Ted rolled up in a wheelchair and looked at us expectantly.

"Oh," I said when I saw him. "I'm sorry. I didn't know you . . . I mean, I didn't realize you . . ." I couldn't finish the sentence, because there was no way to be politically correct about asking him what the heck had happened to him in the last ten years.

"Wheelchair got your tongue?" he asked me. Then he laughed uproariously, and his wife joined in. I had a feeling they'd done that bit before.

"Sorry, Mr. Mulgrew. It's just in this photo"—I turned it around for him—"you're standing. So I didn't expect to see you . . . er. . . . sitting today."

He peered at the photo and nodded. "Yeah. That was before I couldn't walk anymore." Thumbing over his shoulder, he said, "I've got arthritis in the spine real bad. Can't walk more than a few steps without needing to sit down."

Doreen patted him on the shoulder. "He still gets around all right," she said proudly. He put a hand on hers, then took it and kissed it sweetly. I couldn't help feeling some serious doubt while I watched how affectionate and caring they were with each other. Could a guy with arthritis in the back have climbed through the window of Noah's room, murdered him, attacked Skylar, then shuffled back out to run around to his rear door and pretended to be sleeping? In my gut I knew there was no way.

Still, there was that baseball cap. Not giving up entirely on my hypothesis, I pointed to the hat in the photo and said, "You an Astros fan?"

He leaned forward to look at the photo. And then he looked

up a bit sadly and said, "Noah gave me that. His granddad used to play for the Astros and he got it for him, but it was too big to fit his head, and I guess he felt sorry for me shuffling over to the mailbox all bent over. He was such a sweet kid."

And then, I swear to God, tears formed in his eyes and he ducked his chin. Doreen leaned down and hugged his shoulders. Oscar looked at me like, "Game over, Cooper."

"Thank you for your time," I said to the couple.

Doreen looked up in surprise. "Oh! Is that it?"

"Yes, ma'am," I said. "Thank you both. Sorry to have interrupted your Sunday."

She batted her hand at the air. "Bah. Don't you worry about it. We're glad to help."

With that, we took our leave.

On the drive home neither one of us said much until Oscar finally broke the silence. "Sorry that didn't pan out, Cooper."

I stared out the window feeling pretty low. I couldn't shake the feeling that I was failing Skylar, which was exactly what Candice had warned me about when I'd started this case. "It was a long shot," I said.

I called Candice and filled her in on the interview. She was really sweet and said that she'd looked into the Mulgrews' background and there was nothing there that spoke of them being anything other than good people. "I'm going to try to find the missing baseball, though," she told me. "It's a total long shot, Abs, but if it was a valuable ball, maybe somebody tried to sell it."

I nodded even though I knew she couldn't see me. It was all just so defeating.

After I hung up with Candice, Oscar said, "Where to next, Cooper?"

I stared forlornly out the window. "I have no clue, Oscar." I meant it metaphorically, but Oscar seemed to get it, and he drove in silence, allowing me my little pity party until he pulled into a parking garage to an apartment building. "What's this?" I asked. "Where are we?"

Oscar drove up to a space and parked. "I think we both could use a little puppy therapy. Want to meet Amigo?"

I spent the next couple of hours playing with an adorable little pooch and it helped more than I could say.

Later, after Oscar dropped me off at home, I called Candice to see what progress she'd made. "Do you know how many balls Nolan Ryan signed?" Candice asked me by way of hello.

"No, but I'm guessing it's too many to track?"

"By about a thousand," she said.

I blew out a breath and sank into my chair at the dining room table, where Dutch had neatly stacked all the discordant parts of Skylar's murder file. "But we know the killer took it," I said. "And if he took it to sell it, then it's the only way to track him down definitively."

"Abby, finding the ball won't be like finding a needle in a haystack. It'll be like finding a needle in a field of haystacks. There's no way to track the ball when a thousand of them are in play."

I leaned back in the chair and slung an arm over my eyes. Every single lead kept ending in a dead end and I couldn't help but feel we were like firefighters in a smoke-filled room, totally blinded by the smoke as we searched around awkwardly for any signs of life. "So now what?" I asked, because I was out of ideas.

"We wait," Candice said. "We've given Cal everything we have. There's nothing more to do except keep our fingers crossed that Gallagher's weekend in jail loosened his lips a little and he decides to forgo the advice of his counsel and help us."

I wanted to groan. "He hasn't called out to us yet," I said. "And tomorrow after he makes bail, he won't have any incentive besides personal guilt to help us."

"He won't make bail," Candice said confidently. "Not with his criminal record and the assault charges we're bringing against him. Assaulting a federal officer is a big-time offense. The judge won't let him out with anything less than a hundred-thousand-dollar bond. Trust me on that."

I felt a nudge on my elbow and I lowered my arm to find Dutch standing next to me, offering a glass of wine and a winsome smile. "Yeah, okay," I said to her, while gratefully taking the wine from my hubby. "Let's hope he gets shot down at the bail hearing and considers the very long wait to his trial as added incentive to cooperate with us."

"He's really caught between a rock and a hard place," she said. "He can help us and risk prosecution on the obstruction charge, or he can choose not help us and be certain we'll send him away for as long as we can."

I squirmed a little because Candice didn't know the assault charge was bullshit. Across the room the swear jar seemed to mock me. I glared at it. "Let's hope you're right," I said to Candice, turning away from the jar, " 'cause we're all out of new leads and possible suspects to track down."

"At the very least we've highlighted all of the credible weaknesses in the prosecution's case against Skylar, Sundance," Candice pointed out. "When there's a life at stake, the court might decide that's enough to offer her a new trial, rather than take the risk of putting the wrong person to death."

"In most states I would agree with you," I said. "But this is *Texas*, and we're number one in executions several years running." My voice quivered a little as I started to choke up over the futility of trying to find a way to really help Skylar escape the needle.

"Abs," Candice said. "We can't lose hope. Not yet. So hang in there, okay?"

I nodded and squeaked out, "I'll try."

After hanging up with Candice, I trudged over to the couch and sat down next to Dutch, who wrapped his arm around me. "You okay?"

"No," I said, my eyes welling and the tears dribbling down my cheeks.

"What can I do?" he asked.

"Nothing, honey," I said as more tears came. "There's nothing to be done." Tuttle waddled over and jumped up on the couch. She always knew when I needed some puppy comfort, and as much as playing with Amigo had brought a smile to my face and taken the edge off, there was nothing quite like the loyal and unconditional love of your own pooch. I took her into my lap, where she began to lick enthusiastically at my face, and after a time, I was better. "I just feel like I've failed her," I said. "Skylar, I mean."

Dutch leaned over and kissed my cheek. "You did everything you could, dollface."

I turned to him. "Did I?"

He swept his arm toward the stack of photos and witness state-ments on the dining room table. "You've been eating and breath-ing this case for over a week. What else could you do?"

I hugged Tuttle and shrugged. "I don't know," I admitted. "But I can't shake the feeling like we came close to solving what really happened, but still managed to miss it."

Dutch squeezed my knee and got up. "It could still come to you," he said. "But don't try to force it. Come on, help me with dinner and take your mind off it. Maybe something will pop for you later."

I followed Dutch into the kitchen, passing the table and all those photos. I swear they were calling me to take another look, but I'd studied every single horrible image for hours. What more could I see? What more could I do?

Turns out, I wouldn't know the answer until the following day.

Chapter Sixteen

. . .

Dutch woke me as he left for work the next morning. I muttered something about wanting to sleep in and the next thing I knew, he'd put both Eggy and Tuttle on the bed to cover me in squirming, wiggling, furry cuteness, and I sat up, glaring hard at my husband, who was grinning like the Cheshire cat. "I fed them," he said, "but I'm late for work. Can you water them?"

"Watering" the pups was code for "walk them around the block." Which meant I'd have to get out of bed. Something my grumpy ass wasn't much enthused about. "Go, go," I said, waving him out the bedroom door. The pups were digging tunnels in the bedcover, and I lay back on the pillow with a groan, then closed my eyes and had calm thoughts, hoping to influence the pups into settling down and sleeping a bit more with me. Eggy curled up in the crook of my arm, but Tuttle was having none of it.

She wriggled around for a bit; then she sniffed my eyelids; then she settled down to personally groom me for ten minutes, never letting up until I finally curled her into a hug and smothered *her* with kisses. This got Eggy jealous, and he barked in protest. And then I was chasing after them all around the bed, covering them with sheets and throw pillows as they danced and darted back and forth, wagging their tails and having a good romp.

We ended up outside not long after, and even though my worries over Skylar never faded, the walk did both me and the pups a whole lotta good.

Back at home I took a long, lazy shower, then made myself a truly superlative omelet, sharing much of one corner with the pups, and was just about to sit down to eat it when my cell rang. "Dang it," I muttered. The ring was coming from the bedroom, where I'd left my phone.

"Where've you been?" I heard Candice ask me.

"Out for a walk with the pups," I said, realizing she must've been trying to get ahold of me.

"Matt tried to call you several times already," she said. "I was starting to worry."

"Why? What's going on?"

"Gallagher made bail," she said, cutting right to the chase.

"What?" I said, sinking back down in the chair at the table. "How?"

"I have no idea. The bail hearing was this morning, and the judge heard Gallagher's case first thing. He set the bond at two hundred thousand, and Matt thought for sure we'd have Gallagher right where we wanted him back in lockup, but within an hour his bond was posted and he was out."

I glanced at my watch. It was only ten thirty. "Who posted the bail?"

"That's what I can't figure out, Abs," she said. "I've called every bail bondsman in town, trying to find out who put up the ten percent, and no one is owning up to it."

"But how is that possible?"

"The only way it could be is if someone put up the entire

amount in cash. And if they did that, then I can't get the name without a court order."

I suddenly had a very bad feeling. "Candice, we need to find Dennis Gallagher."

"That's why I'm calling," she told me. "I'm coming over to pick you up."

"How far away are you?"

"Five minutes."

"Good. I'll be ready."

I picked up the plate holding my omelet and carried it with me, taking big unladylike bites as I hurried around the house in search of an appropriate outfit, shoes, keys, ID, etc. I'd finished the omelet and put myself together (mostly) about thirty seconds before Candice's car pulled into our drive. Kissing the now sleepy pups on the nose, I hurried out and got in her car with a breezy smile.

"You've got egg on your shirt," she said, the corners of her mouth quirking.

I looked down. "Dammit!"

Candice held out her hand, and I rolled my eyes, digging into my purse for a quarter. She tossed it into a compartment next to the emergency brake. It clanked against a whole lot of its friends. "We are gonna have such a good time on our next girls' weekend," she said.

Candice had made a rule that every time I swore in her car she'd donate the quarter to some future girls' getaway. So far, I was funding the entire trip.

"Yeah, yeah," I said, scrubbing at my shirt with a tissue.

Just then my cell rang. It was Matt. I held up the display so that Candice could see before I answered. "Hey," I said. "I heard."

"Abby, I've got Dennis Gallagher on the other line," Matt said, practically running over my greeting. "He says he needs to talk to you. Exclusively. He wants your cell phone number, but I wouldn't give it until I got your okay."

I sat up straighter in the seat. This was a sudden turn of events. "Give it to him, Matt," I said. "I'll record the call."

"Good," he said. "Good." With that, he was gone.

Turning to Candice, I said, "Dennis Gallagher wants my cell number. He called Matt to get it. He wants to talk to me."

Candice nodded with satisfaction. "Told ya," she said.

"You did," I replied as my cell rang. I let it ring a second time while I switched on the recording app on my phone, then answered his call. "Dennis?"

"Uh, hi," he said. "Is this Abby Cooper?"

"It is, Dennis. I'm here. What did you need to talk to me about?"

"How do I know this is really you?" he asked.

"Because you called my cell," I said as calmly as I could. Man, this guy was a fry short of a Happy Meal.

"How do I know this is Abby Cooper's cell phone?" he asked me.

I sighed. "You know what, Dennis? You don't. But right now you're sounding a bit too paranoid, which tells me that something's got you spooked. How about you just take my word for it and tell me what's up and we'll go from there?"

"Abby Cooper knows what happened in that trailer," he said to me, and suddenly I understood exactly what he was angling for.

"Yes," I said. "I do. I know *exactly* what happened, Dennis. If you help me, I'll help you."

"How do I know I can trust you?"

"You don't," I said bluntly. "But, buddy, what other choice do you have right now? I'm the only thing holding you away from either the frying pan or the fire. Your call."

Dennis was silent for a long time. So long in fact that I felt he was wavering a bit too much. To help things along, I said, "Okay. Call me when you're ready to help me and yourself, Dennis." And then I hung up.

Candice eyed me with raised eyebrows, and I bit my lip. That'd been a bold move, but I needed to jar him away from the idea of stalling for more time. We didn't have it. My cell rang about five seconds later. "Don't hang up on me again!" he said angrily.

"Let's get something straight here," I told him in an even, flat tone. "You do not call the shots here. We both agree to a compromise, or we both walk away and let the chips fall where they will."

"I'm trying!" he yelled back.

"Okay," I said, easing up on him a bit. "What would you like to do, Dennis?"

"We need to talk," he said.

"I'm available."

"But just you. Nobody else."

I frowned. No way did I want to meet this guy in a dark alley all alone. "See, you say stuff like that, Dennis, and it makes me doubt that you're willing to cooperate."

"That's nonnegotiable," he said. "Seriously. I'm freaked-out, okay? I don't know who to trust or where to go. But there's something I need to show you."

Candice, who'd been listening as I held the phone between us, shook her head vehemently. I ignored both her and common sense and said, "Okay. I'll meet you. Where?"

"Alone," Dennis insisted. "No cops. No other FBI people. Just you."

Candice shook her head again, and I ignored her a second time, just as easily. "Alone," I told him. "Where?"

"Be at the Starbucks on Fifty-first and I-Thirty-five in an hour."
With that, he hung up.

Candice glared hard at me for about ten seconds. "It's a public
place," I said. "And perhaps you didn't notice my crossed fingers
when I made the pinkie swear." I held up the crossed fingers of my
left hand and she gave me a gentle punch in the arm.

"Okay," she said. "Let's coordinate this with Oscar and Cox.
Even if the Starbucks is packed, I don't want you in there
alone."

I saluted. "Game on."

An hour and ten minutes later I sat in the chill air of the Starbucks, sipping at my caramel Frappuccino, wishing I hadn't ordered the frozen version because they had the AC on a setting that
would've made a penguin ask for a sweater, when my phone rang.
"Hi," Dennis said. "It's me."

"Where are you?" I looked warily around the café, careful not
to make eye contact with Agent Cox.

"I'm in the park on the other side of the hospital," he said.

I glanced outside. The Starbucks was in the same area as the
Home Depot where Dennis had first met Noah and Skylar Miller.
In the opposite direction was a large park with a running trail, a
playground, and several inviting seating areas under shady trees.
"Where in the park?" I asked.

"Head outside," he said, "and I'll direct you to me." With that,
he clicked off.

I stood up stiffly. I didn't like that the plan had changed, but
what choice did I have? Gathering up my drink, I walked to the
trash bin next to Cox and dropped the drink in while murmuring
to Cox, "He wants to meet me in the park."

Cox gave no indication that he'd heard me. Instead he lazily
turned the page of his newspaper and took a casual sip of his cof-

fee. I knew that Candice and Oscar were also someplace nearby, but neither of them had told me where they'd be, and I think they did that on purpose so I wouldn't be tempted to look in their direction and possibly tip off Gallagher.

More than a little nervous, because I suddenly had a very bad feeling, I walked out into the heat and bright sunshine. Donning sunglasses, I began walking toward the park. It was down at the end of a long street, which was farther away than it appeared, but I walked steadily until my phone beeped and I looked at the display. It was a text from Gallagher. He wanted me to head to the entrance at Lancaster and Philomena, which was a heck of a long haul when you're hoofing it in the summer heat.

It took me ten minutes to get there. I was dripping with sweat when I arrived, and perhaps more than a little peeved. And then I saw him.

Gallagher was standing under the shade of a large live oak tree, wearing a baseball cap, sunglasses, and the same clothes we'd arrested him in. He held his hand up to let me know he saw me too, and I began to move toward him when there was a sound like a hammer hitting the concrete, and all of a sudden, Gallagher sank to his knees. He clutched his stomach and through his fingers I saw a blossom of red. It took me several seconds to put it together that he'd just been shot. Then I was sprinting toward him. Behind me I heard shouts, but I paid them no attention—I simply ran as fast as I could toward Gallagher.

I got to him and dropped down, and he sort of fell into my arms, his face a mask of agony and blood pouring out of his stomach wound faster than I thought it should have. "No, no, no, no, no!" I whispered, cradling him in my arms and trying to ease him gently the rest of the way to the ground. He cried out in pain and I stopped, holding us perfectly still for a few seconds.

Our eyes met and he tried to mouth something to me. I caught only one word. "Noah."

"Hang on!" I begged him. "Dennis, hang on! The hospital is right over there, okay? We'll get you to it. Just stay with me!"

His face had completely drained of color, and his lower lip trembled while his eyes leaked tears that slid down his cheeks. I held him as close to me as I could without causing him further pain, and just kept repeating, "Hang on. Hang on. Hang on."

Somewhere in the distance I heard the sad siren sound of an ambulance, and more shouts, some of which were my name. I ignored all of it and held Dennis's gaze, willing him to stay with me. But he couldn't. And, intuitively, I knew it was over even as he sucked in one last labored breath. With a feeble effort, he pushed something at me. And then his head lolled back and his chest rose no more.

Candice was the first to reach me. I wouldn't let go of Dennis. I cried over him as if he were a dear friend, because in the last moment of his life, we'd connected in a way, and I'd seen him as clearly as anyone but his maker could. He was a man who'd made more mistakes than most, and regretted them all. He'd been trying to do the right thing by meeting me. Of that I was certain.

"Hey," Candice said, in a way that suggested she'd already said it to me a few times. "Abby, the paramedics are here, honey. You've got to let go."

And then she was gently reaching over me to take Dennis's limp torso out of my arms and lay him on the ground. As she did that, something slipped to the ground and rolled next to me.

Through my tears I stared at it. I knew immediately what it was, but the emotion and trauma of the moment prevented me from fully processing the object tucked within a Ziploc bag. I picked up the Baggie, hugging it to me as I got to my feet, and took a few steps with Candice to get out of the way of the paramedics. That's when I noticed that Oscar and Cox had joined us. Oscar was out of breath and soaked through with sweat. "The shot came from that building," he said, pointing to a rather dingy-looking apartment complex with tall wire fencing around it. It looked vacant and ready to be torn down.

"Did you get a view of the shooter?" Candice asked him, wrapping her arm around me protectively.

"No. He was too far away," Oscar said. "By the time I got to the other side of the street, he was long gone."

Cox motioned to Oscar and the pair stepped away to talk to the police officers who'd now also arrived on the scene. Candice shuffled me away from Dennis and the paramedics. "You okay?" she asked me.

I lifted my hand to wipe my cheeks and noticed there was blood on it. My stomach lurched and it was all I could do not to lose my cookies. "Not really," I told her when I could speak.

"Come with me," she instructed, and moved me over to Oscar's car. Reaching inside, she came up with a bottle of water and handed it to me. "Drink," she ordered. I did. "Hey," she said, eyeing my left hand. "What's that?"

I lifted the baseball from Noah's room so that she could see it. On the baseball was some blue scribble, in the form of an autograph, but also, there was a rust-colored fingerprint. The rust was obviously from dried blood, and the fingerprint was obviously that of the man who'd killed Noah Miller.

"Oh, my, God," she gasped, taking the Baggie from me to really inspect it. "You were right. Gallagher really *was* there that night." With pressed lips, she looked back at where Dennis's lifeless body lay. "He was confessing to Noah's murder."

My radar said differently. "You think he was about to admit he was the killer?" I said. "No way, Candice. Dennis just got shot trying to let me know who murdered Noah. I'll give you that he was there that night, but if that fingerprint comes back as Dennis Gallagher's, I'll retire from crime fighting."

Candice tucked the Baggie into her purse protectively and said, "Until we establish jurisdiction, I don't want APD to even get a hint that we've got this."

My attention was drawn back to Gallagher. The paramedics were unwrapping a white sheet to place over his body as bystanders began to gather and gawk, and then I moved my gaze to Oscar and Cox. They were arguing with what looked to be an APD detective who'd just arrived on scene. It dawned on me then that if we lost jurisdiction over the investigation of the murder of Dennis Gallagher, then we'd have to turn over the baseball, which would end up at the bottom of a case file, never to be scrutinized too closely, especially if it revealed who really killed Noah Miller, since by the time the forensics came back, Skylar would most certainly be dead.

I got out my cell and called Dutch. "We need you," I said. "As soon as possible. And bring Brice."

Dutch and Brice showed up about the time that Candice was putting me into her car and offering me another caramel Frappuccino. "Take slow small sips," she advised. "You look pale."

I nodded numbly and took a pull on the drink. My thoughts felt muddled, and in spite of the heat, I wasn't hot. Candice went to the rear of the car and pulled out her gym bag, then came back to me and offered me a T-shirt. "Here," she said, blocking my view of Dutch and the others. "Before he sees you and freaks out."

I looked down at myself and saw the bloodstain on my own shirt. "Thanks," I said, whipping out of the shirt as quickly as I could, thankful that I'd donned a sports bra.

No sooner had I tossed my shirt in the backseat than Dutch appeared behind Candice. "You okay?" he asked me, his sunglasses hiding the worry in his eyes, which I knew was there all the same.

"Yeah," I told him. "I'm fine. What's happening over there?"

"We're taking the case," he said. "APD's not happy, but they've agreed to allow us to investigate since Gallagher was about to deliver sensitive information in an ongoing FBI investigation." He said that like he'd already had a crack at saying it, and I had to hand it to him—Gallagher hadn't been involved in an ongoing FBI investigation as much as he'd been the subject of an informal investigation. We were pushing the boundaries on this one, and don't think I wasn't grateful to Brice, my husband, and all the bureau boys backing me up right then.

Candice turned to him and said, "It's official, then?"

Dutch nodded. "Yep. We've got a few more guys coming down to help canvass the area. See if anybody can give us a description of the killer."

"We may not need that," Candice said, pulling the Baggie out of her bag. "Gallagher was trying to give Abby this when he was shot."

Dutch's brows rose above the rim of his sunglasses and his head swiveled to me. "You were next to him when he was shot?" He said that like an accusation.

"No!" I said quickly. "I was way over on the other side of the street." I pointed to where I'd been standing when the shot rang out.

"Is that blood on your hand?" he demanded.

I dropped my hand to my lap quickly. "No," I lied.

"Goddammit, Abby!" he swore. And I knew he was convinced that I was lying both about where I'd been when the shot rang out and about the brown rust stains on my shaking hands. Dutch turned in a half circle and roared, *"Rodriguez!"*

I set the Frappuccino I'd been holding with my free hand in the cup holder and got out of the car. Before Oscar could come over to get yelled at, I stepped right up to my husband and poked him in the chest. "Hey!" I snapped. "Big guy. Chill the fuck out, okay? We have more important things to worry about right now other than who was where and what was what!"

Dutch put his hands on his hips. "Tell me the truth," he said after I'd poked him a second time for good measure. "Where were you when Gallagher was shot?"

I sighed dramatically and pointed again to the spot across the street. "There," I said. "I swear to God I was right over there."

Dutch swiveled his head from where I was pointing to where Gallagher still lay. The distance was at least thirty yards. "Okay," he said. "The shot wasn't meant for you."

I rolled my eyes. "Duh."

Dutch turned again and I took the opportunity while his back was to me to wave Oscar away with a frantic hand motion. No way did I want him anywhere near where my husband could grill him about why I'd been the closest to Gallagher at the time of the shooting.

Oscar looked a bit confused, but then he seemed to get it, and he gave me a hurried salute and did an about-face, hustling back toward Cox.

Meanwhile, Candice had stepped up to Dutch and was looking in the same direction he was. "Hell of a shot," she said.

"I was thinking the same thing," Dutch agreed.

"Military training?" she asked.

"Most likely," he said. Then he lifted the Baggie holding the baseball. "Wow," he said. "If that isn't the most perfect fingerprint."

"If our shooter spent time in the military, we'll be able to get a match," Candice said. The FBI had access to military fingerprint databases.

"That needs to be done soon," I said. "The clock is running out and we've got to get as much as we can to Cal."

Dutch eyed the ball through the Baggie. "We won't be able to get a positive ID on the blood for at least forty-eight hours, Abs," he said, as if he wanted to prepare me for another round of bad news. "Even if we put this at the top of the lab's list, the fastest they could have it back to us would be Wednesday."

"Why does that matter?" I asked. "If we can get a match on the fingerprint . . . oh, now I see. The fingerprint means nothing if we didn't find the ball at the crime scene."

"Exactly. All we have is circumstantial evidence indicating it *might* be the baseball taken from Noah's room. Until the blood comes back as an exact match to his, there's no way to tell where it came from."

I shook my head in frustration. "Do you think it'll be enough to convince the appellate court to cut us a break?"

"Maybe," Dutch said. "As long as we can identify who the fingerprint belongs to. It could be enough for Cal to make a solid case that this new evidence warrants at least a stay of a week or two until the evidence can be fully investigated."

Candice pointed to the Baggie. "Best get that processed ASAP, then."

We spent the rest of the late morning and early afternoon going through all the motions of documenting my statement and how the ball fell out of Gallagher's grasp as he lay dying. Luckily, we were able to recover his fingerprints all over the Baggie, along with mine, Candice's, and Dutch's, but no one else's, which was good, because another person's fingerprints would've been hard to explain. Then our fingerprint expert, Agent Don Whysall, hovered over the ball, carefully extracted that one perfect print, scanned it into his computer, and ran it against AFIS, which was the national fingerprint database and which held about seventy *million* fingerprint records. He also simultaneously ran it against the military fingerprint database.

I sat behind Don and bit my nails. "Anything yet?" I asked after ten minutes without any indication from Whysall that he had something positive to share.

"Nope," he said.

"But did you run it against all those names we gave you?" I asked. Just to cover our bases, I'd given Whysall a list of names of Skylar's ex-boyfriends, Wayne Babson and Connor Lapkus, along with her ex-pimp, Rico DeLaria.

"Ran them first," he said. "Not a match."

"Crap," I muttered, then settled down into my seat again and continued to stare at Don's screen. And then I thought of something. "What about Gallagher?" I asked. "Did you compare it to his prints?"

"Ran that second," Don said without looking up from his computer, where he was busy typing something. "No match there either."

My knee bounced for a while as I waited, and then I got up to pace a track right behind Whysall's chair. "Why isn't it dinging or something?" I asked him after another fifteen minutes or so.

Don sighed. "Cooper, this could take a while, okay? So why don't you go sit at your own desk and I'll call you if and when I get a hit."

I glanced up at the clock. Skylar's appeal was to begin at ten the following morning. Cal absolutely needed something from us tonight if we were going to be able to help him put a solid case together in time. "How long will it take?"

"Maybe only another minute," Don said, and I got hopeful. "Or, could be a couple of hours. If it doesn't come up with a match, then it could be all night before it's done."

"All night?!" I said. "Are you kidding?"

Don offered me a level glare. "Do I look like I'm kidding? Come on, girl. You know how this works. I put the picture in, and it works backward through time to cover all possible matches, from the most recent on back."

Moodily I shuffled over to my desk and sat there anxiously waiting. Dutch tapped my foot about an hour later. "How ya doin'?"

"Frustrated," I said, nodding toward Whysall. "I would've sworn he'd come back with a hit by now."

Dutch sat down on the edge of my desk. "The crime is ten years old, Edgar. Whoever committed it might not have committed anything else since. Give AFIS time to work. It'll offer up someone."

But I had a bad feeling. "Anything on the canvass?" I asked.

"Nope. Oscar, Candice, and the others are headed back this way. They all struck out. The best description we got was from Oscar, who only saw a blur of movement from the top floor of the abandoned apartment. He says he couldn't even be sure of the guy's race."

I growled. "This case just *won't* cut us a break!"

"Hey," Dutch said, putting a hand on my shoulder. "How about we take a break for a few. Get you something to eat?"

I sighed. "Fine. But we're coming right back here and waiting until AFIS gives us a match."

"Deal," Dutch agreed.

We ate and came right back, but still, there was no match from AFIS. While I sat around rather helplessly, the boys worked Gallagher's murder forensically. The bullet was recovered and Dutch told me it came from a high-powered hunting rifle. The shooter had used hollow points, which explained why Gallagher had bled so profusely. The bullet had caused unsurvivable damage to his insides. He'd never had a chance.

"Are we still thinking military?" I asked Dutch on one of my many tours around the office's perimeter.

"Probably," he said. "The guy was a hell of a shot. Even I'd have trouble making it."

That won him some raised eyebrows from me. Dutch was an excellent marksman.

"If he's got military background," Brice said, taking a seat next to Dutch, "then we'll definitely find him in the database."

I crossed my fingers and glanced nervously at Whysall's desk. His computer continued to whir, but made no pings or dings to let us know that he'd found anything yet.

A bit later when I was sitting at my desk again, Candice brought me some coffee. "Have you talked to Cal?" she asked.

"About ten minutes ago," I said, glancing at my watch and noting that it was now a little before nine p.m. "He's worried we won't have enough to go to court with."

Candice lifted her cup toward Whysall. "He could still find us a match," she said.

"He has to," I whispered. That terrible feeling was taking firm hold in the pit of my stomach again. "We can't lose tomorrow, Candice. They'll kill her, and she didn't do it."

Candice squeezed my arm. "Come on," she said. "Let's do some digging."

I followed Candice out of the office and down to her car. Once we were in and driving through downtown, I asked, "Where're we going, anyway?"

"To Gallagher's."

My brow furrowed. "To his house? At nine o'clock at night?"

"Yep."

"Why?"

"He has a kid, remember? The kid must have a mother, and I'm betting they live together, so let's go talk to her, see if she knew anything about the baseball and maybe even what happened that night."

"Whoa," I said, turning in my seat to face her. "Candice, we *can't* just go over there and start grilling her. She just lost her boyfriend."

Candice's fingers gripped the steering wheel a little more tightly, causing the leather to squeak. "We don't have time to wait, Sundance. Skylar's life is on the line, and yeah, I realize she's likely going to be distraught and she may even tell us to go to hell for barging in on her at a time like this, but we have to try, because waiting around for AFIS to make a connection won't do us jack unless we can put a few more of these puzzle pieces together. We gotta figure out how Gallagher came to have Noah's baseball in his possession, and the only person who may be able to tell us that, now that Dennis is dead, is his girlfriend."

I thought about that for a bit. "Yeah, okay," I said. "You're right. We don't have time to let her grieve. We gotta figure out what she may know tonight. Hell, when I think about it, if Gallagher talked to her about the baseball, *her* life could be in danger."

"Good point," Candice said, and she stepped on the gas to send us racing for the highway.

We arrived at Dennis Gallagher's place not long after. He lived, not surprisingly, about a half mile from Skylar Miller's old house. His neighborhood wasn't as new, or as nice, but it wasn't terrible either. His house, in fact, was a surprise.

There were a couple of cars in the driveway, so we parked at the curb, and walked up the short sidewalk to a very cute, well-kept ranch with a xeriscape garden, a front porch featuring two Adirondack chairs painted a light blue, and a flower box overflowing with blooms along the front window.

We stepped up to the door and heard lots of voices coming from inside, along with the sounds of weeping. I grimaced but raised my hand and knocked on the door. It was opened by a short woman with salt-and-pepper hair, pulled back severely enough to allow tufts to break loose and puff about her head, giving her a rumpled appearance. Her eyes were red and watery and she seemed both curious about our appearance at her door and mildly detached. "Hello," I began. "My name is Abigail Cooper, and this is my assoc—"

The woman gasped and turned around to call into the house. "Elaina! Elaina! It's that woman! That woman that Denny was gonna meet!"

I will admit to taking a slight step back from the door, and beside me Candice edged closer to my side. The door was pulled open by another woman, whose black hair fell around her exotically. She was quite beautiful, even given her tearstained face, and seeing her was enough to give me pause. How Dennis had landed such a beautiful woman I had no idea, because she was truly striking and he'd been nothing special.

She glanced from me to Candice and back again, and said, "Which one of you is the lady?"

I raised my hand feebly. "Me."

She placed two curled fingers to her mouth and bit down as tears welled over the edges of her lower lids and slid down her cheeks. She was one of those women who when they cry, become even more beautiful, and her pain was so raw and so real that I felt my own emotions stir. "I'm so sorry for your loss," I said.

"Did he tell you?" she managed in a quavering voice.

"Tell me what?" I asked.

She took a shuddering breath. "He met with you, right?" she said. "Before he got shot?"

I stepped forward again and took her hand. She was trembling so hard that I was worried she wasn't going to be able to keep standing. "Elaina, is it?" She nodded. "Can we get you some water and have you come out here to sit in one of the chairs so we can talk?"

"I'll get it," the older woman said, disappearing into the house. Candice and I eased Elaina over to the chairs and she sat down, still shaking hard, and the tears kept coming. Candice reached into her purse and offered her a tissue. She took it gratefully.

We waited for the older woman—who I assumed was her mother—to come out and give her the water, and then she left us alone to talk. I sat on the chair next to Elaina and Candice sat down on the arm of the chair. I motioned for Elaina to sip her water, and she did, wiping her eyes again too. "You okay?" I asked.

"He told me once that he wasn't going to live to see his baby grow up," she said, her voice breaking. "He knew."

I nodded and reached out to squeeze her hand. This had to be so hard on her. "We're sorry that we've come at such a bad time," I said. "But this is important."

"They're gonna put that lady to her death soon, huh?"

I kept my expression as neutral as possible. She knew about Skylar. "Yes," I said. "They are. Dennis was going to help us, wasn't he?"

She blinked and fresh tears formed in her eyes. "He didn't tell you?"

I shook my head. "He tried, Elaina, but he never got the chance."

"That guy shot him," she said, her lip quivering and her tone bitter.

"Which guy?" I asked.

"The guy he got the ball from. The guy who killed that boy."

Candice put her phone on the arm of the chair right next to her. It was facedown, and I knew she'd hit the Record button again. She then said, "Elaina, can you start from the beginning? We're coming in here in the middle and we're having a hard time figuring it all out."

Elaina wiped her cheeks with the wet tissue and took a deep breath. "I met Denny a few years ago. He was bad news. Like seriously bad news, and I wanted nothing to do with him. He told me that he fell in love with me the moment he saw me, and he wanted to change, to prove to me that he was worthy of a woman like me. I told him talk is cheap, you know?" Candice and I both nodded. We totally understood.

"Anyway," she continued, "my family and I are really involved in our church, so one day, Denny shows up for mass, and I'm all like, 'Honey, you gotta try a whole hell of a lot harder than that!' So the next weekend he comes to mass again. And then he goes with our church to help build a house for the homeless. And then he starts volunteering for the church, not, like, here or there, but, like, all the time. He helps to make repairs on the church, and he builds three more houses for the homeless, and he volunteers at the soup kitchen, and he helps out with the literacy program. This goes on for a while, and at the end of all that, he comes to me and he gets down on bended knee. We haven't even gone out on a date, and he gets down on his knee and he says, 'Elaina, you may not believe me, but I love you. And I want to marry you. You already know I'm no-good. But you don't know how bad news I am. So I want to confess to you every single bad thing I've ever done, and then I want to confess to you every single good thing I've done, and then I want to tell you how many good things I want to do for you, for the church, for your family, and for everyone from this second on. If you'll just say that you'll think about going out with me, then I promise you, I will do these things.'"

Elaina paused to take another sip of water, and Candice reached into her purse again and fished out another fresh tissue for her. After a moment to collect another deep breath, Elaina said, "So I took him up on that. I asked him to tell me all the bad stuff he'd done. It was all the stuff I figured and heard about, except for one thing. And this one thing was that, eleven years ago, Denny was angry at a lady who'd yelled at him in a Home Depot, and he went to her house because he was gonna rob her, but when he got there and started to break in—he said he heard the gate door open. He told me he hustled around the corner of the house to this little spot where the fence formed a nook and he hid. He said he heard someone coming closer to him, and he was sure he'd been seen and it was the cops, but the footsteps stopped and he heard tapping, and then he heard the window slide up and he knew that someone else was breaking into the house. He didn't want to peek because he was afraid he'd be seen, so he just stood there to wait it out.

"After a few more minutes, he said he heard something that sounded really creepy to him. He couldn't explain what it was other than he knew that something really bad was happening in that room. Then it was quiet for a minute, and then he heard a lady call out the name Noah. It was quiet for a few more seconds and then all of a sudden she screamed.

"Denny pinned himself against the back of the fence, and he said he didn't know what to do. He wanted to run, but he was afraid he'd get caught trying to go over the fence, so he just stood there until he heard the sound of someone dropping to the grass right around the corner, and then they went running to the opposite side of the yard and out through the gate.

"Meanwhile, next door the lady was screaming her head off, and he knew the cops were going to be on their way any second. So he got up his nerve, came out from the side of the house, and started to move along the house toward the gate. He said that when he got to the window, though, he stopped. It was dark in the room, but he said he could smell the scent of blood. He looked in through the window and saw the form of a little boy lying on the floor of his room. He knew then that the guy had killed the little kid, and he froze. He didn't know what to do—he was so freaked-out.

"Denny said that he could still hear the lady screaming from the house next door, and he realized that he was right in the middle of a murder scene. He was so scared that the cops were going to think he'd killed the little boy that he tried to cover his tracks. He closed the window, put the screen back in, and it was when he was about to leave that he kicked a ball that was lying in the grass right below the window. He said he didn't know why, but he bent over and picked it up, stuffed it in the backpack he'd brought, and headed to the back fence to climb over it and run for it.

"When he got home, he turned on the TV and saw the breaking story that a boy in East Austin had just been murdered. Denny said that when he took the ball out of his backpack, it had a bloody fingerprint on it. He'd worn gloves to the lady's house, and he said he never actually touched the ball without wearing gloves, but he knew that if he took it to the police, they'd pin him for murder just for being there."

Dennis's fears weren't misplaced. In Texas, if you're an accessory to a crime like burglary and during the commission of that crime someone is killed, even if you're the getaway driver out on the street and never set foot inside the house, you'll still be charged with murder, which in Texas is also a capital offense.

It's a widely known fact among criminals. I was certain Elaina was speaking the truth about Dennis's motivation for holding on to the ball all these years.

"He also told me that at first, he was happy that the kid's mom was being charged with the crime. He was still really mad at her for disrespecting him, but as time went on, he knew he'd done a bad thing by covering up the other man's escape. Denny had only been trying to cover up for himself, but in doing that, he'd let the real killer go free. I think that's why he held on to the ball all these years. It reminded him of the bad thing he'd done. He felt he needed to remember that to keep him from going back to his old ways."

"And he never thought about getting the ball to the police anonymously?" I asked her. I mean, if I'd been Gallagher and I'd felt as guilty as he'd claimed to his girlfriend that he was, I would've done something about it.

Elaina looked at me as if she'd had that same argument with Dennis before. Perhaps many times. "Denny's favorite show was *CSI*," she said. "He and I used to watch all of them, *CSI*, *CSI: NY*, *CSI: Miami*. On one of them there was a show about some guy who'd witnessed a murder, picking up the leather glove the killer had dropped with the victim's blood on it. They did that thing in the show where they made the camera focus on a small drop of sweat dropping from the witness's forehead onto the glove, so you know that the CSI techs were going to find it, and after the witness sent the glove in to the police anonymously, that's exactly what the CSI techs did. They also found a strand of nylon thread from the bag the witness had kept it in on the glove, and all of that led to them bringing the witness in and accusing him of murder.

"At the end of the show, Denny turned to me and told me that he was worried that some of his DNA might be on the ball. He said it was a really hot night, he'd been dressed all in black, and he'd been scared enough to sweat up a storm. He said, 'What if my DNA is on that ball, Elaina? What if a piece of my backpack got stuck to the blood and they trace it back to me? What if they figure out I was there?'

"Denny had a record. They had his DNA on file. He was scared that no matter how much he wanted to send the ball to you guys, you'd find a way to pin him for that little boy's murder.

"And then you arrested him, and you brought up the murder like you knew he was involved. He called me from jail and said he thought he knew of a way out of the mess he got himself into, but it might cost him some time behind bars. I love him, so I told him, 'You do what's right so our son will grow up knowing his dad was a good man, and I'll be here for you when you get out.' He told me then that he was going to call you and set up a meeting to talk to you about the baseball. He said you were the only one who seemed to get it, and he said he felt like he could trust you."

That hit me like a punch in the gut. Gallagher had trusted me, and he'd been killed for it. "Did Dennis ever tell you anything else about the killer?" I asked next. "Did he ever mention catching a glimpse of him?"

Elaina shook her head. "No."

Candice said, "Elaina, did you put up the money for his bail?"

She shook her head. "Denny said he didn't know who put up the money, but I told him it wasn't us."

And then the hair stood up on the back of my neck. "It was the killer," I said softly.

Candice's gaze traveled to me. She gave one nod and got up from the chair, taking her phone with her to walk to the other side of the porch to make a call. Elaina and I waited in silence until she came back. After pocketing her cell, Candice said, "Elaina, I've called one of our agents on duty. He's going to come here tonight and watch over you and your family. We'll wait with you until he arrives, but I want you to stay inside at all times and not leave your home for the next twenty-four hours, all right?"

Alarm flashed across Elaina's features. "You think the guy that shot Denny might come here and try to hurt us?"

Candice said, "No. I don't. But I don't want to take any chances."

Elaina nodded and then she began crying again. Looking up at us as if she could plead Dennis's case, she said, "He made mistakes, you know, but he was trying. He was trying to do the right thing."

I reached out and hugged her. "He was," I told her. "He really was."

Chapter Seventeen

. . .

A few hours later Dutch and I walked through the door of our home, both of us beyond exhausted and too upset to talk. AFIS had come back with not one single hit on our bloody fingerprint, which meant that the killer had no prior record, and until we discovered on our own who he was, we had no way to identify him other than the clues already left to us.

As Dutch headed into the kitchen to fix us both a small snack before bed, I bent down to pick up Tuttle, who'd come out of her bed and was nuzzling my shin. Tuttle is a cuddle bunny, and really, *really* good at lavishing me with kisses. Eggy, on the other hand, snored away in his bed, with nary a nod of acknowledgment. I took Tuts out on the back porch and let her water the lawn, then settled down with her in one of the patio chairs. It was a nice night, still a bit warm, but dry with just a little breeze. Dutch found me outside and handed me a plate with a sandwich. I took it from him and shared a bit of the roast beef with Tuts.

"We tried, dollface," he said, when he saw that I wasn't so much eating as feeding the pup.

I laid my head back on the cushion, hugged Tuttle, and looked up at the stars. It was like staring right up into heaven. "We missed something," I said, my voice hitching a little. I was struggling to hold my emotions in check. It'd been a terrible day.

"Maybe," Dutch said. "But we're probably not gonna find it before the appeals hearing tomorrow."

Tuttle began to tug on the end of the sandwich. It was supercute. She was trying to be really subtle about it. I fed her another piece of beef.

"You feed her the good stuff and she won't want her dog food," Dutch said.

"She's a good pup," I told him. "She can have some of the good stuff now and then."

"Yeah, well, there's horseradish on the bread, babe. Probably not good for dogs."

I gave her another bit of beef. "She doesn't seem to mind."

Dutch polished off his sandwich and regarded me. "Come to bed, sweetheart."

"In a minute," I told him.

He got up, lifted the plate holding my sandwich from me so that Tuttle couldn't gobble it down, and set it on a side table nearby, so that I could reach for it if I wanted it. He then kissed me lightly on the lips and headed back inside.

I lay curled up with my pup for a long time, going over and over the details of the case, trying to figure out what the heck we'd missed, because the nagging feeling that we had missed something wouldn't leave me. But what it could be, I had no idea.

Dutch shook me awake as dawn was making its way across the horizon. "What time is it?" I said, jerking awake and startling Tuttle, who proceeded to cover me with kisses again.

"It's six thirty," he said. "Come to bed, babe."

I sat up and set Tuttle on the grass so she could water the lawn again. I felt groggy and out of it, but I forced myself to shake that off. "No," I said, inhaling a deep breath and getting to my feet. "I need to work on the case."

"What's there to work on?" he asked me. "Until we get some forensics back on the bullet that killed Gallagher to see if it matches anything registered, we're at a dead end."

I leaned into his chest for a moment, gathering my resolve. "I missed something. I don't know what it is yet. But I missed something."

He hugged me, then released me. "Okay," he said. "Go inside and take a shower. I'll get the coffee on, make you some breakfast, and text Candice, and then we'll head into the office and sort it out piece by piece."

Three hours later, with tears in my eyes, I stood up from the conference table where Dutch, Candice, Brice, and Oscar were all poring over the case, and walked to the corner of the room.

I looked at my watch. It was nine thirty-five. Cal was most certainly at the courthouse, about to go in front of the appellate court and fight for Skylar's life. It was a fight I was certain he'd lose.

"Abs?" I heard Dutch call.

"I'm fine," I said sharply. Of course I wasn't, but I didn't want to hear him or anyone else tell me that we'd done our best, but these things happen. Nothing could be done. It'd been a long shot anyway.

Fuck that. (And for that matter, fuck the swear jar.)

I wanted to save Skylar. I wanted her legacy to reflect what a brave woman she'd been to have overcome her addictions and tried her hardest to create a life for herself and her son, in spite of all the odds and people against her, from her mother, to her ex-husband, to her in-laws, to her former pimp, to . . .

"Wait a minute," I whispered as a thought occurred to me. Turning in a circle, I raced back to my chair. "Wait a damn minute!" Two random clues had just come together in my mind and I was so excited I was shaking.

"What's up, Sundance?" Candice asked.

I shuffled through the array of photos from the crime scene. My hands were trembling and that made sorting through them difficult, so I finally just dropped them on the table and pushed the ones I didn't need out of the way. "Where is it? Where is it?" I asked, frantic to find the one I was looking for.

"Abs?" Dutch said again.

I ignored him. Instead I pushed photos aside until I got to the back of the stack and there it was. "Oh . . . my . . . God," I said.

Oscar got up and came around to my side of the table to look over my shoulder. "What?" he asked. And I understood that he didn't see what I saw yet. We'd missed it a dozen times already, but I needed to show him a comparison before it would make sense.

Without answering him, I dug back through the stack and easily found the other photo I needed. Pushing back from the table again, I walked over to the whiteboard against the back wall and moved the little magnets we used to secure photos and such to the board over the two photos. Turning to the other four in the room, I said, "Notice anything?"

Everyone squinted at the two photos. The first was an image that captured Noah's bed, and the second was the view that captured Skylar's bed. "No," Candice and Brice said, while Dutch shook his head and Oscar stared at me like he didn't get it either.

I pointed to the bedcovers on Noah's bed. Then to the bedcovers on Skylar's bed. Still everyone stared as if they had no idea what I could be hinting at. "It was there all along," I said. "Right under my freaking nose."

"Abs," Dutch said a bit impatiently. "Just tell us."

"Do you see how Skylar's covers have been tossed to the side?" Everyone nodded. "It's because she heard a noise coming from Noah's room. She said she woke in a panic because she heard a noise and raced out of bed. That's what you do when you've been jarred awake and have to run out of bed. You throw over the covers."

Brice frowned. "Okay, so what's your point, Cooper?"

I pointed to Noah's bed. "His covers haven't been thrown to the side," I said. "They've been pushed down and shoved to the end of the bed. Noah was a high-energy kid," I went on, seeing they weren't following me at all. "I figure he slept like most little boys with lots of rolling over and thrashing limbs. And that's what his covers show. That he moved around a lot when he was asleep and got tangled up in his legs a little. What they don't show is someone else's presence in the room, grabbing him out of bed."

"I'm still lost," Candice said.

Oscar raised his hand. "Me too."

I got down on the ground and lay back to mime it out. "I'm Noah," I said. Then, I sort of flopped around on the floor a little, kicking my legs a bit. "Now, it's two thirty in the morning, Noah is asleep, and Dennis Gallagher's girlfriend told us that at that exact time he was around the corner of the house hiding, and then he heard tapping on the window. *Tapping*."

Candice's mouth dropped. "He let the killer in," she said breathlessly. "Noah let the killer in!"

I nodded and got to my feet. Pointing again to the photo of Noah's bed, I took them all through it. "Noah hears tapping, and he's tangled in the covers, so he kicks them free and they end up mostly pooled at the bottom of his bed. He then gets out of bed, opens the window, and lets the killer in. The killer didn't sneak into the room, grab him out of bed, and murder him. Noah's bedcovers would've been pulled all the way to the side after being tangled in his limbs if that'd been the case."

"Okay, so who was it?" Brice asked. "Who did Noah know well enough that he'd let him into his bedroom at two thirty in the morning?"

I moved over to pick up the baseball from the center of the table. "What do we know about this ball?" I asked. Oscar had had one of our techs do some background on the baseball to make sure that it lined up with what Skylar had told us about it coming from Noah's bedroom.

I'd read the report about an hour earlier, as I knew everyone else had. The results were a bit surprising, but I didn't think of its supreme importance until that moment. Oscar said, "World Series ball from game five, nineteen sixty-nine, signed by Yogi Berra, Nolan Ryan, among others. It's worth about eighty thousand dollars. Purchased by Grant Miller at auction in nineteen eighty-six for twenty thousand."

I smiled. "Grant had that ball for all those years. I'd imagine that he wanted the baseball to go to his grandson because it was one of his most treasured possessions. He and Noah shared a passion for baseball. And so did someone else in the family."

Oscar and Candice shared a look. "Chris?" she said.

I nodded. "Chris."

Oscar swiveled his chair and looked like he had something to add. "Cooper, did you know what business Chris is in?"

"Uh, no," I said.

"He buys and sells sports memorabilia."

My brow shot up. "For real?"

"Yeah. When I went to ask him about his mother-in-law, I found him in the office above his shop."

"So Chris would've not only known the value of the ball, but he would've been hard-pressed to leave it behind."

"Especially if it'd once belonged to his dad," Candice said.

I pointed to her. "And the night that Noah was murdered, Skylar told me that Chris had called, she'd given the phone to Noah, and then she'd headed to the shower, so she hadn't heard what they'd been talking about."

"According to court testimony," Candice said, "Noah had insinuated that he had something important to tell him but didn't feel comfortable telling him anywhere his mom could overhear, and Chris had taken that to mean later that Skylar had fallen back off the wagon."

"But why would a kid be worried about his mom overhearing him if she's in the shower?" I said. "I mean, you can't hear anything in the shower."

Candice went back to typing rapidly on her computer.

"So what was it that they talked about?" Dutch asked.

"I think I know. I think that what Noah said to his dad was that he wanted to go on living with his mom. I think Chris Miller was trying to talk his son into changing his mind, and coming back to live with him, and Noah let him know that he wanted to stay put. And since Skylar and Chris were due back in court at the end of the month to meet with the judge, who was going to take Noah's wishes into consideration when they met to either continue the custody ruling or change it, I'm guessing Chris knew that night that he'd lost custody for good."

"Chris Miller has a hunting license!" Candice said suddenly. We all looked at her. "And," she added, "look what photos I found on his Facebook page." She swiveled the computer around so we could see. On the screen were several photos of Chris proudly holding a hunting rifle, standing next to a wild boar he'd obviously killed.

Oscar grabbed her computer and enlarged the image. "That's a Remington," he said knowingly. "Thirty caliber."

"Same caliber we pulled out of Gallagher," Brice said.

"Any military background?" Dutch asked, and I knew he was wondering whether Chris would be ruled out based on the fact that there was no print match from the baseball.

"No," Candice said. "No military record that I've found yet, but he is an excellent marksman, as these pictures show." She leaned forward across the table where Oscar still had her computer to click her keyboard again, and a photo of Chris holding his rifle and a blue ribbon at some sort of marksman tournament popped up.

I felt the back of my scalp tingle. It was all falling into place.

"Okay," Dutch said, adopting his best devil's advocate face. "So, Chris crawls into his son's bedroom, murders him, and slips back out the way he came, taking the ball with him when he went. But what about the knife, Abs? How did he make it to the kitchen and back without leaving any footprints?"

I smiled the smile of someone so relieved to finally have the missing puzzle piece in hand. "Easy," I said. "He'd taken it a few weeks before."

Everyone looked around at one another. Oscar said, "Huh?"

I fished through the murder file again to a page that inventoried the contents of the kitchen drawer where Skylar had kept her kitchen knives. "Skylar told me that the murder weapon was part of a larger high-end knife set she'd gotten as a wedding present. I looked up the knives, and they're crazy expensive, made by a Japanese manufacturer named Shun. According to Skylar, when they split up the marital assets, she got the knives in the divorce settlement. So, not only did Chris know what knife set to buy to swap out for the one in the drawer; he also had an opportunity to do that when he came to Noah's birthday party. My guess is that he switched the knives when he passed through the kitchen when no one was looking, because Noah's party was on the back porch."

"To what end?" Candice asked. "Why swap out a knife when he could've just brought his own to the scene?"

"Remember the smudged fingerprints of Skylar's found on the handle that weren't bloody?" I said. "I think that Chris wanted to make it really clear that the knife belonged to Skylar. I think that he wanted to frame her for Noah's murder all along. I think that he had some sort of elaborate plan to kill Noah using the knife, then murder Skylar, stage her murder to look like suicide, and have everyone think she killed Noah in a rage before taking her own life."

"But wouldn't everyone assume that a killer had broken in, killed them both, and just used a knife from the kitchen?" Brice asked.

Before answering him, I went back to the table and fished around for another photo. Bringing it back to the board, I tacked it up so that everyone could see it. "See this?" I said, pointing to the house phone, lying on the floor near the closet. "That phone was found in the exact same spot where Skylar claimed that the intruder had jumped out to attack her. Now, that's important because when Dioli talked to us a few days ago, he said that when he delivered the death notification to Chris, Noah's dad had shown him his cell phone, which he claimed had rung in the middle of the night but he'd been too tired to answer it, and only when Dioli showed up did he realize the importance of the call.

"That's why Dioli didn't look to Chris as a possible suspect. Chris's cell was his alibi. Also, in the murder file itself, Dioli confirms that phone records indicate that a call was made from Skylar's landline to Chris's phone at the exact time of the murder.

"Now, the really interesting thing that I also didn't connect was that, in the file, Dioli notes that he wanted to present the call at trial to show that Noah had made one last desperate attempt to get help, but, he notes, the DA kicked the call log out because the medical examiner's report showed that Noah wouldn't have been capable of doing anything like dialing the house phone or even hitting redial. He was either rendered unconscious or dead within moments of being stabbed. Dioli didn't investigate the anomaly further because he really likes to ignore things that don't make his case add up. I myself discounted Chris for a lot of reasons, but when I read that the phone call from Skylar's house had been sent to Chris's cell, I'd just assumed he'd been home too. I hadn't even considered that Chris had wanted it to look like that all along.

"Anyway, the way I see it is that, after stabbing his son, Chris's gloved hands literally have blood on them. Maybe the blood has soaked through, so he takes off his gloves momentarily so as not to get blood on Skylar's phone, and he's not worried about leaving a print on it, because he's the ex, and he was just there for Noah's birthday, so his prints would be in the house, or maybe he planned to wipe the phone down after, anyway; the point is that *he's* the one who dials his cell, and while he's waiting for the call to go through, he's walking toward the closet area, and maybe that's when he also picks up the baseball. He's probably worked it all out to establish his alibi this way. I mean, it's believable, right?" Several heads in the room nodded. I continued. "Right—so, he's in the middle of making that call when Skylar walks into the room, interrupting him, but doesn't even see Chris because she's too focused on Noah, who's on the floor.

"As he watches his ex-wife bend down to their son, Chris must've realized that he's left the knife next to Noah, and he's wondering what to do, and then he just decides to attack and kill her, but she gets away. In a panic he dives out the window and runs off, hoping that the call to his cell at his house is enough to establish that he wasn't there. On his way out of the window, however, he drops the baseball, which Dennis then picks up, and he inadvertently helps Chris out by closing the window and putting the screen back in place."

"That's a pretty elaborate plan, Edgar," Dutch said.

"Do you have a better theory?" I asked him.

"No," he said, with a slight smile. "But what I also don't have is a motive."

"I know," I admitted. "Being angry at Noah for picking his mom over him is a little thin."

"I have a question," Brice said.

"Shoot," I told him.

"If Chris switched out the knife, and Skylar swears she used the murder weapon to chop up the salad that night, wouldn't there be an extra knife at the scene?"

I went back to the table and rummaged through the CSI inventory of everything that was in the house that night, including the kitchen's contents. Running my finger down the page, I let out a breath of relief when it landed on the one I was looking for. "There was," I said, and held the list out to Brice. "See? 'One utility knife, wood handle, Chinese symbol. Six and a half inches.' This is the duplicate knife to the one used to murder Noah, which is on this list, here." I picked up a separate list, which inventoried the contents of Noah's room, where the murder weapon was found.

"Utility knife—wood handle, Japanese symbol on blade. Six and a half inches," Candice said. "Sweet Jesus, you'd think they would've noticed a duplicate knife!"

"Obviously someone mistook the symbol on the knife from the drawer for Chinese, and the person who inventoried Noah's bedroom knew it to be Japanese, but still, I agree, they overlooked quite a few things on this case to make their theory that Skylar did it stick," I said.

"We still need a motive," Dutch said. "Or, something usable to bring Chris in for questioning."

Brice glanced at the wall above my head where the clock was. "It's ten to ten," he said.

My stomach muscles clenched. I pulled out my cell and called Cal. It rolled to voice mail. I left him an urgent message to call me back before he went into court. Once I'd hung up, everyone in the room looked grim. "We're so close," I told them. "We can't give up now."

"Abs," Dutch said softly. "There isn't enough to give Cal before the appeal."

"I know," I told him. "And he'll lose. But we'll still have a shot at the Board of Pardons."

"They've never granted clemency," Candice reminded me, her expression pained as if it hurt her to say that.

"True," I said. "But there's always a first time, and no *way* am I giving up now." Turning to Brice, I said, "Have you had any luck rushing the labs on the blood from the baseball?"

"I put in another call about an hour ago," he said. "He said no way can he get us DNA matches until tomorrow, but he will probably be able to narrow the spectrum of possibility down to around ninety-seven percent by ten a.m. In other words, he'll be matching certain isotopes, blood type, and other science-sounding stuff to give us at least a ninety-seven percent likelihood that the blood on the ball is Noah's."

"I like those odds," I said. "And if we can at least nail Miller for shooting Gallagher, we can also grill him about his son's murder."

Oscar said, "In order to get a warrant for the hunting rifle,

Cooper, we'll need to show the judge that we have probable cause, and it needs to be more than what we have on hand, because Miller has money and connections."

I reached again for the baseball. "I have just the plan," I told him. "I'm calling it: two birds, one baseball."

Two hours later I got a quick call from Cal. The appellate court had upheld Skylar's conviction and impending execution. He had an appointment to meet with the Board of Pardons at four, but Skylar was already scheduled to be put to death at midnight.

I had to work hard to slow the rapid uptick in my heart rate upon hearing that, because I couldn't afford to appear anything but confident as I strode down the walk and into that familiar Starbucks.

Chris Miller was sitting in the far corner, watching the door. The Starbucks was empty of anyone who actually worked there. Candice was behind the counter in a green apron, doing her best to appear like an earnest barista, intent on scrubbing down the counter and espresso machine. Brice sat at a table by the window, pretending to talk on his phone, and Dutch sat at another nearby table, wearing a baseball cap, a long-sleeved button-down shirt with the sleeves rolled up, khaki shorts, and sandals. He was seemingly absorbed in the sports page.

I moved over to sit at the table with Chris. He considered me with a steely glare. "Elaina?"

I nodded. "You killed my boyfriend," I said softly, managing also to get my voice to quiver and tears to form in my eyes.

"That's a hell of an accusation," he told me. He wore a confident smile. The kind a snake adopts right before it springs for a mouse.

"But it's true," I told him. "Dennis told me all about you. And I know you were the one to pay his bail."

"You have proof?" he asked me, as if he couldn't believe some lowlife would dare confront him.

I nodded and lifted my purse, taking out the baseball covered in red gore and blue scribbling across the center. "You left this when you killed your little boy," I told him. "Denny gave it to me because he knew you were going to try to kill him."

Chris's eyes widened at the sight of the ball in my hand, but then his confidence returned. "Right," he snapped. "You're delusional."

"Denny didn't know who you were at first," I told him. "But then he saw you on TV at Skylar Miller's trial, and he told me that you were the guy he saw coming out of the window that night. He knew you were the one that killed your little boy." I was of course lying through my teeth, but Chris Miller didn't know that.

"My ex-wife killed my son," he said angrily. "A crime for which she'll pay with her own life sometime around midnight."

I studied him. "Not if I go to the FBI and tell them everything Dennis told me, and give them this ball. That's going to lead to some questions, Mr. Miller. And maybe even a press release."

Miller glared hard at me. "What do you want?"

"This ball is for sale," I said. "One million dollars."

Chris laughed and shook his head. "You have a son of your own, don't you, Elaina?"

I was careful to appear shocked and scared by his statement. "You leave my son out of this," I hissed.

Chris began to draw little lazy circles on the table with his finger. Speaking very softly, he said, "I know where you live, bitch. Don't think I can't take care of you too."

Crap. That wasn't the confession I'd wanted, but I still had a card to play. "You killed my boyfriend," I repeated. "You owe me something for that."

Chris sighed heavily, then reached into his back pocket. I stiffened, but he withdrew his wallet and pulled out a hundred. Tossing it on the table in front of me, he said, "Your boyfriend did me a favor, you know, closing the window and putting back that screen. Made it look like no one but Sky had ever been there. It worked out better than even I'd planned, and for that, you can keep the change."

I shuddered for effect, set the ball on the table without meeting his eyes, and picked up the hundred. Taking a moment to gather my purse, I stood up and waited for him to pick up the ball. The second he did, I couldn't help but smile a little. "That autograph sort of says it all, don't you think?"

Lifting my gaze, I watched as Chris's brow lowered in confusion, and then he inspected the ball. Written across the brand-new baseball we'd purchased an hour before, and covered in smeared blood from Oscar's pricked finger, was the word *Murderer*.

Chris lifted his eyes back to me and realization dawned in his eyes. He then glanced at Candice behind the counter. She was staring at him with contempt. His eyes darted next to his left and saw that Dutch had set aside his paper and was also glaring at him. Swiveling his head to the right, he took in Brice, who'd stood up with a set of handcuffs in hand.

Chris dropped the ball on the table. It bounced once and I caught it, my hand now wrapped in a plastic bag, which I then folded over the ball and dropped back into my purse. "Game over, douche bag," I told him, peeling back the collar of my shirt to reveal the wire taped to my chest.

Quicker than I could've expected it, Chris lunged at me. He grabbed me by the throat and pulled me hard to him as he also kicked the table toward Dutch, who'd begun to spring to my aid. And then I felt the muzzle of a gun at my temple.

"Back off!" he yelled to everyone in the room. It was unnecessary. Nobody dared advance on him with me in his clutches.

It took me a few moments to recover myself, but then I was able to look around the room and assess the situation. Brice, Dutch, and Candice all had their guns drawn and aimed at Miller. He had me by the neck, and he was backed into a corner. I was still holding my purse.

Advantage team Abby.

As Miller shouted for everybody else to drop their weapons, I eased my hand into the big purse and wrapped my fingers around a small canister, placing my thumb just over the trigger. Calmly I said to all of them, "Guys, it's okay. Drop your guns and do what he says."

I looked meaningfully at each of my protectors in turn, but Dutch was very reluctant to let his weapon go. Miller gripped me tighter and shouted at him, and I managed to mouth, *Please* to my husband, who finally did crouch to drop his weapon.

"You!" Miller shouted to Candice. "Get out here!" Candice came out from around the counter, her hands in the air. "On the floor!" Miller yelled next. "All of you get your asses on the floor, your hands behind your back!"

Brice was the first to comply. Candice followed, but Dutch resisted. My stubborn husband. I wanted to yell at him too, but before I had time to beg him to obey, Miller withdrew the gun from my temple and pointed it at Dutch. The warning in my head went off a millisecond before Miller pulled the trigger, and I managed, somehow, to get my elbow up in time to knock the gun's deadly aim away from its target. The gun went off, the bullet went wide, and I spun around to spray Miller in the face with a good dose of Mace. He went down to the floor, writhing and covering his eyes with his left arm. I went under his arm and continued to spray his face, even as I dropped to my knees to land on the out-stretched hand holding the gun. "You. Son. Of. A. BITCH!" I yelled, and he wriggled and tried to hit me with his free hand. I took the blow on the shoulder and just kept squirting him.

And I would've continued to empty the canister, except that Dutch hooked me under both arms as Brice came up on my left to remove the gun from Miller's hand and slap a cuff on him.

Dutch lifted me away, allowing Candice and Brice to twist Miller onto his back and secure his hands.

The whole thing was over in about ten seconds, but I kept shaking for much of the rest of the afternoon.

At two o'clock I was pacing the hallway outside the interroga-tion room, staring at my watch every five seconds and muttering under my breath. At last I heard voices coming from the other side of the hallway and I straightened up when I saw Oscar come around the corner leading Dioli. "Detective," I said, holding out my hand to him.

He shook it even though his face registered a mixture of irrita-tion and annoyance with perhaps a dash of suspicion. "Abby," he said. "I'm here. What's this urgent case involving Skylar Miller you needed me to look at?"

I took a breath. This was going to be tricky, but I couldn't ac-complish what I needed to without Dioli's cooperation. Pointing over my shoulder to the door behind me, I said, "It's in here, but, Detective, I'd like for you to make me a promise before we enter the room."

His eyes narrowed. "What kind of promise?"

"I'd like for you to let me do all the talking. And no matter how much you're tempted to say something, or perhaps even to walk out of the room, I'm going to ask you to stay put until I'm finished."

Dioli's brow folded low over his eyes. He didn't like my conditions, mostly, I suspected, because he couldn't figure out what my angle was. Still, I knew he'd heard that Skylar's last appeal had been denied, and I thought he was feeling pretty confident that I wasn't going to derail her execution. By the end of our meeting, I truly hoped he'd want nothing more than to help me save her life.

After studying me for a bit, as if waiting to see if I'd say more, Dioli said, "Is this gonna take long?"

"No, sir."

"Fine. Let's get this over with, then."

I nodded to Oscar, who spun on his heel and headed toward the observation room while I turned to the door and opened it. Dioli followed me inside.

At the table sat Chris Miller, his face a mass of puffy redness, his eyes still leaking tears. Eyes that held not an ounce of regret or remorse. Which would still work in my favor. I hoped.

Next to Chris sat his attorney, dressed in a suit that likely cost more than all the outfits in my closet. Combined.

Out of the corner of my eye I saw Dioli pause in the doorway as he took note of Chris, but he didn't say a word and came to the table to sit in the seat next to me. Once he was settled, Miller's attorney, a guy named Mel something, said to me, "I've advised my client not to say a word."

I smiled tightly. "Of course you have. And thank goodness he's paying you all that money to advise him to stay silent, something he had every intention of doing anyway."

Mel pursed his lips at me. I ignored him and focused on Miller. "Here's the thing, Chris: I don't need you to say a word. I've got all I need without your input. You're here almost inconsequentially, actually. The person I really need to hear what I've got to say is currently seated on my left, and by the end of this conversation where you say absolutely nothing, I hope to convince him what a very bad person you are."

Without looking at Dioli, I bent down and pulled up my big purse. It was a technique I'd seen Kyra Sedgwick do repeatedly on old episodes of *The Closer*, and I'd always liked the effect of it. "So, first off, I gotta say thank you for providing the fingerprint." I pulled out the baseball I'd brought to Starbucks from out of my purse and slapped it on the table. It made a nice loud thunk. "The print you provided from your left index finger, Chris, ended up being a perfect match to this one. . . ." Reaching back into my purse, I pulled out the actual baseball I'd gotten from Gallagher. The one he'd picked up in Skylar's backyard, smeared with Noah's blood. Next to me I could feel Dioli's gaze tracking my every move. "You may recognize this baseball," I said, smacking it down on the table as well. "It came from your son's room." Then I slapped down a crime-scene photo taken in Noah's room with a view of his dresser and the blood-spattered wall behind it. "And we know *this* ball came from Noah's room because—see that?" I pointed to the small round void on the wall behind the stand where the blood hadn't spattered. "*That* is a void about the size of a baseball. And if you look at the ball this way," I said, turning the baseball around to get the right angle, "you can see that the spatter hit the ball exactly in the pattern it left on the wall."

Chris refused to look at the ball, or the picture, so I continued, pointing to the small stand on the dresser where the baseball had once been so proudly displayed. "That's where the ball your father gave to Noah was sitting the night you crept into your son's room with the knife you'd stolen from your ex-wife's kitchen a few weeks before, swapping it for a duplicate, which is the knife she remembered using to cut up the veggies for the salad she made that night."

Next to me Dioli picked up the baseball and swiveled the photo of the crime scene around so that he could take a closer look at it.

While he did that, I slapped another photo of the murder weapon on the table and then set the second inventory list—the one from the kitchen—down next to it. "And see that, Chris?" I said, pointing to the inventory list. "There's a duplicate knife still in the drawer, and inventoried by CSI."

Chris glared hard at me as Dioli set aside the baseball and reached for both the photo and the inventory list, pulling them close to inspect them.

"And this," I said, reaching back into my purse to pull out another piece of paper, "is the report from our lab indicating that the blood on the baseball—the one smudged by *your* fingerprint— is that of your son. But you know what else is interesting, Chris? Our lab tech found another drop of blood on the ball. It's the blood of a close male relative, likely a father. You didn't realize you cut yourself when you attacked him, did you? It was probably a very small cut, because the drop of your blood isn't any bigger than a dot, really, but it's yours. We're still waiting another few hours for all the DNA analysis to come back, but it's looking pretty good that you'll be definitively identified as having handled the ball at the time that Noah was murdered. But I think what's most telling of all, Chris, is that, after Skylar's trial was over, what I found at the very back of Detective Dioli's murder file was a copy of a list of items that you claimed you wanted out of evidence. Oh, you asked mostly for keepsake stuff, like photos and your son's ball cap, and his mitt, but what you *didn't* ask for, Chris, was this ball. You knew he had it; he showed it to you at his birthday party. And, being the owner and operator of a sports memorabilia company, you had to know the ball's value, and yet, *you* didn't ask for it from the contents of Noah's room, which CSI had collected from Skylar's house, because you *knew* it was missing."

Chris's dark glare turned murderous. I didn't care. I kept going. "And this," I said, reaching into my purse to pull out one more slip of paper before slapping down the hastily gathered witness statement, "is from your ex-mother-in-law. She's recanting her court testimony. Once we showed her that we could pull her bank records, revealing regular monthly deposits—monthly deposits we'd be eager to share with the IRS, mind you—she was more than willing to roll on you. She says you came to her and offered her a deal. In exchange for the testimony against her own daughter, you would set her up rent free and supply her with enough money on a monthly basis to live in the style to which she'd been accustomed when she was living with you and taking care of Noah. What a boon for her," I said snidely. "She didn't have to play babysitter anymore; she just had to sell out her own daughter."

Chris was breathing hard enough through his nose to let me know he really, really, *really* wanted to end me. I looked him in the eye to let him know he'd never get the chance. "We're still going to prosecute her for perjury," I told him smugly, crossing my arms and leaning back in the chair. "And if a copy of her bank statements happens to become part of the public record, which anonymously gets sent to the IRS, then I guess we'll just shrug our shoulders and tell her, 'Gee golly, that's too bad.'"

Next to me, Dioli studied the witness statement. I reached back into my purse and slid a copy of Faith's bank statements over to him along with a copy of the *Austin American Statesman* article Candice had stumbled upon that announced that Skylar Miller was listed as a person of interest in her son's murder. The dates on both the statement and the article were the same. I wondered if

Chris had gotten the idea to include his mother-in-law in the framing of his wife on the day the article came out, or if he'd thought about it even earlier.

And then I dug back into my purse for the coup de grâce. We'd been so lucky to have a judge willing to sign the warrant that I was still thanking my lucky stars. Sliding two bound sets of papers with the word "VOID" in big red letters across their covers to Chris, I said, "Know what these are?"

Chris's eyes darted to the papers and he visibly paled. My smile widened. We had him dead to rights. "I thought you might recognize a copy of your parents' old will. Interesting reading that one. Even if it was written in two thousand three. Seems you weren't their favorite son at the time, Chris.

"See, I had my first inkling that you might not have gotten on well with your parents when Skylar's neighbors said that Noah's grandparents showed up to his birthday party early, then left, and a while later you stopped by. Your dad was going through chemo at the time, and I thought it was a little odd that a man who was seemingly *such* a good father didn't want to hang out with his own father at his son's birthday party. Now, that could've been a coincidence, but we have it on good authority that there was a major rift between you and your daddy-o, Chris. Over some treasured possessions of your dad's.

"It seems that in two thousand two, you started your sports memorabilia company. It didn't do so well at first, did it, Chris? In fact, it wasn't doing well at all. And this despite the fact that some of the items we were able to track, in just the hour or so that we've been working on this, came back as belonging to your dad. In fact, they were listed in his original will from nineteen eighty." I tapped the first set of bound papers for emphasis.

"Your dad was a big collector, wasn't he?" I asked him. Chris didn't reply, nor did I expect him to. He simply kept glaring at me. I picked up the baseball he'd taken from Noah's room. "This puppy cost him a fortune in fact. I'm guessing, Chris, that your dad found out about all the little backroom deals you were making to sell off a few of his sports memorabilia. And as you'd always been a bit of a pain in his ass—dropping out of college after two years, getting a girl pregnant at twenty, and then struggling to do something with your life—I'm thinking that Grant Miller had just about had enough of your ass when he found out that you were selling off his stuff. So, he drafted this puppy."

I put my palm on the second set of bound papers. "In this will, your parents leave you completely out of the picture, Chris. They leave everything to their beloved grandson, Noah. And they even made a bit of a provision for Skylar. Probably a nod to how well they thought she'd been doing.

"And that left you with nada. No inventory for your already struggling business, and no money to live on. You were cut off. From them. And from their money. Your only hope would be to try to worm your way back into their good graces with their precious grandson, but Noah wasn't exactly cooperating with you, now, was he? And your father even blamed you for losing the custody battle with Skylar, didn't he? In the end, he was even taking her side, and, Chris, all of that led you to start thinking about getting even.

"The coup de grâce, however, came with this." Reaching back into my bag, I pulled out a folded set of legal papers and set them on the table. "This trust with the small provision paragraph near the end, which stated that if Noah died before his twenty-first birthday, the money in his trust would be split equally between his parents. And what's really interesting is the very last sentence of that particular paragraph, Chris, which states that if only one parent remains alive, then the whole kit and caboodle falls to the surviving parent.

"On the twenty-first of March, two thousand and five, Chris Miller, you received one million tax-free dollars from this trust. Money that, at the time, you desperately needed. It funded both you and your failing business nicely. The other million, of course, remains in limbo until tomorrow, after Skylar Miller is put to death, when half then falls to you. Of course, you don't need that million now. After Noah's death, your dad was so heartbroken that he made amends with you, and together you even had someone to fight against. Skylar. He died thinking that she murdered his grandson, and he left his entire estate to the *actual* murderer. How's that for irony?"

From the time I'd produced the wills, I could feel Dioli's gaze riveted to me. Good.

"Now," I said, spreading my hands at all the clutter on the table, "maybe you and your attorney, Chris, are thinking that all this is purely circumstantial. But the other thing we discovered from the original crime-scene report was that your fingerprints were on the windowsill of Noah's bedroom. They'd been eliminated because of course you would've been in Noah's room, right? Nothing unusual about his dad hanging out in Noah's room, but the question of *when* those prints were left on that windowsill is gonna become a *big* question at your trial. And given all this other stuff, methinks any jury would likely decide those prints were left on a specific night in July of two thousand four. A night a nine-year-old beautiful boy was murdered in the most unspeakable fashion by the man he loved most in the world. For money. And for the fact that both he and his grandfather picked his mother over you."

With that I got up and left the room.

Chapter Eighteen

• • •

"What do you want me to do?" Dioli asked me when he finally joined me out in the hallway. I noticed he was carrying all the papers and photos from the table. He handed them carefully to me, and it was like he didn't trust them in the same room with Miller and wanted me to keep them safe.

I took a deep breath. He wasn't going to like what I had to say. "In a little over an hour there's a hearing at the Board of Pardons. I want you to go there, but first, I want you to call the DA and confess that you royally screwed up."

Dioli looked taken aback, so I added, "The DA called you to tell you about Gallagher, didn't she? She called to say that we were asking a man named Dennis Gallagher, a man known by APD to have a record of B and Es, about Noah Miller's murder."

Dioli stared at me, and I could see the guilt in his eyes. "And in turn," I said next, "you called Miller and told him we were fishing around, trying to get Skylar off on the appeal by claiming we had a witness to the murder. And when Miller asked you who that was, I'm guessing you told him what you knew about Dennis. That's how Chris discovered that the screen and the window had been put back, and why the baseball he'd stolen from Noah's room had never been discovered in Skylar's backyard. He must've wondered about that for ten years, and when you called to tell him about Dennis, he finally had an answer, but he also knew in that exact same moment that he also had a really *big* problem."

The detective wiped a bead of sweat from his brow, but he didn't say anything. It didn't matter. I knew he'd done it. "You got Dennis Gallagher killed, Detective," I said to him with more than a little venom in my tone.

"Jesus," Dioli whispered, dropping his gaze to the floor. More sweat beaded up on his forehead.

I pressed on. "After you call the DA and *convince* her to support you at the Board of Pardons, I want you to go there and tell them that there's been a horrible miscarriage of justice, and that *you* were personally at fault. I want you to beg them to spare Skylar Miller's life, because you are now convinced, beyond a shadow of a doubt, that she's an innocent woman, and the killer is currently in custody. And then I want you and the DA to file a motion with the courts to have Skylar Miller completely exonerated for the crime of murder. I want her off death row, and out of that jail, Dioli."

The bastard had the balls to look as if he was about to protest, so I brought the big guns out. "And if you don't do everything that I've just said, Ray, I will make your life an utter living hell. The state's attorney is already asking questions about your initial investigation, and all the evidence you not only ignored but failed to provide to Skylar's attorney. I'll go to the press and I'll tell them about how you hacked the investigation together without ever considering Chris Miller's involvement. I'll point out the two identical knives found at the scene, and show how you blatantly ignored that. The missing baseball, the loose screen, the pushed-down bedcovers, the void in the curtain, the phone call made to Chris's cell at the exact time of the murder that couldn't possibly have been made by Noah, and Miller's fingerprints on the windowsill.

"And then I will also point them to a second investigation where you arrested and accused the wrong person for the crime. I'm pretty sure Len Chen is still carrying a significant grudge against you. Think he'd be happy to talk to the press?"

Dioli held up his hand. "Okay!" he barked. "Enough, okay? Enough."

There was an anxious pregnant pause where I wondered what he'd do next, but he surprised me a little when he withdrew his cell phone and made a call. "Lisa? It's Ray Dioli. I need to speak to your boss lady. It's an emergency. I don't care what she's doing—interrupt her and tell her to take this call."

Taking a step back, I leaned my weary head against the wall and fully exhaled for the first time in ten days.

Oscar, Candice, and I exited the car and stared up at the brightly lit condo complex, all three of us wearing identical expressions of happy satisfaction. From a balcony on the third floor, Skylar got up from her chair, set aside her book, and waved down at us. Then she motioned us to the front door.

We headed up the walkway lined with Christmas lights without comment. I'm not sure any of us could speak, actually. I stopped at the locked door and waited for Skylar to buzz us in, and while I did, Candice hooked her arm through mine and squeezed. I laid my head on her shoulder, sharing the glorious moment we'd had a hand in creating.

Behind us another car pulled into the drive. As the door buzzed and Oscar reached for the handle, I looked back to see Cal behind the wheel. While Candice and Oscar headed inside, I held the door open until Cal came up the walkway. "Hey, there," he said warmly, greeting me with an impromptu hug and a light kiss on the cheek. "Happy holidays, Abby."

"And to you, counselor," I said, unable to keep the giant grin off my face.

Cal took the weight of the door from me and I stepped across the threshold over to the stairs and headed up three flights. Belatedly I realized there was an elevator. "I'm getting too old to climb stairs," Cal said, wheezing a little behind me.

"It's good for you," I chided. Looking right, then left, I finally spotted Skylar waving at us from down the hall.

"In here," she called.

Cal and I moved down the narrow corridor side by side, and greeted Skylar with hugs and nervous laughter. None of us said much at first. There was too much emotion and it overtook the words.

At last we were settled into Skylar's beautiful little kitchen, and evidence of her recent move was nowhere in sight. As I looked about the kitchen, and then into the living room, which was nicely decorated in soft steel blues and yellows, with a hint of white tucked in here and there, it appeared like she'd been there far longer. "I love your place!" I told her.

She blushed and swept a hand through her curly hair, which had been cut a bit shorter and which flattered her features quite nicely. "Thank you," she said. "I still can't believe I own it."

Skylar had been completely exonerated by the courts just ninety days before. It'd been an anxious few months for me while Cal and the DA worked together to file all the legal motions and paperwork to get her out of jail. The DA had also been working on a deal with Chris Miller, whose attorney suggested that if the DA was willing to take the death penalty off the table, his client might be inclined to make a full confession to both Dennis Gallagher's murder and Noah's.

That'd taken a whole three weeks of back-and-forth just on its own. I found little satisfaction, however, in reading the confession from Chris about the night of the murder. It'd actually gone down almost exactly as I'd suggested in the conference room to my fellow investigators. Chris had indeed planned to murder his son, frame his ex-wife, and stage her murder like a suicide.

His confession sickened me to the core.

Still, the week was made better by the news that Skylar was going to be set free at the end of September. Next to my actual wedding day (the second wedding day, not the first), it'd been the happiest day of my life.

Immediately following her release, Skylar and Cal had then worked out a deal with the city, in which Skylar agreed not to sue their pants off, and the city agreed to pay Skylar 4.5 million dollars. If you ask me, they got off easy. I'd have asked for double that.

We spent the evening with Skylar toasting her release and exoneration, and we all pestered her for details about how she was getting on and what she was doing, but she was more interested in us. So we laughed at Oscar, who was so smitten with his house, his dog, and his very cute house-sitting girlfriend, and we toasted my recent anniversary to the love of my life, and Candice's impending vacation in Switzerland with her gorgeous hubby over the Christmas holidays, and Cal's new sports car. A present to himself after the settlement with the city. We enjoyed the wonderful things happening in our lives and Skylar seemed to soak it all in like a thirsty sponge.

Toward the end of the evening, we each helped her clear the

table and gathered in the kitchen, where our host had laid out a delicious-looking buffet of tasty confections. While fresh coffee percolated, I noted a group of pictures tacked up onto the fridge. Noah's birthday photo was in the center, and spiraling out from that were the faces of about a dozen other children. "Who're these cutie-pies?" I asked.

Skylar moved over to the fridge and laid her hand gently on a few of the photos. "Those are my kids," she said, with pride in her voice.

Cal leaned over—a pink-icing-covered confection in his hand— and said, "I helped Skylar set up a scholarship fund for underprivileged kids. It's called Noah's Nation, and Skylar is personally sponsoring these twelve little guys from charter school all the way through college, while also helping their moms out with extra food, clothing, counseling—whatever they need."

"All the moms are single parents who left abusive relationships," she told me. "One or two had substance abuse issues and are currently working the program."

I noticed that on the counter there was a shiny new AA medallion. Skylar was still working it too. "Wow!" I said, so impressed with this woman. "Look at you, Skylar. Not out of jail even three months and you're already performing miracles."

She blushed. "Noah would've loved it," she said. "Do you know that Detective Dioli reached out to me in a letter to express how sorry he was for everything that happened? He even offered to volunteer for the Nation. He said he's good with a paintbrush, or for tutoring the kids, or whatever we need." Dioli had retired from the police force shortly after his appearance at the Board of Pardons. There was a rumor that his superiors recommended that he take the early retirement, but I think he probably would've gotten there on his own. His reputation was pretty much ruined.

"And how does his apology sit with you?" Candice asked. I was wondering the same thing. I probably wouldn't have been able to forgive him, and, knowing me (as I do), I'd have told him where to stuff it.

"Well," she said with a sigh, "it's hard. But I know Noah would've wanted me to forgive him, and the cause is so worthy, and I desperately need a little help, so how *can* I turn away his offer?"

"Easy," I said. "You just say no to the person who almost had you killed."

Skylar smiled at me. "Yes, but, Abby, when did you ever learn anything *worthy* by taking the easy route?"

That made me laugh, because Skylar was so right, and I realized I could definitely learn a thing or two about forgiveness from her. Wrapping my arm around her, I pulled her in for a sideways hug. "Good for you, girl," I said. "Good for you."